The Monster Specialist

or

Severus and Lilava

by

Edward S. Louis

The Monster Specialist

or

Severus and Lilava

by

Edward S. Louis

2014

Published by Walking Tree Publishers, Zurich and Jena in 2014

© Walking Tree Publishers, Zurich and Jena, 2014

www.walking-tree.org

Part I of this book was previously published under the title *Sir Severus le Brewse* by Silver Lake Publishing, 2005.

Illustrated by Anke Eissmann.

Cover illustration: "Severus fights a dragon", Anke Eissmann 2014

Series Editors: Peter Buchs • Thomas Honegger • Andrew Moglestue • Johanna Schön
Editor responsible for this volume: Andrew Moglestue

Tales of Yore Series No. 3
ISBN 978-3-905703-23-8

Typeset in Hoefler Text and Lucida Blackletter by Walking Tree Publishers.
Printed by Lightning Source in the United Kingdom and United States

"... for the Freynshe book sayth that Sir Severause had never corayge nor grete luste to do batayle ayenste no man but if hit were ayenste gyautis and ayenste dragons and wylde bestis... ."

Thomas Malory, *Le Morte Darthur*

With thanks to my wife Kristy, and also to Catherine Rock, Stephanie Weidner, Emma Riehl, Luise Wendler and Andrew Moglestue who all helped with the editing of this book, as well as to Tom Shippey, for his encouragement when the manuscript was but an early draft.

Contents

Part 1

Sir Severus le Brewse

1 Severus at Work

[Here we learn of the prowess and character of Sir Severus le Brewse, one of King Arthur's least known but most underrated knights.]

Strong ... for ... such ... a small ... beast, thought Sir Severus le Brewse, as the Father of All Adders wrapped itself ever more tightly about him, squeezing the air from his body.

Normally, Sir Severus did not find himself in such a predicament as this one: though he was brave, he was also prudent about battles. But this snake, though poisonous as are all its brood, stretched to a mere twenty feet long, nothing that would normally take him more than moments and a few easy swings of his excellent sword, so Severus had taken no special care. He had been lured into gentleness by the unusually warm, humming Scottish day with a breeze barely rustling the heather, and had found himself admiring the snake for its age, vigor, and dignity. When Severus confronted it, this serpent did not slink off into the grass or rear up to try to frighten him; rather, recognizing Severus for the kind of foe he was, it puffed a couple of times, realized it had a life-and-death battle ahead, and, fixing Sir Severus with its old, cold, oval eye, glided toward him in a stately coil.

The beast showed such an apparent intelligence that Sir Severus was even moved to consider reasoning with it, something like: look here, you simply must move from this place and take your brood with you, since you are endangering the local settlements, and we can't have you eating any more carpenters, now can we? Severus had even dropped his guard and opened his mouth to speak, since he was a fair man by nature, but as he had done so, the hoary serpent had with stunning rapidity leaped toward him, wrapped itself around him, and begun to squeeze, not a tactic typical of a beast of such age and wisdom.

Now Sir Severus found his arms gripped tight to his sides, his blood beginning to fill up his head and his feet, his life at stake as he stood eye-to-eye with a monster that realized it might very well have gotten the better of him. The serpent seemed almost to smile.

Severus realized he had but one chance to save his life — barring the unlikely appearance of several talented bowmen from the closest village — and he knew his success would depend entirely on timing, so he bored his own gaze back into the serpent's eye, tried desperately not to faint from lack of air, and concentrated on the beast's movements.

The snake flicked its tongue once, twice, tasting the air, debating tactics, then opened wide to expose its fangs, poised, and struck.

9

As Severus felt the forward movement, he ducked his chin to his breastbone, allowing the snake to strike itself into the hard steel above the nose-piece of his helmet, which it did with a resounding clang.

Fighting off the stun from the snake's blow, he looked up to see the fuzzy eyes of the beast, who had never before taken a noseful of steel. Seizing the instant, Severus pushed off with his feet as hard as he could and sank his own teeth right into the serpent's throat.

After that, the fight had gone somewhat more easily, though Severus had had to shake off the nearly irresistible urge to forget what he was doing and spit out a mouthful of adder. First stunned, then hurt, then bleeding, finding himself for the first time in his life on the wrong end of a vicious bite, the serpent had begun to uncoil so as to beat a hasty if indecorous retreat. Severus extricated himself from the unwinding coils, recovered his sword, and struck at the fleeing snake. The most difficult part was chasing down the thing to kill, so that he could return to the settlement to assure the townspeople that they were safe and that they might have reasonable hope of attracting another carpenter. Ascertaining that his task was done and that that particular serpent would feed no more, Severus turned down the hill, found, after a time, Courage, his horse, and in the just gathering evening chill rode for the village.

Later, having delivered his message and recounted the battle to the modest and barely appreciative applause of the locals, having suffered a glass or two of the best local ale, and having encouraged the people to call upon him again should any other such beast trouble them, Severus felt an unusual urge to make his way once more to London. Normally he would pay the obligatory visit to court when King Arthur stayed in the North at Carlisle and would avoid the greater hurly-burly of London, but a voice in the back of his brain urged him south — such voices one often does better to deny, though we seldom can. Allowing Courage a nice rampant pose to impress the locals, he prepared to speed off, but some lingering folk interrupted his plan for an impressive exit.

"Why don't you rest a bit first?" said an old woman. "You look a wee brookit and chitterin' from the cauld. Did yoo fight tha' adder all by yoursel'?"

"Yes, of course."

"Hoo come?"

"Surely, that's simply the way it's done."

"Wouldna it be easier for twa or three knights to figh' the serpent taegither?"

"We can't do that. Each knight's quest is his own. It's a matter of duty and honor."

"Soonds daft, if you ask me."

Sir Severus capitulated, admitting that perhaps it was daft, but then no one had shown up to help anyway and, in practice as well as theory, no one is likely to. Politely resisting some of the woman's haggis but forcing down one more draft of ale, he accepted bread, dried meat and fruit, and some apple cider from the townsfolk. A farmer gave him some oats, which he resisted trying himself, but instead gave to his horse. Then Severus took leave.

As he mounted Courage, Severus turned to some of the local Elders. "You might well prepare some of your young men, sort of train them in case one of those serpents appears again. It's rather a continuing battle, you know, against death and darkness and all that sort of thing. I could return sometime to help and test them, if you'd like. I do occasionally offer seminars. If we could just collect a number of boys and a number of serpents, we could really accomplish something here, though you must be careful of trying anything without me or some other knight to supervise, at least at first." Not a particularly rousing speech with all its qualifiers, and indeed he'd offered it half-heartedly, knowing they wouldn't follow his advice ...

"Maybe we'll start with one, and go on from there," an old man replied warily, scratching his bearded chin.

"Right, capital," Severus mumbled, just a bit disappointed at the lack of enthusiasm, but not entirely sorry to avoid any definitive responsibility. He wondered, though, if the man meant one boy or one serpent.

He rode for some time and thought about what the woman had said.

Yes, Severus agreed, sometimes expediency must dictate the method and approach to battle, but then what would be the use of one's becoming a knight and following one of his favorite pastimes: errantry, the wandering search for adventures by which he nearly defined himself? Knighthood meant more than getting the job done; it meant a way of thinking and a way of living, honor, service, self-sufficiency, detachment from the world's comforts, and, usually, suffering one of his favorite pleasures, unrequited love — Severus wasn't quite sure if requited love would be any better or not. And errantry too had its other rewards: sunshine, fresh air, and, normally, the quiet of the road with occasional adventures thrown in for variety. Often one felt glad finally to be alone and to make one's own decisions, even a knight employed by so great a king as Arthur. Right?

For instance, Severus recalled the time he had spent weeks following a rumor all the way to the backwoods of Ireland that the legendary King of Boars, Twrch Trwyth, had returned and was rambling about the countryside. Then he was especially glad to have been traveling alone. Sir Severus, the knight of all knights who best loved to battle with beasts natural or enchanted, left no path untrodden in his search, and he finally found the ancient boar napping on a lonely hillock near Galway. Being a sporting sort, Severus had waited till the boar woke — losing sleep himself in the meantime — and when the beast poked open a wary eye, spotted him, and tore off down the hill, Severus maintained hot pursuit for nearly two weeks till he finally cornered the boar in a cave out-side of Cork. By that time Twrch Trwyth simply collapsed from exhaustion; he was older now than the tireless young beast that had swum the eternal seas and left generations of young heroes stumbling in his tracks or his wake. Severus had leaped from his nearly-ruined horse's back and prepared to cut the animal's head from its body. The boar simply lay down at Severus' feet and looked at him as if to say, go ahead and kill me if you must, because I'm just too old and tired to keep up this chase anymore — I won't even fight you, so you'll get no glory out of me. At that, Severus had felt as though he had betrayed some natural trust in running the dignity out of a venerable and honorable — and very old — adver-sary, so he simply got back on his horse and rode away, though he did leave the beast a bowl of water before departing.

Severus regained his energy in a couple of days and never heard of the boar again, but his horse took nearly a month to forgive him. As he looked back on that adventure, he realized that, had he not been alone, any other knight would gladly have killed the boar and made his place in history and legend and earned thereby a lifetime supply of invitations to speak at banquets, and that would have been a kind of tragedy in which Severus would not wish to play a part.

Such reminiscence, accompanied by the rhythmic clopping of his horse's hooves, sent Severus into a kind of reverie of memory, and he comfortably slipped into daydreams as that excellent steed, Courage, trotted on into the gloaming, exploring his own waking dreams of good oats, prancing fillies, short, successful battles, and then more fillies and more oats. Severus thought of long summer days of riding, seeing all the beautiful sights of the world, hills and dales, tors and tarns, of apple trees full in the fall, of sleeping warm under a pile of furs when gentle snow covered the ground soft and smooth as samite, of the green shoots of spring, of cooking a simple supper under a May moon, and of his own love, Lilava. Though he feared she might be too wise and beautiful for him in fact, why should such problems interrupt a good daydream, to which he felt certainly entitled given recent successful adventures?

Thinking of Lilava, Severus recalled the tournament he had attended at her bidding in Bath on the previous summer's solstice. He had little joy in tourna-ments, much to the amusement of his fellow knights, such as Sir Dinadan who teased him mercilessly, but on the first day he had done his best, and Lilava had told him he sat his horse well, which he did.

Rather above average height, above average girth in the legs and shoulders, and slim in the waist, Severus, while not of the height and weight of Sir Lancelot or Sir Tristram, looked a bold figure on horseback. He had remarkably strong bones and elastic sinews, and when he felt moved, his muscles had a quick-ness that would have rivaled a mongoose, if anyone in those regions had known about mongooses to put him to the test. While we're at it, he had thick, almost black hair, kept his face shaven after the Roman fashion when he could, and had iron-bright blue-gray eyes that would occasionally make an inexperienced girl swoon until she learned who he was, realized he wasn't a tournament-champion type, and felt silly for swooning over a man who fought only with monsters when so many other popular young knights were still available for flirting.

Lilava would only have urged him to attend the tournament in the absence of Lancelot — she did her best to keep them apart, to avoid their hurting each other. With the great knight absent, Severus took second place on the first day of fighting, behind only Sir Gawain, of whom he also tended to stay clear, since he was the king's nephew, and one does better not to anger the king if one wants to preserve his right to choose quests — and I have said, Severus preferred to select his quests judiciously.

On the second day he did rather better yet. Getting somewhat caught up in the melee, he actually walloped Gawain off his horse with a splendid sword-stroke, not having recognized him. Angered, Gawain refused the hand Severus offered to help him rehorse, and then he spent the rest of the afternoon chasing our hero amongst the field, until once more Severus, hearing a horse bear down on him, turned and without thinking struck Gawain to the ground again. While the queen laughed, the king didn't find quite so funny the indignities wrought upon his nephew, so once again Severus won second place, that day to Sir Bors, who, having returned alive with brilliant stories from the Grail Quest, was a great favorite of the court anytime.

That evening Severus received a far better award than the king could offer — besides of course absolute freedom in choosing adventures — a kiss on the cheek from Lilava, followed by her broad, sincere smile showing her amazing white teeth and her firm assurance that he had easily outperformed every knight on the field, including the winner.

On the third day of the tournament, caught up in the pleasure of Lilava's kiss, Severus had fought without much conviction, in fact quite perfunctorily, poking now and then at someone with the blunt end of his spear just to keep him at a safe distance, and so, not paying attention, he had nearly been thrust from his horse by a young knight whom no one even knew but who caught Severus una-wares. He merely turned and congratulated the youth on a fine attack, but when the fellow, feeling he must press his advantage, refused to accept the lauds and back off, Severus circled him with some astonishing horsemanship — one must indeed praise Courage for that as well — finally grabbed him by the collar, lifted him from his horse, and calmly deposited him among the spectators far enough away that the king couldn't see his ignominy.

When the crowd started to taunt him, Severus made a few weak sword strokes here and there for form's sake, but when the day ended, he won no prize, and

Guinevere — not nearly so bad a sport as many of the old tales make her out — had to talk Arthur out of taking away Severus' prize from the day before.

When he retired from the field, Severus had thought to find Lilava again and get perhaps another kiss, since the first one had shown such promise, but he couldn't find her at all, and believe me he took his time looking. When later he gave up and rode to his tent, he found only a note from her, thanking him for his achievements on her behalf, except for those of the third day, which ended up unexceptional. She mentioned how glad she had felt to see him, hoped he felt the same, remarked on what good weather they'd been having, hoping it would continue, and wished him a nice weekend. Severus' eyes raced to the end of the letter hoping to find the closing salutation "Love," knowing it didn't necessarily mean that, but hoping for it anyway, but to his disappointment, he found only "Your sincere and devoted friend": sincere? devoted? What could one make of such words?

He stayed for the first night's party to celebrate the tournament winners. He had even managed to calm and congratulate Gawain, who had taken "First Place Overall" and thus found himself recompensed for any ill use. He had a drink or two with some of the younger knights who showed an interest in questing and errantry and monsters, and some of them who particularly loved stories even questioned him and listened for a bit, but Severus took no great pleasure in strong drink or overmuch talk of his own achievements, so he gradually drifted away to a silent corner to sit and brood over Lilava's letter, which gave him quite a deal more pleasure than all the noble company. Early the next morning he left, thanking the stewards who had tended the knights. Courage, who suffered a disdain of tournament horses, had felt as happy as his man to ride on.

Such memories filled his thoughts as he rode. Though Courage hardly took the trouble to remember the tournament at all and had his doubts about Lilava's intentions, Severus felt melancholic pleasure in the virtue a knight must surely gain from doing great deeds for unrequited love, and one could hardly have wished for a more beautiful or accomplished love, unrequited or not, than the enchanting enchantress Lilava.

And so he rode on, enjoying that aching, pleasant tension of the errant knight: joy in the presence of the beloved lady versus the solitary quiet of the road, either punctuated by occasional adventures.

II Lilava

[Here appears a brief history and background of Lilava the beautiful sorceress, of whom Severus as yet knew little.]

Lilava came from an island in the Middle-earth Sea, born to a noble family, but not a royal one. From childhood she showed a great affinity for learning, and though her culture hadn't made significant advancements in any technical sense — that is, they felt no particular eagerness to make mechanical war on their neighbors — when she had learned all her parents could teach her, they shifted her on to Heleve, the most knowledgeable woman in the village, who in time left her with the man who governed the island, who in turn took her to the wisest person on the island, whom we would call a physician or magician, depending on the translation.

From her Lilava learned such arts of healing and manipulation of natural substances as her folk had acquired and felt willing to share with one another. She also learned how to buffer events — Lilava didn't like the term magic. Of course no human can fully control or even understand how circumstances grow into eventualities, but in their proper use the powers of herbs and minerals as well as that of speech and movement plus intense focusing of thought and will and muscle can in many instances adjust, subvert, or produce outcomes. One need only understand such activities' virtues, remain hopeful, and never expect too much.

Despite her propensity for study and lack of concern over the common worries of young people, such as her physical appearance, Lilava grew into a beautiful young lady, lithe of limb with enormous dark eyes and silky, flowing, night-black hair that tumbled over her shoulders and down to the middle of her back, when she didn't take the time to tie it in a scruffy knot behind her head, which was seldom, and when she bothered to wash, which happened rather less often. Because of her concentration on her work and because of the self-protective aspects of the arts she'd learned, her folk worried little about Lilava's safety, and when a trading ship accidentally came aground on their shores not long after her entry into adulthood, Lilava departed with it, intending to seek out the distant island home of the woman who had once instructed Heleve, a representative of the Order of Enchantresses, so called to discourage the curious (but not the courageous and devoted) from disturbing them unnecessarily in their study.

She left quietly and hurriedly, as Lilava's folk always counseled travelers foreign and domestic to do, so as not to arouse the Chimaera, that worst-of-beasts, which stalked and haunted the land, falling into occasional fitful sleep that, though it produced minor earthquakes, allowed the people to breathe and grow food to store against the times of its waking. Without anyone's daring to mention a word of it for fear the Chimaera could hear a breath on bare breeze, everyone knew that Lilava hoped to find a means to rid them of their monster. Now in some places a monster may actually increase the tourist trade, but in most places one does better without them, and a Chimaera, about which we'll learn more later, has a particularly bad effect not only on the local economy, but also on everyone's mood, since one never knows what shape it will take or what form of destruction its nasty little mind will devise. Yes, at a safe distance one may say a Chimaera has a little mind, in the sense that it expands little beyond meditating means to cause suffering; in that particular application a Chimaera has a perfect genius.

Lilava did manage a quiet and safe departure, her greatest regret being that she had to leave behind her sister Liletta, a younger and perhaps even more beautiful version of Lilava, and after long searching and many adventures she found Kirkea, a queen among enchantresses. By dropping a few names, including that of her teacher, Heleve, and by sharing a few great jokes she'd picked up in her travels, she gained admittance and proved immediately the finest student with whom Kirkea had ever worked. She'd been born with talent and had acquired considerable skill already: combine a devoted student with an expert and willing teacher and good things happen. Among the advantages of studying with a master, Lilava found that time seemed to move more slowly on Kirkea's island, and so she practiced for some years while hardly aging a day, at least externally. Learning brings with it maturity, if one blends practice with theory, though without proper care it may even bring moroseness — not a good trait for an enchantress, unless she prefers to hear the term witch hissed as she passes. While a good enchantress doesn't take name-calling seriously, a bad witch may try — usually unsuccessfully — to turn the perpetrator into a salamander or something even worse.

Eventually, having spent several happy years on Kirkea's island, Lilava achieved all that she could by means of her own and her tutor's efforts, and since a small, minimally inhabited island hasn't the need for two enchantresses, while the rest of the world, particularly folk such as Sir Severus le Brewse, can find them absolutely, well, enchanting and often useful if not necessary, she caught the eye of some fishermen sailing by, received passage, and set her aim on new studies and new opportunities. Over the next months Lilava traveled to many lands, eventually arriving in Britain, and finding the place thoroughly green and (in those days) temperate and much to her liking, she settled in to stay for a bit, despite the fact that the islands had more than their share of enchantresses. For the most part they kept to themselves, and as each turned out to have different specialties, they seldom quarreled, and when they assembled for the occasional Convention, they always reaffirmed an agreement not to impinge on one another's enchantments except to save a colleague or an innocent bystander in a pinch.

Lilava troubled the other sorceresses (some folk prefer that term to enchantress, particularly those who don't like the type) only occasionally, though of course she ached to learn what she could from them, but every profession has its protocol, so she visited them only briefly and with generous but unprepossessing gifts, asked innocuous questions and spoke little of herself, so that gradually she could add to her learning the little bits of their own arts that they willingly shared. You see, Lilava had the charm of being beautiful without acting beautiful, which won her the friendliness of many folk who would have dismissed her had she behaved in any way other than to make herself appear pleasantly unassuming.

On seeing Sir Lancelot for the first time, when she went to pay her respects to King Arthur's court, she did what women always did on seeing Lancelot for the first time: swoon. She quickly realized, though, that he was hands-off, being devoted to the Queen, even after having had a good fling with the Holy Grail. She knew immediately, too, that he could hardly help her solve her own problem, which was of course to find a knight who could help her rid her land of the Chimaera. Lancelot would never again willingly leave Queen Guinevere, and he wasn't exactly a monster specialist anyway, being in one sense Severus' opposite: Lancelot was a knight of human deeds. He performed great ones, glorious ones, astonishing ones, appalling ones, in all elements except holiness beyond the pale of all the heroes of that time, but though his deeds stretched the limits of human possibilities, they were always fully human deeds. That limitation made him fabulously famous and successful and had all the women fawning over him, but it made him rather sensitive and, more importantly to our tale, immaterial to Lilava's particular needs.

Having greeted the royalty and the fellowship with solemn dignity and some disappointment on her part — she would have liked a glimpse at Galahad as well, but he had by then ascended to Heaven — she was preparing to leave when a man passing by happened absent-mindedly to help her onto her horse, placing his hand beneath her shoe and lifting her quite easily into the saddle. The gentle off-handedness of his courtesy surprised her, to say the least, and when she thanked him, he merely muttered a "Pray, don't mention it" without even missing a step. He seemed not even to realize he had assisted, but merely to have done so as a matter of course.

Something of his touch, even of his hand to the bottom of her shoe, filled Lilava with anticipation, and when she called to him, he turned toward her a pair of iron-blue, distracted-looking eyes: he was Severus, and she immediately felt he might be the man to undertake her quest.

One cannot always trust such feelings — in fact one normally does well to shake them off as no more than romantic nonsense — but Lilava was neither a romantic nor a typical human being, rather a skilled and attentive enchantress, so she took note. She took the trouble to follow him, safely out of sight, for nearly a fortnight, observing his behavior and recording his quests. Over the course of the next two years, she wove her path in and out of his, making strictly detached observations while studying several other knights as well, just in case she might find a better candidate to tackle the Chimaera. To treat matters with strict fairness, I must say though that from the moment she saw Severus and felt his touch, she was rooting for him, since she found his manner reassuring and his countenance attractive — even the most enchanting enchantresses can't always eliminate such considerations, though from a safe and supercilious distance other people may think them petty.

Based on his beauty alone or even on his peerless war record, Lilava would have tried to recruit Lancelot to the task, and her thoughts often returned to that option — who isn't somewhat dazzled by fame? — but each time her good sense prevailed and she realized he didn't fit, nor despite his successes in the Grail Quest did Bors, nor did the hot-tempered and unpredictable though thoroughly skilled Gawain, who, I have it on the authority of one fine lady, was at least as attractive as Lancelot in his way. King Arthur had in his fighting youth slain the giant of St. Michael's Mount on his way to felling a good chunk of the late and weakening Roman empire, but he had retired from questing to rule his kingdom, and Guinevere never would have permitted him to undertake a quest for so beautiful a lady as Lilava (who had by then taken up the practice of carefully scrubbing herself, though still avoiding such customs as cheek-rouge) — odd how one tends to suspect others of one's own flaw. No other knight fit the bill. Even the well-traveled Sir Urry, who had come to Arthur's court to be healed of some terrible sword wounds by the greatest knight in the world — and of course Lancelot kindly obliged him and refrained in the celebratory tournament from sending him back home with more — and who, healed, declared himself healthy and eager for the most difficult adventure anyone could think of, couldn't have done it. No, Lilava became more and more convinced that Severus must serve, and she had come to feel sure that he would willingly do so. Of late, due to his successes and the subsequent scarcity of monsters about, she had heard him moaning to himself of the limited opportunities for monster specialists in those parts.

Lilava was not the sort to shirk detailed research, and therefore she traveled Britain from sea to sea to sea to sea, then went to Ireland and did the same, and Aran, Wight, the Orkneys, the Hebrides, and anywhere else she had heard of knights vacationing. She had finally come to spend most of her time following Severus' paces, about a day's ride behind, interviewing those for whom he performed services to assess their level of satisfaction, checking corpses where she could find them, and even questioning beasts when he spared them, to determine whether he had done so out of cowardice or mercy (always the latter).

Eventually she rode a good deal closer than a day's distance, finally upon occasion even sleeping a mere valley away and, in a few instances when they ended a day's journey far from towns, even residing amidst some tolerable tree limbs above where he slept, to observe his resting habits or just to allow herself to fall asleep to the comforting sound of his steady, relaxed breathing — a good thing for her quest that neither of them snored.

If Lilava had been absorbed in herself as much as she was in her quest, she would have realized that in the increasing number of face-to-face meetings that took place between the two of them, Severus had warmed to her greatly. While preceding their first meeting he had unfortunately fallen into distraction, having just received from Arthur an assignment he didn't like, to defend a petty duke of the populous south who had more interest in acquiring and ruining lands by overbuilding than in kindly governing the locals, he did upon leaving find his thoughts flitting back to the — charming? — girl on the horse whom he had passed on his way out (he had in fact not noticed he had helped her up). On their second meeting he had recalled her to mind with little effort, and by their third meeting he felt thoroughly comfortable with her presence, though he requested no greater liberty than to call her "milady." Gradually they had reached the point of passing beyond the weather and the "state of the kingdom question" in their conversations, and they had enjoyed occasional picnic lunches together. Picnics were easier to hold in those days of fewer people, more public lands, and no particular reliance on hot food, difficult to get or keep when one strayed from courts or substantial homes. By the time they had shared a dozen or so conversations and even a few sandwiches (invented a good deal earlier than our histories tell us), Severus had fallen quite in love with Lilava, to the point where he dared daydream about her as he rode and would even make up ballads about her, which he would sing to Courage as they rode along — the horse remained a tolerant if not appreciative critic. For her part Lilava had done her best not to fall in love, knowing that, given the business upon which she hoped to employ Severus, she had best not get so protective of him that she couldn't allow him to fight the Chimaera once she'd got him home. One can hardly blame her for having a practical side, a trait for which men have come to value women more greatly in ages since.

The "Lancelot question" took quite another turn one summer day as the two happened to be riding along together to the south coast where reports said some sort of curious seabeast had run aground: Severus not only killed troublesome beasts, but would on occasion go out of his way to save benign ones. As Severus had dismounted to fill Lilava's water bottle at a clean little stream,

Lilava had seen in the distance — she had among her many virtues miraculous eyesight at great distances — Lancelot astride his horse and riding fully armed directly toward them. A feeling of dire dread, she could not explain why, had nearly overcome her, and she had to keep herself from fainting with fear, an unusual feeling for one not given to faintness of heart. For no reason she immediately understood, gathering her wits she urged Severus to remount quickly and follow her rapidly into a nearby wood, where she exclaimed that she had heard something that sounded to her for all the world like a bear. No one had seen a bear in that place for ages, so Severus, partly fearing and partly hoping that some terrible monster had been ravaging the local folk, sped into the woods to defend anyone who needed defending.

Even a schoolchild knows what woods mean: places of danger and adventure, one avoids them rather than seeks them out, since they nearly always indicate trouble, at least in stories of knights and ladies, but in that case the woods may have saved a tragic and early ending to our story, for Severus, with a little help from Lilava, got them lost in the trees, and when Lancelot galloped by, only the distance of a cricket pitch or two away, Severus heard the hooves, but could not make out the direction from which they came or whether or not they had any connection with the bear or another monster, so he had merely to let them go by. After a couple hours of his fruitless searching, propounded by a spell of confusion that Lilava wrought with great self-control but with the expense of much energy on her part — and not to mention some rather good acting — they found their way out into a clearing on the other side of the wood, Lilava apologizing profoundly that she must have made a mistake, perhaps induced by too much exposure to the sun or by a hidden desire to see Severus at work — who doesn't like to see how another makes a living?

Severus felt uncomfortable with her explanations, but he let that go when Lilava urged him that they should hurry south on their quest, and they did in fact arrive just in time to save an enormous fish-like creature with intelligent eyes that, having come in too far at high tide, had when the water receded got itself stuck and was suffocating. Mustering all his strength, Severus carefully rolled the beast over a couple of turns until it had gotten enough water under it to shake loose and ponderously make its way back into the current and escape. Severus took the blast of water that it shot heavenward as an expression of thanks, shrugged his shoulders to Lilava and a few of the locals who had sat watching, and calmly enough remounted his horse to ride on.

The missed encounter with Lancelot proved a greater fortune than even Lilava would have guessed. In a later meeting with the Lady of the Lake, she learned that her sister sorceress had had a vision that Lancelot and Severus must never meet in battle. Severus would never seek out such an encounter for pleasure, as some knights did, not having a natural preference for one-on-one battle with other people, and Lancelot, having won more jousts than anyone could count, tended to avoid them as well, but fortuitous events often jerk the course of life one way or another despite our preferences. On any given day two knights might meet, decide they have had too few adventures recently, and challenge one another to fight to keep their skills sharp or just for something to do. From their discussion Lilava realized that her sudden fear had merit: the Lady of the Lake guessed that the two knights must in some way represent opposite principles. Such problems usually produce destruction for one if not both knights, should they happen to meet. One cannot always count that famous battles will end in cool-headed, sportsmanlike draws, as did those famous meetings between Lancelot and Tristram and Lancelot and Gareth; they may as well end in the death of both knights, as in the case of the brothers Balan and Balin. That day Lilava resolved to expend whatever energy she needed to preserve the man who appeared to be emerging as her knight from any such danger as a battle with Lancelot, since the occasional dragon would do well enough to keep him in shape and hone his technique.

She was struck also by the possibility that Lancelot might not kill Severus, but that the fight might end the other way round — a better end for her (though the thought of beautiful Lancelot dying pained her, too), but a disastrous one for Britain. She felt some satisfaction in recognizing that her presence there served not only her people, but Arthur's as well; by keeping the two knights from fighting, she might save Lancelot not only for himself, but for his king — and queen. While Lilava was not the sort of person to lose her focus, neither would she regret helping others if the opportunity presented itself.

And so she set about trying to preserve her knight, assure herself of the rightness of her choice, and find the right time and method to broach the topic with Severus. Meanwhile they had some good times together while decent weather lasted, and before winter came she arranged to have some villagers for whom Severus had done a small service — ridding their village of a troublesome goblin — pay him with a cloak she had woven with a special kind of wool and with a special technique and care (some would say she cast a spell on it) so that it kept the wearer particularly warm. She didn't tell him that she had made it, and the villagers kept her secret; Severus often marveled about that cape, reminding himself to try to return to that village to learn more about it, but he never had the chance or ill-luck to do so, and Lilava had many a quiet laugh over it — funny what sorts of things we'll laugh at in private. As for the goblin, it really was just a pitiful thing and had merely been lurking about, had not even eaten a single child and probably never would have. Severus shooed it out of town with a bit of show to satisfy the villagers, then helped it locate a magic cave door in a nearby valley that would lead it safely home. He even caught the goblin a coney to eat, one that had been troubling the villagers more than had the goblin by eating all the new vegetables from their garden, thus doing the people a second service and making a friend of the goblin, at least as much as one ever can with such creatures. Severus wondered whether he got the cape for the goblin or the coney, preferring the former, that being the kinder deed and also because, not having a vegetable garden himself, he had no particular grudge against rabbitkind.

You may well wonder how Severus found the magic door; you may wonder if Lilava found it for him. Not so: he had a bit of magic about himself, though he wouldn't have recognized it as such. You will hear more about it later. While magic often has a virtue of its own — as well as its drawbacks — in this case it also contributed to Lilava's appreciation of her knight, since, though he said nothing of it, knowing nothing of it, she could sense it, and it made her feel more at home with him.

That odd expression, "at home with," may seem an ill fit with wandering folk, errant knights and itinerant sorceresses, but though the lifestyle changes, human emotions tend to remain much the same. Lilava sojourned far from home, and Severus had not had a home for many years. In such cases one seeks the feeling of home in something else: an activity, a favorite book, or the presence of a familiar and pleasant person. The latter had come to apply for both Lilava and Severus with respect to each other.

When winter fell and travel became more difficult so that "chance" meetings occurred less easily or frequently, Severus at least could enjoy his cloak, feeling warmer than he believed he had a right, though not attributing it to the right source, but Lilava realized the flaw in her joke: while she could enjoy the gift she had given Severus, because she didn't disclose its source, she had no gift from him that she could enjoy as her own in his absence. Such are the emotional travails of this world for men and women.

Lilava of course had accustomed herself to hardship, but even the hardiest of persons enjoys a present now and then, even if a simple and discreet one, particularly if it shows the just and proper affection of a friend. So Lilava spent much of the winter alone catching up on a set of old scrolls she had obtained from a retiring sorcerer in Cumbria. Often as she neared sleep she imagined what sort of present Severus would have given her had he known the cloak came from her, and she played out many sweet sorrowful exchanges in her dreams. But now we must leave poor Lilava for a time to learn more about Severus past and what made him the man he became.

III Sir Severus' Own History

[Here begins the sad account of the plucky Severus' early years.]

Perhaps now you're wondering how Severus had come to be as he was, a knight who by preference would never fight another knight, but preferred to fight only beasts.

To begin with, Severus was an orphan. He had no memory of parents, but had lived for a time with a woman he called "Grandmother," who taught him how to cook vegetables and string a bow, until she died, and then with a very old man he called "Grandfather," as far as he knew unrelated to the woman, who told him stories of beasts, battles, and holy Jesu and who in his own wobbly way showed him how to swing a trimmed-down sword, until he too died. Being forest folk, these people, relatives or not, had few connections with the wide world, and when Severus had laid them to rest, he stayed for a short time alone in the woods until their gardens were empty, partly from his efforts and partly from the rabbits', and he no longer had the heart to shoot the rabbits, since they had become the closest thing he had left to family.

Then he began to wander, bow strapped to his back, and shoes worn and barely clinging to his feet. The old man's cut-down sword seemed to shrink as Severus' own body slowly grew, until one could call it no more than a knife hanging in his belt.

Walking from wood to wood and glen to glen, Severus met folk here and there who would sometimes shoo him off, sometimes share a simple meal and a story before wishing him a good journey to wherever he was going. In exchange, if they had treated him kindly, he would rid their woods of snakes or wolves or whatever seemed to be bothering them most, though he wouldn't return to tell them or ask greater compensation. He never could figure out what to do to improve the weather, about which from his view they most obsessively complained, and one roaring-hot summer he spent several days trying to drive off a field of grasshoppers, but otherwise he felt for the most part that he had tried to repay their simple kindnesses as best he could. Occasionally folk who learned what he had done would thank him, but even they only looked at him strangely and shook their heads. Every now and then someone asked his name or where he was going.

Severus never told them his name, having a natural if to him inexplicable fear of doing so, nor did he mention that he was going nowhere in particular. He had always thought a boy should have some place to go or some sort of purpose, even if it was no more than helping a grandmother peel spuds or listening patiently to an old man's stories. But Severus knew of no relatives, could find no particular purpose, and had found that no particular place seemed like home. Even the word home sounded to him hollow, distant, and a bit mythical.

One day, Severus came to the sea. Having been a forester all his short life, he immediately distrusted but felt drawn to the vast, rolling, slate-gray water. There he took up for a time with some fishermen, learning their craft, but proving unwilling to undertake sea voyages, he returned inland, where he learned to fish lakes and streams, so making a living sufficient to a boy with no prospects and little understanding of his greater talents.

When he was nearly ready to give up looking for a family, he was adopted by some relatives of Sir Gregius the Fat, a country knight who owned vast farms and had a plump wife and many plump children. Gregius, not particularly an energetic or talented man himself, recognized talent when he saw it in others, and though one should not exactly say that he felt eager to exploit it, he would, when the situation permitted him without evoking too much harm, allow others to develop their talents in such a way as to do him some good — a later age would perhaps call him a good businessman.

One day one of Gregius' plump sons, Groomer, was off in the woods with his trained pig trying to sniff out truffles. As he returned home, he chanced to come upon Severus fishing in the lake that supplied his father's lands. He noticed that Severus had constructed a flexible pole from which, by a spin and flick of the wrist, he could cast a line well out into the water, and he judged the young fellow one of unusual skills, if rather on the dusty and dirty side. Having inherited several of his dear father's abilities, including the sense to size up the qualities of another, he hallooed Severus, then approached him superciliously asking if he had a license to fish there. Severus, disclaiming any knowledge of such things as fishing licenses, asked if he had offended God or human by fishing there. Groomer suggested that he had done both, but that he could easily repay any offense by visiting his father and, if he had no gold, paying off the equivalent of the license with a few chores.

Severus, though he had caught no fish — Groomer in fact knew he hadn't, since those waters by then held few fish and none worth catching — asked if he might not work to pay off his debt and also earn the cost of some fruit and vegetables. Groomer, finding the young man both apt and congenial, replied that he felt quite sure his father could find work for the young man on his lands.

Meeting the homeless boy, Gregius found him pleasant enough and happily allotted him employment, congratulating his son on his eye for inexpensive labor. Severus mixed well with the family and other local minor nobility as well as with the other working folk, and he soon developed a reputation as the hardest worker anyone had ever seen, quickly learning the skills to complete tasks in carpentry, masonry, smithing, herding, and training horses more quickly than anyone thought possible, earning first the astonished praise and finally the resentment of his fellow workers. Once having begun a task, Severus often worked at it unstintingly to completion, even if it took several days with little food and no sleep. Gregius, far from a brutal master and attentive to the mood of his many working folk, soon realized he had to find other employment for the boy or risk a revolt from the others and the early demise of his most productive servant, so he deflected Severus' attentions to new duties.

First he tried the lad in food preparation, since he exhibited a natural talent with animals, but Gregius found that, though he applied exceptional energy to the pursuit of wild game, he had great difficulty slaughtering and serving up animals from the barnyard, especially those with which he was on good terms, which normally meant all of them. Next Gregius tried sending him on missions to other villages to negotiate supplies, but the boy had little ability in bargaining, often offering more than sellers asked if he found their wares of good quality and underpriced and refusing to accept overpriced necessities at all. When he came out ahead, he often bestowed the excess on a poor family or an underfed child he met on the pathway, returning home without profit but happy in the belief that Sir Gregius' family, being the wealthiest he had ever seen, would also find pleasure in what he considered the apt redistribution of their wealth.

Gregius of course soon put such practices to an end by reassigning Severus, who on a decent, balanced diet was growing rapidly toward sturdy manhood, to activities that took advantage of his excessive energy and desire to serve: he sent the lad to patrol the forests and hills, which happened at that time to have remained relatively safe, but Gregius knew the world, and so sought to keep them that way.

At first Severus seemed to have found his lot in life. Armed with only a net, a stout oak staff, and a bagful of stones, he rode the hills and valleys like a madman, rooting any ill-intentioned beasts from their nests and, as a secondary benefit, scaring the hair off any would-be bandits. Unfortunately, he rode day and night with such commitment and ferocity that he wore out several horses and terrified the rural folk, who evolved a legend that some sort of ghost horseman haunted the marches, riding down badly-behaved children and transfixing escaped young lovers with his evil stare.

Then one day he actually ran into some experienced highwaymen and nearly got himself killed. Seeing one standing beside the path, relatively well-dressed compared to most rustic bandits, Severus stopped to greet him respectfully and ask his business, and the others ambushed him — the world was no kinder place then than it is now. They would certainly have taken his horse and his gear and probably his life as well, had not something bred deep into Severus' brain taken hold, and he shouted a piercing war-cry, dropping the man closest to him with its force, then began felling one after another with his staff, spinning, leaping outside their reach like a whirlwind, striking them in less than sporting places — you may well fault him for that, but you would probably do the same in his boots. Finally only a single man stood against him, the leader; carrying their best weapon, a large, heavy, and very sharp sword, he cut right through Severus' staff. Only momentarily discomfited, Severus retreated several paces and began pelting the man with stones, just long enough to stay his attack. Then Severus grasped the net from his belt, which he normally used to catch game to bring home for dinner, and cast it about his attacker's feet, jerking them from beneath him. Recovering a small shield from one of the others, he swiped it across the leader's sword arm, knocking the weapon from his grasp, and without further thought he grabbed the sword and with one enormous stroke summarily beheaded the man.

By then several of the highwaymen were beginning to regain their senses. A couple dashed for the woods and were never heard from in those parts again, though a couple others, sure that they had encountered a forest spirit, submitted themselves to his mercy, which he willingly granted. He tied up those stragglers with their own rope and herded them home. Learning of the adventure from his devoted servant, Gregius rescinded Severus' mercy and had the highwaymen immediately hanged, congratulating the youth, whom he was learning to see as at least a nephew if not a son, based on the lad's courage and resourcefulness.

The adventure secured Severus' reputation among Gregius' people, though it afflicted them with even more fear of the youth's exposed ferocity. As for Severus himself, he found the whole thing embarrassing. First, he couldn't believe that he had so unquestioningly executed his assailant. Gregius, eager to encourage the youth to protect his lands, assured him that the man must have been a monster, or Severus wouldn't have acted so. While Severus didn't feel so sure about that argument, he couldn't release his thoughts from an overwhelming sense that his weapons lacked nobility and his fighting methods fell short of laudable behavior. Gregius countered that, as defender of rustic lands he had no need of noble methods, though he appreciated the youth's need for better weapons.

They resolved their differences by auctioning off the belongings of the highwaymen and using the proceeds to seek out the best blacksmith they could find to forge Severus a strong and reliable if not beautiful weapon. The law didn't allow a commoner to carry a sword, and Gregius didn't want to take a chance on Severus' encountering some traveling nobles while inappropriately armed — the youth might out of respect try to greet them and so bring trouble upon his employer — so he had the smith forge a light but powerful axe that one might assume felled trees rather than troublemakers. Next, they found a retired knight, expert in weapons of war but with a preference for rustic quiet, to teach Severus how to use it. A few nasty cuts and bruises (to both parties) later, Severus had thoroughly mastered his new weapon. The knight, like so many others before him, marveled at Severus' talent and rapid progress to mastery, and so asked Gregius about the youth's origins. Gregius, reticent about saying too much, lest he lose so valuable a commodity, told the knight that Severus had come to them as an orphan and had happily become a part of their family as a sort of sergeant-at-arms to their household, aiming to make him seem at once nondescript and indispensable.

Without asking Gregius, the knight, to salve his own curiosity about the young man, made some discreet inquiries, and through a chain of communications he learned of a hermit who lived on the east coast and who reputedly knew something of an orphan who had once been left there. The knight sought out the hermit, and after close parley he returned to Gregius with two other retired knights. They requested that they might take the lad to meet with that hermit, who, impressed with what he had heard, believed he knew something more of Severus. Gregius, faced with what he knew to be the knights' demands rather than requests, reluctantly agreed not only to allow Severus to go, but also to accompany him, to make sure that they accounted for the lad's best interests.

Travel they did, finding the hermit on a windswept cliff overlooking the sea. Seeing Severus he expressed both faint recognition and surprise: he believed he recognized the dark, almost black hair and piercing blue-gray eyes, but Severus had grown remarkably in the intervening years since the hermit believed he first had seen him, as children often do. The hermit asked to see the left side of his neck, where he bore an incompletely healed scar, and his left arm, beneath the shoulder: there, he proclaimed, a boy once brought to those shores by noble but distraught parents had borne the shape of the bear in a brown birthmark. Severus admitted the scar, then rolled up his sleeve.

"Looks more like a boar than a bear to me," Gregius observed poring over it.

"I should have said an eagle," said one of the knights. "Look, there are the wings." He had learned Gregius had an investment in his young charge and didn't want to offend a possible new ally.

"A crucifix, I'd say," said another of the knights who happened to be a particularly devoted Christian, and he crossed himself and looked upon Severus with glowing, reverential eyes.

"A bear — distinctly a bear," said the hermit.

All the others looked expectantly to the last knight, the one whom Severus had first met at home.

"Well," hummed the knight, "I can see why you'd say eagle, or crucifix, or bear. At first glance it reminds me of a nice roast of beef, but as I examine more closely, I believe I'd call it a ... bear."

The hermit clapped his hands, then patted Severus on the shoulder. "Please sit down, everyone. Young man, I'm going to tell you about yourself and your parents, at least all I know of them and you. Once upon a time ..."

Clearly the hermit had waited some time for an audience, for he told a tale that lasted long into the evening about how some years before, he couldn't remember exactly how many, a ship had come across the sea bearing a couple and a baby. They had come all the way from Bavaria in Germania. Their ship docked down the coast from the cliff, and later they had come to its peak to meet the hermit and request his guidance. He was a young hermit then, bold in offering advice, and he heard their tale.

The couple had married young, and without their parents' full consent, so though they both derived from families of quite noble blood, those families denied them the connections and promotions they might otherwise have had. Semperus, the young man, joined the forces of a petty king who knighted him, but had little treasure to reward him for valiant deeds. Fidelia, little more than a girl, became a lady of the queen, but never won her affection and so languished on the social fringe while Semperus traveled and fought, trying to win glory and reward. He never did. Fidelia's beauty grew as she matured until in her husband's absence she attracted the attention of all the single men at court and several of the married ones as well. She felt so besieged by their expressions of love that she failed to attend court at all, first causing their enmity and later their renewed pursuit, which she resisted first valiantly and later almost violently, beginning on her own to study weapons of defense so that if necessary she could protect her husband's honor and her own. While he spent most of their first years away harrying, when he did return they always found their love renewed, and Fidelia bore two sons, who looked to grow into healthy and productive young men.

Though Semperus fought bravely and well and generously turned over all that he won in war to his captain, he failed to win that captain's gratitude, as sometimes happens with men of greater power but lesser worth. Once upon returning, the captain heard rumors at court of Semperus' wife's beauty, as well as many unkind stories by men who maliciously claimed to have taken her virtue. Jealous of his soldier, the captain began to spread rumors that Fidelia's second son was not Semperus' son, but that of another knight with a particularly bad reputation for seducing other men's wives — the first boy looked so like the father as to be an exact copy, while the second so balanced the parents' features as to look little like either. While Semperus loved his wife, seeing little of her caused his trust to wane, so that he believed he must test his wife's faith and that they must not have another child unless he could prove her spotlessly true. He found no evidence of unfaithfulness, yet fueled by rumors the fire of his jealousy grew in him, as it so often will in men. Though he vowed to keep distance from her, physical love will take its course, and in due time Fidelia became pregnant with their third child.

Semperus fumed and fretted over what to do, since given the rumors about the second child, the couple soon became the joke of the court with the appearance of a third. Unable to stand the rumors any longer, Semperus challenged a taunting, rakish knight to single combat and killed him, giving his captain a reason to complain of him to the king. The king's anger at the impromptu duel provoked a further reduction of their fortunes, making them outcasts at court, since, though he had basked in his reputation for romantic intrigues, the knight had upon Semperus' challenge denied any carnal knowledge of Fidelia.

By pleading with their families and by collecting what he could of his plunder, Semperus bought his first son a knighthood to be bestowed by the king at his majority, and he bought the second son a place in the Christian church, which was just then making inroads into that country. Those purchases devastated what wealth they had, and Semperus had never, despite her sincere protestations, regained his trust in Fidelia, who pined away at having lost his affections as well as her reputation and place at court — what young lovers ever foresee such eventualities? Severus was born at midnight during the full moon of Midsummer's Eve, a child unwanted by his parents — in those days signs that he should in time become a werewolf. As his father, who had become a Christian, rode with his few faithful friends to a chapel to have the child baptized, the party found themselves accosted by a pack of wolves, normally known in that place not to attack people, but Semperus' companions rushed upon them, and the wolves circled, growling and biting at the horses, so that Semperus, scrambling from his horse, lost the baby briefly into the pack.

He recovered it, scratched but alive, fearing that one of the wolves had bitten it, but the wolves disappeared as suddenly as they had appeared, and the men and the child escaped the mauling they'd feared.

When they arrived at the chapel, hidden in the woods — Christians had not yet won welcome to those lands, where many people perceived them as dangerous zealots — they told the priest the story of their journey, and he at first refused to baptize the boy, fearing him an aglœca, that is something born on the fringes of nature, either illegitimate or by an accident of nature of more-than-human strength or tainted with the mark of the beast. Those men, among the few local converts upon whom the priest could count for support, at long last convinced the priest to do the baptism, though he proceeded reluctantly, and when upon making the sign of the Cross over the boy, a rumble of thunder galloped across the sky, he hurried through the rest of the ceremony and urged Semperus to bestow the boy elsewhere, since such children tend, he said, to destroy their forebears and destroy whatever powers hold sway, be they good or ill.

Semperus returned home with the boy with no further incident, but Fidelia, who had not yet converted, resented what her husband had done. In time, unsure of what to do and troubled by the stories that circulated of how her baby had brought the wolves to him, then sent them away, she went, too, to the priest in the forest, made her conversion, and heard his advice. When she returned, after long arguments with her husband, they both agreed that, fearing for the boy's safety and their own, they must give him up. They knew well that no one in that region would take him — superstitions had great power there, as they often still do — and so they agreed to take him far away to try to find him a home where he could grow up without the taint of his early history.

They traveled to the west of Germania as far as the sea, where they had hoped to find Fidelia's elder brother, the child's maternal uncle in those days being the first choice for placing a child for rearing, but they learned he had sailed across the sea to Britain. There they sought him, but failed. Worn and weary, their relationship breaking up from the strain, they happened to find the hermit and so left the boy to him, requesting that he place young Severus with a good family, so that they could return to assist their older sons in ascending to the positions they had bought them. Only half reluctantly they left, sailing back across the sea, whence the hermit had never heard from them again. Those were hard times, and the hermit, who had thought to place the boy with a childless couple at court or at least with a family well off from the practice of some craft, could at long last find only an old couple who lived in the forest and practiced woodcraft. Their only son had long ago sailed over the sea with a warband seeking adventure and had not returned. They wanted company, and as they were aging rapidly, they would need more help, even that of a young boy, with the many chores of woodland life.

"Yes, your father was Sir Semperus and your mother the beautiful but sad Fidelia, so you have noble blood on both sides. You may also, though, have the taint of the beast in your blood."

"If I was bitten by a wolf, why do I wear on my arm the mark of the bear?"

"Maybe it isn't a bear after all, but a wolf?" one of the knights suggested.

"It's a bear," the hermit responded, "because you didn't get it from the wolf's bite, but from your birth: nature marked you as the bear's kin, so the wolf feared to harm you."

"Sounds like a silly superstition to me," said Sir Gregius, feeling grumpy at the realization that he must now lose the youth who had served him so well, since such duties lay below his blood.

"Maybe," answered the hermit, "but now, since you know who he is, you must see if you can find a knight who will train him. If he has proven himself a warrior

30

and of no danger to the folk who have housed him, he may turn out to be a hero instead of a monster."

"I suppose you don't know any such knights?" Gregius asked the hermit.

"Knights? Of course not. That's your job. I'm in the wisdom business, not the fighting business."

Gregius looked around.

"I may know someone," the first knight said, "and there we will take him to learn, if he will go, to study with the knotty old root of a woman who trained Sir Uwayne. Yes, a woman, but she will charge you nothing, and if she is still alive and can do half so good a job, she will make a fine knight of him — and without our having to go through all the silly business at court."

And so they took him to Lady Lynne of the Welsh Border, who was in fact still living if rather less hardy, and while Gregius felt rather sorry to give up the youth, Severus promised in time to return to repay the man who had served almost as his foster father, or at least as a good employer.

Severus spent two years with the lady who trained young knights in quick and ready combat and kind and gentle manners. She worked him hard, commanded him firmly, fed him rustically but healthfully, and watched him endure both a strict training regimen and the growth spurt from youth to young man. After the first year Severus began to call her "Aunt Lynne," and before the end of the second year he thought of her, despite her age, as a second mother. But she had aged considerably, and their second year together saw a bitter winter, and a cold spring claimed her body for the earth and released her soul to Heaven. Before she died, she complimented Severus on his accomplishments, but assured him he had much left to learn, and she gave him a talisman to carry to Sir Gareth and Arthur's court, adding that above all of Arthur's worldly knights, Gareth best understood courtesy, and since he had once fought Sir Lancelot to a draw, he could teach Severus the full range of the techniques of knightly combat and just living. "Tell him I said you are a young man of quality, like Uwayne, a woodsman, like Percival, but wearing the mark of the wolf," she said. "He will understand."

"I was told it's a bear, milady."

"All right, a bear, then."

When Lady Lynne died, Severus found a country priest, and the two of them gave her body Christian rites and burial. With some other artifacts she had left to him, Severus was able to buy a fresh horse, and so carrying the talisman, a metal brooch in the shape of a hawk, and all that he had learned, Severus rode for London, expecting to find Arthur there in the spring, but once again having lost what family he had.

He kept largely to the backroads and the woods, partly preferring them, partly unsure of his newly-acquired social skills. Arriving in London in early summer, he learned that Arthur and his folk had already gone north to Carlisle. With more than a touch of relief at leaving the larger settlement, he began the long ride north, which, with intervening adventures of small consequence, took him much of the summer. He found Carlisle in August and immediately sought out the famous Sir Gareth, once disparagingly called "the man with the beautiful hands." His arrival at court caused even less of a stir than had Gareth's many years before, for while Gareth had posed as a kitchen hand, drawing the disparaging nickname from Sir Kay, Severus arrived when nearly everyone had gone off hunting, which turned out an advantage to him, since he'd never enjoyed crowds.

He did, though, find a joyous Sir Gareth, who had remained behind to witness the birth of his first (and to be his only) son. Mother, Lady Lynors, and baby were doing splendidly, and Gareth, having spent several days with mother and child, happened to be taking a celebratory walk in one of the gardens when Severus arrived. The young man had asked a porter if he might see the famous knight. The porter had found Severus quite dirty and ill-kempt from a long journey and an even longer spell of training in the woods, but Severus' face, with its wide, iron-blue eyes and unpretentious gaze, inspired a sense of honesty if not absolute comfort, so the man showed him in.

"Do you know, good Sir Knight," Severus asked, "where I may find the knight and gentleman Sir Gareth?"

"You do not equate the two, knight and gentleman?"

"I intend only to suggest that the great lady who sent me to seek him called him explicitly one of the two greatest living knights and the greatest living gentleman."

Who, however humble, wouldn't have felt a glow of pride at hearing himself described so? "You'd best not tell that to Sir Lancelot, young man, but tell me, please, who sent you, and why to me, for you have found whom you seek."

Severus smiled and bowed, then handed Gareth the hawk broach Lady Lynne had given him.

"Ah, I have seen one of these before. Sir Uwayne once gave me one, telling me he had gotten it from a remarkable woman who had trained him in knighthood. He said that if I should ever be given another, then I would treat the young man who gave it to me as well as I treated him."

"I believe, Sir, that knowing your reputation for goodness, the lady sent me to you as she did with him. She said to tell you that, though I may not be of the quality of Sir Uwayne or of the craft and holiness of Sir Percival, I have learned much, and under the instruction of a great knight, I may learn more."

"You praise me above my worth, for though I remain a knight in the service of the greatest of kings, Arthur, I have practiced no errantry and even little

32

war since my happy marriage several years ago, and I have never tried to train a young knight."

Severus looked at him half discouraged, half hopeful, and with a plea in his wide eyes.

"Yet I don't say I couldn't do it, if my effort were to serve my king and to train a worthy squire. May I ask your name and quality?"

"Sir, you may, but to tell you the story may take some time, and I wouldn't presume to ask so much of you." You see, Severus had learned well his lessons in manners as well as those in combat.

"I perceive you have ridden far, though you look fresh for someone who has done great labor. Perhaps if we sit together over food and drink, which I must do anyway, you'll feel less that you're wasting my time."

Severus smiled, for in fact hunger had been gnawing at him for some time. "Sir Knight, you have as great courtesy as your reputation portends."

"Let's call a kitchen porter, then, and have a bite, and afterwards you shall have a wash to make yourself more presentable to the king. If your abilities match your courtesy and your desire to learn matches your demeanor, I believe Arthur will let me undertake your training."

IV Sir Severus and Sir Gareth Travel South, then North

[... wherein we learn how Severus attended a tournament then fought a troll to earn his knighthood.]

Severus and Gareth not only got acquainted, but quickly developed quite a friendship, and meeting the strange but mysteriously interesting young man, Arthur willingly designated Gareth his mentor. Many of the folk of Arthur's court, both noble and common, welcomed him, though many did so perfunc-torily. The hunting dogs fell all over themselves trying to lick his face, showing an immediate affinity as though they recognized him as a captain of their own. Even Sir Kay, who had learned his lesson about underdressed visitors, welcomed him, though with a noncommittal harrumph. To Lady Lynors he became as a brother, and to her little son an uncle, and to Gareth the most quickly develop-ing young knight he had ever seen, as Severus learned over the course of a fast year all that Gareth could teach him of large weapons, military tactics, and the insider's wisdom of the practice of arms. He had then only to test what he had learned to prove his mettle: by then Arthur knew what Gareth had learned of Severus' family, but Severus had still to perform deeds worthy not just of praise, but of knighthood.

33

Through the winter he served as watchman along Arthur's northern borders, having accepted a task that few sought. Slow months with little adventure followed, as another cold, snowy winter descended, and Severus, assigned to a lonely outpost, learned more about the art of simple survival than about courageous deeds. So when spring came, Gareth, concerned that the rewards his student won should match his progress, decided that he must accompany the young man on a worthy quest.

In late March, Severus was recalled from the Great Wall of Hadrian to the south of London to participate in a tournament. There he joined Sir Gareth's team against Sir Gawain's. He was thrown from his horse only once in the jousting, by no less than Sir Percival, while unhorsing nine opponents himself. Accustomed to wild riding and maneuvering, and trained with a war steed by the excellent Sir Gareth, Severus performed superbly in the melee, though unused to competition. Having fought only for his life and not for fun, he got a bit carried away. On the third day Sir Lancelot sauntered by to have a look, happened to find Gawain's forces taking a beating, and, feeling inexplicably drawn to intervene, surreptitiously entered the field himself, though not in his usual colors.

With Lancelot's aid, of course, Gawain's forces immediately began to gain the upper hand, much to poor young Severus' mystification, for he had thought his own team headed for certain victory. Lancelot watched the vigor of the young man, first marveling, then growing angry that through his aggressiveness Severus was placing other knights, particularly the younger and less well-trained, in danger. Lancelot galloped over to intervene. Severus, suddenly finding in his peripheral vision an enormous man who rode his horse like an icon of knighthood bearing down on him, turned and, in the heat of battle, struck the world's greatest knight such a blow that he nearly ripped Lancelot from his horse, and the sound of the blow echoed like the cracking of the ice across a lake as winter first begins to thaw.

The severity of the blow stunned the knight, who had seldom in his life felt such power, and of course once he regained his balance, it jelled his anger into something bordering on murderousness. It also surprised Severus, who had until then not fully felt his own strength. A lesser knight would probably have found his death in that blow. Severus backed his horse away, dropping his sword to the ground, but Lancelot had raised his with the intention of bringing it down in two-fisted fury, when Guinevere screamed and Arthur boomed out in his rumbling baritone, "Stop, I command you!"

Their voices barely pierced Lancelot's wrath, just enough to make him realize that he had in fact entered a tournament, not a war, and exerting the greatest of his self-control, he pulled himself back, nearly causing his horse to tumble, since it too had hardly recovered from the reverberations of Severus' blow.

Severus had regained enough of himself to understand what he had done, that he, not even a knight yet, had struck a nearly deadly blow to a full-fledged knight, though he knew not whom. He leapt down from his horse, approached the mounted knight on foot, threw off his helmet, and bowed deeply. He looked up into the iron mask of Lancelot and without flinching but with sincerity spoke.

"Sir Knight, I don't know who you are, but I humbly beg your pardon for overstepping my bounds. I am a young man in my first tournament and have not yet learned self-control, having allowed the heat of the moment to catch me. Nor have I done any public speaking, so I hope my simple apology will do. If not, swing away and have done with me, since I would rather die than offend the ideals of the knighthood I seek. Sir Gareth has taught me well, but I have much to learn, and I accept responsibility if I have erred."

You can guess at the effect that speech had on Lancelot. Despite its sentimentality and verbose formality, Severus delivered it with such sincerity and candor that the great knight, having himself regained composure, had to keep himself from laughing — not at Severus, but out of sympathy with his excess. Looking at Severus' face he remembered the innocence of his own youth, but he felt rather than saw something dangerous, and he began to wonder at the impression of urgency that had drawn him into the kind of tournament he would largely avoid. He no longer needed glory, and as a veteran fighting man with instant reflexes, he would have posed a danger to the younger knights — much as did the new young warrior.

Now that bit of reasoning took quite a lot of thinking for Sir Lancelot, who, while the greatest of soldiers and the handsomest of men, hadn't the brightest mind. He noticed he had kept the young man waiting for some time, so needing to say something, he removed his helmet and spoke: "I would possibly have done the same thing myself, so I can hardly forgive you, but if you feel the need, I do, forgive you that is, though I should rather praise you for strength and skill; however, a knight ought indeed to know when to curb them, and you look rather young — you say you're not yet a knight? — and who are you, anyway?"

Though not an artful speech, it drew appreciative ahs from the crowd, and several women swooned, since, after all, Lancelot had delivered it, and that's what they did when he spoke.

Severus bowed again. "Thank you, Sir, for your generosity, and I hope I have not earned your enmity, since I wouldn't willingly harm anyone. I am Severus, not a knight, but training to be one. May I ask your name, Sir?"

At that question the crowd tittered with laughter, and Lancelot regained his usual majesty.

"More likely, young man, in times to come we will be friends and comrades-in-arms rather than enemies. Ask Sir Gareth my name." And with a flourish and a wave of his helmet to the crowd, Lancelot ramped his horse and cantered off to the wild applause of the crowd — at least of all those who hadn't fainted.

Smiling, Gareth rode up to Severus. "My young friend, you have just met Sir Lancelot, the man who knighted me, and the only man from whom I wished to accept that honor."

"Brilliant of me."

"Not so awfully bad — you've given him and everyone else here something to think about. You have learned about tournaments, some of the good and bad, and you have come out of an encounter with the world's greatest knight unscathed, at least physically. Cheer up."

Gareth then turned to Arthur. "My lord King Arthur, I believe we have provided worthy spectacle and competent feats of arms for these three days, to your honor and to the greater glory of God. I believe also, meaning no detriment to my team, that today should go to my brother Gawain, since his team has fought the better, though I offer in our defense the energy of this splendid young man, who I aver has come near to earning his knighthood. Will my brother accept victory for the day, and will my king give his benediction to the tournament?"

Arthur, first making sure that a physician had revived Guinevere, raised a hand to Gawain, who removed his helmet and waved it in the air, signifying his acceptance of the cessation of hostilities. Arthur then spoke to Gareth and the crowd. "I grant Gawain the day, though I should call the whole a draw, since both teams have performed marvelously. Congratulations to all, and our thanks to Sir Lancelot for his courtesy and generosity in joining us. Sir Gareth, your trainee has fought well, and I agree that he nears the honor he seeks. When his courtliness matches his vitality, I bestow upon you, Gareth, the discretion of knighting him. To all who have participated and attended, may God bless you, and may you enjoy the remaining festivities!"

As a governor of people and icon of history, Arthur had of course to choose his words carefully and balance his judgments. With Guinevere recovering nicely, he hurried off his party to the feast, and the knights saluted one another and retired to their tents to prepare for the party. Severus, feeling rather sheepish already, began to feel even more so as the many knights and squires granted him only a nod in response to his offers of congratulations.

He saw to his horse's comfort and quickly retired to his tent, where very soon Gareth visited him.

"Do you know what you did wrong today, lad?" Gareth asked.

Severus of course had done nothing but think of that since his encounter with Lancelot.

"Oh, yes, I got carried away, I fought wildly, I struck the World's Greatest Knight without even looking to see who he was, I spoke out of turn, I ..."

Gareth held up a hand to silence him.

"Nothing."

"What's that, sir?"

"Nothing. You did nothing wrong. The error lies in the tournament system, which is why I attend them only when the king requires me — same with the other veteran knights. You notice that Sir Lancelot appeared only when he could keep himself clear no longer, his competitive fire kindled, and then he entered incognito. We arm young men, urge them to fight, then get angry when their blood rises or when someone gets injured. We must train in the event of war, yes, but we have turned training into public spectacle, into entertainment that rouses spectator as well as participant to violence. Do you know that somewhere out there tonight one spectator will kill another, arguing over the details of what they think they saw today? Foolishness! They treat old soldiers like meat, young ones like fodder, and one another like numbskulls."

"But I attacked Sir Lancelot and nearly injured him."

"Nonsense. He attacked you, and you did what I've trained you to do, which works in war, but wins only enemies in peace. I fear I have done you disservice, though frankly neither of us could have done much about it. If you want to be a knight, by these means you must do so. But I have in mind something else that may fall more to your liking and mine, as well: a means by which you may earn your title without killing any other knights. Given what Arthur has said, I would be impolitic to knight you now, though as far as I'm concerned you've earned it. As much as I love Sir Lancelot as my friend and mentor, that buffet you gave him will echo in people's memories for years. And I warn you, for his sake as well as yours, you may want to avoid him for a time. But one may gain knighthood by other means, some of which require more courage and a broader range of skills than does tournament fighting or even real war. I have spoken with my wife, and she agrees that you and I must make a journey."

And that's how the two knights happened to be riding north in April, when the sweet showers had eased, having drawn daffodils and violets and green shoots from the ground that had just shaken itself free of the last snow — north, past the land of the Caledones to the highlands.

When Gareth had broached the idea of a different sort of quest, Arthur leapt at the suggestion, eager to send Severus elsewhere for a time to avoid trouble, and had appointed him, with Gareth's help if he wished, to ride to the Highlands of Scotland, whence stories were brewing about some increasingly troublesome monster in a place called Ben Novis.

"God may not have designed you for a tournament fighter, my young friend," Gareth said as they rode. "You concentrate on what's before you rather than opening your thought to the whole circle of battle, which can make your back vulnerable — you're young, and we can work on that. But that concentration and your instinctive response to sudden adversity may make you an excellent knight errant, and maybe you will do even better against beasts than you do against men."

"Yes, I believe I should prefer that."

"Tell me why you think so."

"I have had my encounters with beasts, yes, my first as a baby, a hermit told me, as my father took me to baptism. Then again, as I rode watch on my lord's lands in the South, one nearly caught me unawares at night. I had seen the red eyes following me as I rode, and when I turned back, I saw that the thing had followed me. When I stopped, it leapt for me — creatures seem always to be leaping for something — and I barely dodged it. Can you imagine a poor wolf leaping for a horsed rider? Well, I found it wasn't such a wolf as one may normally see, but a huge thing with foul breath and enormous haunches, and I had quite a time with it. Got free of the horse so it might run away if it wished, and faced the thing with such weapons as I had — thank God for the full moon, which allowed me to see it clearly enough. I'm certain I slit its throat at least twice, but it kept coming back for more and scratched me up thoroughly. Finally I pounded the thing practically to a jelly with my staff, then cut it to pieces with my knife and burnt the pieces in a fire. Then the oddest thing happened. From the fire I saw — I must have been suffering from fatigue and dehydration — I saw arise a cloud of smoke that took the shape of a man shaking off the pelt of a beast, then rising into the breeze and disappearing into the night.

"Must have been a werewolf."

"Do you believe in such things?"

"You saw it; I didn't. Perhaps you will become a monster specialist."

"Have we such knights?"

"None that I know of."

"Not a bad thought, though."

"You don't fear fighting other men?"

"Not fear, exactly — you may say I find it distasteful."

"Yet you get along well with animals; they seem to like you, even sometimes to adore you."

Severus' horse neighed.

38

"I can communicate with them. We can reach an immediate understanding. They know what I'm thinking, and I know their intentions. If they intend no harm, we make friends; if they wish to harm, they know that I know, and I know they know that I know, and they know ..."

"Got it."

"Right. The hermit called me an aglœca, which I take to mean that he considered me some sort of beast, thus kin to the animals and better able than most to understand them."

"You don't talk to them?"

"Not exactly — I'm not begotten. But I can read them better than I can writing and better than I can people."

"Aglœca. I've heard that word, though I think the continentals use it more than we do, largely in their faery tales."

"The hermit said nothing about my coming from the Otherworld."

"I've had little experience with it myself. You do have something odd about you, but I'd call it forthrightness, which one doesn't see often in people, rather than anything elven. Should we work a bit on your reading as we travel?"

"I should like that."

"If you can't read well, how will you ever know if the stories the poets write about us are true?"

"Do you think someone will actually write our adventures?"

"You never know."

Gareth and Severus rode at a steady but unhurried pace over many days, stopping to right wrongs and rescue folk in distress. Well, to tell you the truth, I must admit that what they did was help a village complete a dam before rains flooded their river, help a sheep farmer repair a wall to keep his livestock in, and rescue a hunting dog who had gotten itself backed up by some wild boars. You may think those tasks unsuitable to noble sorts, as most knights did, but Gareth and Severus were more the type who like to keep busy, and they preferred to leave behind them people who honored knights rather than those who despised them.

The hardest part of the journey came once they'd reached Scotland: they heard tales of so many ghosts and monsters that they needed two weeks to sort them out and find the one Arthur had sent them after on the mountain known as Ben Nevis — Arthur had gotten the name wrong, though certainly close enough for us to forgive him for it. Locals spoke a different language than any Gareth or Severus had heard before, and they knew little Latin, so communication moved slowly, and when the two errants clarified their purpose, the people, affirming that they did have a monster who, when they least needed him, rumbled down from the mountain to steal, maim, and kill, made explicit that they didn't believe outsiders could or should handle it. And who can blame them? They wanted to take care of their own monster rather than feel incompetent at needing someone else to do it.

So Gareth and Severus, bound by honor to see their quest through, waited, and they didn't have to wait long. The people had a summer festival in which they celebrated a local meat dish that they considered their particular claim to culinary fame, but that no sensible outsider would touch. Of course the monster came down from the mountain to dismantle the festival and dismember a local drunkard or two who hadn't the good sense to sleep it off withindoors. Our heroes had made the mistake of eating the local fare and paid the price by missing the festival woefully sick, disgorging the contents of their bellies all the way down to the lining. In a day or two, when they'd recovered, they renewed their offer to fight the monster, but by then the locals thought little of men who couldn't hold down their food, especially food fit for lairds, so they waved them dismissively up the mountain to meet their fates. All they could learn amounted to this: the monster had great weight, huge feet, and an enormous appetite — it had cleaned out the remainder of the picnic supplies — and that it moved quickly for its bulk.

Now you probably know that most monsters turn out to be bad men or bad or just hungry animals, but Severus believed the case otherwise: he smelled something odd in the air, and the only facts he could get from anyone about the monster bore out his nose — those who had glimpsed it said it carried a club and looked like a huge, lumbering stone.

They climbed watchfully and circled the mountain, but by day they could find nothing — Severus had expected as much. They set up camp, near an outcropping and not far from a small tarn, in case they should need more water, and with the dusk they built a large, happy campfire. You may well call that silly, since such a thing may as well attract as repel a monster, but our heroes did in fact intend to attract it: for that reason they had taken up their quest.

They ate a sparse dinner, still feeling a bit queasy, and sat and talked by torchlight about tactics for fighting monsters, when Severus suddenly sniffed something and jumped to his feet. "It's near," he said, "and I know what it is, though I don't know the name or how I know."

"Tell me."

"It's a large magic-earth cave-dwelling ... thing. I don't know the word for it," Severus said, grasping his sword, then instinctively tossing it aside and fingering about for his longstaff. "It smells of earth and spells, and it's very old. It knows we're here, but I think that may help us." Snifff. "I don't smell fear, but it has power like stone."

40

"Troll," Gareth said, shuddering.

"What does that mean?" Severus asked, but Gareth had not time to answer.

Not far from them, at the base of the outcropping, a large hole opened in the earth, and from it came a smell of dusty stone and desert earth, and the troll, for that is in fact what it was, leapt out and landed not far from them with a thud that shook their tent down, leaving them just time to roll free of it.

"Hoo, haw," it boomed, fingering an enormous wooden club.

"Who are you, and what do you want?" shouted Gareth at it, trying what one normally asks ghosts, not knowing if trolls respond to it as well.

"Stirr hungry, sirry man, haw!" it said inhospitably. "Hooo!" it shouted at Gareth, the power of the voice and the dusty death-smell nearly knocking Gareth off his feet.

"Better let me have a go at it," Gareth said, regaining himself, but Severus had already moved forward.

"Now look here, my good fellow," said Severus, striding calmly toward the troll with his hands holding his weapon behind him, so as not to look too aggressive. "We simply can't have you troubling the village this way. Can't we make some better arrangements to get you fed?"

"Feed on your fresh and bones, rousy man," the troll rumbled. It looked to be made of stone: two tall, hinged stones for legs, an oblong stone body, a round stone head, and two stout but oddly flexible stony arms.

"Not very kind of you, though I suppose that's your way, if no one's taught you better," said Severus, who took the staff from behind him and began to twirl it in circles, spirals, and figure-eights before him.

"Fancy twirring, makes me hungry," said the troll. Gareth found remarkable that he could understand the troll better than he could the locals, but he had no clear notion of how to help his young friend.

"Two things may fix that, good fellow, either food or death: choose one now!" Severus called.

"Food, now. You wirr do." The troll raised his club and brought it down right where Severus stood, but the young man bound aside, twirling his staff, and struck the troll's weapon arm solidly and rapidly.

The staff bounced off the troll with a resounding thwack.

Before the troll could remount its club for another swing, Severus had struck it several times in different spots, looking for something soft, but finding nothing but flesh hard as stone.

"Haw-haw, hoo!" laughed the troll.

41

"Torch!" Severus called to Gareth, who, knowing nothing better to do, raced for their torch and relit it while Severus gamely battled the troll.

The troll had incredible strength, but modest speed, so Severus raced round and round it, striking here and there ineffectively, but getting the troll dizzy with trying to keep track of him. The monster wasn't accustomed to anything other than folk running from him or dying beneath his club. Eventually Severus spotted two small, uneven eyes in the round, stony head, and when he found an opening, he thrust his staff-end right into one of the eyes.

"Ow!" the troll bellowed. "Nasty you, thing!" And though wobbly with dizziness from trying to keep up with his adversary, he redoubled his blows, so that the whole mountain seemed to shake.

"If you've had enough, you may still go back in your hole and never bother anyone here again!" Severus offered, but everyone knows trolls seldom give in, and with a horizontal swipe of his club the monster sent Severus' staff flying from his hand. Severus dashed for his sword, but the first swipe of it confirmed his instinct as the blade shattered against the stony body.

"Haw, hoo-haw!" the troll laughed, rubbing its injured eye, and Severus realized he'd have to find a better weapon in a big hurry. His own hand stung from having his weapon jerked from it, and he saw a fey yellow light emerging from the troll's injured eye, as if it were healing or gaining some additional power as a result of its injury. He took his iron sword-hilt, recovered his staff, and ran for the cave entrance.

"Run, rittre man," the troll called with a laugh, "run to my rair!" and ambled after him. Gareth had followed with the torch in one hand and a hammer in the other.

"Same idea," Gareth breathed, "but we must be quick!" They found a chink in the hard stone of the troll's doorway. Severus thrust his sword-end into it, and Gareth brought the hammer down onto the hilt of the sword, breaking off stone-shards with a crack. In a second the two men gathered shards and prepared to fire them.

"Eyes and mouth," Severus whispered.

"Two at once, hoo, bad manners!" The troll had reached them and was preparing to take them both with one swing, but the men pelted him with the stones, plugging his eyes and mouth and causing him to reel and drop his club — who doesn't make his door out of something harder than himself?

The troll let out a yell that echoed into the valley like thunder.

"Downhill, toward the water!" Severus hissed, and the two men, quickly picking up more stones, hurried toward the tarn, Gareth clutching the torch and Severus hurling stones with one hand, then the other, at the angry, injured troll.

They ran to the edge of the water.

"What now?" Gareth asked, hearing rumbling footfalls right behind them.

"Take one side of my staff; when I say 'now,' run right for him and catch him at his knees!"

"Knees?"

"Here, where the legs hinge — now!" For, you see, you may often tell a cave troll by the fact that his knees hinge backward.

The troll was almost upon them, and they sprinted with all their strength toward him, gripping the staff on either end. The troll, coming rapidly downhill and following the men more by smell than sight, couldn't stop himself, and the staff caught him right across the knees and sent him sprawling into the water.

"Bbbrraawwww! No-bbbbbbbb," the troll sputtered and bubbled.

"We must hope he's too heavy to swim: water conquers stone," Severus said, panting, "and that the water's deeper than it looks."

But the troll was clutching for the bank and beginning to draw himself out.

"One last effort," Severus said, and he leaped onto the troll's round head and pushed it with all his strength into the water. Gareth with all his strength tried to pull the stony fingers loose from the bank.

The struggle lasted for several minutes. Air bubbled up as the troll struggled so that the whole tarn seemed to froth over. But finally the troll sank deep into the water, his body too heavy and Severus' strength too great for him to rise.

"I can't believe you did it," said Gareth to a wet and dirty Severus, who emerged looking grim and tired.

"We did it," Severus said.

"I've never seen anything quite like it. Cave troll. What a story that will make!"

"I wish we could have reasoned with him," Severus said.

"With a cave troll? Reason with earth and stone?"

"Worth a try with anyone or anything."

"You did try."

"And failed."

"Tell me you're not proud of our victory."

"I am," Severus said. "My blood is pumping and my muscles swelling with pride — but I wish they weren't. I wish they weren't."

"My friend, you have won your knighthood — isn't that wish enough? Even Arthur or Lancelot wouldn't deny you now."

"There are more of them."

"More?"

"More trolls, or at least one more. I can smell it."

The men strode grimly back to the cave entrance. There they indeed found another troll, half hiding, a small troll, and it was moaning horribly. When Severus approached it, it flinched and growled threateningly. Severus stopped, sighed, and spoke.

"I don't know if you can understand me, but I'll try. I'm sorry for what we've done. But you must not harass the people. Leave them alone, and no harm may come to you. Trouble them, and we will return. I promise by God that I will not seek you unnecessarily."

It spat a cloud of red dust at them, and with a terrible, painful, howling whine disappeared into the dark hole in the earth, and the cave entrance sealed behind it.

"We could chase it down."

"I may not. I will keep my promise."

"Did you take that awful sound to mean it won't attack or that it will not call others more terrifying than its lord to attack?"

"Its parent."

"Oh. That other was its ...?

"Yes, sad, isn't it?"

In the morning from the foot of Ben Nevis the two men departed for the south. When they stopped at Carlisle, they found Arthur and his court there, and before the king at early mass Gareth knighted Sir Severus. Arthur said that he should be called Sir Severus le Brewse.

Some say that the surname came from Severus' creative use of his oak staff, or that it implied he served as a bridge between the animal kingdom and the human one. Some say that it was a joke, because the water bubbled up around the cave troll as he drowned it or because he did much of his work in rural regions amidst the brush. Still others say that it was suggested by Sir Kay, because Severus showed no particular fondness for beer. And yet others say that it meant nothing at all: Arthur had heard it among the Franks, liked it, and used it, and in later years it became the surname of some of the kings of Scotland.

Ʋ Sir Severus' Adventure in Ireland

[... wherein the knight learns more about the world and himself.]

$\mathfrak{S}$hortly after their safe arrival at Carlisle, a story began to circulate about how in the northern Highlands Sir Gareth and a squire killed a troll as tall as a mountain. Sir Gareth, a gentleman through and through, did all he could to set people right, but you know how stories work: once someone tells them, one may try and try without success to correct them, as politicians have long known. While the story gained popularity for some time, few scribes recorded it, because if Gareth found someone writing it down, he would insist that Severus had done the heroic deeds while he had merely assisted, and of course no one wanted to hear or read that — some even began to accuse Severus of trying to creep into the story to aggrandize himself.

At the same time another story began to circulate that at a tournament in London Severus had treacherously attacked the peerless Sir Lancelot from behind, and when Lancelot turned to defend himself and remonstrate with the young knight for uncourteous behavior, Severus had trembled and cringed at the great knight's feet, begging clemency.

Yes, you know how stories sometimes work.

And things got worse yet for the new-made knight. One afternoon at a feast Sir Aggravayne, who, often at Sir Mordred's instigation, sought and provoked more than his share of trouble, felt moved (or allowed Mordred to move him) to confront Severus with the stories and any others he could invent. First he said that Severus had glommed onto Sir Gareth to take credit for his adventures and win an easy knighthood; Severus merely shrugged and moved away. Then he said that only a cowardly knight would strike another knight from behind, and only a treacherous one would do so to Sir Lancelot; Severus glared at him, but decided to leave the feast. Finally Aggravayne grabbed Severus by the shoulder and said that any lowborn knight must either kiss his boot or be run naked into the Solway Firth. Two other knights who were sharing Aggravayne's jest laughed menacingly.

When Aggravayne took Severus' shoulder, he realized suddenly that the young man was quite a good deal larger and stronger than he had noticed — Severus almost seemed to grow as he turned about to meet his antagonist's gaze. Aggravayne tapped him on the nose condescendingly and said that Severus ought to challenge him to a joust, if he were a worthy knight.

"Challenge away yourself, then," Severus answered.

"Ha, I should gain no honor from the likes of you," Aggravayne said, "but maybe we should throw you in the firth anyway," and he attempted to tap Severus on the nose again.

But before he could, Severus struck him such a lightning-fast blow on the chin that Aggravayne fell back, out cold, among his comrades.

"Who's next?" Severus asked quietly and grimly of Aggravayne's companions, who began calling to the other knights that Severus had treacherously killed their friend.

"He's not dead," Severus said, as other knights, who had only been watching the spectacle with half-amused inattention, now began to surround them, "though I suspect he will sleep for a bit."

Severus asked pardon of the older knights, in case he had breached proper etiquette by striking first and requested that they excuse him from further festivity. They mumbled, and he departed with no more trouble.

By the day following two other new stories had begun circulating, one from Aggravayne's friends about how the new knight had, in response to their comrade's gentle teasing, struck him in the face without warning. Those knights who had no particular reason to favor Aggravayne told how Severus had defended himself in an effective if rather base way against some rather brutal hazing. In the afternoon Arthur, looking to prevent a quarrel between factions, asked Severus to attend him, and Gareth, wishing no harm to come to his charge, accompanied him to the royal hall.

"Well, my young knight," said the king, "I can expect from you either heroism or trouble."

"I apologize, my king. I wish only to serve and honor the institution of knighthood."

"King Arthur, if I may speak in my friend's defense: you saw the Lancelot incident yourself; I saw the troll-battle, and you have reason to trust me; every senior knight who saw the Aggravayne business says that Severus acted in the right, if a bit unconventionally."

"I believe you, Sir Gareth, but I also value peace and unity within my halls. I do not judge Sir Severus in any way to blame, but I do believe that we all may benefit from his undertaking an adventure. Severus, you seem to do well with monsters and beasts. Word has reached us of a magical adventure in Ireland, the land west across the sea, that no man has achieved, though one Irish knight, according to legend, won a boon there. You will find it some distance from the great and ancient passage tomb that lies in the northeast, along a river called Boyne, on a green hilltop. You must find the spot by inquiring. You will meet, so stories say, a gatekeeper, a ram, a cat, and a beautiful maiden who inhabit a cottage. Your task lies in finding the meaning of this strange story. Sounds deceptively simple — that often happens in cases of magic — but if you complete this quest, you will bring our court great honor, for no one has been able yet to understand, far less achieve it. Do you accept this adventure?"

"Most willingly, my lord."

"You will not have Sir Gareth beside you."

"Though I value that great knight's friendship as much as anything in the world, I happily undertake it alone, knowing that he has greater duties than to continue my education."

"God bless you then, son, and fare you well. When you conclude the adventure, return to us, if you can."

"I will, my king."

And Severus took the next ship he could get across the Irish Sea, and on that journey the wind howled and the waves tumbled, and Severus got as seasick as any man has ever been in this world. When the ship landed and he had recovered enough to move, he fell to the sand and kissed the earth and vowed to himself — he was ready for no more vows to kings, let alone to God — that he should never sail the sea again unless he could not avoid it.

When he had recovered, he undertook to find his adventure. Immediately he noticed this strange occurrence: people who greeted him seemed almost to know him, until he introduced himself and asked directions. Then either they would not help him or could not. He spoke such Latin as he had learned, but people either claimed to know nothing of what he sought, or if they offered help, they gave him wild directions that sent him far afield, if he trusted them enough to test them at all. Finally, having at least located the Boyne, he took passage on such boats as would have him, sailing one way, then another, with few leads on his target. He found the passage tomb, an enormous mound with its front covered in gleaming white stones. Two more months went by, though, before he could get any word of help whatsoever, and after he had learned that nearly every other cottage claimed to have been the site of one adventure or another at one time or another, though none fit the description of his quest.

He finally got help as he walked along a road he had tracked several times, but something in the air kept drawing him back — plus it offered a lovely view of the valley and the river. He found shambling along a woman who looked older than the river itself, and passing her he wished her good day in Latin. When she responded in kind, he asked her if he might take the liberty to ask her a question, whether she knew where he could find a magical cottage with a gatekeeper, a ram, a cat, and a beautiful maiden.

"Aye, young men are always seeking such adventures. Many a cot in Eire has such adventures, though they have consequences, and a gentleman should not seek a maiden but with honorable intentions."

"Forgive me, madam, but I should have said I did not come to seduce young women, but to unravel a mystery. I am a knight on quest — I tell you that not to try to impress you, but to speak the truth."

"Then maybe I can tell you something useful to you. But before you hurry off to your adventure, would you do the kindness to walk an old woman to her gate? Age catches up with everyone eventually, you know, and the young should remember it will catch them sooner than they think, if death doesn't find them first. Surely a knight errant can spare that much time to assist the needy."

While Severus found that speech thoroughly gloomy, he found it also true, and so he gave the woman his arm and helped her along the road, carrying the bundle she had been toting, which he found quite light, then up a steep walkway that he hadn't seen before to a cottage well hidden in a large copse of pine trees.

Before the cottage stood a simple wooden fence, with its forged iron gate guarded by what appeared a stone gargoyle, tall and broad with a grotesque countenance and a long, sharp tongue pointing half an armspan out of its ugly mouth. He looked it over for some time, then turned to address his walking companion, only to find that she had disappeared. Then he heard her laughing from inside the gate.

"Madam, are you all right?"

"Yes, young man, and so, at least thus far, are you."

"I have your bundle here. And may I ask for directions, if you know ought of my goal?"

"The bundle is not mine, but yours, and you have reached the next stage in your quest."

"I don't understand."

"You have reached the place you seek. You would not have, had you not agreed to assist me. Knights must first accept and perform their vow to serve. And few men can carry that bundle, though it differs for each. Open it."

Severus did so, and from it flew several small blackbirds, which then disappeared down the hill toward the river.

"Can you explain the contents to me, please?"

"Those were your sins, mercifully few. For most men the bundle feels heavier than lead. Since they already carry their sins, twice that weight means more than they can bear. Now you must pass the gargoyle and the fence."

Severus examined the gargoyle, but he could neither hear nor smell nor feel anything, so he passed it and tried the gate, but found no latch and no way to swing it free. The low wooden fence seemed to pose no problem, so he tried simply to jump it, only to find that as he started to jump, it grew higher before his eyes: as he jumped higher, the fence grew higher. He scanned round the building, but the fence enclosed it entirely.

The old woman laughed.

Taking from his pack a short sword, he dug a trench beneath the fence, but as soon as he tried to slide underneath, the dirt rapidly filled in the hole, prohibiting his entrance. "Madame, would you forgive me if I damage the fence? I will repair it before I go."

"Do your worst."

"You mean my best?"

"Whatever."

The tone of her voice made him careful, so Severus brought a controlled, focused, ringing blow down on the top rail with his short sword. The blade broke, and the blow sent a painful vibration up his arm.

Wondering if this puzzle were beyond his powers, he meditated for a bit, then took his staff, which he had carried tied to his back, and began circling the fence, looking for an apt spot. He found not the lowest point of the fence but the flattest ground and there dug a small pit. He stepped back two dozen paces and ran toward the fence with his staff before him; when he reached it, he planted his staff in the pit and used the length of the staff to throw himself into the air. The fence tried to rise to meet him, but he just cleared it, falling into the soft grass inside.

"That was inventive — never seen anyone try it. Are you injured, young man?"

"Not much, I think. You say others have gotten in by other means?"

"You must figure that out for yourself."

"What about the gargoyle? It troubled me not at all."

"Just a dead old stone, there for show. You'd be surprised how long some men spend trying to figure it out. Ha!"

"Shall we go inside?" he asked.

"Not yet. One more test: first you must wrestle me."

"I beg your pardon?"

"You heard correctly."

"Madam, even in my rustic youth I have never seen or done such a thing. I would sooner fail in my quest than harm you."

"You have no choice. You must wrestle with me later if you fail to do so now. Come, let's have a go and get it over with."

The old woman waited no longer, but stepped up to Severus more quickly and aggressively than he thought possible, and she grasped him around the waist and began to squeeze and lift. Severus felt the air being forced from him, but could hardly allow himself to fight until he found that if he didn't, he would in a short time pass out. So he returned her grip and squeezed as well, squirming, shifting his weight to get air and footing.

"You have the joy of youth in you. I have seldom if ever wrestled anyone like you," she said. "I have from the first liked you: you have something unusual about you, and that's a fact."

Severus assumed she intended to keep talking, so he listened politely but remained silent to preserve his strength.

When they had tried their respective grips for about an hour and neither could make an inch of progress, the woman relaxed her grip and stepped back.

"You have passed this test, and you have wrestled fairly and well. I was hoping you would."

"Hardly a test of wrestling in the traditional sense — may I ask its purpose?"

"Like you, I am more than I seem. I am no human woman, but the embodiment of Old Age. I will get you eventually, but not today. You cannot as yet feel my strength: long may you remain immune to it! And yet you respect age in others — an unusual trait for a young man, indeed. And yes, now you may go inside, though I hope you have no designs on escaping with the maiden."

"I don't know exactly what I'm seeking — no one has told me. I come because my king sent me and for the sake of adventure."

"Then if you're not too tired, go right in. Having matched me, you may keep your youth as long as any man can."

Severus tried to mask the fact that he was still breathing hard. He looked about for any tools that might assist him, but finding none, he knocked on the front door of the cottage and entered.

Inside the door sat a short, plump, cheery-looking man who stirred what looked and smelled like a kettle of soup.

"Well," he said, "you've made it past the gatekeeper. Few do that, so you may feel proud of yourself."

"I greet you, sir, and thank the powers that be for preserving me."

"Good, a mannerly young fellow. Have a look around, if you'd like. I'll light some candles, as the day has nearly spent itself."

He did, and Severus looked around the large room that must have taken half the inside of the cottage. It had a tall, pointed ceiling, a great fireplace with a broad mantle, a large, sturdy table in the middle, and several chairs and stands. On the table sat a huge ram, looking sleepy and contented. On a small chair by the fire sat a cat, its wide eyes taking in Severus unblinkingly. At the western window sat a girl, as beautiful as Severus had ever seen, embroidering golden leaves on a beautiful cloth. She looked at him and smiled and called him a greeting.

"I am Severus of Britain, newly knighted," he said.

"Welcome, young man! Oh, you are quite handsome, and don't try to deny it. Hugh, do put out an extra bowl for soup so he can join us — he must feel famished after all his adventures."

Her face lit up the room, especially when she smiled, and her sunny disposition so surprised him that he forgot to ask her name.

"Thank you, miss," he said, at least not failing in his manners, "though I should like first to learn what I must do here."

"No must, just may," she answered, smiling again, "though I should recommend the soup first, if you'll forgive my seeming pushy."

Severus looked to the kindly man. "May I join you, as the young lady suggests?"

"Of course! Though as you see there's no eating at the table. Choose a chair, and I'll bring you a bowl."

Severus could not help but sit near the maiden, who smiled dazzlingly and continued her embroidery. "I shall soon finish this new shawl for Elli; her old one has gotten so worn. Funny name, that, but she comes from the North, as you may expect."

The man dished out three heaping bowls of hot soup, cut slices from a loaf of crusty bread, and dipped three cups full of cold stream water, and they had a pleasant repast together, talking about the weather, the sorts of birds they got there, and the virtues of various medicinal plants that grew on the nearby hillsides. Severus learned about several artful stitching techniques, and the two politely asked him about his adventures up to that point. The soup warmed and restored him, but not so much as just sitting next to the girl, whose glow filled him with ease and confidence.

By the time they had eaten and talked, night had fallen, and the man asked Severus if he would prefer to sleep and attempt the remainder of the quest in the morning, when he had rested.

"I fear you will find me impatient, but I feel quite ready and prefer to stay the course to its end, now that I've gotten here, if of course you don't mind."

"Not at all," said the man, and the maiden smiled her gleaming smile.

"First thing: lift the ram off the table, if you don't mind. He's too heavy to move, at least for me and most folk, and we would like to have the table to use at least for visitors like yourself."

"Quite so." Severus, thinking he could move the ram easily despite its bulk, stepped right to it. The ram looked at him with some surprise touched with disdain, flattened its ears, and settled itself further, if that had been possible. Severus braced his back, bent his legs, grasped the ram, and lifted — and could not budge it. He tried different grips, different angles, till, finally, setting all his body and mind and will to the task, he lifted the ram, which bleated with surprise, and carefully set it down beside the table.

He rose up, not entirely satisfied, but shook out his arms and stretched his back.

"Well done!" said the man, who shook his hand warmly.

"Good show!" said the girl and kissed Severus on the cheek, causing both to blush.

Severus felt so happy that he hadn't noticed that meanwhile the ram had shaken itself and gotten up, and the cat had come down from its chair, taken the ram's neck hair in its mouth, and led it right back up on the table, where it settled down again. The cat stared at Severus for a moment, then nonchalantly returned to its chair where it shut its eyes, looking pleased with itself.

"Blast," Severus muttered.

"No worries," the man said. "You've done as well as anyone's ever done. There's no keeping him off in the long run. At least the cat left you alone."

"What does it mean?"

"Well, you see, the ram represents all the troubles of the world. Pretty heavy, aren't they? Few men can take them on, but no mere man may relieve anyone else of them for long. And the cat, well, is Death. Most men who get this far she will shake and toss in the fire, leaving them to escape if they can, though she gets us all in the end. At the very best she leaves our troubles on the table and leaves us alone to deal with them.

"That's all there is for now. You'll be needing some sleep, and you can bed down in the spare room. Would you take a cup of ale with me? I have really fine stuff in a crock here. Or if you'd prefer the water, which you know is good, too, for those who have the taste for it, you may have that instead."

Severus accepted a cup of water, and they talked for another hour until the others bade Severus good-night, and each retreated to a separate room. Severus let his memory recount the events of the day, and he tried to keep from his mind thoughts of the beautiful young lady, until sleep instead of she caressed him with dreamless ease.

In the morning Severus rose to find that the young woman had prepared him a breakfast of warm wheat cereal, goat's milk, and dried fruit. The man had gone out for supplies and to report how well a young knight had done with the mysterious adventure, and Elli had left the gate for her morning walk up and down the road, as she always did, should any other knights come calling.

As they sat and ate and talked, Severus finally got past his shyness enough to remember his manners and ask the girl her name.

She laughed, got up, and, having kissed his left cheek the night before, bent over and kissed his right cheek.

"Sir Severus, I am Youth. You have done so well here partly because you understand me and love me. But not even you can possess me forever!"

The front door opened, and the man stamped his feet and entered with his arms full, causing Severus and the girl to move apart and blush again.

"Good morning, birdies! I see that you have had breakfast. Good. In case you haven't guessed, young man, I am Good Will, and though you may feel welcome to stay a few days, you have achieved as much as one can here, so you may also leave as soon as you're ready. I will not hurry you away, nor may I urge you to remain — so life gives us each a course to follow."

Severus looked to the maiden, saw she had a sad expression, and noticed a tear slowly descending her cheek. She nodded assent.

"I believe, then, I must thank you for your hospitality and go, though my heart finds much to keep me in this place."

"Yes, my good knight, we do best to love our youth for as long as it may last; once gone, it will never return, though one may recapture a bit of it in children and in imagination. But you have the glory of achieving your adventure to take home with you."

"Yet there sits the ram, comfortable on the table."

"There he will always sit."

"And I'm so pleased," the girl said, "that an Irishman has done so well — none ever better!"

"I'm sorry, miss, but I'm not Irish. My parents come from Bavaria in Germania

"Can I have been wrong about that?" the girl asked the man.

"Not at all, miss," Good Will replied. "Whoever told you that, son, was wrong. Early this morning I spread the word of your success among the powers that live amidst the hills, valleys, and streams of these parts, and they recognized you as Ireland's own, not just afterwards, but even as you approached. Some of them even wished you success, which they seldom do, though they gave you no help on the way. Some goals you must win by yourself."

"Puzzling."

"I would give you a lock of my hair to take with you, young man, but a time will come when you'd wish I hadn't. As I will carry my memory of you, perhaps you will carry one of me." She hugged Severus and as she did so surreptitiously slipped something into his tunic pocket.

"Always, or at least as long as my memory holds."

As he passed through the front door and down the short path, the man and maiden bade him good health and long life. Not knowing what to say in return, he merely said that he hoped the earth poured its blessings upon them. He noticed then that someone had collected his belongings and placed them together inside the fence. He wondered if the fence would let him pass more easily from the cottage than to it. He took his bundled gear and tossed it over the fence, then leapt over after it. He heard the fence groan a bit as he passed, but it didn't move, and he landed on his feet comfortably, though feeling a bit sad, on the other side. As he walked down the road to begin his journey home, he spotted the old woman ambling toward him.

"Good morning, madam."

"And the rest of the day to you as well, young man."

"No one about this morning?"

"None so far, and I suspect many a year will pass before we see the likes of you again."

"May I carry your bundle up the hill for you?"

"You have carried your own, and that's enough. But this much will I give you for your kindness: should we meet again, and that is by no means certain, I will treat you gently."

Severus walked the hills and fields, then found a riverboat, and finally with great reluctance boarded a ship for a miserable journey back to mainland Britain. He made his way south, and with persistence located the hermit who had once told him his family history, but who meanwhile had moved from the open hillside to rather cozier quarters inland.

"Yes," the hermit said. "As I told you, your parents were Bohemian."

"You said Bavarian."

"Yes, Bavarian, that's right."

Then he told the hermit of his Irish adventure.

The hermit looked about to make sure no one was listening — normally unnecessary when one is a hermit — put his hand on Severus' shoulder, and spoke quietly. "All right," he said, "they came from Ireland. But I didn't want to tell that to the knights who brought you here. They tend to dislike Irishmen, and I wanted you to have a fair chance in life. You're what they call 'Black Irish,' with the dark hair and features, but with your light eyes you could pass for Bohemian or Bavarian — you looked like a good lad and I didn't want them to fail you because of their own prejudice."

"Do you know that they had prejudice?"

"No."

"Then shouldn't you have given them, and me, a chance? Don't hermits value the truth?"

You may think what Severus said there a bit harsh, but how would you feel if someone had misled you and others about your heritage?

"Young knight, I apologize, but when you have seen more of the world, you will understand, if you don't already. I assure you that the rest of the story I told you is true: I changed only your parents' country. Tell me now: how have the courtly folk treated you?"

"Fine."

"How?"

"Like something lesser than themselves, because, not knowing me, they prefer to believe my family in some way ignoble."

"Would they treat you better if they knew you to come from a people some of them believe inferior to themselves?"

"And yet I would treat them and myself honestly."

"If you can do that, young man, you will have accomplished an unusual quest indeed. In fact, I should think it quite possibly unique among men. And if you ask my advice, I suggest not that you lie, but that you keep your origins to yourself."

Severus talked with the hermit for some time, and when he departed, he rode for London, figuring Arthur might have reached there by that month, but he rode slowly, not especially eager for court, though his duty took him there.

In due time Severus reported to Arthur's court and told his adventure. The more mystical types enjoyed it thoroughly as they worked out the mystery, but those who preferred tales of battles and tournaments found it quite a bore: no gallant horsemanship, no marvelous weapons, no legions of soldiers killed. I suppose that's why the Romans say "De gustibus non est disputandem." No one at court recorded the tale, though Sir Gareth told it to his children in the years thereafter — sad to say, he didn't live long enough to tell it to his grandchildren, but that is another story. And you may take comfort that Severus had learned from it, as we'd hope he would.

We need add only one more point of narrative interest here. When he had gotten back to mainland Britain and recovered from the obligatory seasickness, Severus, having given up his horse before sailing, had to find a new one. Not far from the dock he found some rough men angrily beating a young, spirited horse they couldn't tame, the beating having gone past any stage at which they or the horse could ever have had productive relations thereafter. Severus never liked to see an animal harassed, even those who, because they posed a danger to

themselves or to others or because they had aged beyond repair, deserved to be dispatched quickly and painlessly. So he interrupted to stop the men, which of course stirred their anger further, but directed it at him rather than the horse. When one fellow, not knowing that he was dealing with a knight, tried to snap Severus with his whip, Severus dodged, caught the whip, and jerked him to the ground. The others left the horse to avenge their comrade, fallen in the dust and muck, and faster than the eye can see, Severus pulled his staff from behind his back. As he did so, something felt warm in his tunic pocket and, glancing in, he found that it glowed brilliantly. He opened the pocket to examined the contents, a gift from a friend, and an idea struck him.

"Wait!" he called to the advancing men. "I would like to purchase the horse which you apparently neither need nor want."

"And what do you offer in exchange?" asked one man dubiously. The others laughed, figuring a man must be simple if he wants a wild horse or if he intimates to bad men that he has treasure. Such fellows will often examine whether they may gain something of advantage in exchange for abandoning violence or merely in addition to it.

He pulled the glowing object out of his pocket, as eager to see what it was as they were.

"This," he said, and he held up before them a golden leaf, which caught the rays of the sun and sent them dashing every which way. He knew, of course, who had given it to him and also that he was certainly undervaluing it, but he believed the maiden would have felt glad to know that he had used it to save a horse from getting beaten to death.

"And what is that, young sir?" the man asked.

"A golden leaf."

"And how do we know that it is real gold, and not just some toy?"

Severus, who had no material aims whatever, felt himself almost too attached to the leaf to give it up, so he knew they would, too.

"See for yourself," he said and tossed it to the man, who caught it as the others crowded around to see. He saw in the man's eyes the first impulse to try to keep leaf and horse and beat Severus as well, but they all became so quickly captivated by their new treasure that the man said, not even paying attention, "Well enough, then: take the horse and good riddance. What a beautiful bauble..."

"And I will need the bridle, too."

"Take it, and be gone with you."

As Severus left them, he noticed them looking out of the corners of their eyes at one another, and he wondered which of them would end up with the leaf and at what cost to the others. "Under God, I call it then a bargain," he said.

As quickly as he could he tried to gain the horse's trust, managed through gentle cooing to get the bridle over the horse's head and lead it away. He didn't dare yet to try to ride it, but he took it at a jog, wanting to get the horse as far away from such bullies as he could. With a final glance back he noticed they were already starting to shove one another, and he suspected they would remain so occupied for a time. Once he had made some distance, he got the poor, skinny animal some decent food and water, and he saw in his new friend's eyes appreciation, if tempered by doubt.

And that is how Sir Severus acquired the friendship of his horse, Courage, with whom he shared many adventures.

Severus had by then assured himself that he liked traveling far better than courtly life, and that he preferred adventures of mystery and magic and monsters to those of fighting men, so with Arthur's approval he took the life of the errant knight, and in the following years had many successful adventures, until he gained a reputation as the man one sought out for those quests necessary to peace and prosperity but beneath the dignity of most knights. He cherished his youth, but grew into a fine man, as fine a monster specialist as those or any other times have seen, and he undertook many quests of which no tales tell, until those which you shall find related next. For now we return from the backgrounds of our characters to the adventures they shared, and we rejoin them in the spring following Severus' battle with the serpent in lowland Scotland.

VI Sir Severus and Sir Lancelot

[Here we return to the main thread of the story: the adventures of Severus and Lilava, with some connection to Lancelot.]

Whether from a lunch of red apples, bread and honey, and fresh milk, or from the pollen in the air, or from the light hum of mid-spring over the grass and a throbbing breeze through the trees, Sir Lancelot lay by the lake and slept. Lilava, at that time serving as attendant lady of the Lady of the Lake and beloved of Sir Severus le Brewse, quite happily sat in a nearby aspen (which is why, they say, in parts of England the aspen quakes yet, because of her trembling) watching Lancelot as he drew in the deep breaths of spring sleep under the sun. For, as we have learned, like most ladies of her time, Lilava loved no man so well as she loved Sir Lancelot, except for Sir Severus.

Yes, the ladies in that time and place loved Sir Lancelot, since he was tall, strikingly handsome, the most successful knight in all the world, and, when he wasn't mooning over Queen Guinevere, friendly enough, if not especially attentive.

Most ladies also realized that if they ever wanted to hold a man in their arms, they had better look elsewhere than Sir Lancelot, because he spent nearly every waking hour — when he wasn't tumbling other knights over their horses' cruppers — lost in his love for Guinevere.

And that is, as we have said, one reason why Lilava had also come to love Sir Severus le Brewse. He was also tall, reasonably handsome, and though he wasn't especially prominent at tournaments and court feasts (in fact, he seldom attended them at all, since he had no special heart for fighting his fellow knights), everyone at Carlisle, London, or anywhere else that was anywhere in the courtly world knew that when it came to fighting dragons and other beasts, no one could match him, not King Arthur the giantslayer or even Sir Lancelot himself. And Sir Severus le Brewse, though he didn't care for courtly life, could be charmingly and devotedly attentive when he wasn't in immediate pursuit of a dragon or some other menace, and if one could find him.

That is also why Lilava sat perched that warm spring day in an aspen tree watching Lancelot as he slept: not only to watch the first knight of the realm, but also because the knight of her heart, Sir Severus le Brewse, was riding around the bend of a river scarcely a half mile away and directly toward the sleeping Sir Lancelot. She wanted to be sure that they did not accidentally meet in combat.

Lilava, having by that time trained with the Lady of the Lake in the spells of love and other especially useful magic, in addition to all that she had learned through childhood and youth, was trying every charm she could think of to keep Lancelot pleasantly and deeply asleep. The Lady of the Lake had once prophesied that should Sir Lancelot and Sir Severus meet in battle, one or the other would die, and despite his superior knightly skills, it might be Sir Lancelot. For as all enchantresses knew, Lancelot was, despite his personal beauty, like Severus an aglœca, that is, something other than normally human, and as close kin to dragons and giants as to other men, because his skills and natural abilities lay beyond the spectrum of most human accomplishment. That fact accounted for his continued success and also made him the kind of opponent that attracted Sir Severus without his taking time for the normal greetings and recitation of lineages and battle histories that would typically precede a chivalrous joust.

Now of course Sir Lancelot's history is another story entirely. Let it suffice for the present that though he was descended from Joseph of Arimathea, somewhere in the whirl of time one of Cain's kin had married into the family, thus tainting the line with Giant's blood, occasionally leaving in some descendants a taste for such things as battle and adultery. Of that blood Lancelot had received an especially significant dose, so that, though in his best moments he longed for all that's good and holy, when his blood ran hot he now and then lurched a step toward the unfortunate and even the infernal — thus his inability to shake free of his love for Guinevere (and also her fatal attraction for him) and his failure in the Quest of the Holy Grail.

Lancelot, though, was a different sort of aglœca than Severus, and therein lay the particular problem between them. Sir Severus bore the mark of the bear, connecting him to beast and bird, while Lancelot bore a taste for sin, into which only his continually renewed vows of faith kept him from tumbling headlong.

So to avoid an untoward end, the Lady of the Lake had once called both knights, Lancelot and Severus, to her and made each swear that he would never willingly fight the other. Being good knights and true, they had so sworn, and both had always kept that vow, though of course anyone may make a mistake in a pinch.

Lilava aimed to make sure that the pinch didn't come, at least until she could secure the proper knight to complete her own quest and free her folk from the Chimaera.

To be fair we must note that Lilava was, despite being an enchantress, a lady of feeling. Not only did she want neither of her knights to harm the other, but also she wanted to be sure that they were spared the embarrassment of meeting, not recognizing each other, and, finding an opponent of beyond human strength, having to break off in the heat of battle because of their vows of mutual safety. In such an instance even a breaking off might be too late to save a life, since Lancelot and Severus were as able knights as the world has ever seen.

On this particular day, as on most days, Sir Severus was riding alone. He enjoyed the solitude of a sunny day when he could unlace his helmet and ride slowly, with his eyes closed and his face upturned to the sun. He enjoyed the sound of the stream licking at the rushes, the smell of leaves bobbing in the breeze, and the feel of warmth on his smooth forehead. Some days he would stop to fish, hoping to catch nothing as long as he had another source of food. Because he did not willingly engage in quarrels with young men or in fleeting amours with young women, Sir Severus' face was free of lines and his glance free of sorrow. When he met a hermit or found a chapel, he would stop to pray — having as yet had no particular experience that led him to confirm his faith, he felt nonetheless moved to religious expression and tolerance, if not zeal. When he met poor folk, he would give what few alms he had. When he met a graceful maiden, he would smile, drop his eyes, offer a greeting and assistance if she needed it, and then ride on. When he met a knight who insisted on a joust, he would, if he must, fend off blows, get his opponent tired with striking, bore him into submission by striking seldom in return, share with him a kind word and a simple meal, then ride again on his way, happy to meet the solitude of the road again and dream of Lilava until he should happen along another monster. Many young knights who may unluckily have fallen on foes bent on their destruction had instead gained experience by jousting with an excellent knight who intended them no harm — much of Sir Gareth's wisdom passed through Sir Severus to the next generation of knights. Yes, sad to say, it was a short-lived generation.

Only when he met a monster would Sir Severus' blood begin to roil, his nostrils dilate, and his eyes flame for battle. Then a mountain of water could not have washed the battle-heat from him till he had subdued his beast or dragon, burned its carcass, and laid a fang or a claw or a scale on the nearest chapel altar as a sacrifice to God.

That is not to say that Sir Severus was a man with no fear or of virtue and virtue only. For instance, not being an especially good swimmer, and having had his bouts of seasickness, though he fished avidly, he had never particularly learned to like deep water. And as for virtue, the deft body of a trim maiden, or her soft, thin fingers, or her ruby smile could on occasion, especially if he had not found a chapel in which to pray in the past few days, make his head spin and his knees weaken. So he stayed away from lakes and seas, and he tended to shyness, and though he had never sought out swimming lessons, he did have a special affection for Lilava, the lady of the Lady of the Lake, whose odd dark eyes made him feel like he was suddenly flying, despite his fear that Lancelot stood first in her heart.

While most men knew that Lancelot was first in their ladies' hearts, they were accustomed to the idea, and they learned to live with it. So did Severus.

The fact of the matter: they learned to live with it or they died for it. Since personal challenge was the only respite for a knight whose lady (however chastely) loved another knight, and since no man had survived a serious personal challenge against Sir Lancelot, most knights were quite willing to accept a comfortable second place in their ladies' hearts, enjoy a little dalliance despite their fantasies, and complain over a cup of ale or two to close friends only.

Sir Severus did not complain. About anything. To anyone. That is perhaps why, despite his difficult introduction to court, most knights of Camelot gradually came to admire if not like him and even willingly accept his oddities, such as his drinking only seldom and his attending mass, but sitting always next to the door. And Britons in general felt happy to be relieved of troublesome beasts. They did not, however, especially trust Severus as they did Lancelot, since human nature will seek someone to whom to complain about love, war, politics, and British weather, and anyone who does not complain regularly may just be hiding something — at least so they thought. And Severus did not reveal his heritage, not because he withheld it, but because, after a time, especially with Sir Gareth's support and the gradual winning over of the king (because he did so much dirty work with so little expectation of glory), no one asked it.

Sir Severus did not complain, though, chiefly, as we have seen, because he was a happy man: he loved a woman, Lilava, whom he did not possess and who did not possess him, but for whom he had a more than mild attraction; he served the world's best king, Arthur of Britain, who was served by the best knights in Christendom or anyotherdom, and he made a living doing what he did best, which was making mincemeat out of such creatures as most brave men quaked even to imagine.

Lost in the joys of daydreaming about the bloody beheading of a dragon and of claiming a victory kiss from the exotically beautiful and intellectually accomplished Lilava or of roaming wild, barren mountain ranges far from villages and towns, Sir Severus relaxedly opened his eyes as he rode directly beneath the aspen tree in which sat Lilava, energetically working her way through every spell she knew to try to make him turn and go the other way. She hoped he would willingly disappear into his daydream or simply fall asleep and trundle by without falling out of the saddle and hurting himself, just so that he might not find her sitting there, poised over a sleeping Lancelot, and wonder what she was doing. Severus had always proven, though, for some reason Lilava hadn't quite fathomed, remarkably resistant to magic.

So as you may have guessed, when he passed under the aspen tree, Severus yawned, stretched, and looked up.

When Severus spotted her, Lilava smiled broadly and nervously and, one must say, not with complete sincerity. She certainly did not want to give Severus the idea that she was following Lancelot about the countryside, and thus fall in the estimation of a man to whom she might make a better claim. Neither was she ready yet to tell Severus she often followed him.

"Greetings and blue skies to you, Lady Lilava."

"Greetings and a swift horse to you, Sir Severus."

"Is it a hurry you're in to get rid of me?"

"Not at all, my dearly honored knight. But I have heard that beyond yon wood and ridge lives a giant, and one who enjoys terrorizing local farmers and occasionally even eating a milkmaid," said the lady, trying to come up with something plausible and not likely to insult.

"He hasn't threatened you, has he?" said Severus, straightening in the saddle and a bit too abruptly jamming his helmet back on his head.

"Indeed not, Sir, so do not fear for me. I have not even seen him myself, and he may indeed be no more than a rumor." Lilava felt bad about simply lying, so she tried to ease her conscience a bit with conditional clauses.

"Rumor or not, I will find out for myself, if for no better reason than to secure your safety, Milady!" So saying Sir Severus quickly spurred his surprised horse, who was not at all himself happy to be yanked out of his own daydream, but who plucked up his own courage and gamely carried his master off the road, into the wood, and toward the hill.

Lilava sighed with relief and peered down at the sleeping Lancelot. He might have been made of stone except for the slow, slight rise and fall of his breastmail with the measured breathing of deep sleep. No baby in all of Britain bore a more placid, contented expression, though, we may be thankful, most slept without breastmail.

Meanwhile, Severus was mazing his way amidst the trees, feeling partly stymied and partly angry at his slow progress, for he was not one to keep a giant waiting. By the time he urged his horse through the trees, the poor beast was hardly ready for the hill ahead, but did his brave best. The hill itself was gravelly and difficult to climb, but Severus was not about to give any giant the advantage of seeing him pull his horse up over the crest of the hill, so by the time they got to the top, panting and sweating, neither was entirely unhappy to find no giant, but only a green moor that stretched off into the distance under the spring sunshine.

At that discovery Severus felt rather perplexed; he would not for a moment have guessed that the lady would even conceive of deceiving him, so he was forced to believe that the giant must have heard him coming and fled, though he saw no evidence of farms or farmers, let alone milkmaids, to be terrorized, or that the fellow was otherwise no more than a bare rumor. When he looked back down the hill, figuring to question the lady about whether he had taken the wrong direction, his horse gave him a look that suggested that, should they go back the way they had come, Sir Severus would have to do the carrying, so the plucky knight simply sighed at missing a worthy battle, the relieved horse sighed at avoiding a tricky decent, and the two set off across the moor together in favor of some other adventure to come.

However, they were to ride for some time without meeting an adventure of any sort. In fact, they had had little excitement in some time. Before the encounter with Lilava, they had in a month not met with anything but tender feet and saddlesores. About a month back on his way to the Great Tournament at Westminster, following directions from Lilava, Severus had found himself riding in circles, round and round where the field would had to have been, but never quite finding it. The only thing he heard at all was Lancelot screaming that he had been struck in the rump by a stray arrow shot by a lady who was hunting. He never actually saw Lancelot, but had heard him clearly, and he did finally locate the lady on her way back from Westminster, who told Severus that she had indeed shot the World's Greatest Knight and had apologized profusely, pleading that some magical force had diverted her arrow from what she had thought to be a sure shot, sending it off at an impossible angle directly into Lancelot's soft hindquarters. While Lancelot had gone away perfunctorily forgiving the young lady, the lady departed miffed that she had missed what looked to be a substantial buck, not to mention that she had encountered the World's Greatest Knight in a foul mood.

Following the young huntress's directions, Severus found himself continuing to circle the tournament field, though he was sure he could hear the clashing of swords and the cheers of the onlookers in the distance.

Ultimately, Severus had tired of circling, realized that he didn't really want to fight at the tournament anyway, but had merely thought of it as a break from the tedium of errantry, and so had happily turned his steps toward the open plain beyond, where he might take his time, lay his head back, and enjoy the unusually sunny spring. That decision was one his horse was quite happy to accommodate.

But now, faced with only more open spaces and not a hint of a giant about, Severus was beginning to feel lost for a purpose in life. I would not go so far as to call what he was experiencing existential angst; that is something of another place and another age. But he was feeling itchy at least to do something knightly and would even have almost gladly accepted a joust with a passing knight if he could have found one. Where was Sir Lancelot when one really needed him, sleeping by a brook? Sir Severus paused, looked about, and turned north, thinking that the direction he had least often taken lately, wondering why the thought crossed his mind of Sir Lancelot sleeping by a brook, and hoping to find something new.

He got something different, if not new: rain. The good weather had lasted as long as one could have reasonably hoped, but then he got rain.

Buckets of it, barrels, rivers and oceans of rain, days and days of slogging through spongy, gummy, seepy sod, of slipping on hillsides and sliding on rocks, of hoping one's armor did not rust and that the rot did not settle in to kill one with itching. An entirely sunny spring in Britain was, after all, more than anyone might reasonably hope for.

So Severus and his poor horse fumbled on, staying on the edges of woods for some cover from the steady downpour, gradually moving north, till one afternoon out of the misty gloom appeared a castle looming ahead under the rain, a large and impressive castle that certainly promised adventure.

The drawbridge was up, so the best Severus could do as he came to the castle was to shout, since no one seemed to pay any attention to his coming. In fact, after shouting for some time, Severus began to wonder if anyone was in the castle at all. Why would anyone leave such a magnificent castle unattended?

As he was just about to turn and ride off to get soggy somewhere else rather than lose his voice shouting at an empty castle, Severus heard a small voice calling from above.

From a window high up protruded a small but lovely face and an arm waving a handkerchief. Then the young woman sneezed, twice.

"Good-day, Thir Dighd," she said and sneezed again.

"Good-day to you, Lady, and may we all see one soon."

They both looked at each other for a moment, but said nothing. The young lady sneezed again.

"Whad do you wand, Thir Dighd, thtanding oud in da raid? Forgive me: I have caud a code."

"Terribly sorry," Sir Severus replied. "I am a knight errant in search of adventure. What is this castle?"

"Thid id da cathle Carbonek, odderwide knowd ad dee Cathle of Adventure, or dee Cathle of King Pelleth, or dee Grail Cathle."

"King Pelles? Grail? As in the Holy Grail? Thad ride. She sneezed violently. "Thorry."

"That's all right, poor lady. I have ridden long in search of adventure, and I would dearly love a chance to see the Grail." Sir Severus was known as a pious, if not perfect, knight.

"You're doo lade."

"Too what?"

"Doo lade. Lade. You should have come before."

"Too late?"

"Yed. Da Grail Qued hath been ashieved. Ha-spppt! Thorry. Da Grail hath athended do Heaven forever."

"Oh. And King Pelles: may I speak with him? He must have stories to tell!"

"Indeed he dud. But he id not home ride now. He had gone to da coath' to ged away from da raid."

"To get away from the rain? Can't say I blame him."

"I had to thday home becaud of my code. I'd led you in, but then you'd ged id, doo, and everyone here — ha-thtooo! — ith in a bad bood becauth of da raid, anyway."

"Thank you, fair Lady. You say the Grail Quest has been achieved?

"Yed. I thoud everybody dew dat."

"I hadn't heard. I was out of the country — called away to fight a two-headed giant in Denmark. Turned out to be a whole family of them, so it took a while. Since I've been back, I've had a hard time finding anyone ..."

"How doth one knide fide a family of gianth?"

66

"Well, you start with one, then see what happens from there," Sir Severus answered.

"Thpppt! Thorry. Good-day, Thir Dighd. I'm dot allowed do thday in the damp doo long. Ride nord if you theek advendure!"

With that the lady sneezed again, waved as vigorously as her cold would allow her, and then disappeared into the darkness of the castle.

Imagine that, thought Severus, turning his horse back toward the trees: the Grail achieved, and no one had even told him. But then he did not make a special effort to keep up on court news. North to adventure, the lady had said; then north he would go.

Severus wouldn't have thought it possible, but the rain increased again, and he rode into a small copse of extremely green trees of a sort he didn't know, hoping at least for a little cover, since Courage was starting to get irritated at the mud and fumbling.

"Choke you up, choke you down, choke you under a field brown." A high-pitched, whiny voice trundled down from somewhere above amidst the trees.

"I beg your pardon, I didn't quite get that."

"Choke you up, choke you down, choke you under a field brown. And no, you mayn't have it, stupid knight."

Then Severus realized he had found — or been found by — a rain gnome. They can create a good deal of trouble in their fashion, and they are forever riddling, often with their real purpose well hidden. By then Severus had little choice but to try to solve the riddle, for if you don't, once a rain gnome has gotten hold of you, he may keep you soaked for weeks or even drown you, since as a rule they have little else to do.

The first thing that came to mind, rain, obviously wasn't the answer, but only the unskilled will leap after the first answer without carefully considering it.

Just as the gnome was starting to laugh — an annoying sound much like the bray of a donkey, but an octave or two higher — Severus said "Shame," silencing the gnome briefly.

"Dance a lot, chance a lot, lives among a handsome lot — if that's what you like — " the laughter followed again.

Since he had been thinking recently of Lancelot, that name came readily to mind, but everyone knows Lancelot never liked to dance, so Severus chose otherwise. "Queen Guinevere," he said, "though that's a poor riddle."

If you ever run into a rain gnome, one does best not to antagonize them, nor to praise them, which often makes them stick around, but to play out the game as boringly as possible and hope they just go away.

"Ha, smart guy. Well then: has a fall, cries for all, tumbles down a fireside squall."

That wasn't as easy as it sounds. First of all, you may notice that the gnome broke the etiquette of the riddle-game by asking them all himself and not giving Severus a chance. Second, you may notice that the answer might as well be rain or Adam for that one. Gnomes don't usually use religious subjects, being generally opposed to them, but they may try anything with a difficult opponent, and one hesitates to take the obvious answer, though the third riddle is always a good one to use to hide the obvious answer and so outthink your opponent.

"Rain. Now that's three, and you may go, or at least permit me, master gnome."

"Go soak yourself, fool. You're no fun at all. Yaah!" And the rain gnome climbed higher in the trees, hoping for another victim, but Severus knew few people would come that way on such a day. He ducked back out from under the branches and returned into the rain, which lasted only a few minutes more as he continued north. The he turned also west, finding there a welcome hiatus of clear sky.

He had just time to make a fire and put out some fodder for Courage when the rain started again. He thought he could hear echoing in the distance the laughter of the rain gnome, who, though Severus had won the game, seemed intent on continuing his antics. Yes, sometimes they act that way, and sometimes they have nothing to do with it: British weather is just like that.

VII Severus Errant

[Severus finally gains a lead on a more serious adventure.]

Eventually the rain eased to a mist, and after a couple of days' riding along a green but rural path, Severus came to a spot where the way forked into minimally worn paths, one around a hill ahead, the other up it. Severus first thought the way around the hill the less travelled, but then noticed they were both worn about the same. He had not had much luck with hills lately, so he nearly took the easier path around, but feeling obliged to meet any and all challenges, especially considering his recent isolation, too much even for his predilection for solitude, he took the high road, leaving the low path for another day. Besides, as he peered up the hill, he saw what appeared to be a beacon near the top and took that for a sign.

Not so very long later Sir Severus realized he had made the wrong choice. The rain had picked up again, and as he looked down, the bottom of the hill was completely obscured in mist. That fact was only partially mitigated by his observation that the top of the hill was now smothered in mist as well, and the beacon that he had seen before had disappeared entirely. Figuring that he might as well just go on, Severus and his horse struggled with the slick grass and the turf slipping out beneath them, indeed struggled manfully and horsefully until they finally managed to crest the hill.

Patting his beleaguered horse and looking ahead, Severus saw emerging out of the gloom an ancient stone circle. Stone circles always promised magic and almost always demanded adventure, so Severus alit and led his horse forward. If the horse had struggled bravely to get up the hill, and he had, he set his hooves all the more stubbornly to keep from being dragged into the stone circle.

"What's wrong?" Severus asked. "You've seen stone circles before. You've even been inside bigger ones than this."

The horse simply looked at Severus with disdain for the knight's limited human intelligence, shook his head, and locked his legs in place, unwilling to move a step forward.

"Well, perhaps you're smarter than I am — " at that, the horse neighed " — but I am, after all, an errant knight, and what sort of knight would I be if I overlooked a chance for adventure and glory?   And what sort of horse would you be if you let me? It's not as if we've worn ourselves out with adventures lately."

Speak for yourself, the horse would have said if he could, and believe me, this horse was unusual enough almost to be able to do it.

"Well, all right then. I'll just go on alone, and it's you who'll be waiting here by yourself, feeling silly and left out," Severus said.

You just do that, the horse almost said.

So Severus stepped boldly up to the circle, then almost did not step in, because as he reached a gap between stones, he felt an icy wind blow out of the circle toward him, a wind such as he had not felt before, not a wind even with winter's deepest natural chill, but a wind with more than a touch of malice.

He steeled himself and pushed ahead, and as he did, the wind increased its force, so that, hard as he tried, he could not go forward. When one cannot move a force, he recalled, yield to it and let it defeat itself, so he tried to take a step back and turn to let it go by. He could not do that either: the wind had caught him round about as the Scottish adder had done before, and it was quickly chilling all the body heat out of him.

Severus began to breathe rapidly and flex his muscles to generate heat. Building his energy, realizing that the cold would soon freeze him to the spot and turn him hard as one of the standing stones, he prepared to throw all his weight forward in an act of calculated desperation. With a quick thought, he remembered watching the priests at mass, and he crossed himself and leaped.

As he made the sign of the cross, the wind immediately stopped, and he was propelled rapidly into the circle. He had just time to gain his footing before running over a very old man, whom he now saw kneeling in the center of the circle.

The man was red and withered as a dried apple, and the expression on his face as he stood up was not a happy one.

"Severus, what are you doing here? This isn't your quest!"

"You know who I am?" One can perhaps forgive Sir Severus for asking the obvious in such an unusual circumstance.

"Of course I know who you are," growled the old man. "You are a horse-brained knight — " Severus thought he heard an offended whinny from outside the circle " — who can't even tell if a quest is supposed to be his or not. Why, I heard you spent two months pursuing the Questing Beast, and everyone knows that is Sir Palomides' quest. I take that back: you're not a horse-brain. Your horse is in fact smarter than you are."

Both paused upon hearing an approving neigh from without.

Severus responded, a little hurt, "I am, after all, a fighter of beasts, so I naturally thought the Questing Beast was my task when I heard Sir Palomides was dead."

"He's not dead," snorted the old man.

"And when I learned that, I gave it up," Severus snorted back. "Not my fault if rumors aren't true. There just aren't that many monsters left in the world anymore."

"Thanks to the likes of you," the old man retorted. "And don't think it's a much better place without them. Ask me, some monsters are better folk than a lot of knights I've met."

"Please don't get irritable," Severus replied. Now that the heat of battle was cooling in him, he felt a desire to placate the old man and find out what he was doing here. "May I ask, old sire, what is the quest of this circle, and whose quest it is?"

"I am not a sire, Sir; I'm a monk, Brother Adam, as a matter of fact — spare me the jokes — and as long as the quest isn't yours, why should you care whose it is?"

"Just curious, I suppose."

"Curious! As if that were a reason for prying into other folks' affairs. I have an inclination not even to tell you about the quest you should be going on."

"I should be quite happy to learn what quest I should be going on, Brother, or why am I not fit for the one at hand."

"Now where is that horse? Perhaps I'll send that horse of yours on the quest, and you can stay home and get a job — blacksmithing might be nice, or maybe something easy to understand, like shoveling cow dung out in the fields."

By then, as you can imagine, Severus was nearly ready to give up and simply leave the stone circle, but he had the feeling that he might as well stand firm and take whatever abuse the monk intended to offer, which he did, hoping that he might learn of a proper quest to undertake. The monk went on berating him for some time. Severus kept his eyes fixed on the haranguing monk, but eventually let his mind wander to pleasanter matters, such as sunny days, forests, and the Lady Lilava.

"... and stop letting your mind drift to pleasanter matters while I'm talking to you!" the old monk finally shouted. "Now, as I was saying, this quest belongs to a soldier who is too caught up in worldly matters and needs a lesson that he is not the only creature in the world. As knights go, you, Severus, are a more generous and serviceable, if slow-witted, sort. You are not at all greedy or envious, you attend mass periodically, though you don't really understand it yet, and though you let your mind creep into lecherous thoughts, you live chastely. So get out of this circle before your presence here ruins it for someone else. And if you want to know where to find your own quest, the one meant for you, go southwest to the sea. You will find a boat departing from Cornwall. Get on it. I don't think you'll be disappointed with your companion. Your fates are linked — pity for her. Now get going! I don't know why I help these people. They blunder around, wandering into each other's quests, missing their own, and I'm supposed to sort things out for them ...." The monk went on in that fashion as Severus tried to sneak out politely. As he was doing so, the monk disappeared among the stones. No wind stopped Severus' egress.

The quest would require sea coasts and boats, Severus thought — not one he would willingly have selected for himself. But that bit about the companion seemed intriguing.

There, outside the stones, was his horse waiting for him, with a look that said: don't ask me — I told you so. Feeling that the animal was right, he felt disinclined to ride down the difficult hill before them. Fortunately, the rain had stopped, the sky had cleared, and the moon shone brightly, giving the landscape a dusky gleam, so Severus walked his horse down the hill. As they reached the bottom, the horse, figuring his knight had had his share of difficulties, even nudged Severus' neck to let him know that he was now forgiven and might expect to ride guiltlessly. Severus mounted and rode only until they could find a dry patch in a grove where they could rest comfortably for the night. Neither complained that night, though both slept fitfully for hunger, their provisions having run low. The horse dreamed on and off of apple groves, and Severus dreamed often of Lilava and of where a boat leaving Cornwall might take him, and of whether or not he could even board one without embarrassing himself, considering his fear of water.

Fortunately, after a short ride the next morning, horse and knight found the dwelling of a hermit who took them in, prayed with them, fed them, and told them where they might stop not far away to load up on provisions for their trip to Cornwall, though the hermit, being himself from the east, couldn't imagine why one would want to go to Cornwall for a boat rather than to Kent. Severus inquired if the hermit had seen any other knights passing that way recently, and the hermit replied that he certainly had, Lancelot, in fact, who claimed to be on his way north to find some sort of stone circle.

"Odd," said Sir Severus, "since I was just there myself, that we didn't pass on the road. Perhaps he went by in the night, as we slept." The hermit could find no better answer.

"There was a lady here a short while back, also," the hermit added. "Quite beautiful at that, though of course I'm not supposed to notice. She was inquiring after a Sir Severus."

"I am Sir Severus," Severus exclaimed. "Who was she?"

"She didn't say," the hermit said. "But I would hope, if I were you, and if she posed no peril to my immortal soul, that I should find her."

Hermits, while being hermits, are nonetheless human.

Severus thanked the man profusely, promised that he would pray daily for the next week for the hermit's soul (which he did), and happily took his leave as the warming sun welcomed him to the road. He met no adventures over the picturesque landscape of Cornwall until he believed he could hear the roar of the sea in the distance. Only half eager to get there, he camped for the night in a spot with plenty of sweet grass for his horse, then rose early to a windy day, riding south by southeast along a path, directly into the rising sun and toward the sea. Finding nothing but plain, he turned west, still hearing the call of the sea before him.

Not long thereafter, Severus heard a horse galloping toward him. He could not see the rider well, because the sun shone directly in his eyes, nor could he hear him clearly, though Severus knew he cried out a challenge, since the wind blew from directly behind the assailant. Realizing he had no choice, since he must either defend himself or get thrown, Severus grasped his spear firmly and returned the charge, though all he could see coming toward him was a blaze of light, the light of the sun engulfing the attacking rider. Assuming that he might have met misadventure and thereby death, Severus quickly if perfunctorily crossed himself, said a prayer, aimed his spear by guess, and prepared to receive the oncoming shock. Just as the galloping enemy's spear touched Severus' burnished armor, enemy spear, horse, and knight disappeared into thin air.

Severus slowed his relieved horse and found himself still facing the rising sun, but as well as he could tell, entirely alone.

Severus turned his horse about in a neat circle, but found the field bare, save himself. Puzzled, he trotted on, till as the sun rose clear of his eyes, he could spot a dark-haired woman, dressed all in white, standing ahead, the sea stretching out behind her. She appeared to be swaying, and as Severus stopped to get a good look at her, she swooned and fell.

Quickly at her side, Severus propped up her head and cleared the long, black hair from her face.

It was Lilava.

As Severus continued to stroke her forehead, she came to.

"Silly men," she said, "always crossing themselves. Do you know you almost got yourself killed by doing that? Either you or he would have, that's for certain, had I not gotten him out of there."

"He who?"

"Lancelot. Yes, that's who was charging you. He often gets his directions confused, and when he gets in the mood, he just can't resist a joust, though more often than not he'll just pass by. Not so sporting, either, with the sun at his back — must have been some sort of evil spirit moving him. I had a spell going to swerve him just a little to the side so that you wouldn't strike each other, so you could see who he was and call out for him to stop, since I knew you couldn't see because of the sun." She stopped for a breath, then continued. "And then you go and cross yourself, almost ruining my spell, so I had to throw everything I had into it at the last moment and send him off into space. And now — let me breathe a moment, since I've spent myself."

"Where? Where did you send poor Sir Lancelot?"

"Oh, nowhere awful. Probably to Scotland or Wales — somewhere far away, that's for sure. If it weren't for you we could all have had lunch together, and then he could have gotten on to his stone circle."

"Well — sorry. How was I to know? And Lancelot, how did he get here? I just heard from a hermit that he was heading north, while I was heading south."

"He was supposed to get to the adventure at the stone circle — one I hear you tried to enter — which should, if all had gone right, have sent him elsewhere. But events don't always go right, and knights sometimes do their best to go on the wrong adventures."

"Word does get around."

"Well, that wasn't your quest. But this one is. Please stop stroking my forehead and help me up. Ooo — you should have seen some of the fellows who tried the Quest of the Holy Grail: hadn't a chance."

73

"Missed that one myself. Not sure I'd ever have been ready for it, anyway."

Lilava rose, delicately brushed herself off, and curtsied. "Well then. Welcome, Sir Knight, to the adventure of the Chimaera."

"'Sir Knight'? You know who I am, Lilava," Severus said, somewhat hurt.

"Of course I do, but this quest is serious business, so we should begin formally. You can always choose not to go if you want, though this quest has been especially appointed to you."

"By whom?"

"By God, of course, silly, and by the earth, and time, and King Arthur, and all the Order of Enchantresses."

"Who are they, the Order of Enchantresses?"

"Too many questions for now. Save them for later, when you need them. Please follow me, if you don't find that too difficult."

"I don't find it difficult at all," said Severus, and he didn't. In fact, he happily followed the beautiful Lady Lilava down to the coast, enjoying her smoothly swaying figure and his daydream as they went.

"Your daydreaming is all right, even, I suppose, flattering, but don't suppose that you're really going to do that."

"Do what?"

"What you were daydreaming about."

"How could you possibly know that?"

Lilava stopped, glanced at him with a look that clearly said "silly man," and continued on to a small but solid sailboat that was moored upon the beach.

"What will I do about my horse?" Severus called to her retreating form.

"Don't worry; I've seen to that," she answered without turning around.

Severus heard behind him a neigh, but not the one that he was used to hearing. He turned to watch his horse trotting toward a filly that nickered on the opposite end of the field.

"Oh." Severus doubtfully followed Lilava to the shore.

"Well, are you going to help me in?" Lilava asked as he arrived beside the boat.

"Look here: is there any other way to get there?"

"Of course not. Oh, I see. Afraid of water, are we? Fine thing for a full-grown knight. Never learned how to swim?"

"Not really. I sink like a stone. And worse, I get seasick."

"Well, learn to swim, but not right now. You are with the lady of the Lady of the Lake, and though this is the sea and not a lake, I'm not entirely without influence here, nor am I unskilled with medicines." So saying, she lifted the hem of her dress and helped herself quite gracefully into the boat.

"Do I go without you, or are you going to pluck up your courage? Just take one step, and we'll go on from there."

Severus yet hesitated, with a little smile on his lips.

"Does time alone with me on a sailboat frighten you that much?"

"Well, if you put it that way."

Severus stepped forward and gingerly put one foot in the boat. Then, losing his balance and feeling himself lurch forward, he fell into the boat, which was immediately propelled forward into the wash.

"Now, Sir Knight, the quest officially begins, and you should pray to God for success and thank your guide for the chance to pursue it."

"More formalities?"

"Yes."

"Right, then. Yes, I will pray, and thank you!"

"You may not want to thank me when you realize what you've gotten yourself into."

"What who got me into?"

"Free will, you know: you have, and so have we all, at least with respect to some choices."

"I'm not always sure of that, but for the present I'll take your word for it."

VIII Lilava's Quest

[Severus learns from Lilava the nature of their quest, and Severus tells Lilava a story.]

After flailing about for a bit and trying not to cry out, Severus finally managed, with Lilava's cooing encouragement, to calm himself and hang his slightly green face over the edge of the sailboat, which, catching a breeze, was moving rapidly into the current and away from shore.

As the coast fell away behind them, clouds gathered, and one last English rainstorm bade them farewell, soaking them both thoroughly and rocking the boat nauseatingly with its accompanying winds.

Even after the rain had stopped, Severus did not find the trip easy, despite the excellent company. The time might have allowed him the opportunity to woo, had he wished it, but, frankly, his mind was more involved with such concerns as "When will we get there?" or "Why did I agree to do this?" or

"I don't remember having eaten that much, so I wonder if what I'm seeing over the side of the boat is part of my insides" and other such peevish if justified sentiments. Let it be recorded that Lilava remained remarkably patient through the whole ordeal; in fact, she felt even somewhat relieved to learn that her knight was not one of those who refuses to admit that he simply can't do something and so asserts that the problem must lie with anybody else but him, and she appreciated the fact that though she knew that his sufferings were a bit self-indulgent in his own mind, he did not permit himself to verbalize a single complaint. She found her admiration for Severus growing even as he experienced his worst moments, and she mixed for him a potion against motion sickness.

By the second evening, having adjusted to his seasickness and having eaten some bread and a couple of apples from the basket that Lilava had had the foresight to pack for them, Severus found himself feeling better and eager to reach their destination more because he was curious about the adventure than because he was afraid that he was going to be emptied even of blood and bone by the time they got to wherever the waves were taking them.

"Wherever are the waves taking us?" he asked.

"Feeling better, are we?" Lilava suggested.

"Yes, though I hope I'll have a day or two to recover before I have to fight any sort of really nasty beast," Severus answered. "Though I'm all for giving the opponent a sporting chance, I do prefer to feel sturdy myself."

"You'll have nearly another day before we get there. Here: have a drink of water with these mint leaves in it. It will clear your head and make your mouth taste better."

"You know where we're going?"

"Of course."

"Where?"

"Where I come from."

"Where is that?"

"Halfway around the world."

"Around?"

"Yes, around. Round. Didn't you know?"

"I'd never thought about it, actually."

"All that time riding around and looking at the sun and the moon and the horizon and you've never noticed?"

"Speaking of the sun," said Severus, glancing at the first rays of daylight over the circle of ocean, "how is the weather there?"

"Bright. Warm. Much better than Britain's."

"How could it not be?"

"Ever been to Siberia?"

"Surely I've not. Why would I — or you — go there?"

"Shamans' gathering."

"The Order of Enchantresses?"

"The man may be trainable after all. I know you're feeling better, but you'd better watch your hands — we're not that close yet, you and I."

"My hands? My hands are right here." Sir Severus sounded more puzzled than pleased Lilava.

"If those are your hands, then what's that — yeeeee!"

More quickly than Severus could move in his weakened state, a giant sea squid had wrapped one of its tentacles around Lilava and was doing its best to pull her from the boat. As she tried to work up a spell, the wily beast twisted a coil around her throat and pulled tightly, preventing her from speaking a word.

Green and wobbly or not, Severus leapt to his feet, drew his sword, steadied himself amidst the boat, which was now tossing back and forth from the writhings of the many tentacles, and began hacking at the monster.

After a stroke or two Severus began to feel his blood rising again, and with increasing strength he lopped off one tentacle, releasing Lilava from its tightening fury. But before he could check to see if she was all right or even congratulate himself on some fine sword work, Severus found himself eye to eye with his angry opponent, who intended with its last breath to take one out-of-place knight to the bottom of the sea.

Now as everyone knows, desperation adds fight to the basest of creatures, and this particular opponent was far from the least of its kind, full grown, strong, and with a good deal of malevolence come from more than one successful tangle with a hungry shark. With its tentacles waving and its mouth opening wide enough to swallow more of Severus than he could comfortably lose, the beast worked enough of its coiled bulk around the boat to get some leverage for a spring as Severus bravely fended it off with his sword. As the squid leaned back for one final, desperate attack, and Severus braced himself to keep his feet and parry, the beast's eyes suddenly became dull, the tautness disappeared from its coils, and the head slunk down over the edge of the boat, nearly flipping the small craft over and nearly sending its inhabitants, alive and dead, into the bubbling sea.

With a swift kick Severus sent the body of the squid rolling over the edge, then thrust his body against the backlash of the craft to keep the boat from overturning. With his left hand he reached out to grasp for Lilava, lest, spent from the encounter, she tumble into the sea, but what he caught instead was her hand, and as they pulled toward each other, Severus heard her quickly whispering. The boat rocked twice dangerously, then quickly calmed in the now sanguine water, red more with the light of the sun than with the blood of the squid.

"You all right? I feared that I'd lost you," he said.

Lilava smiled slyly and held up in her right hand a nasty-looking blade about the length of a forearm. It was dripping with the squid's blood.

"Base of the head, where the tentacles join the body," she said. "Works every time, as long as one can get round the shell."

"Yes, I know," Severus replied. "I don't know how I know, but that's thespot I would have gone for myself."

"Exactly," Lilava said. "You have a sense for these things. I knew I had the right knight for this quest."

Severus smiled proudly, but then had second thoughts.

"I almost wonder if you couldn't manage it on your own," he said doubtfully, "after what you've just done to that seabeast."

"Certainly not," Lilava said calmly. "It will take both of us, and even then our chances aren't very good."

"So glad to hear it," Severus said, more to say something than for any particular meaning he attached to the phrase, as he stood admiring the dripping Lilava in the light of the rising sun, which showed that she was not only as beautiful as he had always thought, and able with a dagger which he might have guessed, but also more firmly constructed than he could even have wished.

Over the next day, Severus and Lilava got to know each other tolerably well. One doesn't spend any length of time on a small sailboat with only one other person and not get to know the person well, unless one's companion is a complete troll — or vice versa. In fact, by the time they spotted land ahead, they had exchanged histories and hopes and had so come to enjoy each other's company that they felt sorry that the voyage must end.

On their final evening afloat, Severus lay with his head in Lilava's lap. As she stroked his forehead, she said, "Tell me a story."

"What sort of story?"

"Something exotic with exciting adventures."

"I could tell you a story I heard about giant rats in Sumatra, but I'm not entirely sure where Sumatra is."

"No, that won't do."

"What would you like?"

"How about one of your adventures?"

78

"Oh — anything in particular?"

"Any one will do."

"Well then, let's change spots: you lie down, I'll stroke your head, and I'll tell you about the time I met a vampire."

"Vampire? Really? Where?"

"In eastern Germania. Tall, thin fellow with thinning gray hair and long canine teeth. Kept following me around, showing his teeth with a wicked smile and saying, 'I am a vampire!' or some such rot. I suppose he'd heard I fight monsters and so he came about looking for attention. He'd hold his cloak open, both hands outstretched beside him as if he had bat's wings, and he'd follow the girls about, hooing like a wolf and, if they'd let him close enough, biting at them."

"What did you do about him?"

"Mostly just left him alone, because he seldom really touched anyone — more show than substance. Then one day when I'd got back to my lodgings tired from chasing away a pack of wolves — they too had been more show than actual trouble, though I know what they can do when you get a bad bunch of them with a wicked leader — and I was about to sit down to a bit of dinner, I heard something shuffling behind me, and there the fellow stood with a nasty-looking iron hook in his hand as if he were going to plunge it into my back."

"What did you do?" asked Lilava, her eyes properly wide and appreciative.

"I whipped out my staff and struck him in the knee. Knocked him right down. I'd hit him rather hard, so he couldn't get up, and he said something like, 'You can't do that to me! I'm a vampire,' though he said it rather forlornly. So I said, 'Well now you're a vampire with a bad knee. People will hear you limping along behind them and run away, so just give it up.'"

"What happened to him?"

"He eventually got up and hobbled away, and I had my dinner, a nice, lightly-spiced meat with some rather bland boiled vegetables and I think it was rhubarb pie. When I left town I saw him sitting at a crossroads wearing normal clothes and a traveler's hat and carrying a clothing bag — looked like he was waiting for a carriage to take him away from there. I offered him a ride, but he ignored me — perhaps he didn't like horses. I had some other business in those regions, and a couple months later I heard a story from a villager about how a brave knight had destroyed a scheming vampire who had terrorized a village for two hundred years, how the knight had thrust a sharpened staff through the monster's heart, sending him to hell. You know how these tall tales get started. Sorry. Not much of a story."

"That's all right. I don't like vampires anyway."

"How do you feel about dragons? I'll try to put you to sleep with the story of how I once dealt with a Gaulish dragon."

"Sounds marvelous."

"Marvelous indeed. That's my job, as you know: dealing with marvels and monsters, much like yours, in a sense. There. All set now? Good. Here's what happened."

The stars danced over their heads as Severus told how he had heard of a dragon among the Gauls. One seldom found real dragons anymore by that age of the world — normally just an overgrown serpent or a wild story cooked up to cover someone's excesses. But in that case the dragon had been real, and one of the nastier sort at that. Rumor of it had reached Severus all the way in Britain, so he had boarded a ship — yes, he had to explain, a ship, and as usual he had gotten emaciatingly sick. But youth heals quickly, and he had soon located a squire who could speak both English and Gaulish to guide him, which saved quite a good deal of the time that hunting a beast normally takes.

The world seemed bigger in those days, even if some stories do say that Arthur had, in his early years as king, fought his way an entire triumphant course to Rome.

The squire and guide, with little help from locals along the way, had by discreet requests gotten them into the eastern regions of Gallic lands. You may think that simple enough, but Gauls didn't like to give directions to strangers, and squires didn't like to stop for directions: they considered it beneath their dignity, that they should be able to find anything they wanted by natural sense of direction and persistence. A knight does well to find an apt and humble squire, as Severus had, particularly lucky since he had neither great wealth nor reputation. But as any attentive person knows, luck does play a part in adventures, and one has little choice but to feel thankful for the good and endure the bad.

While distant from their goal, they had received largely diffidence or insolence from those they questioned; as they neared, they met with grim laughter and outright scorn. Yes, they had a dragon in that place called the "Golden Banks," a beautiful spot where the hillsides along the river shone like sunlight and the ground gave up its riches to healthy crops with easy tilling. The land bore riches of all sorts, but rumor of such plenty, if it draws gentry to rule it and peasants to work it for them, attracts dragons as well. A great dragon, one of the fiercest of its species, had, learning of the golden shores of the river, flown there from the North, found the location, excesses of treasure, and taste of the wealthy burgesses to its liking, and had dug itself a barrow and settled in. Anyone who had tried to reclaim the land or even bargain with the dragon for use of part of it had met with a fiery greeting and felt fortunate if he lived to see the following day. No one yet lived on those banks, they learned, and few close to

81

them would even talk about them, thus making directions once again difficult to get, except for one thing: from a distance, Severus could smell the dragon, and as soon as he did, he realized what he was up against.

The knights in the region just laughed at his inquiry, insulting him for thinking that any such fellow, young and inexperienced in the world, would have a chance with a hundred good men against such a foe — even a thousand wouldn't help him with a dragon. They would have nothing to do with him.

Severus knew that, but resolved to complete his quest, first freeing the squire of service, paying him what he had (which wasn't much), thanking him, and wishing him well.

Severus rested for a day, took a balanced meal of proteins and carbohydrates, drank fresh water, said as many prayers as he could remember, and tried to get a good night's sleep. In the morning he stretched, cleansed himself, checked his weapons, and set off to meet the dragon.

Dragon fights are not nearly such a sure thing as we have often heard in stories. Knights lost them far more often than they won them — we simply do not hear their tales, since no one returned to tell them. And a knight does well to know what sort of dragon he faces. Some dragons were once men who through greed and a taste for horror and blood metamorphosed into dragons. They will sometimes speak if one confronts them, and one may recognize them because they show disdain for anything other than treasure or violence. Yet their vanity can make them vulnerable. Others, barely the size of people, can fly and will use their tails and teeth as weapons and their claws to steal or kidnap what they want: as a rule they seek food rather than ransom. Still others, more like overgrown lizards, slither thoughtlessly along the ground, and one may feel tempted to take them as less dangerous than their more visually impressive cousins, but they move with astonishing rapidity, have poisonous bites and even poisonous skin — one must not even touch them — and show an unguarded ferocity that belies their simple nature. The largest and worst sort of dragon, the great fire-breathers of the North, could in the ages of old devastate settlements, landscapes, even whole countries, such as they existed then. Naturally large and armed with all sorts of defenses, those most impressive of beasts suffered from enormous vanity, which the occasional bright knight could use, if he could get close enough to question one and scope it out. Typically their defenses had somewhere a seam, such as an opening between scales on the belly, that the knight could exploit, but of course the dragon knew his own weakness and did his best to keep it carefully covered. They would sometimes talk and sometimes not; one never knew without confronting them.

While one can't find any easy dragon, that last sort is the worst: they live long and show great cunning and malice if anyone disturbs them. They may sleep for years, even centuries, in an earthen barrow, so that people with luck may even forget them if they leave them untroubled, but some day some unlucky soul will wake them, and once they wake, only large quantities of blood and the recompense of some new and vast treasure will return them to sleep again.

You have probably guessed which sort of dragon Severus found: that last and worst sort. He didn't know that yet, but he suspected it, since the rumors had traveled so far. And as he was nearing the barrow, he found the land more and more scorched and useless. In that last stage the dragon would at least no longer be hard to find, so he dismounted, patted his horse on the rump, and sent it back toward the nearest town, where he would recover it in time if he could.

To fight such a dragon a knight needs special weapons, and Severus had armed himself for the worst. A wooden or leather-covered shield does no good whatever. Some knights select an iron one, but metal conducts heat well, so while it may keep fire-breath at bay, one can't keep hold of it for long — not to mention that unless one forges it extremely thin, it weighs a ton. Earthen substances have some merit, but stone also weighs too much, clay is too brittle, and no one knew of such exotic substances as diamond. Severus had made a special shield for just such occasions. He carved the frame of light, pliable linden wood while it was yet green. Over the outside surface he wove a cover of the hardest iron alloy he had ever found, thinly forged into chain-links, with a substance he had bought from the son of a miner from the far South, a gray, fibrous mineral that refused under any circumstances to burn. He melded them together with a glue he had gotten from a wizard whom he had once freed of a troublesome ghost, leaving a rough, but hard and fireproof surface. He had then covered the rough surface with a green slime he'd found in a northern bog — he had heated it at a forge until it had become resinous, then he had taken it outside and thrust it in a snowbank until it had hardened, giving the surface a dull sheen off which even sharpened objects tended to glance without doing much damage.

While other knights had beautiful shields with painted or engraved devices to show their affiliation, lineage, or faith, Sir Severus carried the ugliest shield any knight ever saw, but one as nearly impregnable as anything from its time.

Though he had great skill with a staff and less with a bow, the staff wouldn't serve against a dragon, so he threw over his back a smaller, but tightly-strung bow with which he had fair accuracy up to 100 feet — greater distance or lesser accuracy would do him no good alone against a dragon. He carried the best sword he had for the purpose, long and light, sacrificing some strength for speed, with a short, rounded hilt and a tip as sharp as the blade-edge. He carried a long, straight dagger and a four-pronged iron hook attached to a long rope. He carried a leather pouch of fresh water. To maximize mobility he wore a light, leather armor coated with special soap to make it slick and help retard heat. He wore a short iron helmet with layers and layers of soft leather padding inside; while most helmets had metal visors, his had one of the hardest, clearest amber anyone had ever seen, though he tried not to use it, as even that would obscure his vision (he had gotten that from a dealer in exotic items from the East). He wore tight leather gloves and light, soft leather boots without greaves or metal studs or covers. As best he could, he girded himself with courage.

You may find the description of Severus' habiliments too particular, but rest assured that Lilava quizzed him carefully on the details, the reason for which you will learn later in the story. You will also notice that Severus put to good use the time he had spent learning in Sir Gregius' smithies.

Despite the depredations of the dragon, when he reached the Golden Banks, Severus appreciated the name: dark, rich soil, a climate for growth, and the rolling banks shimmering golden in the morning sun — certainly a shame that no one could cultivate it, impossible to do with a dragon about.

He sniffed, noting the direction of the wind.

After a short walk around a turn, he found the barrow just atop a particularly steep section of the bank, no doubt of it, and he could even hear the dragon snoring: it must have fed well to have reached so deep a sleep so soon after attacking, only a few months before — the only bit of information he had gotten from the local Gauls.

Severus neared the barrow as quietly as he could, but the snoring became irregular, and with a loud snort or two, it stopped, followed by a short silence and then a hint of the sound of sniffing. Severus had a great sense of smell, but nothing even remotely close to that of the dragon. If you've ever seen one, you know a dragon's barrow is no cinch to enter, even if you can find the original opening of the passage, which, unless you arrive just after the dragon has exited, you will find blocked and probably protected with spells.

In Severus' case he had no difficulty with the door. As he approached from the side of the barrow, the tip of the dragon's thorny tail flicked out of the earth, wagged a few times, and retreated inside.

No question now about the ethical implications of trying to attack a sleeping beast — the dragon had wakened.

Severus positioned himself with the sun at his back and waited for the beast to emerge. He silently reviewed all the known strategies for dealing with dragons, all the riddles he had ever learned, all the historical points of weakness by which dragons had fallen in battle — then he tried to clear his mind, breathe slowly and deeply, and remain alert.

Still the dragon didn't appear. Severus had to restrain himself from tapping his foot.

Once, twice, the tail emerged, then retreated.

Still he waited.

Then something else: a tongue — it flicked out whiplike, but silent, then retreated as well. The dragon clearly had no intention of fighting with the sun in its face. Notoriously patient, except when someone has robbed them, dragons will wait till the advantage lies with them.

Severus never felt right about attacking first, but he realized he must force the issue or yield advantage to the dragon, who could if he wished wait until Severus fell asleep, which would eventually have to come. Watching, timing the tongue by its periodic emergence, Severus pulled an arrow, aimed, waited, then shot. His arrow grazed the edge of the tongue before it slid back in, and the dragon let out a shriek, which echoed horribly along the bank, down the river.

Then the noise really began, as the dragon slithered about its chamber, gathering itself to attack whatever or whoever had dared to interrupt its beloved sleep atop its beloved treasure.

A claw grasped the edge of the door and used that leverage to pull the body through it. Dragon body began to pour out, extruding itself in great slithery coils, and before the head could appear, Severus shot several more arrows at it to test the hardness of the skin: they struck hard, but fell to the ground without making a nick or dent.

Severus positioned himself at an angle, so that when the giant head of the dragon popped out through the barrow door, the beast had no direct angle on him, but would have to crick its neck. He timed a shot so as the dragon opened its mouth whether to speak, growl, or breathe fire, the arrow might enter first.

He fired, the dragon's mouth opened, and the arrow hit, breaking a front tooth.

The dragon bellowed with pain, and the howl shook the ground, leaving Severus unsure of his feet. He looped the bow over his shoulder, dodged aside, and covered himself with his shield as the burst of fire that followed shot past him, singeing his elbows and boots.

If that arrow had not struck a tooth, but had buried itself down the dragon's throat, the battle would have ended with no more ado. Severus was what he was, a monster specialist, but at any given instant he was not especially luckier than you or me. As he looked past the shield, the dragon was beginning to rise up and coil itself for a full frontal assault. The gold eyes turned a fiery red. It was an old dragon, long, leathery, unyielding, with no taste for irony or sarcasm: only for blood.

It showed no intention of talking.

Another burst of flame sent Severus diving behind his shield. He felt the iron on his helmet heat up so that his head almost felt on fire. He had to abandon either shield or bow; he dropped the shield, got off several arrows — two missed, one struck the hide, two struck the face beside the eyes, all fell harmless to the ground — while the dragon restoked its fires. Then Severus tossed the bow aside, grabbed the shield, and dashed behind the barrow, which was just tall enough to obscure the dragon's view. The dragon slithered around after him, and Severus circled the barrow toward the opening. From there he could either dart inside for protection or dive for the river below if his shield failed and the dragon's heat became too much for him. He hoped to outflank the beast and find a place to attack.

At full speed he careened around the barrow to the front, and before the dragon could pull the full length of its huge torso around the barrow in pursuit, Severus pulled his sword and thrust it through the thorny tail, affixing it to the ground.

Oh what a bellow issued from the dragon then, louder and angrier than before, and the sheer force of it threw Severus to his back. He rolled to his feet and dashed in the front door of the barrow as the dragon tried to redouble upon itself to release its pinioned extremity and aim its next burst of fire. Severus poked his head out the door, dodged inside from the fireburst, and, dagger in hand, stepped out, looked for the dragon's eye, and threw.

The shot hit its target with a dull splat, and Severus dove out the door and beneath a claw as the dragon, too angry and in too much pain to hold back, spent all its fire in the direction of the front door of the barrow. It flung out the other claw as Severus slid by, pounding his shoulder, but failing to pierce with the claw. It pulled the sword from its wounded tail as Severus stopped his slide. With his good shoulder he gathered his final weapon, swinging the iron hook over his head. The dragon glared down at him and opened its mouth to attack, but had no more fire to breathe. Severus threw the hook, caught it in the dragon's jaw, and pulled with all his might down the slope.

Weakened by pain and loss of blood from its damaged eye, the dragon pulled back against Severus' strength, but its feet began to slip beneath it, and when the large, heavy head lurched forward, the dragon could not keep itself from going head-first down the bank. Having jerked the dragon forward, Severus tried to clear aside as the dragon's mass bore itself down the slope toward the river. With a final flick of its tail as it passed, the dragon caught Severus' calf with one of its thorns, and then the beast's neck broke under the weight of its own body, which slid the rest of the way into the river. Steam rose from the water with a hiss, and the dragon's body twitched for some time before settling into stillness.

Severus sat and watched as the skin and muscle dissolved into dust, leaving only the great bony structure of the beast behind — it had been a very old dragon.

Severus felt little better off himself. The thorn, which had borne a poison, he had pulled from his calf, but it was already working its evil magic as the poison spread, numbing the parts of his leg that didn't throb with pain. At first he feared that he might die, but then he thought, what better way for a hero to die? If only he had done so for someone who might appreciate such a deed, someone such as Lilava, rather than for a people he little knew and who cared little for him. With his last waking thoughts on Lilava, he had passed out.

The next events he remembered involved his riding into the town where he had excused his squire, feeling sick and weak, with his wounds bandaged, his leg painful, but at least not numb, carrying two of the dragon's teeth, including the broken one, and a great bag of treasure from the barrow. He had no recollection of having gotten that far himself.

The people there hadn't believed his story until they went to see the dragon's carcass for themselves, and even then they insisted that the treasure belonged to them, not to him. He negotiated a settlement that more than covered his travel expenses and allowed him sufficient funds for a proper convalescence, and as soon as he was able to stand the ride and stomach the voyage, he had returned to Britain.

Having finished his story, Severus continued stroking Lilava's beautiful hair, thinking her asleep, wondering how much of the story she had heard.

"You're welcome," she said sleepily.

"Oh, you're awake. Welcome for what?"

"Who do you think tended your wounds as you lay otherwise dying and set you on your way back to civilization, or at least such as one finds there."

"Who?"

She batted her large, dark eyes at him.

"Was it you, then? I would have wished it so."

"I followed you, just in case you were to find trouble. And, oh, you did."

She yawned.

"I thank you with all my heart."

"As I said, you're welcome. You'll recompense me for it."

"You still haven't told me much about this beast we're soon to fight."

"Yes, it's — oh, is that land in the distance there?"

As they neared shore, Severus spotted a broad, white beach that ended in woods, with a mountain rising behind. Lilava cut the sail, and they ran smoothly aground with the white wash billowing around them.

"I wonder how my horse is doing?" Severus spoke his thought aloud.

"Well, I should think," broke in Lilava. "I found him a proper companion — though they may behave improperly, if no other adventure interrupts them," she added with a smirk.

"Adventures? Horses have adventures?"

"Certainly. You didn't think the world was made for you alone, did you, Sir Arthurian Knight?"

"I suppose I hadn't thought of it."

"Apparently you haven't thought about much." She smiled slyly.

"I'm learning."

"I hope so. You'll need every bit of wit God's given you when we meet the Chimaera," Lilava warned.

"Wit?" Severus asked. "You mean I'll need more than strength and courage and a special ability to fight monsters?"

"That's why this quest is yours and mine, and no other's," Lilava answered, "because fighting monsters is your special talent. But if you survive this fight, and I hope you do, you'll live by your wit, not by your strength alone."

"Thank you."

"For what?"

"For hoping I'll survive. And for suggesting that I may have enough wit to manage it. Perhaps you're growing to like me now that I'm not retching over the side of a boat anymore."

"I liked you before. But I have a better reason for wanting you to succeed — yes, even better than liking you. If you don't defeat the Chimaera, it's going to eat my sister and then me after her. With or without the help of a knight, I have known since childhood that I must face the beast. But I have seen in a vision that my sister must join me — something I would have wished on no one and particularly not on her."

"Tell me about your sister."

"I know little about her. I haven't seen her for years, since I left home, but I carry her image ever in my heart, and I have always felt bound to her in a way that, through visions, I am only now coming to understand. But why do you ask about my sister?"

Before Severus could reply, two horses came trotting down the beach toward them.

"Horses!" he said. "Let's see if we can catch them."

"We won't have to," Lilava said with a smile. "I've called them to meet us."

"You are remarkable."

"You've only just noticed?"

IX The Greatest Monster Battle of All Time

[Here Severus and Lilava confront the enemy they have sought.]

They rode through the cool overnight and on into the next day, past several small villages with neatly-trimmed fires, through a long wood with little undergrowth, until they emerged out of the trees. Before them rose the foot of a mountain, its top reaching majestically into the clouds. Lilava stopped to look and take a breath.

"My home is there," she said. "We will reach it in an hour. I have been gone a long time — nearly too long. There, for good or ill, you will find your adventure — our adventure."

Shortly they reached a small city, full of many low buildings, mazy streets, and many people who looked like Lilava: trim, long dark hair, dark eyes, high cheekbones. They hurried out to greet her and welcome her home.

The people greeted Lilava with great pleasure: hugging, kissing, crying, dancing, but they restrained themselves from vocal outburst. They took her away as quickly as they could — she waved to Severus as they pulled her toward what looked to be the center of the village. Others patted Severus on the back, kissed his cheek, and from what he could understand of their words and gestures, made him feel welcome. He tried what Latin he knew and found that thereby he could communicate relatively successfully if a bit fumblingly with his hosts.

By evening they had given Severus such food and drink and hearty welcome that he was beginning to feel quite himself again. With the help of an old couple who had lodged him, fed him, and poured him a hot bath, he had even learned a few words and phrases in the flowing, musical local language, enough so that when Lilava joined him later, looking sponged and brushed and shining, to check to see if he was comfortable, he amazed her by addressing her in her own first tongue with a sufficiently tuned accent that she might have thought she was listening to someone who had been among her folk far longer than a few hours.

"How did you learn so quickly?" she asked. I've been paying close attention and using, as you would say, the wit God gave me. And it's not so awfully different from Latin, at least to the extent that I know Latin."

"Not so very different," she agreed and quickly informed him of her day's activities, chiefly reporting her adventures to the people and learning the status of their village in her absence. They had lived for some time free of the Chimaera's depredations, but recent rumblings from the mountain, lightning, and quakings of the earth had left them certain that they should not long remain at peace.

89

Her return, they'd hoped, showed great good fortune, especially since she'd returned with a famous and gallant knight.

"They said famous?" Severus asked.

"Oh yes."

"I wouldn't say famous."

"To them you are now famous, at least here; as for the rest of the world, if we fail here, that won't matter."

"And if we succeed?"

"Then we shall have to figure out if that matters or not."

After they had sat and chatted together for some time with increasing warmth and friendliness, Severus finally pried his eyes off Lilava to look out the window of his comfortable hut toward the mountain. There, standing at the window, her face glowing in the growing darkness, he saw looking back at him Lilava. But not Lilava — Lilava but — younger? Then he looked at the real Lilava sitting next to him, then back to the window again. Both women laughed. "Twins," Severus proposed.

"No," said Lilava, "but close. She is Liletta, my, hmmm, younger sister. But not younger by much."

Liletta smiled, said something in her native language that Severus could not understand.

"'By more than a year,' she says. Liletta can understand a little of your language, but she can't speak it, though she's pretty good with Latin. She told me to ask you, are you the famous knight who's going to save us from the Chimaera?"

"Not so famous," answered Severus, "but certainly willing to do whatever I can to save you. Though I believe I will need more than a little help to do it." He looked into Lilava's eyes. She smiled and began to hum a low, rolling tune, like the sound of water moving in the distance. Liletta joined in, first humming, then singing gently in higher-pitched counterpoint. Severus found himself transported by the song. He imagined deep, green woods with flowing streams and stars under a clear sky. He could feel brisk coolness in the air and smell its clean breath. He felt a need to find a stream among the trees and to drink from it.

"Where are you going?" Lilava asked. Severus realized he had risen to his feet and taken several steps to the doorway.

"I didn't even realize I had moved," he said, abashed. And then he laughed, recognizing the power in even so gentle a song sung by the right singers.

"We have strong, too," Liletta said, melodiously if imperfectly, in language entirely understandable to Severus.

"We will be there with you, Sir Severus," said Lilava quietly. "We trust in your abilities and courage — and our own."

Severus looked deeply into Lilava's eyes for quite some time. When he glanced back at the window, Liletta had gone.

"She is beautiful, isn't she?" asked Lilava smiling.

"Indeed she is," answered Severus.

"And though she is no enchantress, she is very brave. We will all need our courage when we face the monster. The part of the day that I didn't spend with the elders, I spent with my family. I haven't seen them for years, and my sister has grown up, as have I. You see, this adventure is the very reason I left this place, to prepare for my part in it. I foresaw it years ago: death and destruction for my people, unless I could do something to stop it. For that I will need my spells, my sister's courage, and your strength and heart. But for now, let's enjoy the stillness of the night."

Sometime later, Lilava got up to go.

"Leaving so soon?" Severus asked, disappointment evident in his voice despite himself.

"You didn't expect me to stay here, did you?" Lilava asked.

"Well, no, but I don't think this old couple would mind if you stayed just a bit longer. Considering what we have soon to do. And you look so wonderfully — " here Severus was looking for just the right word, but finally gave up " — clean."

"So do you," Lilava said. "But they would mind. We may not be at Arthur's court, but that does not mean that people here have no propriety. And, you see, the old couple are my grandparents."

Lilava curtsied slightly, then added as she left, "Rest well, Sir Severus le Brewse, for soon you will face the greatest adversary of your life, and you will need every bit of your strength, mental as well as physical. Tomorrow we really must talk more about the beast."

Severus half-listened; he was caught up in the smell of her that wafted in the door, her skin, her hair, and the light that glistened in her dark eyes. He did not even stammer out a word as she turned into the darkness, but walked to the window and watched her slim form retreat into the night.

When Severus awoke, he found Lilava nowhere about, so he began to wander among the folk. Through the day he learned what he could of them, their history, their land, their character. Beginning at noon they began to prepare beneath a vast tent a feast in his honor; he watched the people busy with food preparations, though always with one eye searching about for the movements of Lilava. They roasted white meat and fowl and fried fish in large pans; sliced huge plates of white cheese and yellow cheese and orange cheese; filled enormous bowls with a rainbow of fresh fruits; decorated platters full of yellow beans and green beans and white beans and orange peppers and red peppers and yellow and green squash and onions and spinach and fried mushrooms and heaps of fragrant herbs all splashed with olive oil and sprinkled with salt; baked bread loaves of all shapes and sizes, their aroma wafting warm and scrumptious among the meat pies and fruit pies and vegetable pies; opened great jugs with fresh water and lemonade and casks of red wine and white wine and honey wine and sloshed milk out of great wooden pails into jars where they sweetened it with honey; tore open burlap bags full of figs and dates and olives; scrambled eggs and poached eggs and folded them into omelets; and spread trenchers with salted nuts and dried seeds and crisp biscuits.

Such a feast people prepare for heroes, usually after they win or before they die. As they cooked and arranged, they talked and sang and drank — Severus joined the talk and songs when he could, but avoided strong drink, since he wanted to keep his wits about him. Nonetheless, as the afternoon ran its course, he began to feel drowsy. He had already noticed a number of those about him dropping themselves into chairs and nodding off, a couple snoring from the floor, and one or two who seemed to have fallen asleep on their feet — he found that odd, but reasoned that people do have their own customs. He also noticed the afternoon sunlight wavering outside the tent, as though heat waves rose from the ground, and in fact the air felt heavy to him, but no so hot as to produce visible waves, and his thoughts began to loop and wobble and his speech slurred and his head felt too heavy to remain on his shoulders and everyone seemed to have fallen asleep and he began to fall into an abyss the color of wheat and ....

"Severus, wake up! Don't let me down now! Wake up! Severus!" "Hey, what?"

"Wake up, man, something's happened!" "What, what has happened? I was just having a little ..." "Nap, I know, and so has everyone else, and something's wrong." "What's wrong?" Finally Severus' eyes focused on Lilava, who stood right before his eyes, shaking his shoulder and looking worried. "Look around; what do you see?"

"Well, people preparing food, vast quantities of it, and singing and — hey!" As he cast his eye around beneath the tent, he observed that all the food was gone, and all the people sleeping, except for one or two who were groaning and rubbing their eyes.

"We must find quickly who or what has come here. The feast has the magical virtue of ritual; without it we stand at less than full strength, and we leave the people with fear rather than hope — that's no way to fight the Chimaera."

"Is it here, the Chimaera? Has it stolen the food?" "Do you sense it here? I don't. But I feel something ... something." Severus already stood shakily on his feet, as though he had risen instinctively in his sleep, and he began unsteadily hunting about, listening, sniffing. "Not Chimaera — though it could have been — but something different: it feels human, not bestial. I can sense it, but I'm not sure what," Lilava said, her eyes dashing here and there, her expression puzzled. She lightly shook a woman who had been peeling fruits, but who now had wakened. She just sat there with an empty expression, her face and body limp as a wet wash rag. "Wake up, Samala. Get busy, now, and wake the others as well, get everyone up! We must search and keep our guard."

"How long have I slept?" Severus asked Lilava.

"Don't know, but I wouldn't exactly call it sleep. You look awful — something has cast a spell over the place. You have resistance to such things, so whatever it is may still linger close about. We may be able to catch it, if it has struck you as recently as I suspect."

Yanking himself back to full waking, Severus happened to look outside the tent and see again the heat waves rising in the sunshine. No, he thought, not rising, but moving, as though away from the tent. Odd, that movement, something strange in it, unnatural ...

Others began to rise from the spell, shake one another, stretch, move stiffened and uneasy limbs.

"There," he said, taking up a carving knife from a table, having left his weapons aside. "Lilava, look."

They both watched the odd waves of yellow heat moving quickly away from the tent, leaving behind it a trail in the dust.

They dashed after it, Severus trying to head it off, Lilava drawing what others had possession of their senses to grab weapons and follow. Severus raced past it and cut off its retreat; Lilava caught up from behind it, so that whatever the source of the strange power, they had it briefly at bay: it seemed no more than a wavering light. Lilava reached down, picked up a handful of dust, and tossed it overtop of the apparently bodiless waves.

As the dust fell, scattering about, it gave the waves a vague but suspicious outline.

Other people soon followed Severus and Lilava, armed and angry, and they surrounded the indefinite shape, which then began to rise, as if, though they were to enclose it, it would simply fly away above their heads. Severus thought he could hear from within the wavy emptiness a low mumbling. As Lilava had done, he took a handful of dust and tossed it over the mysterious intruder. Others did the same, and as the dust covered it, it began to take on a more definable shape, which Severus thought odd, but recognizable. He noticed that Lilava was chanting rapidly in a low tone, and she had taken from her cloak a short staff with a metal tip that she pointed at the rising figure. The figure began slowly to descend to the ground.

The last few feet it fell, landing with a thud. What sat for an instant as looking like a large, dusty, hump-backed animal with a human head emerged into full sight as a dusty woman trying to rise and drag a huge, heavily-loaded sack.

"Must get out of here," the voice said, laden with exhaustion.

"Who are you," Lilava asked, "and what do you want here?"

"I want you to go away, Lilava the Enchantress, and never return here again," said a female voice. The intruder had by then taken her normal shape: a woman of middle age, high forehead, tired, hazel eyes, and dusty, graying hair, her natural dignity ruined by the fact that she was covered with dust and clung to the enormous bag she no longer had the strength to move.

"Please answer my questions," Lilava insisted.

The woman rose to her feet, tried once more to tug the bag, then fell again in the dust. Severus took her arm and helped her up. She pushed his arm away and began trying to clean herself off, but succeeded merely in raising a cloud that more completely covered her head in a crown of dust.

"I am Corsicana, of your neighboring island. I studied with your teacher, Kirkea, though clearly I learned less than you did, except for one important thing: I learned to let sleeping dogs lie. I know why you have come here with your brave Arthurian knight, and I know what you intend to do — I am not without my own skills — and I will do everything I can to keep you from doing it."

"Why would you want to stop us, since what we do, if we succeed, will benefit you and your people as well?"

"I am weary, and you have caught me. Will you not allow me the dignity of a wash and a drink before you question me to death? You'll find in my sack what you're missing, though I don't know how much good it will do you now."

Dismissing the others, who reluctantly gave her up to Lilava and began sifting through the mish-mash of food that had so recently looked like a feast but now sat jostled and dusty in Corsicana's great sack, Lilava led her fellow-enchantress back to a spring where she washed her body, then back to the tent where she cleansed her throat with diluted white wine. Severus sat with them as they talked, and he listened, following their conversation in their own language as well as he could.

"No reason not for me to tell you everything now," Corsicana said, "since I can do no more to stop you. I have spent my power with that final spell, which you neatly voided. I have sought you since rumor spread of your sailing here and have followed you since you landed. Kirkea knew what she trained you to do, and I learned it from her, so that, though I knew you'd gone far away, I kept an eye out for your return. After all this time, I knew that I would waste my breath begging you to forgo your quest, so I set myself to stop you."

"But why?"

"I am older and smarter, if not more powerful, than you are, and I know what will happen if you fail — and maybe even if you succeed. You must not fight it." She whispered, "You must not wake the Chimaera. Why would you want to do it? Your people live happily enough for now. It may sleep for a century — who knows? — and not attack even your grandchildren. Once you have loosed it, who knows how far it will go in vengeance? Will you, who can't stop it here, stop it from decimating my people, or those of the other islands or even the mainland? Can you tell me, Lilava, where it will stop, once you have piqued its wrath? Go throw yourself and your knight into a volcano if you wish to die, but leave the rest of us, people whom you owe no harm, to live in quiet."

Lilava listened patiently, then shook her head. "Do you live in peace and quiet, or in fear? Do you live normal, happy lives, or do you skulk about, living stunted, miserable lives? You have food; you have wine. Tell me the truth: when is the last time some fool insisted on sacrificing a child to keep this monster or some demon at bay? I thought so: I can see it in your eyes, though you have tried, I suspect, to stop them. Madness! Stupidity! Someone must stop it for good and all. Have you thought at all that we may win?"

"Ha! Impossible. The dream of a proud child."

"The dream of anyone who believes in, who hopes for, a life of peace and freedom. Someone must eventually try it; I have prepared for it since childhood; I have found a knight who may do what a hundred knights can't. We must wait no more, but try what we can do."

"You can do nothing against it. Have you ever faced it, seen what it can do?"

"Once, when I was very small, it came down from the mountain. My parents took us, and we fled into the darkness of the caves. Before we could hide, I saw it descending ..."

"But you have not seen it at close range."

"I saw it, I felt it, and we all knew its devastation."

"Look." Corsicana pulled her robe above her knees. The skin of her legs, scored and puckered and mottled, showed the scars of burns that would never heal. "You see, young Lilava the Enchantress, what happens to the luckiest of those who confront monsters. These burns I got from a dragon, and a dragon is a mere mortal beast, not an immortal horror from the roots of time, not a — Chimaera. And you don't know the prophecies. Yes, everyone knows the old saw that 'no man shall destroy the Chimaera,' but in our prophecies, no woman shall, either; in fact, a woman shall unleash the horror from its own island upon the world! The wide world holds more wisdom than that of your tribal elders, young woman, and if you have a shred of concern for your neighbors, you will take your young man and return whence you've come and leave again the people

95

you left long ago to tend their own demons, so mine may do the same. You will notice that I sought no harm to you and did no harm to your knight beyond a little heavy sleep — pretty light spell compared to what a monster can do. I interrupted your ritual to deter you from your task, and clearly I should have tried something more drastic, though you will receive no harm from me now, I promise. You have reduced me to pleading."

Lilava sat in silence for a long time. Corsicana sipped her drink. Severus waited.

Shortly a man appeared to inform Lilava that some of the food had not suffered salvaging, but that they might make a nice meal yet if they wished. The elders had gathered and wished to meet with them across the table.

Severus rose and touched his hand to Lilava's cheek. "I know what you're thinking. Let's learn what they have to say."

"Corsicana, I must turn you over to the elders, though I believe when they hear you out, they will ask you to join us as well. We must make an informed decision, not just for our people, but for others as well."

"The secret to enchantment," Severus said, "comes when soul, heart, and mind meet. You have labored long, but let's hear what they have to say."

"What do you know about enchantment?" Lilava asked.

"Only what you've taught me," he answered.

Corsicana's spell had had power, but while the food workers still felt woozy and irritable from its effects, they had managed to save quite a lot from the mess the enchantress had made by stuffing it all together haphazardly. She offered her apology, which the elders had little choice but to accept, explaining her purpose to do no harm, but rather to avoid it. Over the revised ritual meal, which the elders conducted with great sobriety, she told them what she had learned of the Chimaera, its powers, and the prophecies that surrounded it. They listened carefully to her, but also to Lilava, and they quizzed Severus at length on his training, his adventures, and his motivations.

"Corsicana," asked a small man with black hair and a neat, graying beard, "why should we believe you, since the only knowledge we have of you is that you tried to steal our food?"

"A distraction, my lord. You have no shortage of food, so I would do no harm by taking it, but I hoped to draw your attention away from any confrontation with the Chimaera. We have no wish to see it roused, since we believe therein lies our own destruction."

"And you, Sir Knight," asked a tall man with a beard so long he tucked it into his belt, "what makes you think you can succeed against such a monster? The best of our soldiers have never done so, and the Chimaera did not originate here. While we welcome you for your own sake as well as Lilava's, do you not see that your quest may bring death not just to one people, but to many?"

Severus stood and nodded gravely. "You ask a fair question, sir, and I can only reply that I don't know the answer. I have pursued and fought many beasts in many lands — Lilava can tell you of some of those battles. So, apparently, God wills me. Unlike others of my order I find no pleasure in jousting or swordplay against other men: you may say my heart doesn't lie there. I followed Lilava to undertake this quest because she believes it is my quest, and I believe her when she tells me so. If you contend I have allowed my reason to be guided by my love, then I avow your argument has truth. Perhaps she loves me, too — you may ask her that yourselves. But I tell you truly, hearing of this quest, I would have come anyway, not because I know it mine, but because, if you wish me to, I will try it. The attempt does not feel wrong to me, and I have come to trust my feelings about such things, but if you decide that I should pack my gear and leave, I will pack my gear tomorrow, tonight if you prefer, and make my journey home, or at least away from here. I come to serve, not to destroy."

"You, Lilava," said a woman with long black hair mottled with gray, her face aged, but her movements controlled and almost youthful, "have left us for many years, and we know the purpose of your studies and wanderings. But do you know that the time has come for what you seek, or have you so fixed yourself upon it that you can't see whether the quest represents your own wish or our greatest good?"

"You ask fairly," Lilava replied. "If I urge my own wishes, I have failed my people, whom I've sought to save. If I intuit correctly and have seen rightly, I offer a chance for freedom from our fears and constraints, and I believe we come in good time: my heart forebodes great sorrows, not if we try, but if we fail."

The elders heard them, and many more spoke their wishes also, and they debated until the stars had risen, and they resolved only to continue the debate when sleep had cleared their thoughts and the morning sun should warm their deliberations. The elders, having assurance of their cooperation, wished their guests formal welcome and retired. Lilava found quarters for Corsicana, then she and Severus bade each other good-night.

Lilava looked downcast.

"Can I have been wrong?" she asked.

"For now don't worry. You have acted with an honest, generous heart. You may yet prove right and complete your quest. If not, what adventures we have already had! And who knows what adventures lie ahead?" He kissed her gently on the lips.

"Why do I believe your sister is waiting for you?" Severus asked.

"Severus, are you sure you've never studied the arts of wisdom and magic?"

"Only such as you have taught me and one gains by living." As she waved him good-night, Severus noticed clouds forming over the mountain and spreading into the valley and wondered if that meant they should have a storm overnight.

Severus sought his bed and dropped onto it with a sigh. Thoughts of Lilava swam in his head and moved his body, but the blessing of healthy sleep fell over him like a blanket and he eased into a gentle doze.

Severus was pulled from his thoughts by a blast of fire that broke the night sky and came billowing off the mountain down onto the drowsing city. It exploded and rumbled, and before it faded, Severus could already hear the screams of folk rushing for cover and fleeing from the mountain toward the fastness of the wood. He groped for his sword and helmet and ran out the door into the city. Amidst the confusion he saw Lilava running back toward him. He donned the helmet and twirled the sword in his hand absentmindedly.

"Dragon?" he called to her.

"Not so lucky," she said. "It's the Chimaera. Looks like you don't get to wait even until tomorrow."

"What exactly is the Chimaera?" Severus asked.

"It's many different things, not just a "she," as the old stories say. It shifts shapes, seeking the one most dangerous to the enemy who dares confront it. No time to explain it fully. You'll just have to see it for yourself. Here's your chance to prove yourself, and I certainly hope I've picked the right knight, because otherwise, very shortly I'm going to be an early breakfast, and so are you." She sighed. "Now it comes to this, and I have waited years for it, I wish I hadn't brought you into it — for your sake, not for mine."

Severus began to cross himself, then stopped.

"Go ahead," Lilava said. "No stone circles here. Can't do anything but help this time."

Lilava took Severus by the hand and led him through fleeing people directly toward the fire. Severus did not resist or say a word, but he did wish that he had had a chance to warm up a bit, so he twirled his sword as they ran toward the base of the mountain.

"The elders must accept what we may do for them. We're on our own now: no others can help us or save us, except as God guides them," Lilava shouted as they ran.

Clouds poured darkness down from the mountain, and despite the warm weather, a cold wind struck their faces. As they raced round the last corner of buildings and walls into the brief plain that stretched up to the mountain, Severus saw, standing upon a plateau beneath the mountain's shrouded peak but above the city, as strange a beast as he had ever seen: the head of a serpent, the body of a lion, and the feet of a goat, and it spewed volcanic fire. As Severus appeared before it, the Chimaera stilled its fire and looked at him, puzzled, then seemed to rear its snaky head in laughter. As Severus and Lilava watched, the beast dissolved before their eyes into a mist, then emerged from its own mist in the shape of a dragon.

"I thought you said it wasn't a dragon?" Severus asked, confused.

"Keep watching," Lilava said.

As they looked on, the mist appeared again to swallow up the dragon shape, and as it quickly dispersed, a giant arose before them, but a giant even beyond those of Denmark, thirty feet high, with a war-club twenty feet long and a wart the size of a large child on the end of its nose.

"Angels preserve us. Just what is this thing?"

"Shape-shifter. It came out of the root of the mountain years ago — no one's sure before that, though legends in many places report it. In times past it would demand to be fed young people twice a year, but now it will someimes sleep for years, or go wherever else it goes, with little more than a whisper and a rumble deep in the mountain. As I foresaw, it was due to rise again. We've gotten back just in time for you to see me eaten or to save the lot of us. You must attack the Chimaera. But you won't be alone; I'll be with you. As I told you, this is my quest, too, since childhood. That's why I became an enchantress, though I must admit magic does have other advantages besides fighting impossible monsters. I don't think I can do it alone, and I really don't think we can succeed together, either, but our chances are better with two of us, or three, or however many more may join us, if we keep our wits about us. Liletta too may be able to help us at need." She paused to look deeply into Severus' eyes. "We do have our wits about us, don't we?"

The beast, having gotten insulted by their having ignored it during that rather long speech, had once again changed shape, this time into an enormous salamander that was slithering down the foot of the mountain toward them.

"How do we fight this thing?" Severus asked, the beast rapidly approaching.

"Prudently," answered Lilava.

Seeing the beast wiggle near and open its mouth, Severus thought prudence might require waiting no longer to fight, so he leaped toward the beast, raised his sword high, and, meeting it on a landing above the plain of the city, struck toward the center of the Chimaera's skull.

The beast disappeared in a puff of mist, and Sir Severus's sword pierced the earth two feet deep before he could stop the blow. As he yanked the sword free, the mist reconstituted itself several feet ahead, then rapidly condensed into the form of a small dog with very large, round, sad eyes. It opened its mouth to bark, but instead spoke in a thin, pitiable, raspy voice.

99

"Why do you want to hurt me?" it said.

Severus glanced at Lilava. "What do you think of that?"

"Don't trust it," she replied.

"Why shouldn't you trust me, Lady Lilava?" it said. "Have I ever done you harm?" A tear fell from its furry cheek. Severus found himself wondering how anyone could fear such a creature.

"How many homes have you burned? How many people have you eaten or killed?" Lilava's voice, as she addressed the beast, began to sound unkind. How could she accuse such an innocuous beast of such foul deeds? he thought.

"Good knight," said the ingratiating animal, "maybe you have come to kill me. Others have come so to this mountain, strong young men of this people, though I don't know why. Often I have hidden here in the dark, cold and hungry, alone, for fear of them." As it spoke, Severus found himself doubting Lilava, wondering why she had brought him there. Why should he accept the word of an enchantress anyway, or the word of someone in monkish habit in a stone circle who might as well be a demon as a holy man?

"Do not trust these people, sir knight, or they will harm you as they have tried to harm me. I have been lucky to escape them. I know that you will be my friend."

Severus, confused, turned to Lilava, wondering why he had allowed himself to be lured here, wondering if the enchantress intended to kill him along with the poor animal. Lilava was concentrating, mumbling something, her eyes riveted on the poor dog, her right hand turning in a circle.

"Look what she is doing to me!" the dog called to him. "She will kill me if you do not save me!" Severus turned back to the dog to see its body roiling and bubbling like a wave, expanding and compressing, contorting into odd shapes. "Take her away! Save me! Fulfill your vow to protect the undefended!" The voice began to lower into a deep rumbling growl, and as Severus began to move toward Lilava to stop her in the midst of her terrible spell, angered at her cruelty toward the poor beast, a fortunate instinct urged him suddenly to duck.

That urge saved his life, as the Chimaera, now changed again, its head like a lion, its body a serpent, and its feet the claws of an eagle, had swung its talons directly for his throat.

Severus felt the helmet ripped from his head, and he staggered and fell, nearly losing his sword as well. In a twinkling he had rolled onto his feet again, just in time to stave the onrush of the now slavering beast and to meet it obliquely with his own rush. With several quick, passionate strokes of his sword, he sent the beast tumbling over the edge of the landing toward the city.

"Quickly," Lilava said, "we must catch it before it burns the city to cinders."

"Lilava, I'm terribly sorry. I can't believe I thought ..."

"No time for that now. Hurry!"

They darted down the hill and followed the beast, which now, in the form of a great cat, was flinging about as many of the outlying buildings as it could get between its teeth, ripping them like balls of yarn, tearing the city to shreds. As Severus closed, his sword raised, the Chimaera raised its back and hissed, then spit a ball of fire directly in his face.

Severus dived out of the path of the fire and rolled to his feet. Then the cat spat a shower of fire over Lilava, who, fast at Severus' heels, quickly made an umbrella of water above her head that exploded into steam as the fire struck. The explosion threw Lilava backward, and she disappeared into a ball of dust and water droplets.

Once Severus realized what had happened, that he had given the beast a chance to attack them, and before he could realize that Lilava might be dead, the blood rose in him, filling him with the fire of battle, and with all his strength he sped upon the cat and struck it such a blow with his sword that it sprawled sideways into the city. When it rose, it disbursed again into a mist, in the midst of which Severus could see two thin, red eyes glowing like embers. Before Severus could move, the mist engulfed him, and the fiery red eyes bore down on him and scorched him.

"Puny man," a voice lower than the depths of the sea said to him. "I am as old as time. I have more shapes than the wind, more strength than mountains. You will feed me and add power to my wrath, as has your sorceress."

Severus felt the sword, under the power of the Chimaera, heating in his hand, hotter and hotter, till it glowed red, then blue, then white. With the courage that comes only when one realizes that horror, pain, loss, and death will culminate in a moment, Severus began to spin, as fast as he could, swinging his sword round and round in great circles, turning and turning, till the sword burned into his skin and he screamed out of pain and desperation, screamed every ounce of effort and passion and humanity that he could muster, screamed with the joy of battle and lust for revenge, screamed resistance in the face of death and the pleasure of contest from a place deeper in his body and soul than he knew existed, and at the height of his scream he released his sword, throwing it with all his strength into the eyes of the mist. He spun in a spent heap onto the ground, embers raining around him.

The sword sizzled up into the sky right through the Chimaera, and the mist was blown into a thousand pellets of icy rain, antithesis of the fiery eyes, that fell heavily upon the dust.

From that place deep inside, Severus pulled himself back to consciousness. He did not know how long he had been out cold, perhaps only a second. Jumping to his feet, he tried to get his bearings. The city, beyond those buildings and walls already felled by the monster, looked clear: his scream, filled with the spirit of battle, and the point of his sword, thrown with all his might, had blown the beast into fragments. He turned toward the mountain, saw a shadowy shape, tall and oblong, with long, column-like legs darker than night, painfully ascending the mountain's foot. As it did so, it stopped suddenly. There on the plateau where Severus and Lilava had first confronted the beast stood the enchantress, alive as spring ... and angry. Her face was set — Severus could see her clearly under the glow of the moonlight, staring into the center of the darkness of the beast — and she was circling her hands in opposite directions and chanting slowly and carefully.

The Chimaera, reconstituting itself, tried to climb to attack her, twice, then a third time, grinding its way toward the steely enchantress. As it moved, it took the form of a rock-troll, merging with the stone of the mountain, and it lifted its rocky fist to crush the tiny woman whose spell held it at bay. The breath of night itself paused alongside Severus' heart in that moment.

Then from beneath the mountain from a point past the city came a song, a call rising in crystalline notes in a small but clear voice that splintered the night like rain. In that song, though Severus could not understand the words, lived courage, sacrifice, and love. The rock-troll shape, trying to turn first toward the voice, then back again toward Lilava, began to wobble, and the shadow crumbled into itself. For a long instant the shadow seemed to have gone; then with a wail rising from profound bass to a wheeling soprano, the Chimaera rose as a mist again, turned to meet the voice behind it at the base of the mountain, standing at the edge of the city, a perfect copy of its enemy who stood above on the mountain. There below, Liletta continued to sing out a song brighter than moon¬light, drawing the monster's attention from her sister above, who had climbed a level and was chanting more loudly and slowly thrusting her hands forward, as though to push the beast into the ground.

In that instant, the beast hesitated.

An instant, no more — then feeling no magic to impede its anger, the Chimaera concentrated all its power into the shape of a falcon and dived upon the helpless Liletta.

But that instant's hesitation had given Severus all the opportunity he needed to muster his courage and resolve and speed. He raced to fill the distance between himself and Liletta, and as the beak of the beast was about to bore into the heart of the courageous young woman, Severus himself dived, his hands outstretched for its throat.

He caught the beast at full stretch, just as its beak was about to sink into the breast of the brave but helpless Liletta. Severus and the Chimaera rolled aside,

Severus clinging tightly and coming up on top with his hands grasped unyield-ingly around the falcon-shape's throat. The eyes glowed red, but Severus ignored them, focusing only on keeping and tightening his grip, so that the Chimaera could utter no words to deter him from squeezing the life from it. As he clung, pressing the monster ever more tightly, the Chimaera heaved in a breath and began to dissolve. The mist condensed into a tiny sparrow that slipped through Severus' frustrated fingers and flew off as fast as it could fly.

That time Severus did not hesitate. On his feet and after the bird, he pursued along the base of the mountain, beside the wood, across a stream, leaping over a bog, then sped back and up the side of the mountain, till monster and man came together, exhausted, gulping for air, at the brink of a ravine that fell into obscure blackness beneath. The sparrow drooped and faded into the shape of a small, contorted, hoofed and winged man, hovered just over the edge of the ravine, inches from Severus' avenging grasp.

"Come, sir knight," growled the misshaped beast, "for we are both spent. Grasp me with your last breath, for I am your Devil, and we will fall together into the abyss. Your life for mine, and the folk of the city may live safely. A fair exchange — come now, before my strength returns and I squash you like a fly."

Severus prepared to jump.

"Don't jump!" Lilava called from behind him. "It will deceive you to kill you!"

Severus returned his eyes to the beast just in time to parry the claw that raked at his eyes. Knowing he must give no quarter, he stretched forward and swung his fist, striking the floating creature squarely in the center of the face with a splat.

Water droplets flew in all directions. As Severus nearly lost his tenuous bal-ance, the ravine opened beneath him. Then he felt a grasp upon his belt and found himself yanked away from the plunging edge and pulled to the ground on top of a panting Lilava.

"Odd time for this sort of thing, don't you think?" he said.

"Severus, look!" said Lilava, pointing over the edge of the ravine and up the mountain.

Beyond the steep drop the beast scrambled up a slope, having taken the shape of a fiery scorpion.

From Lilava's look Severus knew that she feared they had lost their hold on the beast even as they had nearly subdued it. "We may yet take it, dear one, if we can think of something. Here — " he reached down for a rock " — can you make this stone icy cold?"

"I have little strength left, but ..." Lilava concentrated and touched the stone, which within Severus' fingers froze over until it nearly stuck to his skin — the cold eased the burning of his palm, then got so cold that it nearly began to burn as well. Lilava dropped to the ground beside him.

"Well done. Let's see how the world may cast our luck." He aimed, reared back, and fired the ice ball up the slope after the Chimaera.

It struck the scorpion's fiery foot, releasing a hiss of steam, and the body writhed in midair. Then all the feet struggled madly for a grip, but the ground beneath it gave way, and the scorpion-shape tumbled down toward the abyss and fell headlong into it. Severus peered into the chasm. Transmuted again, the beast clung to the cliff. One claw clung to the edge, but the other swept Severus from his feet. He rolled back and pushed Lilava out of the way, and as the beast pulled itself to the top, Severus poised to throw another stone, then cast it into the eye that rose above the surface.

He crushed the eye to a jelly, and the scorpion body dropped into the abyss, leaving behind only the crunching sounds it made as it struck and bounced from outcrops on the way down and a small blob of blue jelly that rested on the edge of the drop.

Lilava propped herself on one arm, and Severus stood and watched as once more the remnant of the beast began to move, tremble like a pumping heart, and take a new shape. Severus wiped dust and perspiration from his eyes, and when he focused again, he saw sitting there on the edge of the precipice a figure that looked oddly familiar.

"You," Lilava said, "only smaller. Or not quite you, but close..."

"Not I, but my ..."

"Father," said a voice like Severus', but a frequency or two lower and with a different accent.

"No father of mine."

"And why not?" said the voice, panting, and the chest shook like that of someone who had run from the Greek coast to Marathon.

"Everybody does the father thing. You already tried 'the boy and his dog,' and now you think I'm going to grow teary-eyed over my father. I'll just get another stone and ..."

"Wait!"

"No."

"Do you know who your father is?"

"Yes."

"No you don't."

Severus found a rock and turned toward the Chimaera.

"It's rebuilding energy," Lilava said. "Best to put it out of our misery."

104

"I am your true father, Severus. Why do you think they call you aglœca?"

"How do you know about that?"

"How else would I know?"

"Then why would you try to kill me?"

"You tried to kill me, and then I didn't know who you are. Now I know."

"Severus, don't listen to it," Lilava said. "It's trying to regain the power of voice, to use it as it did before."

"Why do you listen to that poor woman?" asked the beast. "Has she done anything for you but nearly get you killed?"

Severus could feel the power of the voice beginning to overcome him again, and he raised the rock to throw it.

"All right! Don't, please! I will speak to you normally."

"Then take your own shape and stop trying to fool me."

"Severus ..."

He interrupted Lilava. "I'm sorry; may I not let him say his piece? Tell me, you, why I should not plunge you into the abyss and allow these folk to have done with you?"

"Because in plunging me, you plunge yourself. I know that you have followed in your heart the teachings of the Christians, and for you to kill me now, while I am helpless, would constitute murder. You see, I cannot take my own shape, for you have spent my strength."

"Then take some shape other than that."

"The shape doesn't matter. I am your father either way, not by mere blood alone, but by the deeds you do in battling me."

"Severus ..." Lilava interjected.

"The hermit in Britain told me my origins, as did the people of Ireland who claimed me as their own."

"They would claim you to win your power to do their bidding."

"You claim me to distract and kill me."

"I claim you to tell truth before I die, since you have already killed me. Yes, I am dying, but before I do, you must know the truth of your origins. I fathered you upon your mother at her husband's request: he was impotent and could father no children. You walk with my blood. You are, like me, what these people call a monster, and if you beget children, they shall be monsters like you, if you can father them at all."

Lilava rose to push the beast into the abyss herself. Severus caught her arm and stopped her.

"We have wearied our magic, this bad woman and I," said the beast, "and nei-ther of us can do you any more harm unless you deceive yourself."

"Then show me your true shape."

"What you ask will kill me. I am tired."

"If you don't, I will kill you anyway."

"Then for you, my son, I die willingly, answering your request."

As they watched, the beast began to mutate, waves of faces and shapes emerg-ing from parts of its body, until the waves began to settle. Finally it took the shape of an aged lion with a long, graying mane, but with human eyes: Severus' own eyes.

"This shape is my own, for, you see, I was regal once. Will you do me this last kindness: send the woman away, that I may die alone save my kinsman. I have little inheritance to offer you, but I have given you speed and power and persis-tence, and if you stay with me, I will give you the secret of your royal blood and how to use it. That much good I may do before I pass into nothing."

"I will not leave your side," Lilava said.

Severus turned his face to her. "I have no intention of asking that, ever," he said, smiling.

"Sir knight: you will need this!" Liletta appeared, having climbed behind them. She tossed Severus a rope. Severus caught it and made a wide loop with one end just as Lilava screamed.

The beast, which had quietly felt its strength returning, had sprung for them.

Lilava dived aside, a claw just missing her. The second great paw had struck Severus, who, while he had turned aside from the full brunt of the blow, felt a claw cut deeply into his arm, and painful poison crept into his veins.

With every ounce of will he could call from himself, he turned, flipped the noose he had fashioned over the head of the lion-shape, which in its charge had run past him. He held tightly to the end of the rope, as the beast turned about and sprang again straight for him. Severus spun aside and jerked the rope with all his strength, adding his to the beast's. It flew past him in full career across the chasm and into the rocks beyond, striking them with explosive force.

Like a pounding breaker, the Chimaera broke against the rock and tumbled into the abyss, a few small drops clinging to the steep wall of the mountain.

Some drops began reconstituting into a small, thin, bulbous cloud, which, caught by a gust, drew up the mountain as an ember up a flue. It disappeared into the rising morning with a weak cry.

"We must treat you," said Lilava. She took an herb from her pocket, chewed it, and placed it on the open wound on Severus' arm. With a small blade she made a cut in the skin above the wound, allowing the blood to flow, then tied a tight tourniquet above his elbow. Liletta tore a cloth from her hem, poured water from a leather pouch to saturate it, and applied it to Severus' forehead.

"It got away," said Severus. "After all that, the Chimaera eluded us." He groaned a palpable groan and laid his sweat-soaked head upon the ground.

"You expected to destroy it?" Lilava asked, beginning to regain her breath. "I didn't know, Sir Severus le Brewse, that you suffered so from pride. Do you think you, one little man, can remove evil from the world with some miserable fighting, no matter how courageous?"

"That's why I became a knight in the first place."

"Then you should retire and become a hermit. The only evil you can remove from the world is your own. Don't believe the monk from the stone circle. There will always come another monster to fight, in one form or another."

"But the Chimaera: won't it take shape and return again to your city?"

"It will take shape again, yes, but not here. The wind will take it far away, to a place where people have never heard of it, and it will rise in a different form, a quest for some knight of another place and another time. The Chimaera will live as long as people live to fight it and maybe beyond. But you have achieved your quest, and if I can save you, I have achieved mine."

"So I have. And I believe either way you have succeeded as well. You have freed your people of a great evil." With his good hand Severus brushed a blotch of dust from Lilava's face. "Liletta?"

"She's fine. Not a scratch," Lilava answered.

"Just one more thing."

"What's that?"

"I am sorry that once again I placed you in danger by listening — I found the voice so fascinating. Do you know if what it said, about my father, about me, is true?"

"Don't be sorry." She kissed his lips lightly. "Today, and for all time, you are a hero. And know — look into my eyes so that you may see and hear the truth — know the truth: your father was your father, the beast a beast."

"A hero. As great as Sir Lancelot?"

"Sir Lanc-e-who?"

In time, as the temperature rose with the sun reflecting off the face of the mountain, Lilava and Liletta helped Severus to his feet, and they walked painfully but with satisfaction down the mountain to Lilava's home.

X The Myth of the Eternal Return

[Severus must come to grips with the completion of the quest.]

As Lilava and Severus neared the city, they saw people rushing toward them. Some men placed Severus carefully on a litter and hurried him to comfortable quarters where Lilava, along with the best of their physicians, tended his wounds.

Other than at the city's edge, near the base of the mountain, the Chimaera had done remarkably little damage. No one had been killed, though several folk who had peeked out to observe the battle had suffered burns. Most had hidden safely and intelligently, and within days they would return the city to normal operations, even if they would need months to make repairs.

But upon his return to health, what honor they showed Sir Severus! For days he was the toast of every feast, dance, and picnic, to some of which he was even invited.

Lilava recovered quickly. Severus endured a long convalescence. Though the physicians determined relatively quickly that the poison had, as a result of Lilava's immediate ministrations, not done sufficient damage to kill him, it had chilled his blood, much as if his body bore the effects of continual fear. His mind felt free; he had fought such a battle as knights in their most foolish dreams imagine, and he and Lilava had won and survived. But his body, even his will, threatened to succumb to enervation, to passive listlessness, and the loss of energy hurt Severus more than would pain.

So he celebrated, ate and drank, tried to rest, and fell more and more restlessly in love with Lilava — not that love that acts and serves and joys in the beloved, but the sort that maunders in melancholy, for the poison had, while not killing him, frozen his will to live and left his thoughts vague and hesitant.

Lilava had tried to speak with Severus about what troubled him, but he felt uneasy even speaking about what he felt and could hardly have described it if he had tried. One day she persuaded him to take a ride, and he reluctantly agreed. They both mounted horses and set off at an easy trot. They rode for an hour, then another, then another, until finally they could see the coast in the distance.

"Where are we going?" Severus asked.

"Not far from here," Lilava replied.

They turned down a hill into a steep valley. Riding with great care, they found a waterfall with a grove beneath. In the midst of the grove stood an open space with a small pool.

"Why did we come here?" asked Severus.

"For you to bathe in the pool."

"Why there?"

"You have lost your will. This pool has sacred waters. If you immerse yourself in it, you will feel the life returning to your limbs and, more importantly, to your heart."

Severus felt at first irritated that they had come so far for what looked to him a silly idea. He got down from his horse, looked at the pool for some time, and thought about it. Lilava also dismounted, then waded into the pool. Severus could see that, though small, it got deep quickly, as within a few steps Lilava had waded so that only her head showed above the sparkling water.

He stripped to the waist, tried unsuccessfully to pray, and dived in.

The water felt freezing cold, but immediately as he submersed himself, Severus began to feel better. The cold seemed to jar his limbs and wash the troubles from his mind. Thought seemed to fly from him like a flock of sparrows flinging themselves in all directions. He bobbed and tried to swim, but his body just sank until he drifted down and felt his feet touch the bottom. He felt at first as though he could just stand there until he eventually drowned, but then a thought struck him that, if he did so, he would abandon Lilava and never see her again. He felt that to die then would be wrong, and he felt life, the desire to live, rising in him again. Just as he began to run out of air and take in water, he felt an arm grip his. Kicking powerfully, Lilava was pulling him back to where he could stand on the bottom with his head above water.

"Never have learned how to swim."

"You won't be able to do it very well, but I can teach you a bit. Not here, though. We've come here for something else. Do you feel it?"

"Yes, I think I do."

"Good."

She moved toward the edge of the pool and pulled herself out, her clothing soaked, and she poured several handfuls of water over Severus' head. "Let the water cleanse you, body and soul," she said.

He did.

"You may get out now, if you wish. You have made yourself new. You are not the man you were. No one departs this pool the same man he was when he entered it. Do you feel better?"

"I think I do. Yes, I do."

They rode to the beach and there sunned themselves dry, then rode home before nightfall. Just before they entered the city, Severus asked, "Did the pool really do anything for me?"

"Oh, yes."

"How do you know?"

"Do you feel as though it has done something?"

"Yes," he said hesitantly.

"What?"

"After the battle with the Chimaera, I felt old and tired, as if the poison had eaten up the last of my youth and any hope I had of regaining it. Now I feel strength in my legs again, and the breath draws more easily into my lungs. My heart feels lighter."

"That's exactly what it was supposed to do."

"Did the pool do that, or did you?"

"What do you think?"

"You're a remarkable enchantress."

"You've told me that before. I was beginning to think you no longer believed so."

"I never doubted. Will you leave here with me?"

"I don't know yet. We must find out."

"How?"

"Tomorrow I'll show you. Tonight you can enjoy the feast again, and you will sleep better."

As they dismounted from their horses, Severus caught Lilava in his arms and kissed her.

Even the best of knights can celebrate or suffer for only so long. After an evening of feasting, song, dance, and testimonials, Severus again felt the need to do something, and he particularly wanted an answer to the question he had asked Lilava.

In the morning he told her, "I don't know what to do with myself."

"You can become a hermit and seek to eradicate evil from your soul, as you have tried to do from the world."

"Yes, I may."

"You can go home to the Round Table."

"Britain seems so distant now. And the land is lovely here, too."

"Yes, I know. I'm glad you like it."

"What does a knight do when he finds no more heroism to be done? I see no more quests here, no more monsters or beasts to fight, giants to chase away, folk to rescue, and I have asked a question to which I await an answer."

"No, for now you will find no other monsters here, other than the typical human kind, and those kinder than you will find elsewhere, I think," Lilava answered. "The Chimaera chased all others dangers away for the present — what would dare face what the Chimaera flees? More will come someday, I'm sure; I don't know when. If you want, you could wait here to fight them. Till then, rest, enjoy yourself, learn about us, fall in love."

"Too late for that."

"Why?"

"I already have."

"I know. I wanted to hear you say it for yourself, free of enchantment."

"Oh, I am certainly enchanted."

"I cast no spells on you!"

"But you did, knowing or unknowing. You yourself are the one spell from which I hope never to recover. And how about you? Do you love someone, Lilava?"

Lilava smiled.

"Will you marry me, Lilava?"

"I don't know that yet, either. We must find out."

"You know, of course, that I oughtn't stay indefinitely. I should return to my king, to ask proper leave and proper blessing, since I have entered his service."

"Perhaps. And after that we will return?"

"We can talk about that. It seems a reasonable option. Though my heart feels fixed, my soul yet wanders: I feel a need to return somewhere, but I'm not sure of the place."

"First we must answer your questions."

"Yes?"

"I know how. We must speak with the elders, but first with Corsicana. We must find to where, if anywhere, you may return."

When they found her, Lilava asked if she had any knowledge of where they could seek the answers to some personal questions.

"Why should I help you find those answers?" Corsicana asked.

"You have yet to make restitution to our elders. I believe if you offer to help me, they will release you to go home. I assume you want to go home?"

"Oh, yes, and there, if you go with me, you may find the answers to your questions."

Lilava pled with the elders for Corsicana's release, and having seen the happy ending to their problem, they granted her request and offered for their journey a better ship than the tiny craft on which Corsicana had come. The three set off that day for Corsicana's home, not a long journey in good weather, which they got.

"You realize that when we arrive, you will find yourself at my people's mercy and mine?" Corsicana asked.

"As you did, with my people and me," Lilava replied.

Corsicana laughed. "You don't look worried, and you need not. My people don't like enchantresses; they have no particular love for me, other than when I'm gone doing something to try to save them. When I return, I see always in their eyes fear and mistrust. We three will not even visit them; we don't need them to find what you seek. Before I studied enchantments, we lived under the protection of a white wizard, immensely old now, infirm of body, but sound of mind, at least when I left. He has some tools that may give you what you seek. I can't use them, but you have some powers beyond mine. There is our shore — we will reach it soon if the wind stays with us."

They landed in a small, wooded cove and managed to disembark without drawing attention to themselves. They traveled by foot north along the coast for two days and found the old wizard, stripped to the waist and sunning himself. He greeted Corsicana, introduced himself as Ambrose, excused himself, ambled into his simple, thatched hut, complaining of aching knees, and returned a minute later wearing a long, tattered blue robe embroidered with figures of stars and planets and moons, animals and plants, signs and equations of all sorts, and a tall, broad-brimmed black hat.

"Don't mind the outfit," he said. "It's just for show. But I don't believe you'd worry anyway, young lady; if I don't mistake, you practice the art yourself, and you have with you as sturdy a knight as I have ever seen, who I think loves you more dearly than sunlight."

"Not such a great trick," she replied, "for you to deduce those conclusions."

"Ha! You're right — good for you. But you must have come here for something. What do you wish me to do for you?"

"We have some questions for you, sir, if you'd be so kind. Corsicana suggested you may have means to help us answer them."

"Questions, is it? I once did better at that than I can now. Too old, you know, though I suppose once we get matters going, you can do most of the work, both of you together, for I note something odd about your companion as well. Do you, sir, bear the mark of the wolf?"

"Mark of the bear, I've been told, sir."

"Oh, yes, bear, right — should have got that. Yes, yes, just let me go back to my laboratory — " he winked " — and get something that may help us. Now where did I put that old thing? Let me go inside a moment."

They heard sounds of someone rooting around, tossing things here and there, stubbing a toe, then shuffling back to and through the door.

"Here it is." He held up an ellipse two handspans long and about three inches thick of soft, murky glass. "Magic mirror," he said.

XI Severus, Lilava, and the Magic Mirror

[Severus and Lilava try to learn about their future.]

"How do we use it?" Lilava asked.

"Pretty easy, if one has any sort of talent for it at all. Place it down, so, where the sunlight shines on it, so, and then you must stand over it and look in, concentrating on your question. Concentration is the key. If you let your mind drift, you'll see all sorts of strange colors and shapes that don't mean anything. If you want the answer to a question, you must focus your mind and heart on that question. Short attention span gets you nowhere. Now who wants to go first?" He looked at Corsicana.

"Not I — I haven't come for myself, but to help them find you," she said.

"I will go," said Lilava, "but please answer me this: will I see what must come to pass or what may?"

Ambrose laughed. "You still have your free will, my dear. The mirror shows you choices you can make and the events that may hinge on those choices. Neither any creature nor any mirror can tell you what shall happen to you. Would you want anyone to do so? The world will take its course regardless of you and me, but our lives, if we're lucky or blessed, may take such turns as we wish. But you must look in the mirror alone — anyone else looking with you will distract you, and too close proximity will cause the surface to obscure its images in confusion."

"I'm ready then." Lilava stepped up to the mirror and bent over it as the others watched her, back a few paces from the mirror. She stood over it for several minutes, hardly moving, barely seeming to breathe. Severus saw the expression on her face change slightly, then again, and her breathing quickened and then slowed, and then she seemed impassive, almost dispassionate. How can she, he thought, seem to care so little about her future? When she turned her face from the mirror back to him, her eyes shone and a hint of a smile crossed her lips despite the care he found in the wrinkle in her brow. She nodded slightly.

"Your turn?" Ambrose said to the knight. "Clear your mind of all else but your question, then watch without trying to guide the images you see. Let them inform you, but not overcome you."

"What did you see?" Severus asked Lilava.

"Look for yourself first," Ambrose interrupted, "so that you may view the images without prejudice."

A thought crossed Severus' mind that he might not want to know anything about the future, but since Lilava had brought him, had herself looked in, and seemed to believe he would gain by looking, he strode to the mirror, focused his thoughts on his question, and peered in — Severus had seldom had trouble concentrating.

At first the surface of the mirror looked cloudy, barely translucent, and he saw nothing more than hazy, gray murk. Then the surface began to move, like clouds blown across a broad sky by a strong wind, and as he concentrated, the clouds resolved into figures who played out a story before his eyes.

He saw himself and Lilava sailing back to her island. They found welcome from the people there, married, and made for themselves a happy life. They had two children, a son and a daughter, whom they raised in the pleasures of life far from court in a place where people, freed of worry over the Chimaera, found no reason to attack or oppress others, but lived in gentle harmony, supporting one another, avoiding undue strain on their minds and bodies. They taught the children, as well as they might, to live well. They loved each other fully and faithfully. The years spread out before them full of summers and falls and springs with few troubles, but few adventures. Their children grew healthy and productive and strong, until they left the island for their own quests, seldom to return. In time, Severus and Lilava fell into the common patterns of life and grew restive with them, but they had grown too old for travels and quests and battles, so, quietly resentful of each other, wondering if they had missed anything exciting, they lived out their lives loving each other, but with an unspoken distance between them that remained unresolved to the end of their days. Then even as dust covered their empty bodies, so did clouds cover the mirror's images. The clouds slowed briefly, then began again to roil and fly, and a new scene began to emerge from their misty shadows.

Severus saw himself on a boat, leaving Lilava's island. On the shore, which grew more distant by the instant, he could see her standing. He waved to her, but she stood still as stone, her gaze fixed on his ship. He turned his attention to the waves, fighting seasickness, then navigating a storm. After long days he reached the southwestern shores of Britain, landed, and with the help of a local

hermit found his horse, Courage, who, happy in his new masterless life, feigned not recognizing him, but eventually gave in and carried Severus to London. Trouble had arisen at court: some envious knights, led by Mordred, the king's illegitimate son, had insisted on making public the long-tacit affair between Lancelot and Guinevere and had obligated Arthur to make war upon his long-time friend, ally, and champion. In Arthur's absence, Mordred had taken over the throne and, supported by a powerful faction that sought to unseat Arthur for its own gains, threatened to take Guinevere against her will and assassinate Arthur on his return.

Never a favorite at court, especially of the Mordred faction, and having been long away from British eyes, Severus sought unsuccessfully to moderate Mordred's stance and to mediate for Arthur and restore peace, but Mordred, after a brief and fruitless attempt to win Severus to his side, had ordered him imprisoned to await his captor's will. Severus escaped miraculously, on his way to execution diving from a bridge into the Thames; Mordred's folk, knowing by the famous stories that the knight couldn't swim, believed him drowned. But Severus caught a lucky current and, having had the foresight to store his horse and gear outside London, regained them and rode in full haste to Arthur to inform him of the plot.

A spy of Arthur's had caught Severus' flight from London and followed him. When he reached Arthur's forces camped on the edge of Lancelot's lands, Severus sought the king to expose Mordred, but the spy followed close behind and cast doubts upon Severus' story — envy may taint both sides in a conflict — suggesting that Severus had come instead to raise trouble between Mordred and his king to distract Arthur from his business with Lancelot. The spy, you see, was a double agent, his true loyalties lying with the usurper rather than the king.

Severus recalled the source of his distaste for court life, then, watching the clouds begin to obscure the images in the mirror, refocused his attention.

As a test of his loyalty Arthur sent Severus to Lancelot's stronghold to demand individual combat in the name of the king and knightly honor, leaving him with no other choice but to prove his innocence.

Severus issued his challenge, and Lancelot accepted. Severus had thought to engage his brother knight gingerly and use the encounter to communicate with Lancelot what had happened and try to win him to peace with Arthur, but Lancelot, offended not only by the charges against him (which were of course true) and also by the fact that Arthur had sent against him a knight of so little reputation in human combat, charged with all his might, giving no quarter.

Severus, at first sorry for the situation, soon, finding himself beset by the greatest of knights in full career, felt his own blood rising, and the encounter that the wise enchantresses had feared took place outside Lancelot's stronghold with the massed armies watching.

The battle, among the greatest of its kind ever to take place between two knights for its display of courage, stamina, and martial virtuosity, lasted the entire day, first one knight then the other seeming to gain the upper hand only to have a culminating stroke foiled by the other's quickness or defensive skill. Courage, though not particularly experienced in jousts or sword combats, served his master well, swerving, dancing, weaving, darting, as Severus needed him to do. When both horses were nearly dead from exhaustion, the knights dropped to their feet and fought toe-to-toe with swords until the last light of day dwindled on the horizon.

When their swords gave out, dented and bent with hundreds of blows, they selected other weapons. Severus tried once more to speak to Lancelot, who had in the past admired anyone who could keep up with him in combat, but found his opponent grimly silent. Even when other knights began to call for a truce and a draw, since darkness began to turn the matter into one of mere chance rather than skill and right, Lancelot merely selected a new weapon and attacked again, unmoved. When Lancelot chose a mace on the end of a chain, Severus relied on his trusty staff to deflect the blows that swung about him almost invisibly in the growing dark. Having missed a stroke so powerful that it drove his mace into the ground, Lancelot stumbled a step, and Severus, by then fighting only on will and the automatic response of instinct, struck on the crown, then the clavicle, then the knee, sending Sir Lancelot sprawling into the sweat-, blood-, and dew-streaked mud they had churned beneath their feet. The blows struck home with perfection, and Severus, expecting his opponent not to rise, swung the staff down in a warning blow, intending by its proximity to his opponent's nose to show that the battle had reached its end. But even he underestimated Lancelot's will, and the great knight had already risen to one knee to unclog himself from the muck. Severus' blow, where he intended it to communicate a message, instead struck Lancelot flush on the forehead, and Arthur's champion fell dead without even a sigh to issue forth the departing ghost.

Some knights would have expected from such a victory their king's praise and reward, but when word had passed through the darkness that Lancelot had been killed, both sides claimed foul and treachery. Arthur, sadder than he had felt to that day in his whole life, spared Severus' life because he had forced him to the engagement, but banished him from his court and his lands forever for having killed his greatest champion.

In the meantime Mordred had played his hand, fortified London, and prepared for Arthur's return. Arthur, mourning, failed to take proper precautions, and when he reached London he and his forces found themselves beset on all sides. Severus, grieving at his victory, had joined Arthur's army in disguise, and he fought well for his king in the battle that followed. But without Lancelot, Arthur's army fell. Severus, struck in the chest by a stray arrow from Gawain's bow, stumbled to the periphery of the battle, unable to staunch the wound. He learned from a squire that Mordred had won the day and thus all of Arthur's kingdom, and Guinevere had died trying to escape, and his thoughts drifted back to Lilava as the last drops of life left his body to fertilize British soil. Again the images faded, and the mirror clouded over.

Once again the clouds whirled and raced, and new images began to dot the mirror, then take full shape. Severus saw himself again sailing, but this time with Lilava at his side, as they returned to Britain together to pay mutual respects to Arthur and his court. The drama unfolded much as it had before, but with Lilava, who had stayed clear as Severus had approached Mordred, working a spell to release him from his captors, saving him from nearly drowning in the Thames. Together they rode to Arthur and nearly persuaded him of his danger, but the king's advisors showed no trust of Lilava, and the king dismissed the would-be friends from his service. Knowing nought else to do, they rode then to Lancelot's stronghold to learn if the great knight might not, learning the brunt of the situation, negotiate peace where they could not.

Finding them at his gate Lancelot admitted Severus and Lilava to his castle, but suspecting them of treachery, he challenged Severus to prove his case by individual combat. The famous Sir Bors fought for Lancelot, and Severus un-willingly fought and defeated him, trying desperately to do him no harm. His method of less than full engagement angered Lancelot, who then stepped in to Bors' place. Lilava pleaded with Severus not to fight him: should he defeat Lancelot, she said, Arthur's court would fall, and Mordred would begin a reign of terror that would keep Britain in a Dark Age for centuries.

Lancelot gave Severus no choice: he attacked. Being inside the castle walls, he forsook the joust, and they undertook battle with swords. The result followed what Severus had seen in the previous vision, except for the final stroke: know-ing, as Lilava told him, that he must not kill Lancelot, he withheld the final stroke of his staff. Lancelot, recovering his footing, rose and, in the dark, caught Severus first in the leg, then in the face with his mace. A third blow, as Severus tried to rise, split his chest; Severus' life departed his body as Lilava held his head in her lap and Lancelot stood nearby, watching by candlelight and, once the heat of battle had passed, wondering if he had killed friend or foe.

Clouds again covered the scene and obscured anything beneath the surface of the mirror, only once more to give way to the winds of time that cleared to show wild landscapes such as Severus had never seen before: long, enormous moun-tain ranges that seemed to stretch from sunrise to sunset and from ocean to sky; vast waters with waves whelming sandy dunes and green, sodden fields full of working farmhands; islands rising steep from the sea; rivers that stretched for lifetimes into forgotten plains that turned to deserts unfathomable; courts of kings and queens whose skin and eyes and dress reminded Severus of nothing he had seen before, exotic with perfumes and fruit trees bursting with food and blossoms — to those places he and Lilava traveled, until in a far land in the East a warlord who had feigned welcome to them turned on them instead, accused them of spying for his rival, and set his minions upon them. By Severus' skill and Lilava's magic they managed to escape, both gravely wounded; Severus recovered, but Lilava, far from any proper medicine, died upon the floor of a cave where they hid, Severus too weak to offer her the love and comfort that would make her last moments tolerable, and his failure broke his heart. By the time he had regained enough strength, her spirit had departed, so he burned her body and buried her ashes with the last tears he would shed in his life.

He worked his way west, gradually came home to Britain, where Arthur's court had fallen. Arthur and his illegitimate son Mordred had killed each other, Guinevere and Lancelot had retired to religious houses, and the land stood in a chaos of civil war as rival chieftains struggled to re-establish a central kingship and invaders began to pour in from the continent. Once again he took up a life of errantry, riding slowly along backroads and amidst the hills and forests, trying to stay away from the petty squabbles and the gangs of bandits that assaulted passersby, discomfiting any who dared confront him. When Courage died of old age, Severus sailed to Ireland, where he spent many gentle years traveling the coasts and rural ways, dismissing the occasional ghost or bogie and warning the occasional elf to return to the Otherworld without causing any trouble. Eventually, weary of wandering, he retired to a religious house to become a brother, where he tended their animals, performed their smithing, and prayed the hours as diligently as anyone ever had. In the peace and obscurity of that quiet life he found ease and hope of mind, if not balm for his lonely heart, and in time he died and was buried among the holiest of the members of his order. The priests and monks never learned his history, other than that he had been a knight, as several of their order once had. They knew him as a quiet, gentle brother who ended his days seeking holiness, and they laid him in an unmarked grave.

With that vision the mist rose again to obscure the mirror. Clouds assembled, wavered, then stilled, forming a surface opaque and lifeless. After waiting a moment Severus decided the mirror would show him no more, so he looked at Ambrose. "Thank you, sir."

"Use wisely what you have seen," Ambrose said.

"Thank you for bringing us here," he said to Corsicana.

"In time, sir knight, you may not thank me, but I accept your good will," the enchantress replied.

Then he turned to Lilava, who looked at him intently. She stepped near and brushed a drop of water from the corner of his eye.

"You have seen neither fact nor necessity," she said to Severus. "Is that not right, Ambrose?"

"Quite so," replied the wizard. "I don't know what you saw, but most people, if they are asking about their future, see directions their lives may take according to the decisions that lie before them. Judge the value of what you have seen, and feel no obligation to take it with any seriousness whatever. I have seen people rise from the mirror laughing, I have seen them crying, I have seen them elated, and I have seen them confused, even dazed. This much advice I will add: choose carefully and be good, but be light of heart! Our days pass quickly. Now I will return to commune with the sun, as I was doing when you interrupted me." He nodded to Severus, winked at Lilava, tossed his robe haphazardly into his hut, and plopped himself in his chair on the beach, his face turned up to the sunshine.

"Ready to go?" Corsicana asked.

"Yes, but where?" Severus asked Lilava.

"That depends on what we decide," she said.

"That depends on your answer to my questions."

"Ah."

"Look," said Corsicana, "I know you two may want to take your time, but I must get home; I have my own elders to meet and my explanations to make. I'd offer that you come with me, but I'm not sure they'd want to meet you — they tend to distrust strangers, especially those with unusual abilities. Since you'll not be safe here, I suggest you take your boat and return home, or to this Britain place of yours, or better yet take a vacation somewhere you've never been but where they welcome the trade of outsiders. As for me, I would happily bid you 'so long' — may it be so long till I see you again that I don't remember you. I say that not as an insult, but because I have to reconsider my profession and my own place here."

Lilava and Severus offered their best wishes, and Corsicana with no more ceremony left them, walking north along the coast.

Before they could leave, Ambrose called to them, following from his hut with his arms full. He had doffed his robe and hurried toward them dressed only in trousers cut off at the knees, sandals, and a band of cloth tied round his forehead. "Here," he said, "take this bit of supplies with you. Nothing magical, you understand, just some decent fishing gear and citrus and herbs and emollients and a few biscuits such as you may need at sea."

"Your kindness and foresight would give all magicians a good name in the world," said Lilava, thanking him.

"Not all," he answered, "but more than this age believes. And to think what they will do to the poor people they call magicians in ages to come: ugh, shocking."

They looked back at him once. He sat stretched in the chair before his hut, a piece of shiny metal beneath his chin reflecting sunlight onto his reddening face. He waved at them vaguely, or it may have been a sign for them to hurry along.

"Would you like to tell me," Severus asked as they approached their boat, "what you saw in the mirror?"

"I'm not sure I should. Don't you understand what you saw as a gift to you alone, to weigh as information you may use to make your own decisions?"

"A gift, yes, but to share so that I may use it better."

"Tell me first, then, if you wish."

Brought to the point of telling, Severus considered whether or not he should unburden himself of what he had seen, of all its sorrow and pain.

"Let's sail before the dark falls. We can talk as we go."

"We can watch the moon rise. It has nearly reached full and will help light our way. May I use your staff?"

He gave it to her, and in its end she stuck a metal orb, which when she stood it in the front of the boat gave off a faint light. "This device will also give us some light. I think we do well to sail rather than to trust in the locals' kindness toward strangers."

"Which way shall we sail, south or north?"

"Let's go a bit west."

"And decide as we go?"

"Yes."

Severus recounted his visions to Lilava. He changed little, trying to remain as truthful as he could allow himself, given the nature of what he'd seen.

After he'd finished, Lilava remained quiet for some time. Finally, "Heavy," she said, "but you have told them well."

"Thank you. And you?"

"All right. They weren't much better than yours, if you must hear them, but not without their rewards. I saw five visions."

"Five? You stood over the orb only for a few moments!"

"How long do you think you stood there? No longer than I, I think. The visions work as quickly as dreams, and because we ask the questions, the narratives develop and end only as possible answers to the questions, with few extraneous images."

"Tell them if you wish, not because you think you must."

In Lilava's first vision she saw the deaths of her parents and grandparents while she and Severus traveled in the East. She saw her own death there, as she lay at Severus' side. In her second vision Severus left alone for Britain to pay his respects to King Arthur. He never returned. For a long while she waited, helping her folk and tending her village, never marrying, finally traveling again among the islands of the Middle-Earth Sea, learning bits and pieces of her craft that she never had a chance to use, one day finding herself caught in a storm and dying at sea.

The third vision showed her returning to Britain with Severus, and as in his vision, he took his last breaths in her arms, having died in the battle with Lancelot. Lancelot in sorrow allowed Lilava her choice, that she either might stay safely within his stronghold or depart freely to the world. She left, sought out her sister enchantresses, found them busy with affairs of state, trying to foresee the coming events, but unable to prevent their evil course. After the war they dispersed to their several elements, and she wandered alone for some time, finally, wrought thin by deprivation and sorrow, allowing herself to die by exposure to the elements on a frozen hilltop far to the north.

When a new vision appeared, she saw herself bidding Severus wait for her while she sailed north alone to Britain to convene the Order of Enchantresses so as to prevent Mordred's rise to power and Arthur's fall. But they could reach no agreement, and though they managed to prolong the peace, the same people finally made the same bad choices, and civil war ended the reign of King Arthur, though the Enchantresses were able to bring about a brief and unstable peace thereafter. Allies from Germania eventually came at a young king's behest, to help him defend the peace, but seeing lands ripe for the picking, they soon became invaders and took what they could win of the islands for themselves. She never managed to get home to Severus, who, finally seeking her, met a storm off the British coast and drowned as Lilava watched the ship from a promontory, determining by means of her art who had died in the wreck.

Her final vision showed the two of them remaining together among Lilava's folk. They married, had children, raised their children to be such adventurers as they were themselves, and shared many exciting adventures at home and abroad. Off one of the Greek islands they found a great sea-monster that haunted the coast, devouring its fishermen; they encountered that beast, and together they destroyed it, freeing the island folk of their sorrows, but in that adventure found a sorrow of their own: they lost their son to the monster as he fought bravely and fiercely, but without the maturity and skill to survive against such a powerful beast. The family had other adventures together, but their hearts never recovered from their loss. Their daughter married and left for her husband's home on the distant mainland. The couple aged, never losing their love, but each partly blaming both self and the other for loss of their son — they died without reconciling themselves to it.

When she had finished telling her stories, Lilava sat pensive, shivering as their boat sailed slowly west. Severus placed his cloak over her shoulders and kissed her forehead.

"Maybe we can use what we have seen to guide us from bad decisions. Ambrose assured us that the visions don't bind us; they merely suggest possible results from possible choices. I do have a feeling that I must return to Britain, that I have something there yet to do — in addition to those events I must, if I go, avoid."

Lilava took his hand and kissed it. "We have choices far beyond those we've seen, and we may yet make the story turn out as we please, at least in terms of how we treat each other. We must decide now whether to sail north or south."

"What do you propose?"

"To answer your questions. Yes and yes."

"Which questions? Oh, the old questions! I am very glad of that. What helped you decide?"

"I had already decided in my heart. I hoped for external validation, but that was silly of me. We must make the best decisions we can, live our lives, and love those we love."

Wind had kicked up behind them and filled their sail, propelling them rapidly but comfortably west. The moon had risen high in the sky, where it sat lopsided and bright and beautiful, its light pouring down on them like a shower.

"South then, or north?"

"Neither."

"Oh?"

"The whole world stretches before us. The wind takes us west, and I take that for a sign. No, we mustn't decide on that alone, but it does offer a convenience. I know a place in the west, a beautiful coast with beaches and orange groves and flowers as big as your head and quiet little villages. The language differs little from Latin, and in one great settlement they have many priests and churches, and there we may get married and take our rest and find out what it's like to live life with the one you love."

"Will we have adventures?"

"Let's start with one, then see where we go from there. But isn't there more to life than adventures?"

"For one thing you will have someone who each day tells you he loves you and then strives to prove it."

"You will do that for me?"

"You shall have to wait to see for yourself."

"And when we have spoken and shown our love, what will we do then?"

"We can talk about that."

And they did.

Part 2

Severus and the Two Kings

1 In a Dire Strait

[... wherein Severus and Lilava unwillingly fight a battle in the strait of Messina.]

In weather pleasant but hot, in the south of the green and varied land of Europa, Sir Severus le Brewse, Knight of the Round Table, and Lilava the Enchantress sailed west on the Middle-earth Sea.

They had been traveling for about a day and had the good fortune to catch an easterly. They had grand success using the fishing gear that Ambrose the Sage had given them. His emollients protected their skin from the hot sun, which burst off the wave caps like glowing embers. They refreshed themselves with a cool drink of citrus squeezed into the sweet water in their waterskins.

Through Ambrose's thoughtfulness and foresight, they enjoyed greater comfort asea than they had in any previous journey. Having accomplished many adventures together and separately, they felt particularly happy about simply being together, freer of burdens than they had felt for years. They continued to talk over their future, each revolving in mind the scenarios and choices that they had seen and shared, the panoply of images that had risen from the fogs of Ambrose's magic mirror. As everyone knows, visions may prove a dubious blessing, but they will certainly provide good conversation on a long sea voyage. At night Severus and Lilava took shifts steering west while the other reclined for sleep, and despite busy thoughts neither had trouble drifting into deep sleep, cradled by the rocking of the waves and entertained by the bright garden of stars sketching pictures over the vast night sky that stretched like a blanket far above them.

"We should think of the best place to go now," Lilava offered before she slid into sleep. "I have seen beautiful places in Hispania, and I hear that the Greek Islands are nice this time of year. Or in the west of Britain we may seek Arawn, a great friend of the Lady of the Lake and King of the Otherworld. If we can find him, he may let us vacation there. His lands spread out almost endlessly, or at least, having seen them, one wishes they did. Boad and green and lush, they fall away into singing dales or rise to snow-capped peaks."

"For my part, you may choose," Severus said.

"Good answer," Lilava replied just before sleep wafted her into the even broader, deeper, unpredictable lands of dream.

Well into the next morning and refreshed by rest, they sat together in the stern of their boat, tacking into the gentle breeze that had blown up from the west to still their progress. Still, they enjoyed the flow of cooler air over their faces, relaxing until they spotted a ship on the horizon.

It seemed to sit there in the distance for some time, then finally to turn toward them, growing gradually from a speck into a veritable bulk, its broad, golden sails unfurled. As Severus and Lilava realized that it must inevitably cross their path, Lilava gathered her energies should she need a spell, and Severus took stock of available weapons, since the ship appeared, as it loomed close enough for perusal, accoutred for battle. Armed men lined the deck, and when the ship got close enough for hailing, a herald called to them from the prow, which rose high and stately above the sea.

The man addressed them in a tongue unknown to Severus, but that Lilava recognized as distantly akin to her own. She replied as best she could, guessing by what she had heard at inflections and phrasing foreign, yet familiar. Severus caught some of her words, but found the accent strange and the whole of the speech confusing. He noted, however, Lilava's tone: one of confident command rather than deference or inquiry. The ship's herald listened carefully, then paused a moment, licked his lips, and spoke again in Lilava's native language, though with the occasional odd word ending — close enough that Severus could understand what he said.

"My honorable master wishes to speak with you. He believes he knows who you are, and he intends you no ill, merely desires to, ah, consult with you about a matter of grave importance to him and his people."

"We have business in the west," Lilava answered, again with the commanding tone, "but if your master wishes, we would happily speak with him, if he would parley from his own deck. Our boat is small and allows little room for guests."

Severus caught a resonance of magic in her tones, the kind that says without saying, "Hear me and do as I ask."

The ship had pulled alongside their small craft, and the soldierly men aboard looked down on them, each with a hint of a smile that troubled Severus. Severus noted bows hanging at their sides and arrows quivered at their backs. Examining their faces, he got the sense that they hadn't been listening to Lilava — perhaps someone had coached them on how to avoid magic. The herald, breathing heavily and looking confused, departed the prow for a moment — he showed the effects of the power of Lilava's voice. Shortly he returned with regained composure.

"My master requests the honor of welcoming you aboard ship. He offers food and drink in exchange for, ah, conversation. He assures you that he wishes you no harm, but that he rather seeks knowledge you may have that may help him honorably defend his people. You may board at your pleasure."

Too much wishing and maying going on here, and too many claims about honor, Severus thought. He glanced at Lilava's eyes and saw that she didn't trust the ship's crew any more than he did. He also knew that asea in their tiny craft they could do little to defend themselves, and clearly Lilava knew so as well.

"My knight and I will parley with him if he would," Lilava answered. "Please ask him to come forward."

Beyond doubt Severus heard the rumblings of magic in the undertones of her voice.

The dull face of the herald stared at her for a moment, then disappeared from the prow. In a moment a shortish, balding man with broad shoulders and brow and extremely wide eyes looked down on them, grinning. He wore a long, red robe, open, but clasped with a shiny black gem at the throat, and he had a crown a-tilt on his head. He spoke in Lilava's tongue, but with a slight hiss in his accent that impeded the rhythmic roll of his words.

"What a happy accssident! I believe I have found personss of the ssort I sseek," he said. "You have ccertainly impressed my herald — he ssits here babbling now. But may I offer you the hosspitality of my ship? The greater comfort will I'm ssure provide you resspite from the rolling ssea. In fact, I musst sspeak to you, for my people sstand constantly in peril, and if you are who I think you are, you, Sseveruss and Lilava, possess the key to ssave them." He grinned, the wide, white smile shining like whitecaps in the sun.

Severus noticed that the bowmen, though they hadn't aimed, had taken arrows in hand. "Without egress we have a better chance at arm's length than at bow's length," he whispered to Lilava in Cymric, hoping the hissing captain wouldn't understand.

"I don't know the language your companion sspoke to you, madam," said the shipmaster, "but I guess that he encouraged you to accept my offer. And I require both of you, ssince the problem I musst ssolve iss a mighty one, worthy of your skills. Come: enjoy the hosspitality of my gallant ship, my home away from home. I insisst."

* * *

After several minutes in the master's undeniably homey cabin, Severus and Lilava had got accustomed to his strange, sibilant speech, and they had also learned that he had found them in fact not by accident, but by vigorous searching. Following Lilava's lead, Severus had refused repeated offers of food and drink. Having reached the brink of death in grim battles, and having an inherent distrust for such creatures as their insistent host, Severus found the thought cross his mind that he should not only avoid giving the man any additional advantage, but also that he should with all speed simply kill him. Severus felt confident he could dispatch the little man — who looked far less imposing in person than he did peering down from the deck — without much trouble, even though the master had requested that Severus leave his weapons outside. Conscience held him back: though he felt they faced danger, he could not yet prove it, so he waited and listened, unwilling to kill or even do harm unnecessarily.

"Yes, you are right, madam and sir, I have sought you in person. No one else will do, since you and only you have destroyed the Chimaera."

Lilava, Severus was sure, had no intention of mentioning her sister, who had certainly helped in the battle, and he felt glad that the master apparently knew nothing of her — best to keep each mess as simple as possible. He also felt surprise at how quickly the story of their battle had spread, apparently across the seas.

"And yes, sir, you can, if you wish, kill me — my thoughts tell me you have been considering it. Your physical powers outstrip mine, though perhaps not by so much as you think. But you would gain nothing by doing so, and you would then have to kill every one of my soldiers. And: you would have no ship to sail. They have orders to destroy this ship if any guest, let us say, overcomes me, and, I am sorry to admit to you, I have had them destroy your boat already. What need have you of it now, eh, since my craft provides much more comfort? Perhaps you may guess that my men would not follow that order to burn their own ship, since they would forfeit their own lives in doing so, but their loyalty has often surprised even me. They have positively dedicated their lives to me. What confidence, wealth, and a little magic can accomplish never ceases to amaze me. Ha!"

Severus wondered if the man could read his mind or his face only, or if he simply had the intelligence to guess well. One thing he knew for certain, because he had a sense for such things: they were dealing with a man, not a monster, though perhaps a monstrous man. Though the master had plenty of gall and probably a good deal of cunning, he had no whiff of the beast-nature about him.

"May we know by what name we should call you?" Lilava asked the master.

"You ask politely, and I appreciate you even more for that. Knowing your power, I shouldn't tell you my name — you for one can discern the value in a name, the power one holds over another by knowing it. But to show you my magnanimity and good will toward you, I will tell you. You may call me, as my father and mother did, Abracadabrax, but that is cumbersome — try carrying around such a name for a few years, and you will see. Other peoples, those on lesser terms with mine, call me The Witch King — not always, I think, out of kind intent. My people call me King Abra; when we are not among them, you may dispense with the title, for we shall be friends. I am a bit more than a mere shipmaster, you see! And I will call you Lily and Sevy, no? Ha! Lilava and Severus, then, since that you prefer. And no, my people are not witches, nor would I call myself one, though I have sought such learning as the world offers over land and sea. Come, won't you have a drink with me? I suspect you, madam, have acquired such unsavory epithets as 'witch' in some places — please pardon me for saying so. But let us drink to a profitable association."

"Thank you, no: we may not drink other than the fresh water you see us carrying. Pre-marital ritual requires that discipline among Severus' folk," Lilava said. Severus didn't nod agreement, nor did he contradict her, preferring to let her plot their course among people she knew better than he.

"Does it so?" Abra exclaimed. "I have never encountered such a barbaric, ah, let us say chaste, ritual. I should certainly not submit to it, but then you may have more filial piety than I. Not that I preach impiety — I defer to the gods as well as any man — but I enjoy my little indulgences, and I find that the gods do not trouble me if I allow them proper libation, ha! You, my good sir, look a pious man to me, correct? You defer to the gods?"

Severus hesitated for a moment over whether he would describe himself as pious, drawing out the first syllable of his answer as though to avoid overcommitting to it. "Yes, though where I come from, people tend, at least publicly, that is, to profess devotion to one god only. I do my best to follow God's teaching and to serve my king, if that you would call pious."

"You choose one god among them, then, and profess loyalty to that one alone?" Abra asked.

"Most, many, of the people believe that there is only one God, Creator and Savior, whose will they, we, serve."

"Only one? Really? Ha! Ha, ha! What a notion! Only one! And do people you have met elsewhere hold that view, or does it remain peculiar to your people?"

"Many believe it now, since the worship of God has grown and continues to spread."

"And yet I heard your hesitation. Even your people have not accepted the idea fully. Such a complex and interesting world, full of varied creatures and ideas, to fall under the auspices of one god only. But 'live and let try,' I say. I must ponder the idea and observe how you get on with such an odd belief — and whether your only one god will have the wherewithal to protect you."

"Protect us against what?"

"Too bad you will not dine or at least drink with me, for the food and wine have such excellence as I'm sure you've seldom experienced. These cool fruits refresh like no others, the northern cheese is magnificent, and this dry red wine truly delectable. But already you grow impatient. Have you never heard the expression carpe diem, as the Romans say? I would not have told you so soon the request I intend to make of you, but I have always myself aimed to expedite business that must be done, so I suppose I should admire that same trait in others. Yes, we have a task we must complete, you and I, and though what protec-

131

tion you can invoke will help us, I have never heard of anyone other than you two who I have believed could accomplish it. So I sought for you. And I have found you. Yes, you must undertake it for me, and I believe I can convince you. You may even succeed, ha ha."

"As I said when we boarded," Lilava interrupted, "we have our own business in the west, and ..."

"In some cultures, I hear, shipmasters have the privilege of performing wedding ceremonies, so you need not worry about that business in the west. And I'm afraid the duty I must place before you can't wait."

"How did we get from 'conversation' to 'duty'?" Severus asked.

"You may put the prospect any way you like, so long as you perform the task," Abra said, in a grimmer tone than he had used before.

"What task do you wish of us?" Lilava asked.

"Something inconsequential, I should think, to two persons who have rid the world of the Chimaera."

"Hardly rid the world."

"Oh, it will return then? Ah, not here, but somewhere, yes, in time. Well, let's say then that you defeated it — close enough? Heroes who have defeated the Chimaera should have scant trouble with this next little problem, er, two problems."

"Please tell us the situation exactly."

"Well, you know, in the strait between your island and the mainland lie two monsters, one on either side ..."

"You can't mean Scylla and Charybdis?"

"Precisely, madam. As I said, no great difficulty for such accomplished warriors."

"Impossible."

"I think not. At least it had better not be."

"Even the greatest wizards and soldiers of the ancient world could not destroy them; the lucky ones merely survived them."

"Then you must find a way to do better. You see, they impede, how shall I say it, my commerce. The way around them takes too long, while a free passage along the coast would speed matters immeasurably. I have lost far too many ships in that channel, and I have lost too much trade by avoiding it."

"What makes you think you can convince us to attempt the task for you? If you know the stories, you know that the most dangerous of enemies has experienced ill fortune not only against those monsters, but against us."

"I considered that you might feel reluctant to serve me out of the goodness of your hearts alone. I am willing to offer treasure, but you don't seem the types to be won over so. May I offer you treasure, treasure such as, given the quality of your clothes — forgive my bluntness — I doubt you have ever seen before? No, ha, I did not expect that to work, so I have taken steps, yes, steps."

Without rising from his chair Abra emptied his wine cup and flung it against the door of his cabin. It shattered with a sound like the sudden falling of hundreds of massive rain drops. The door opened, two eyes peered in, a shadowy head nodded, and the door closed.

"You really, really should try one of these apricots," Abra said, chewing one, then another with gusto.

The door opened again, and through it two shadowy figures shoved Lilava's sister Liletta, her hands bound behind her and her mouth gagged. They maintained a tight hold on her.

"Forgive me, but I took the liberty of collecting, on my way to find you, a reason that would assure me I could win your loyalty. No, no, stand still, sir knight." He nodded, and his men immediately yanked Liletta back through the door. "And I assure you that beyond such small discomfort as you have just observed, we have done the girl no harm or indignity whatever, besides, ha, insisting upon her presence on our little excursion. And no harm will come to her so long as you agree to accompany me, even if you should — how shall I say it? — not manage to return from it triumphant. Then we will take her home and allow her such treasure as may serve to compensate your family. And should you triumph? Well, the treasure may mean little to you, but I have no doubt your people can use it anyway, and the young lady may then depart with you, no serious harm done to anyone save the monsters."

Abra's men closed the door before Lilava could catch her eye.

* * *

Abra allowed Severus and Lilava only a single cabin to share, which he locked as he left them there. They got no further glimpse of Liletta. The sparse cabin had few comforts, and by then they had spent enough time alone together to feel no particular need for what some prudish people may have called propriety; they trusted each other entirely. Though neither could sleep, Severus convinced Lilava to lean her head against his shoulder so he could stroke her hair and ease her mind. In the distance they heard the sound of thunder.

"Storm building in the west?" Severus asked. "Maybe we got lucky to have fallen into Abra's hands."

"I should rather take my chances with the sea than with our self-styled Witch King."

"The good thing about this business," Severus suggested, "is that your sister may now attend you at our wedding, assuming of course that we survive the ordeal."

"Not a big help, my love."

"I know, but a small help must do in a pinch."

They spent the night talking of monsters, as lovers sometimes do.

In the morning a servant slid them breakfast through a hole in the door, and shortly Abra himself relieved them of their confinement so that they might walk together on the deck.

"I have no intention of keeping you prisoner," he said. "You see, I am working for your welfare as well as mine and my people's. I merely thought you should have an uninterrupted night of, let's say, talk to consider the obvious rationality of my proposition. A marvelous thing, rationality, for the invention and promotion of which all learned people must forever value and thank the Greeks, my ancestors on my mother's side. But now that you have eaten and taken some air, we must have the rest of our conversation, for you have a difficult task ahead of you, and we must plot a strategy. No, no, you need not see the girl again now. Ah, trust my hospitality! Though I practice a bit of sorcery and, well, what you may call piracy, I am no barbarian, nor should you think of me as such. But now to business: tell me all you know of the monsters of the strait, and I shall tell you what I know, and we shall see how and why this venture shall accomplish as much for you as for me, treasure or not."

Scylla and Charybdis, Abra explained to Severus, guarded the two sides of the thin strait that separated Sicilia and mainland Italy. Scylla, with her dragon's body and six voracious heads, and Charybdis, the great whirlpool that draws sailors irrevocably to the bottom of the swirling sea, allowed no one free passage. Scylla had once consumed six of the famous Odysseus' men, and Charybdis had nearly got the wily one himself. They had never ceased to wreak havoc among travelers along the Italian coast. Of course Lilava had told Severus much of them during the night, but Severus didn't mind getting Abra's take on the facts, so that he might get a better sense of the man's veracity. How, asked Abra then, could his guests free his ships from their terrors, either by magic or might? For he believed them as capable as anyone he had met.

"Now, as I have said, my ships must sail all the way around the island to avoid these troubles: many days and much profit lost. But certainly your people would be overjoyed, too, to find themselves rid of those monsters?"

"We avoid them," Lilava answered.

"Live and let live," Severus added.

"Now, if we have free trade through the straits, so will you, and with that greater freedom of movement I can trade with smaller peoples, such as yours — I mean that in terms of numbers only, not quality." Abra tried to smile engagingly. "And you, sir knight, would they not add to your reputation another chapter of courage and victory?"

"I have never really sought reputation."

"Then of course, milady, we have the matter of your sister, my other guest."

"So we have."

"And none of us would wish her other than complete happiness and a long life."

Quietly seething, Severus was beginning to wonder if he were losing his ability to detect monsters and if his conscience had once too often stilled his hand.

"No untoward actions now, my good knight — no good will come of such thoughts. You will see: we will all gain the benefit of our working together."

"I have been thinking, King Abra, that if your less savory epithet bears any truth, the woman we saw may not be my sister. Perhaps you have discovered a spell that can create resemblances and affect the perceiver in such a way as to believe them true."

"Young lady, you need merely unleash your athletic friend here upon me, and when later you find your sister's body, should you live to see it, you can surely identify it to your own satisfaction. Now I tire of discussion. You really, really must make your decision with no delay. You may have no more time to consider or attempt to practice spells or counter-spells, to reason and decide. You must choose and act."

Severus looked deeply into Lilava's eyes. "As for me," he said, "I will fight."

Lilava replied to Abra, "I ask only this much of you: give us one hour to consider by what means we may fight the monsters. They may in fact lie beyond our skill."

"You shall have it, and I have no doubt of your skills, either of you, and if as I believe you are choosing to assist me, I promise you will not regret it. You will preserve a life much worth living, serve your own people, and save not just me, but the world a good deal of suffering through ages to come — too good a deal to refuse! And I will be generous: you will have several hours to meditate a plan. We are already sailing south for the strait, but you have plenty of time to, ah, strategize before we arrive, ha! And I will stand with you every step of the way."

Abra removed himself to the stern of the ship, and Severus and Lilava stood in the prow looking glum and considering what to do.

"Stand close and speak as softly as you can," Lilava said. "I have little doubt he will hear everything we say anyway, if he has any real magic about him. Titles, everyone wants titles, having earned them or not. Even having earned, who needs them? Look at the trouble we have got into by reputation alone — and so soon after having won it. Who runs faster than Rumor? If I thought it would help, I would sink the ship and drown the lot of them, but who knows if we could reach Liletta in time?"

"And, er, you know of course that I don't swim very well. You might find yourself on your own looking for her, since I have difficult time enough just trying to remain afloat."

Lilava smiled and stroked Severus' cheek. "Yes, I know, but I wasn't going to mention that. No need to look sheepish: we all have our limitations, and you do swim better than you did, and I should find us something on which to float anyway."

"I see land in the distance, which makes me wonder if we should simply go ahead into the strait and have our little battle, though we be less well-armed than we'd like. And hearing you tell of it, I think I may have a chance against this Scylla creature, if you have a notion of what to do with the whirlpool."

Lilava spotted the land, too. "Too soon: I need time to think and gather my energies. Something, in the far reaches of my memory, and that only a chance, if I can recall it ..." Lilava didn't feel at all confident, for while she felt Severus had a chance against Scylla — a living, breathing creature, horror though it was — Lilava must deal with a force of nature, something beyond the reach of one's ability to cause it fear and confusion, something with a power beyond that of living matter. Lack of sleep hindered her memory as she searched it for spells.

"Sit here by me and put your head in my lap. I'll stroke your hair to help you think," Severus offered.

"No, that will put me to sleep, and I will need every instant we have to concentrate — but thank you. If I had not many times seen you fight, I would believe you too gentle a man for knighthood, and I mean that as a compliment."

"Then while you think, I will see Abra about what sort of weapons he will spare me. Too bad we don't have with us the Lady of the Lake. Didn't you attend her once in Britain? Maybe she would know something about water spells."

Water, Lilava thought, and her mind began to turn with the power of the whirlpool itself. She had learned much as a lady of the Lady of the Lake, who wore the supernatural like a cloak about her person. Yes, she had spells for moving the elements, but would they work here, Lilava thought, in a different clime, and at sea rather than among inland waters? And had Lilava the power, even could she recall the formulae, to use them? Think, Lilava said to herself, remember; assemble each part of the puzzle. Savor the words.

In the stern Severus discussed weaponry with Abra, who was fiddling with a hawser. "I am so glad you have decided to serve, er, join me in our task. Yes, we must consider what best may work against these monsters. Six heads and a dragon's body, difficult enough for a troop, let alone one, er, two or three men, regardless of their courage and skill. We shall have to attack in a small number — can't risk too many on one venture — and you shall get no parley with her, the monster, that is. We are not dealing here with men, but with great, seething, volatile powers, a creature as old and angry as the fires beneath Etna and a maelstrom as immitigable as death. But you have a stout heart and a fine musculature and — blast this knot! — here, you, come get this! Now let us get my swordsmith and see what we have." One of the sailors took the rope from Abra as the king and Severus sought the belly of the ship.

Abra had in the hold quite a number of weapons, and the swordsmith warily offered Severus some impressive blades, but the knight had a different idea in mind. "I will take these star-shaped dirks — where did you say you got them? — and these two broad battle-axes, one for each hand. Had I six hands, I should ask for six of them. No, a shield's no use here, I think, if I have the right picture in my mind. And my staff, I'll just sling it over my back so. Severus twirled the staff, slipped it in a halter, and slung it over his back, dropped the dirks into a pocket of his short jacket, and swung the axes rapidly in each hand to test their heft and balance. The swordsmith looked uncertainly at Abra, but the king just shrugged, his round eyes beaming at Severus' easy skill with the weapons.

"Remarkable dexterity," he said.

"Smith, may I use your grinding wheel? I should just like to take it bit of weight off here and there. And if you can, provide me a small bow and a dozen arrows."

"Make it a half-dozen," mumbled Abra.

When Severus had armed, he strode forward for Lilava, expecting to find her cross-legged in the prow, meditating. She stood waiting for him, with a hint of smile on her face which had, despite the dint of the sun upon it, grown pale. But her deep, dark brown eyes gleamed, and her lips were steady. He knew what she would say, and he smiled.

"I have it. I'm ready. Ready as I'll ever get."

"And so am I," he said. "Though I should feel better, sure, if Liletta were with you, and you were both safe, while I deal with Scylla — though I must admit I have no notion of what to do with Charybdis."

"I can think of no reason," Abra offered, "why your sister should not join us, young lady. I had thought to bring her, to wait at my side, and your knight's confirming my thought assures me I was right. Guard: get the young one and bring her to the small boat."

"I prefer to do this task alone," Lilava said, casting a glance at Severus. "I would have you assure me of my sister's safety, regardless of how I fare."

"Nonsense. Who better than loved ones to help in a pinch. And I and my guards shall stand watch nearby, should you need us." He moved to the port bow to oversee the lowering of a tiny boat little more than a dinghy.

"I preferred not to have her involved," Lilava whispered to Severus, as they drifted starboard to talk. "She can't help me this time, and we will face great danger."

"She may help more than you guess, if she has her sister's natural resourcefulness. She has helped before when we most needed her," Severus said. "And I have a sense that she will stand more safely with us than apart from us. And you can be sure, with her in our presence, that we will have a chance to save her. We will fight for us, not for Abra."

"I was already fighting for us. I need no more pressure than that."

"Then trust me. The greater danger may lie away from us, rather than with us."

A deep, distant rumbling interrupted their talk.

"Do I hear the thunder coming nearer?" Severus asked, examining the heavy, dark-blue sky that looked to be creeping toward them from the northwest. A brisking wind had freshened and was blowing them rapidly southeast. The coast loomed in full view.

"Ready the skiff!" Abra hissed to one of his guards, and he and a comrade drew out a small, open boat that had lain hidden under animal skins, and they quickly lowered it into the sea toward the east. "Maybe thunder, or maybe the thunder of Charybdis being herself — we lie close enough to hear her roar."

Knowing the king would betray them, Severus cast a disgusted glance at Lilava and armed quickly, and two of the guards lowered Severus and Lilava into the boat, then kicked it off into the current. Abra appeared at the bow, grasping Liletta at the elbow. "On second thought, I will keep the young lady here with me. She will give you reason to complete your task and return to me. It would be a pity were she to fall into the rough sea meanwhile. Good voyage to you, and good luck, and may the powers of earth, water and wind bless you with the will to prevail."

Abra had cut sail and turned into the wind, holding as steady as he could, while the boat that carried Lilava and Severus turned and sped directly into the strait. Lilava just caught a glance a Liletta's terrified eyes before they passed too far away for Lilava to do more than wave hopefully to her sister.

"Bad luck there — I had thought that if Abra had put her in with us, we could make a run through the strait and lure him after. Monsters may take the larger meal rather than the weaker seeming."

"He's too smart to put us in a position to escape. We had done better to fight him aboard ship," Severus replied. "But something stayed my hand. At first I

138

saw no necessity, then I felt sure we should lose Liletta, and then — I'm not sure why, but I felt I must not kill him. His magic may have worked on me."

"Sometimes one must accept the feeling and go with it. But I fear I haven't enough power to execute my plan. I can think of nothing better, but it calls for a depth of concentration and power I have only once attempted."

"Have no fear, love: I trust your strength as I do my own. We will return for her," Severus said. "You feel confident that you remember the words you need?"

"Confident, no."

"I can always count on you for honesty."

"Well, most of the time."

"Hmm. Rumbling again, not this time from the sea to the south, but from a storm: it approaches rapidly from the west."

"Not rapidly enough, I fear."

"Haven't we enough trouble without a storm?"

"I am counting on the storm. At night, when we heard the rumblings, I began to wonder if a storm could help us escape. When you reminded me of the Lady of the Lake — oh, my time with her seems so long ago now — I recalled her spells for the water and wind spirits. I don't know if they will work. She balances the forces of a lake, and we have the whole sea before us. No one can control the weather, but she knew how at least to guide it, within her element. I don't know — I don't know for certain that I can do it. But I have the idea firmly in mind, if I can effect it. Tell me truly: can you deal with Scylla?"

"Since we keep to honesty most of the time, then, I must tell you that I'm not sure either. Is one ever sure? I tell myself I'm sure, else how can I fight at all? Doubt breeds defeat. Like you, I have a plan, and I will use the skills that God and practice have given me. As for Charybdis, I feel at a loss. I must count on you, and I do. If we fail — well, why consider that? Together we will seek the path that all shades follow. My heart tells me that we have already faced worse, and yet one doesn't always fall to the greatest enemy.

"Ah, my love, you are a sorceress, the kindest, most beautiful, and most loving ever, and I am a fighter of monsters who loves you. Let's go cheerfully, since go we must — I wouldn't have believed a small boat could go so fast! Let's live the moments of battle, awake and complete. We may fight, I think, with clear conscience, though we fight for Abra's good as well as Liletta's and our own. With confidence and commitment we will win."

"A speech worthy of a Roman legion commander!" Lilava said, admiring. "Let us steer as well as we can toward the mainland. Too close to Scylla we still have a chance, since you must engage her regardless. Too close to Charybdis and we both may fall. The storm comes on rapidly — good, we may have luck with us. But now I must concentrate. No more words, love, until we have survived or walk the paths of the dead together, whatever and wherever they may be or lead!"

The wind howled at their backs as the blue northern sky tumbled gust-over-cloud upon them. As they entered the channel between island and mainland, rain began to spit; thankful that the boat had a rudder, Severus leaned on it with all his weight to steer toward the Italian shore. Lilava muttered syllables indecipherable to Severus.

Through the kicking and neighing waves, they neared the coast and the rocks. In the distance to the west, they could hear the rumbling of water, and not far a-starboard the roiling sea approached in rounding, piling waves, petering out just out of range. Behind them, the storm followed as though Lilava had roped it, as if she were pulling it behind them like a domesticated beast. When they got close enough to shore, Severus checked his weapons, kissed Lilava on the forehead without looking in her eyes, and dived into the surf. Lilava, already concentrating, allowed the boat to drift toward the peril of Charybdis. Glad Liletta was out of the immediate danger, though Lilava knew she could have used her sister's help, she slowly began another incantation.

Severus found pebbly ground churning beneath his feet and for an instant feared he wouldn't get his footing, but a wave burst behind him and pushed him forcefully toward the shore. He hit the short beach at a run, turning straight south along the coast, his eyes poring over caves, crevices, and crannies. He carried an axe in each hand and pumped his arms powerfully and steadily as he ran.

Amidst the rushing wind and pounding surf, he nearly failed to hear the sound of padded feet, claws withdrawn, that slipped behind him from the deep shadows of the rocks. He sensed the presence before he heard it, turned, dug his feet in and whirled both axes in intersecting circles as rapidly as he could.

Scylla let out a roar of pain as an axe-blade cut a claw cleanly from the arm she had stretched to grasp her victim. A vertical swing of the axe severed a head that had bent over to bite what the claw had hoped to grasp. She slid in the sand, kicking up an enormous billow, and shrieked to a stop, striking Severus head over heels backward with the sweep of another powerful limb.

When Severus regained his feet, he planted an axe in the ground and grabbed the dirks from his pocket. A cloud of sand stood between him and the beast, and the dust threatened to blind him, burning and scraping his eyes. Another claw emerged, swinging, razor sharp, and Severus ducked it, close enough that he could smell its metallic sharpness. When it swung back, he parried with his remaining axe and cut the second claw clean away, the sharp edge digging into his shoulder as it flew by, sending his blood spurting onto the beach. He dropped the axe and rolled, covering the wound with sand to dry the blood and stop the flow, and leaped to his feet only to be felled again by the bellows that broke from the beast's mouths. Scraping himself up, he saw the heads emerge as rain pelted down, flattening the dust cloud, giving him a view of his targets: four heads left. The beast must have lost one to a previous hero — good, he thought: one weapon fewer he needed. Severus readied the dirks, and as the heads emerged, taller above the sand than Severus would have guessed, he choked down the pain that seared in his shoulder and pitched them in rapid succession toward the angry eyes that leered down on him.

Two hit. Three missed. Two healthy heads to go. Both descended at once, screaming horribly.

He dodged aside and rolled, picked up one axe and fired it at the neck that flung itself at him, parting the head from the body. One head to go. It rose up above him, leaving the breast open.

He rolled again, grasped the other axe, rose, and with both hands flung it into the center of the beast's breast.

It struck home, but the last head descended anyway. Severus pulled his staff from behind him and jammed it into the open mouth.

The impact broke the staff, which splintered, the sharp end piercing through the palate into the beast's brain. The heavy head fell, striking Severus before he could duck and knocking him unconscious, the other end of the staff, propelled into the sand beside him, missing his head by inches.

Too bad, the thought crossed his mind, as his awareness tumbled into growing darkness: I liked that staff — will have to cut a new one now.

* * *

Lilava, standing in the boat, chanting, drifted toward the opposite coast. The water that had choked and frothed moments before had calmed. The thought grazed her consciousness that the maelstrom of Charybdis had retracted itself, and she should escape it. Despite her concentration, another sort of roaring sound entered her mind from the shore where she had left Severus, and part of her said she should paddle there as quickly as she could: he needed her. Then she felt a bobbing beneath her feet, and the rain began to fall in earnest. The wind, a northwester before, began to twist and sheer, forcing her to sit down lest she lose her footing, as the water beneath began to churn malevolently. Concentrate, she thought. Concentrate. Did Abra want them to fail? Concentrate. Had Severus a clear notion of his enemy? Concentrate. What were they doing aboard ship to Liletta? Concentrate. Would they find a Land of the Dead where she and Severus might at least dwell peacefully together? Concentrate! Lilava dug into her thoughts and poured all her focus into the chant, a version of the spell she had learned from the Lady of the Lake to quiet a wind, but that spell

141

reversed, and the spell to call the feminine wind, that spell, too, reversed: she wanted, needed the whirling, remorseless, male wind, the great spouting torna-dic wind drawn against its course, at her will, to oppose the whirling turmoil of the sea, spin against spin, female against male, water against air, depth against height, that each might still the other and fall together into peaceful oblivion. I hope, Lilava thought, that Abra was right in calling Charybdis female, or I shall make one horrible row. Concentrate! Stay at the edge of the whirl and con-centrate! Come wind to water, and water to wind, and find your mate! Come, elements, and spend your hate! With all her strength Lilava chanted the great spells of the elements that speed them to tempest, that wrack the sinews of the chanter to the limits of endurance. Come wind, come water, propel yourselves to love and slaughter! Lilava wasn't sure whether she had chanted the words or merely thought them.

Then, rapidly, the water before her and the wind above her began to churn and whirl. Hold on! Concentrate! Water to wind, and wind to water, son of clouds, and sea's daughter; find your elemental lover! smother rage, unfurl and cover!

Rain crashed down, and lightning snapped like a whip, and the wind threat-ened to rip both Lilava and her tiny boat into jots. Charybdis, as though hearing the call of the wind, opened her swirling maw, drawing a great chasm of water into her groaning depths, with Lilava teetering on the edge.

But before the maelstrom could swallow Lilava into her great gyrating chan-nel, from above the swirling wind spun itself into a towering spout that rushed into Charybdis' hub, and, whirl to whirl, sucked the water back up from the sea bottom. Gyre to gyre they contended, joined, fed upon each other, each shout and groan echoing under the dome of blue-black clouds, lightning electrifying their cries, until in a great spout volumes of water rose into the sky, absorbing the wind that had drawn it forth, and they plunged together into the gray-white froth of sea. With one final blow the north wind shot the clouds south through the strait into the open, flattening sea beyond. Lilava's boat bobbed and rocked, rose and fell, then lurched backward, but she clung on, until with one last heave Charybdis cleansed her roaring spirit, spurring a vast wave that caught the boat and whisked it at terrible speed toward the Italian shore.

Exhausted, bone-weary from wind and spells, Lilava lost consciousness as Charybdis and her great windstorm spouse disappeared together into the new-born quiet of the sea, seldom to trouble travelers thereafter.

* * *

When she awoke, Lilava heard the sounds of footfalls and of wooden ob-jects being stacked together. She lay beneath a warm, but evil-smelling cloak, stretched otherwise comfortably upon soft sand.

142

"We've done it again, you know," Severus said softly, dropping his head down to kiss her on the cheek once he noticed she had wakened. "After the great wave deposited you on shore, the sea stilled almost to mirror-glass. You'll see for yourself. I've collected a bit of food and started a fire. Night will fall soon. At first light we will have yet another task before us, but for now eat a bit and sleep. I can't tell you how happy I was to find you alive."

"You talk rather more than you did."

"Sorry."

"Not at all: I'm glad for it. Tell me what happened to you, since I am at least as glad to see you as you are to see me. I thought I heard such screaming from out there, though I had to strike it from my thoughts. You see ..."

"Rest a bit for now, and try to eat something. We'll talk as we row in the morning. We've had a rough time of it. Abra certainly never expected to see us again, but he shall, he shall. Here: try this."

"Some sort of fish soup, is it? Hmm. Not bad, really."

"Nor good, but it's something in a pinch and will warm you, though the wind has stilled almost entirely, so we shan't have as cold a night as I expected."

"The storm?"

"Gone in a great flurry, as though it dropped into the sea. Tomorrow I'd like to hear all about how you did it."

"Tough day of work for you? Oh, my — let me tend that shoulder. It looks dreadful."

"Not so bad, the shoulder anyway. Bit of a tough day, but I've had worse, and so have you. That cloak's pretty awful, isn't it. I threw it over you for warmth, but since I've been around you, I've got more accustomed to clean things, and I can tell you don't like it much. Let me find something better. You don't want to know all that I found in Scylla's cave, but a few of the items will prove useful tonight and tomorrow." Severus hunted until he found a cleaner cloak for Lilava, replaced the foul one, then sanded the roughness off a new wooden staff as Lilava drifted to sleep.

* * *

In the morning, once Lilava had tended Severus' shoulder and he had checked and patched their skiff, they set off rowing for north of the strait. From among Scylla's horrible artifacts Severus had recovered two large, iron-reinforced linden shields, a stronger bow and better arrows, and a rope with grappling hook. He'd strapped the new staff in a halter over his back. Lilava did her best to cast off the utter exhaustion that her spell had cost her, and Severus did his best to shape a plan for dealing with Abra and freeing Liletta.

Once they set off, they found him sooner than they expected. He had already put out to sea — one could hardly mistake his ship with its broad, golden sails — but not far from the spot where he must have moored for the night, in a natural harbor on the island, just northwest of the channel. As soon as they got within earshot, Abra greeted them.

"Well, my friends, you seem to have fared better than we feared. Such a storm blew through as I have seldom seen, with such groaning and grinding of elements as would raise the long dead from the depths of the sea. I had intended to face all the trouble with you, but the wind caught us by surprise and drove us ashore just over there. Your sister, dear lady, nearly despaired for your life. I believe she has survived the night — you must board and see for yourself. Such resilience and resourcefulness: you have astonished us all!"

Within earshot also means within bowshot, and just in time Severus got the still weary Lilava behind her shield as arrows whizzed from the deck of the ship past them thick as a flock of birds. After the first volley, Severus perfunctorily returned fire with the arrows Abra had allotted him, then hid behind his own shield to avoid the second volley. Having discerned a pattern, Severus armed then with the arrows he had recovered from Scylla's cave, and he fired with precision at the sources of the attack. Three he missed, but two he hit, and those hits sent the remaining archers scrambling for cover.

Severus spoke hurriedly to Lilava. "I had hoped to get aboard first. Ah, well. This won't be easy, but we must try it. Someday I must learn to swim better, but here goes. Keep well covered and distant from their bows, but drift no farther away than you must. Abra may believe they have no need to allow Liletta to live any longer, so we must act quickly." He stopped short of articulating his fear that she might already be dead — he knew Lilava was fighting the same thought.

Checking the axe at his belt and the staff on his back and taking the grappling hook in his hand, Severus dived into the sea and swam for the ship with all his might, trying to stay beneath the surface for as long as he could. Abra had begun to set out for the open sea, but the current was against him, and his ship moved slowly. With a burst of strength Severus surfaced beneath the bow and swung the grappling hook overtop one of the gunnels, then raced up the rope. He reached deck behind several of Abra's sailors just in time to catch Abra's eye. He struck down one man in his line of fire, then saw Abra clasping a living but shaken Liletta. Smiling, the king tossed Liletta, her hands still bound behind her, into the sea.

When the other sailors turned to face him, Severus spoke, taking from his pocket the dirks he had recovered from the battle with Scylla. "Any man who opposes me tastes one of these dirks, each dipped in the poison of Scylla's blood. Flee me now!" Severus hoped not to have to use them — the thought

of wielding a poisoned weapon appalled him, offended his sense of honor — but with Liletta's life at stake he had to use what weapons he could find, the greatest being the fear he could generate in his adversaries. Two men ignored the warning and, armed with short swords, came for him.

They fell writhing to the deck, one with a dirk in his forehead, the other with one in his throat.

The remaining sailors scattered for cover.

"Archers!" Abra called. "Shoot the girl if she floats on the water. Shoot the woman in the boat. And shoot this man on my deck!"

Severus sent another dirk flying for Abra's heart, but whether by magic or an ill throw, the king dodged it and slipped beneath deck. Severus had just time to grab a stray water-sack, and to avoid the archers, then he had no choice but to throw himself over the side into the sea.

Beneath the waves Severus could feel the water around him penetrated by arrows, but the ship, tacking, sailed rapidly away and quickly lost him in the whelm of waves. Bobbing to the surface a moment later, he drank from the water-sack, emptying it, blew air into it, and retied it tightly, then used it as a float. He kicked toward the direction where he guessed Abra had dropped Liletta into the water.

Unable to see far over the waves, Severus floundered for some time, wearying himself but unable and unwilling to give up the search. Long he floated with the aid of the air-filled sack, long he kicked, with no ship or boat in sight. The pain in his shoulder, which remained from Scylla's sword-sharp claw, grew into a spreading numbness, and the desire for sleep, either by some spell of Abra's or by the strain of his labors, grew into a nearly irresistible necessity. Thoughts and memories loomed and bobbed almost tangible, floated through his mind, whisked away, followed by more, until he didn't know which was a memory and which a fantasy. He felt an impossible, unendurable sadness that he should never see Lilava again, and that, so close to saving Liletta, she must also lose the sister she loved. He felt his awareness darkening and his consciousness drooping when four hands pulled him from the waves just before his own hands would have slipped from the slowly deflating water-sack. Dim shapes and sounds played in his mind like raindrops that patter the borders of sleep.

* * *

"We thought we'd lost you." Lilava and Liletta looked down at him as he lay in the bottom of the boat, his feet hanging over the edge into the water.

"And I have never in my life been happier to see anyone. How long have I lain here?" He felt Lilava's hands moving about his face, stroking water and salt from his eyes.

"Not long. We shall reach shore soon. We could hardly chase Abra in this bit of a boat."

"I remember hearing someone chanting, someone repeating Abra's name among others I've never heard."

"Yes, as he said himself, names have power, and I tried to use his, to call another storm to track him, but I'm weak from our labors, and if one is to succeed in bringing it, the storm must want to come for its own ends."

"Abracadabrax, Abracadabrax, over and over again."

"Yes," said Liletta, "sister tried, and so did I, but to no avail."

"Perhaps we do best to avoid spells directed at people, to leave such men to God," Severus offered, "in which case you didn't fail, nor could you. We all make our choices, and events will take their course."

"Sounds a bit sentimental to me," Lilava replied, wishing for at least some vengeance against the man who had abducted and nearly killed her sister.

"Liletta: are you — well?"

"Yes, brother-to-be, brother-already. My wrist and feet hurt from the binding, and my mouth from the gag, but otherwise Abra did me no harm and permitted his men to do none — though I admit I feared it."

"Who causes fear should feel fear — that is my hope for Abra," Lilava mumbled.

"I fear you haven't seen the last of this Witch King," Liletta sighed.

"Witch, ha! and probably no king, either," Lilava answered. "Nought but a pirate if you ask me," Severus added.

Together in their small boat they paddled for the island shore. They could do nothing about Abra, who had escaped into the broad sea, so they found a landing, took a day to rest and get their bearings, and set off overland for safe ground, aiming to avoid the pirates of the northwest coast. Traveling mostly at night until they could find a friendly tribe, gradually they made their way along the coast. Once they had again found safe waters, they bought another small boat with the weapons and flotsam Severus had collected from Scylla's cave, and they sailed gently home, returning Liletta, and finding themselves once again praised and feasted as heroes.

There, according to the rites and customs of that people, Severus and Lilava were married, with Liletta attending her sister.

And when they could celebrate no more, once again Severus and Lilava, with a company of tried sailors, set sail for the west. They sat together in the prow to feel the breeze, and Lilava spoke. "Let us try again for the place of which I told you, called Valencia, in Hispania at the western end of the Great Sea, but east of where Ocean opens up to the vast world of the North and South. There we will find orange groves and greenery and markets and festivals and a Christian community where we can marry after the fashion of Britain as well, if, having married here, you still wish it." She smiled, glancing at Severus from the corner of her eye, wondering if she should see a hint of doubt. She saw none.

"I want nothing more than your love. Having wedded here, we are married; if you are willing to confirm it according to the practices of Britain as well, I am all for that, too."

"Willing, eager. We may need to go back there, and we don't want the lack of proper ritual to stand between us."

"We have fought the Chimaera together. We have subdued Charybdis and Scylla and survived Abra's betrayal. We have married. Nothing will stand between us now."

And so they sailed together, wishing no better company, but only a little peace and quiet.

II At Sea Again

[... wherein Severus and Lilava find their post-nuptials interrupted by more sorcery and water.]

After a week of relaxing in each other's company in Valencia, Severus and Lilava had recovered from their labors and the long journey to the coast of Hispania. They had found a small chapel where a priest married them according to Christian rites. But even as they lounged, in the back of his mind Severus realized that they had a longer journey yet before them, all the way back to Britain. He kept thinking about all that the magic mirror had shown them, and he felt deep down a nagging sense of duty to King Arthur, that an unfinished task lay before as well as behind him.

Tasks, he thought, always tasks.

"Tell me what you're thinking," Lilava said, lying beside him on the clean, white sands as they stretched out, listening to the sea. Lilava had once again been teaching Severus how to improve his swimming. She had told him to release his tension and let his body movements flow as he did in battle, but water had never felt to him his natural element. "On second thought," Lilava continued, "don't tell me what you're thinking. I know it by the look on your face. Why do men always think in terms of tasks to complete?"

"I don't know why, love, only that we do. Each duty stands like a tree in one of these orange groves. When I have picked the fruit or seen to the health of the tree, I go on to the next, until I have tended the whole grove, the grove,

148

I suppose, of my life, though now of our life together. You sought me out for a task, you recall, probably because you knew that I think that way. It has its advantages when need imposes, though it makes real rest difficult to find."

"Not a very good metaphor: when you have tended the trees and picked the fruit, you must then start again, growing, tending, picking. One never finishes the job. What will you do when you have tended all the trees, rid the world of its monsters? And yes, I found you for a task, but please don't blame me for your character. And I married you not to give you more tasks, but so that we may free ourselves of them, so we may on one not-too-distant-day live a bit, together."

"Will we ever free the world, even ourselves, of monsters? Like a grove of infested fruit, the problem seems only to grow more difficult. King Abra: when we met him, I though he was a man, not a monster. I may have erred. He may be the worst sort of monster. A dragon simply defends its hoard. Charybdis merely spun her waters, whether sailors came near or not. Creatures such as Abra do evil by choice. They seek out not only their own good, but ill for their victims."

"Yet we need not see him as evil by nature. Perhaps he considers what he does a kind of good."

"You say that about a man who tried to kill your sister, you, and me, who used us all on the chance that he might make life a bit easier for himself? How can that sort of behavior come from anything but evil?"

"Evil may be no more than misunderstanding, the absence of a yet unidentified good, or the presence of an undeveloped or latent good. Abra may yet learn good."

"Are you speculating, or do you believe that?"

"No. I was speaking hypothetically. But do you believe you understand the nature of evil?"

"I'd have to consult the philosophers for that. I have always gone more by feel than reason. I sense the monster, and the monster senses me. If I find it malicious, I try to immobilize the malice. If it will not desist in malice, and I must and can, I destroy it, but I'd more happily just set it right or send it away."

"So that someone else must deal with it."

"Someone else has already been dealing with it, but if I make myself plain to it, no one else may have to deal with it, so I have eliminated, or at least for a time assuaged, an evil."

"And relieved someone else of responsibility for it."

"Someone who hadn't the wherewithal to remove it."

"Do you find that's what monsters are: embodiments of evil?"

149

"I once thought so, but no longer. A monster is a grotesque. It distorts nature in some dangerous way and so threatens nature and her other creatures. A monster may not always intend harm, and yet may do it. Sadly, though, I have found that often they do intend evil, and apparently God has fashioned me in such a way to oppose them. But people too may do evil and sometimes may be evil. We may think evil even if we don't do it, or we may choose to continue in it or to avoid it or to fight it in ourselves or others. We may give in to it so far that we no longer recognize it as evil. But once people know evil, and they have chosen it, and once it has got a full hold on them, they seem to believe that they place themselves in peril if they then try to avert it, as though it had grown inextricably into the fibers of their hearts. That, I think, describes our friend Abra. I believe that if you put him to the test, he would be able to tell you, 'Yess, I know what evil iss, and I choosse it, and you musst hardly expect me to give it up.'"

"Good imitation. I don't remember that you've ever done sarcasm before."

"I may be wrong about that. I hope so. Such thoughts grieve me and weary me, since they force me to question not only my life, but my own nature. That fellow seems to bring out the worst in me, the urge to destroy rather than amend. Does good destroy evil, or can only another evil destroy evil?"

"You, my love, are not evil."

"I hope not, and I hope I never will be."

"Any quest you've undertaken, even one among them: would you now undo it now?"

"No, none. But choosing the next one burns me to the quick."

"Dear, dear: you're on vacation. You have married me. Love me, rest, and mend. By doing so you may serve God and the world for a time, at least until your next task."

"Would I could do so always."

"Maybe you can."

"For now philosophy has exhausted my thoughts. I will try again to swim — you've taught me much, but now, as you've preached, I must practice. Will you go with me?"

"Poor dear, not for now. I've wearied myself as well. I've never felt so tired as after Charybdis, not even from the Chimaera. Nature seems to have taken from me what I asked of her, strength for strength. And I need my strength to love you, my philosopher. Go swim, and I will watch. Meantime I will look at this old scroll that the priest lent me. It is a piece by a man named Vergil, a story the priest called 'Dido and Aeneas.'"

Severus rose from the sand, kissed Lilava on the lips, ran to the surf and dived into the waves. Slow, smooth strokes, he thought; try to relax, and remember to breathe, and don't swim out too far. Just so far I will go, then pace evenly along with the shore. As he raised his head to breathe, he would glance toward Lilava, her back propped up, her long legs stretched out along the sand, her face bent on the manuscript.

When he had swum past where he could twist his head to see her, Severus turned round to return, staying an even distance from the shore. The pull of the current wanted to draw him out, so he exerted himself the greater to stay close — good exercise, he thought, though I don't feel confident with it yet. The sun, the water, the long months of battles had stripped some of the reserves from what he had once felt must be a bottomless well of energy. He had to build himself anew. His shoulder injury had healed to a thin scar and an occasional light burn, enough, when he stretched, to recall Scylla to mind. As he concentrated and relaxed, the swimming became easier, and rhythm contributed to endurance. He glanced to the eastern horizon and saw something floating.

No doubt, he saw a boat, small, but sailing rapidly toward him. He continued swimming, slowed his pace a bit, assumed the ship just a fishing vessel returning. He thought he spotted a ship far distant, little bigger than a dot to his eye. Then could see the larger craft no more, but certainly the boat he had distinctly discerned was closing, and rapidly. His swimming pace slowed, making him feel as though he were sinking, so he picked up speed to stay more easily afloat. Larger waves struck him, sucking more energy from his muscles, so that he decided, regardless of the boat, he must return to shore. He looked up for Lilava, but couldn't spot her — must have swum farther than I realized, Severus thought. He heard a voice that seemed to come from behind him, from the sea rather than the shore. He turned back to listen.

The boat, he could see, was definitely sailing toward him, and on the deck he could see but one person, rather tall, a woman, standing and waving. She looked familiar. Severus stopped swimming, trying just to tread water so he could see. The woman on the boat waved again and called him by name. He heard her clearly. He recognized her.

She was Guinevere.

What was Guinevere doing off the coast of Valencia?

"Severus!" she called. "Oh, Severus, I have looked long for you. Your king needs you! You must sail with me, and no delay! Enemies have attacked from within and without, and Arthur is recalling all his loyal knights from the four corners of the world. Will you not heed the call of your king at need?"

The sight so astonished Severus that he began to swallow water, but he tried, treading water, to speak. "My lady, this request makes no sense: why would King Arthur have sent you, and alone at that? What trouble of such magnitude has come to the world?" Collecting himself, he dog-paddled toward the boat.

"You must come, Severus! The circumstance allows no time for questions. Come because you would save your king and queen, because all goodness has not left you, because you believe in right and honor and peace." As she spoke, the boat drifted further out to sea, beyond Severus' grasp.

"Hold her still, my lady, and I will board. You and the king may count on me, but I must understand what we have to do, and I must bring Lilava, too."

"No time! Hurry, board, and we must sail!" The boat again drifted beyond reach, and Severus' breath was beginning to fail.

"Please, just hold her still. Have you no one there to help me up? I can't catch you."

"Come Sseverus, come. Sswim with all your sstrength! Sswim to ssave your queen." The voice, while still feminine, had taken on a familiar, sinister sibilance. The boat drifted more quickly than before until it sat well beyond Severus' reach, and he began to despair of catching it. Then, bobbing, beginning to gasp for air, he understood the sibilants: from only one person had he heard that peculiar speech.

"Abra!"

"Come, Sseverus, ha!" And Guinevere, or whoever or whatever creature or phantom at Abra's bidding had taken her shape, turned away, and the boat sped for open water.

He knew he would gain nothing by calling out, and as the waves rose and fell higher around him, he lost sight of the boat entirely, if it had been more than an illusion. If ever Severus were to panic, that was the time: the boat had led him far out into the water, farther than he had ever swum, and his limbs felt already numb and unresponsive. His stomach felt sick from the bitter water he had swallowed, his movement in the water had left him disoriented, and the effort to remain afloat had drawn him near the limits of his endurance. He tried to bob as high as he could, to catch the upward movement of a wave, to look around. On the third bob he spotted shore, and doing his best to draw air — never easy for him in this element so foreign to him — he tried to relax and begin a steady, easy backstroke toward shore. He hoped that Lilava had seen the boat, too, that the illusion had not worked on him alone, and that she would bring a boat for him. Beyond that, he must reach shore or die. The current, also pulling out to sea, held him, making his progress slow.

After several backstrokes he would turn over and take overhand strokes, spotting the shore to maintain his bearings. He grew dizzy for lack of air and sicker from swallowing more water, but he had no choice but to swim: he hadn't enough air left to call out, and the wind, blowing out to sea, would simply have caught his voice and carried it away.

Sometimes, particularly for a person in good training, the body can achieve remarkable feats of strength or endurance beyond what the mind believes possible. A trance-like state overtakes the mind, and the body moves as if beyond the mind's power, beyond the power of fear to paralyze it. So Severus swam.

Stroke, he thought, and ignore the cramping in the muscles and the hands, the neck and the feet. Just fifty more strokes: count them off. Puff, puff, four, three, two, one. Stroke, just twenty more strokes. Anyone can do twenty strokes. Puff, cramping! Easy: three, two, one. Ten more strokes, only ten — any child can do it! Ten, puff, no, can't do it, and the body begins to sink. No, just ten strokes, ten! Puff, three, two, one. Five more! Only five, two, one. Only — falling, burning, burning under the water, the lungs, burning.

At the edge of consciousness he felt a grip. Something had got him. Too dark to see. Something. Pulling, pulling, pushing. Cough!

"Breathe, breathe, oh dear breathe!" a voice said from somewhere on the other side of the darkness.

His head swirled, and his lungs still burned — signs of painful life, but life.

From the deck of a small boat Severus woke to consciousness and rolled over and tried to suck air, but he turned and got sick over the side. Air would not come, and he got sick again, and he thought that for the second time he would suffocate. "Breathe!" the voice called.

"Breathe, my only love, please breathe." The air came in finally in a rush, and Severus lay on his stomach, drawing air like a sprinter who had run past his natural distance. Then he felt a body collapse atop his, and as his eyes regained focus and his skin began to tingle, he saw and felt Lilava's hair, wet with sea-spray, gleaming blue-black in the sun, strewn over his face and back. She rose, and when he turned over, he saw her eyes full of fear and love, hope and dwindling despair.

"Oh, God, my love, I thought I had lost you."

"We have to stop meeting like this."

"We must get you away from water."

"Did you see the boat, the boat with Guinevere?"

"Guinevere? Why would she come here? I saw a ship on the horizon, that's all — I don't know whose."

"Abra's."

"Are you sure?"

"I think so."

"Did he do something, something to lure you out? Oh, Guinevere! You thought you had seen her, calling to you, I guess. No — must have been an image wrought by Abra to lure you or both of us out to sea, too far out."

"The Witch King."

"I doubted him, but he must have some magic. Such an illusion as that isn't so hard to create, if it was an illusion and not just a confederate. I gave him too little credit for his ability, too great a credit for any remaining scrap humanity. He must have following us simply to destroy you. He is a monster after all, and we will treat him as such when we find him."

"I'm glad that you found me."

"That wretched manuscript — I got caught up in it and lost sight of you. When I scanned the beach, then the horizon, and could find you nowhere, I grew terrified and called for a boat. Two men brought this one for me, but when they heard my incantations — oh, I must have looked a sight to them! for I was gathering all my strength — they ran off. I rowed straight out, and finally glimpsed you, rowed as quickly as I could — I'm sorry, dear, sorry I took so long. But you! How could you believe that silly illusion, and why should you follow Guinevere anyway?"

"She is still my queen."

"And I am your wife."

"I would have tried to help anyone who had called to me, begging. So would you."

"I would have better sense than to follow an illusion."

"You would have better sense, but you know illusions better than I do. I'm glad you row better than I swim."

"So am I. When you have finished getting sick, come here and hold me. The current should ease now and maybe push us back toward shore. Odd, though — the current seems to shift one way, then the other — hasn't anyone heard of tides here? We can row back when you feel better."

"I feel better, thank you." Severus sat up, rinsed his mouth from a water bottle he found on deck, and pulled Lilava to him. He held her as close as one wet human may hold another.

But the current did not push them toward shore. It gave way to a tide that drew them out to sea. Despite their rowing, neither had the power to resist it, and they soon drifted far beyond view of land. As night fell, the waves rocked, and a storm blew in, tossing the little boat like a buoy. The only comfort the storm gave Severus and Lilava was the occasional swallow of fresh water from the rain that they could collect in their hands or from the bottom of the boat.

By morning the storm had passed, but the wind had shifted from due east and had blown them south. "Oh what I would give for one or two of those oranges of which we ate so many in Valencia," Lilava said.

"One for me, too, please," Severus added. "What will happen if we lie here and imagine ourselves eating oranges? Will that make things better or worse?"

"Let's try and see."

"This much good we can consider a blessing: Abra has not found us, either because he didn't want to or because he assumed we would founder. If we can catch a westerly, we will reach your home, if we aren't dead by then."

"Let's think about fruit."

They floated for two days, blown east again by a strong wind, until they sighted the rocky coast of a small island. Their boat broke up on the rocks, but they managed to swim to shore. There they found a small number of inhabitants, friendly enough, who spoke a language rather like to Lilava's, something akin to that of Valencia, and from them they got food and water and directions to a harbor. In the harbor they found a trading ship — not one of Abra's — bound for the land of the Goths. One of the sailors had come from Britain some months before, and he told Severus of trouble there: the king at odds with his best knights, and according to rumor a younger knight, the king's nephew or son, the man said, hoped to unseat the king. Arthur indeed had need of all his forces — perhaps Abra's vision had told Severus the truth, whether with good or ill intent.

The sailor's story seemed either a hint from God or the hand of fate directing their course. Severus and Lilava talked all night, and in the morning they arranged for passage on the ship through the strait of Gibraltar and north up the coast. Had Severus' vision come not from Abra, as they had assumed, but from some other source trying to get them to return to Britain, and if so, did it wish them to return for good or ill? Severus felt that either way they must go, since he had yet to discharge his duties to his king. Lilava agreed, deciding at last that she must accompany Severus as he had accompanied her, and perhaps the Lady of the Lake could teach her some means by which they could avert the tragedies they had witnessed in Ambrose's mirror. Lilava disguised herself — such men as those sailors would have killed one another trying to get at her — and the two bought passage in exchange for Severus' labor as a sailing hand.

Within a month they'd got farther than they'd hoped, all the way to the coastal land later called Brittany, where they sought news of Britain and King Arthur.

Even there they had to remain discreet, since Arthur had both friends and enemies on the continent. Looking thin, weather-worn, and far less than noble after many harrowing travels, Severus and Lilava eventually came to the marches of the lands of King Ban, the father of Sir Lancelot. Having gained entry to see him, they received a less cordial reception than they'd hoped, but no less welcome than they could reasonably expect, given familial preference for Lancelot and Severus' loyalty to Arthur. For many long days they had received no news.

Arthur, the king told them coldly, had banished Lancelot on a charge of treason, on the assertion that he had seduced and dishonored Queen Guinevere. Everyone knew of Lancelot's love for Guinevere, but all good people, Ban insisted, knew that love a chaste and good chivalric service. Mordred and Gawain, traitors both from Ban's point of view, had insisted the king not only exile Lancelot and his followers, but also besiege them as well, which the king, too weak and easily prevailed upon by bad council, had done, throwing the full force of his remaining army upon Joyous Guard, Lancelot's stronghold. Too well protected by nature and Lancelot's own loyal soldiers for Arthur to take the castle with less than his entire army, the walls held, the siege continued, and the armies fought to a stalemate. Mordred had insisted on keeping not only London, but also Carlisle fortified against treacherous invasion, so Arthur and Lancelot fought on bravely, but pointlessly: with Lancelot less than committed to battle, their strengths balanced equally and waned rapidly, while Mordred's influence grew. Ban, who had not trusted Severus from the moment he'd met him, had in mind that he should keep them both prisoner there — why should he allow freedom to even one more of Arthur's knights? — if Severus were a knight at all, which his appearance belied.

There again Lilava proved her mettle. With spells so subtle that even Lancelot's family could not perceive them — mixed in with a great deal of good will and utter honesty — she assured Ban that they sought Lancelot's good as well as Arthur's and wanted no more than to find a way to bring champion and king together again for the safety and honor of Britain. Severus proved his quality as well with a few obligatory jousts. Though out of practice, he performed well enough, keeping his saddle and neither sustaining nor causing serious injury, since Ban's best knights had joined Lancelot to defend his castle in Britain. Finally, with the charge that they try to help his son, Ban provided them supplies and means sufficient for them to sail the French Sea — once on the British coast, they would have to fend for themselves.

"I see little that two persons alone can do for my son or for King Arthur, but one must respond to proper devotion and stoutness of heart. I must admit, sir, that I don't trust you. I sense in you something dangerous, something antithetical to me and my son, but since I can't identify it or articulate it, and since you have proven your courage and skill, and since one must in evil times occasionally allow chance to work its course, particularly for the good of this family I will assist you. If you have lied to me or told me less than truth, may God punish you for it!"

Though they had certainly not lied, they had told Ban less than the full truth, if one were to consider true the visions of Ambrose's magic mirror, in which

Severus either fell at Lancelot's hand or felled that champion by his own. Can one ever tell the truth, the whole truth, and nothing but the truth, as philosophers ask of themselves and judges require of all?

A reluctant King Ban bade Severus and Lilava follow the will of God, and they departed in fair weather for Britain. They left Benwick on a brisk and clear morning, but found the coast of Brittany and most of their sailing swathed in fog. Disembarking at a small, Cornish port town after a foul trip, and nonetheless calling their good wishes to the captain, they heard once again the peculiar sibilants of a familiar voice.

"Fare you well, travelerss, ssince you have got where I mosst wanted you. I have learned more about you and your fate — I have ssources, you ssee — and with proper choicess you will bring King Arthur'ss power tumbling to the turf. Do well and sserve me yet, ha, ssince from chaoss will the trading Witch King prossper. From food to weaponss, all will rely on me, ha!"

"Abra!" Severus whispered.

"Abracadabrax, Abracadabrax, slow in the fog like feet caught in wax, Abracadabrax ..." Lilava, using the power of his name, tried a spell to hold him, and though they heard him squawk, he disappeared into the mist before they could catch him.

"Can he have intended us to come to here?" Severus asked.

"I don't know. And if he did, did we come at his bidding or because of some larger or greater movement of the world, or simply because, doing our best, we followed our choice?"

"Once thing for sure: I've come to hate that hiss in his speech — snaky and devilish."

"A good batch of sibilants of your own, there."

"You're not comparing me to our friend?"

"Of course not, love — only reminding you we have a little hiss in all of us, or maybe just a little mark of the bear."

"True enough: you do well to remind me."

"The devil may serve God, too: so say the priests. But as for me, I will devise a spell, and I will teach it to all the children I meet, so that they will remember and teach their children. Then in speaking his name they may thwart that man and his family for fifty generations."

"Can't say I blame you. Now we must try to learn what we can of Arthur and Guinevere."

* * *

157

$f$or several days Severus and Lilava hiked the small towns of Cornwall, inquiring discretely about Arthur and his troubles. Everyone seemed to know that Arthur was at war with Lancelot, and many whispered that Mordred was waiting for his chance to seize the throne. Gradually they pieced together more of the story, filling out the picture they had seen in the magic mirror — much to their concern.

Gawain's brothers, except for Gareth, were malefactors who promoted the fortunes of their Orkney faction regardless of the general good. They claimed to have caught Guinevere and Lancelot in the act of adultery while the King was away. Lancelot had since argued in their behalf that he had merely heard suspicious noises in the hallway and gone to Guinevere to determine if she was safe, but he had nonetheless been obliged to flee the immediate attack led by the Orkney boys, who had offered Lancelot no quarter.

In Lancelot's absence, once the king had returned, the malefactors had insisted that Arthur try Guinevere and burn her at the stake if no one would champion her cause. Given the Orkneys' power at court, despite Gawain's refusal to participate in anything that slandered Lancelot or the queen, Arthur felt obliged to instate the Trial-by-Combat, knowing that Lancelot would find a way to rescue Guinevere. He did, but in the process Lancelot had accidentally killed Sir Gaheris and — to Severus' great sadness — Sir Gareth, raising the unquenchable ire of Gawain, oldest sister's-son to Arthur, who demanded the siege against Joyous Guard, since by that action of murder Lancelot appeared traitor indeed, to friend as well as king.

Severus grieved beyond grief at the news of the death of Gareth, who had proven his only friend at court, a man brave in battle, true in character, generous in heart — his one true ally among Arthur's folk. Few of Arthur's knights had ever surpassed Gareth in the skills and virtues of chivalry, and no one had surpassed him in human kindness.

None of the locals knew more than that of current events, or they would tell no more than that to strangers, though some hinted at more dark business in Carlisle, where Mordred was fortifying his army. The magic mirror, as Ambrose had warned them, had not spied out all contingencies. With that much knowledge and a greater sense of the inevitable sadness of the world, Severus and Lilava began the long trek across the moors to the north.

Walking hand-in-hand as the sun cut an opening in the clouds, they saw a horse approaching, and Severus heard a familiar whinny.

"Can that be — I don't believe it!" Lilava breathed.

"Sure and thank God for old friends: it is the horse himself! Courage! Alive and, by the look of him, well, too! Can such things happen by chance alone? Then all things in Britain haven't turned to sorrow. Horse, you've been on your own so long that I wouldn't even ask it of you if the need were not so great, but can you bear your old companion once more, and his wife with him?"

Surprises happen even in old stories, and Courage gently brushed Severus' face with his nose, then whinnied twice, nodding his head. Then, from just beyond a hill, appeared a beautiful white mare. She pranced up beside Lilava as though she had known her since foalhood.

"If appearances tell truth," Severus said, "we each have a horse, and I should love to get as quickly as we can to Winchester to learn the rest of the situation."

As they mounted, they passed a number of foals, of mixed colors, who whinnied in their wake as though they wished to join in the adventures themselves. The horses, neighing as they passed the foals, carried their riders with surpassing swiftness all the way to Winchester.

* * *

Even the best of horses need time to make the long journey from the Cornish moors past Exeter and the great monument on Salisbury Plain and on to Winchester. Winchester, uncertain with the rise of Mordred, bore its own dangers, but a knight in the garrison there recognized Severus and had in fact been one of the few to admire him at Arthur's court, having risen from similarly rustic roots. Severus gave him a brief account of their adventures, leaving out the least believable instances, and of their plans to join Arthur and assist him as they could, so the knight gave both Severus and Lilava tokens of safe passage to the north. The knight, Sir Evelake by name, gave them what remaining news had come to the south.

Arthur had demanded from Lancelot Guinevere's safe return, and Lancelot, seeking peace, had unwillingly complied. The king had her accompanied to Carlisle, ostensibly into the care of Mordred: the prince had largely forsaken London, where among the people loyalty to Arthur remained strong, thus leaving Winchester safer as well. He had retreated full-time to the north, where he hoped to gather support from troops stationed along the old Roman Wall.

With Arthur's unhappy agreement, Gawain, seeing no reason to spare Lancelot nor to limit their attack since the queen had been safely recovered, had redoubled the assault on Lancelot's castle, to the detriment of his army, which dwindled by the day. Having Arthur out of the way and Guinevere in hand, Mordred had made official proclamation of his own ascent to the throne in despite of his father and had made overtures that Guinevere should become his queen. And Mordred's army was growing, not only with soldiers from the north, but particularly with mercenaries hired from abroad, in Germania — worse and worse the news. Pausing only to hear the full course of the sad state of events and for a hurried meal and a brief sleep, Severus and Lilava rode on, feeling they had little time to spare.

They stopped to rest again at Oxford and to collect their thoughts, and they talked long into the evening. Knowing what they must do, finally they resolved.

"I don't like it, but we must part soon," Lilava said, "I to Carlisle to save Guinevere, and you to the east to try to resolve Arthur and Lancelot. I had prepared myself for what we should meet in London, but Mordred's relocation adds miles and doubts to the journey. If the king and his best champion cannot join forces, Mordred will attack Arthur from the west while he continues to waste his strength on Lancelot in the east. If Mordred has his wish, we may give up hope of peace and law, for he will march back and take London when no king remains to hold the loyalty of the people. He has already sown the seeds of foreign invasion — you know what loyalty he will get from the mercenaries — and Britain will descend into a time of darkness from which she may never recover. Love, I would never wish to part from you, but I have come to appreciate your sense of task, and as in the case of the Chimaera, we now share it. Because we have seen what may happen and know the devastation further rebellion may cause, we have an obligation to try to set things right. Let us enjoy this night together, then ride north in the morning, you to the east, I to the west. When next we meet, we must in the meantime have spent every energy to bring peace to our time."

"In my heart I would return to our honeymoon in the orange groves, but in my head I know as you do what we must try to accomplish. In all we do, we love each other, for now and always. Think of the days we spent in this green and lovely Britain — ah, they seem a century ago — I riding alone, errant, wondering if I should spend all my years so, and you, building on your skills, searching for the knight to share your quest. Now let's rest, and may the stars shine on these next hours together and the sun make few courses in the sky until we can hold each other close again."

"I needn't remind you that you must avoid battle with ..."

"No, my love, you need not."

III What Ambrose's Mirror Didn't See

[While Lilava seeks help for Guinevere, Severus aims to restore friendship between Arthur and Lancelot, and together they attempt to save Britain.]

*L*ilava rode Dancer the white mare — for that was her horse's name — north toward Carlisle, but she had in mind to go first to the waters of Cumbria to see the Lady of the Lake: the fortunate enchantress may sometimes get help from an old mentor.

An attentive person will always ask a creature its name, not only because names have power, but out of simple courtesy. Nearly every creature prefers to be called by its own name rather than to be gratuitously given one by some passer-by. And so Lilava had learned her horse's name. Why the mare had chosen the name Dancer Lilava had no idea, since she wouldn't likely have seen anyone dancing, but the point, at least until one knows the creature better, is to ask what, not why. The why comes when one has come to know the creature better and gain her trust.

Lilava whispered steadily and calmly to Dancer as they ran, aiming to make herself feel and sound familiar, to make their course a partnership, and to give their relationship a feel of mutual equity. Lilava had not expected that Severus would find Courage waiting for him, since the horse had always had a bit of an air of solitary superiority, and Lilava suspected that he valued his own freedom more highly than his relationship to his knight — not that one could necessarily fault him for that, since one expects in all creatures a natural desire for freedom. Yet the horse had appeared, miraculously, one might say, at their greatest need, showing loyalty beyond hope, and he had brought along the perfect companion for Lilava. Together the new partners in adventure rode faster than an echo, as silent as dusk. They kept as well as they could to the flatter, rural ways, since Lilava wanted not only to move swiftly, but also to avoid having anyone try to stop or follow them. Covered in only an ordinary cloak, she had little protection beyond what speed and the spur-of-the-moment spell could allot her. For two days their luck held, and the night sky shone bright with a full moon, allowing them to run best when they were most likely to avoid detection.

On the third day, as they entered Cumbria, a fog settled in, and that too proved fortunate, since Lilava knew the land and could draw protection from the additional cover of the mist. They followed the river and came to the edge of the Windy Lake no more than forty miles south of Carlisle and close enough to the lair of the Lady of the Lake to call her forth. Lilava could almost hear the whisper of the Lady's voice in the steady breeze that whisked down the long stretch of water.

Near a copse Lilava dismounted and bade Dancer take her leisure carefully, then she stepped to the water's edge and called to her former mistress and
teacher, bending her voice into the breeze and projecting it skimming across the
barely moving, crystalline surface. "Lady Nineve! Chief source of the Power
of Magic in Britain, Lady of Waters, I need parley and your advice, if you will.
Hear me, Lady of the Lake, and answer!"

For some time the water lay nearly still, rippling only gently at the touch of the
wind. Then not far from Lilava the water began to bubble, then to churn, and
from beneath the surface slowly emerged a human shape. "Lady Lilava, practi-
tioner of the Power, why do you call upon me, and how may I help you?" Nineve
emerged as though stepping across the surface of the water. She walked up to
Lilava, a look of concern in her eyes, and touched her hand to Lilava's cheek.
"Speak, my dear, for trouble has begun to echo even beneath my waters, and I
would see you at least free of it. I thought you had gone from this land, and
you must have returned but recently: I hadn't sensed your presence until this
past hour. I fear that means either your strength fails you, or I have lain too long
in thought and too far from action."

"Dear teacher, I have traveled far and long, and would dearly love to tell you
of many adventures, but necessity urges speed." Lilava examined Nineve's face,
a face she knew well, still unlined with age, but stretched, as though thin with
care, such as she had never before seen it. The gold-white hair hung loose about
her shoulders, and the green eyes looked watery, less crystalline. Lilava considered how to approach the problem without offending and yet without dallying.

"I'm sure you know more immediately than I the troubles of Arthur and Britain. That news has spread even to us, newly returned from the Continent and
beyond. But we have seen, Severus and I, the unfolding of possible futures. We
must try to save Britain from the looming storm, and I must save my husband a
death that, in his goodness, he has not earned."

"Yes, I see that you love this man, and that he loves you. I have heard the
troubles growing, but, as you sense, my powers have weakened. I know only a
little I can do, and that must lead me to try to preserve the king. Times and the
world always change, but you are right: now we face an age of darkness, nor can
I can see a way to avoid it.

"Long have I meditated, and those great Powers to which I still have access
I have consulted, but the time seems ruled by evil tides and evil men. Even
among those Powers, some work for good, but as many now work for evil. Morgan, too, weakens, she who has wrought great ill. Old friendships have broken,
the nascent sense of law has weakened, and the good that once grew in chivalry
has failed. People desire no peace, and they wish no law, only what power they
can acquire. They apply it to amass the wealth they steal and to try to control

even others' fates. All the good that Arthur had set in motion has stilled and crumbled at his feet.

"You must know that if I could understand what to do, I would do it. I bear complicity in the fall as well. When in our youth we gain power without wisdom, we misuse it without guessing consequences that seem distant beyond worry, or we wait, hoping someone else will know what to do to set things right. I tell you frankly: I don't know what to do. Can you tell me, Lilava? I have grown weary beyond my years with the weight of the evil that dwells here — we think we can avert it with impunity, but it spreads, filling every nook and path, like smoke, until one can't escape it. I am still young, Lilava, in the practice of the arts, and yet look at me, already bent with the aches of body and mind, as though I were some ancient Merlin. People have come from far and wide to learn from me, but now I know little and tire easily. What must I do?"

"Oh, Lady, I can tell you only what I must do. I came here hoping that from you I can learn the words that will save Queen Guinevere and slow Mordred's progress. The queen inspires Arthur, and Arthur civilizes the realm. Without them, all falls into chaos. And I must know everything, anything, that may help me save my husband when our crisis comes. I have no time to guess what I may do and what must lie beyond my strength. I must have the will to do what can be done. I must move swiftly and choose without fail."

"No one can avoid failure, however diligent she remains in study and action. If you believe I know something of value to you, then come, and we will talk, and what I can offer to do to help you, I will do with all my heart."

"You mentioned that others have come to you?"

"Yes, Morgan, believe it or not, once the strongest sorceress of Britain, actually sought me — I dismissed her inquiries, and never will I trust her. And not more than two months ago came a swarthy man from the far south — a silly fellow, styled himself a sage and wizard, but no more than a pirate."

"Abra."

"Who?"

"Abracadabrax — calls himself the Witch King."

"Yes, the very man. A fool."

"No more than that?"

"Sadly, somewhat more: a powerful fool, not as much in the arts as in the growing wealth at his disposal. His folk harry coastal settlements, and he provides Mordred with mercenaries and weapons, and he claims also to furnish him magic, but that is only a deception — though maybe a lucrative one. When he came here, I sent him running with only a little hooting and some bad weather. But we may talk more openly inside, and you must need refreshment. Come with me."

163

A passerby with eyes firmly fixed on the women at that moment would have seen something remarkable: they would have seemed to vanish. The Lady of the Lake, skilled in her arts despite her weariness, dwelt in the midst of the greatest source of her power, the wide, deep lake waters. She removed Lilava to her lair, where, having eaten, through the long night they talked. Lilava told of the voyages, of the Chimaera, of Charybdis, of Abra, of the magic mirror and what she guessed lay ahead, all that she thought would help Nineve advise her. By morning Nineve shook her head, partly in wonder, partly in admiration, partly in near despair.

"Once my student, you have far surpassed me. You knew, for instance, that the Chimaera would respond to certain sounds, certain harmonies, or you learned so, anyway. I have little to give you now but the love I have borne you from the time we met, that of the teacher for her most diligent and appreciative student. You have the faults we all have as the curse of our humanity, but you have the rare gift of a truly good heart, as well as a strong mind, and from all I can see, so has Severus. That gift will not bring you success in itself, but succeed or fail, you will have love, the greatest gift and the greatest curse, because with it comes unsurpassed joy and unassuageable pain.

"Hmm — these few trifles I yet can give: I will teach you how to speak to Guinevere. You know what pain has troubled her heart, and I fear she has insufficient will and goodness to survive even with your help, though you must save her if you can. If she dies, both Arthur and Lancelot will despair, and Mordred and his evil will certainly prevail. She must live, if only as a symbol of respect, cooperation, and beauty — for well or ill, she inspires men. I will teach you also how to speak to Mordred: as you have rightly assumed, you can't stop him, only slow him — you can't take away free will, and he chooses evil, and he has absorbed much of Morgan's strength of character.

"I can teach you where to take Severus should mortal injury occur; he may avoid it yet, but if not, you must keep your wits about you to save him. I will attend the battle, when it comes, for Arthur's sake; should he fall, I will take him to Avalanna, where, God knows why, dwell the finest physicians in the land. We will save him if we can. I can't help you then, since I must concentrate on him. But I know who can help, if anyone can, if you recruit his assistance, which is by no means certain. He is my good friend, and he will be there, at the battle, for the conclusion affects his folk as well. He is Arawn, King of the Otherworld. He must assure that the evil of our days does not overflow into his own realm, and he has great, but not impenetrable, power to stop it. He will be dressed like the other soldiers, but you will know him by his raven hair, eyes dark as midnight, and the glow in his face — not everyone sees it, but you will — and by the emerald broach with which he fastens his earth-brown cloak.

"And I will give you this last gift: a cloak, better than the one you have. It makes the wearer the nearest thing to invisible a creature can be without breaking nature's laws. Yes, I have used it often, and I will miss it, but your need is greater than mine: I do not attract quite the attention I once did. Besides, I must try to save a king who may have no chance to avoid death; you and your husband must save a land from centuries of shadow. Take also this iridescent stone: it will gather light, hold it, and shine forth even in darkness — odd, what sort of magical bits one collects. And I add this reminder: by any means you can, prevent Severus and Lancelot from meeting in battle. You understand why: though they are both good men, Nature has made them enemies, and evil will come of it regardless of who wins or loses."

"I hear and thank you, mistress. And I'm glad Arawn will attend with you. Yes, I met him once years ago. He is both great and largely good, a noble ally in peace or in a pinch."

* * *

In the morning Lilava parted from Nineve. She could hardly find sufficient thanks to show her appreciation to her old mentor. Lilava embraced her, kissed her on the cheek, and asked her blessing. Dancer waited not far from where Lilava had left her. Lilava fed the horse with oats she had got from Nineve, and as soon as Dancer had eaten, Lilava mounted, and they began the day's ride for Carlisle.

Nineve gave a final gift of a swirling fog blowing north off the lake, no problem for the sure-footed mare and additional cover for Lilava in her ride. Lilava believed she had never seen a horse swifter over rustic ground. As they ran, Lilava first hummed a tune, then sang it in Dancer's ear, then whistled it many times over: an old tune, musically like the 'Non Nobis' that the Catholic priests sing, but with the air of the folk song from which — though few remember — that devout chant comes. She gave the tune words of her own, teaching the mare how she should call her at need:

> Come, Dancer,
> come when I sing for you.
> Come, Dancer,
> if you hear me whistling.
> Dancer and Courage, too,
> Most honored and true,
> Help your friends save their queen and their king!

By evening they entered Carlisle unnoticed among the last traffic through the guarded gates at the end of the day.

Lilava surprised a stablehand who had neither seen nor heard her approach and boarded Dancer there as near the city gate as she could, yet close enough to get as full a view as possible of the stronghold where Mordred had taken power. She had first to find Guinevere, and what better place to look than at the best protected place? The stablehand, wary of speaking but not uninformed, given his job and the public nature of wars at hand, gave way before the spell of Lilava's gentle cajoling and was able to confirm her fears: Mordred was building a well-provisioned army either to meet Arthur on his return or march out to engage the king, depending on the course of Arthur's siege and the speed of Mordred's own preparations. She ordered the man to feed and water Dancer, but not to tie or restrain her.

Mordred must not be allowed to march, she knew — Arthur must meet him with Lancelot at his side and at the best of his strength, not pinned between two forces. Rumor also hinted that Mordred had every intention of making Guinevere either his queen or his concubine, by choice or by force. Lilava knew that Guinevere would never consent; Lilava must save her not only humiliation, but also death at Mordred's hand or her own.

She considered waiting to gather better information and to try to gain conventional access to the queen, but seeing the massed garrisons and knowing that she had no time to waste to save Guinevere, she slipped through the next gate using relaxation spells on an inattentive guard and through the third with a group of serving girls carrying food. Nineve's fog had followed her all the way into Carlisle, giving her a double cover as darkness spread around the city. Considering the structure of the stronghold, she guessed as to where Mordred would most likely have secluded the queen, and using a stout vine she scaled a wall and dropped lightly into a garden.

Slipping quietly among the trees and shrubs, she found that she had guessed well and had arrived none too soon.

Through a balcony doorway she saw Guinevere standing, confronting a fuming Mordred.

As she watched, Mordred raised a hand above his head as though he would strike his fist down into the queen's face.

Guinevere stood unflinchingly, facing him. He shouted something Lilava could not comprehend, grasped the front of Guinevere's cloak in his fist, flung his hand past her face without striking, turned and stalked off. Guinevere remained where she had stood, her frozen face, even in the limited light of evening, looking blanched.

Recalling what Nineve had taught her, Lilava begun softly to whistle bird calls, and then barely audibly she first hummed, then sang a slow, haunting, lilting tune:

Far has he gone,
farther on
than words can find him.
But he will stay true
as you always knew
for ever love will bind him.

Two you love,
Two love you,
Another would deny them.
You love true,
they do, too,
and the best will yet defy him.

The song gradually pulled Guinevere from her stupor, and she came to the door listening, wondering what she had heard. Shivering, she spoke, "Is someone in the garden?"

Softly, softly Lilava sang the song again and then answered. "Yes, my queen, a friend who would ease your sorrow."

"I fear no one can do that now, and yet from your song I can believe that you know my troubles."

"I know them well and with God's help will ease them."

"No one can do that, at least no one here, while war continues and the earth teeters in the sky. Tell me: who are you, and how did you get past the guards? You risk your life here, and with a word I — or another less kind — could bring your death."

"And with my words I will bring you life, or the best chance for it, if you will let me."

"Did he send you?"

Lilava guessed Guinevere meant Lancelot.

"No, but even now my husband seeks him out. We would bring King Arthur and Sir Lancelot to accord and return the country to law and honor." She tactfully placed Arthur's name first to avoid embarrassing the queen.

"Too late for that, I fear, for even God seems to have abandoned us."

"Not yet, my lady, while our hearts remain true and our courage holds. I know what you face here, and if you will let me, I will free you of this place and take you to a safe haven."

"I know of no safe haven while Arthur and Lancelot make war and Mordred prepares to unleash his armies."

"I can show you one that even Mordred won't breach. It will bring safety of body and soul, though perhaps not of heart. That at least is a start until we find what more we can do. Have you courage enough for it, my queen?"

Lilava had never really acknowledged Guinevere as her queen, but in questioning her courage, she had to make some obeisance or lose her advantage. She saw Guinevere struggling with the choice.

"How do I know I can trust you?" Guinevere asked.

Lilava held next to her face the iridescent stone — it caught what moonlight filtered through the mist and illuminated her face. "You must choose to trust me or face Mordred again soon. I don't know yet what you have suffered from him, but I would see you suffer no more. If you would save Arthur, Lancelot, and the land you love, come, and I will help you do it. I am Lilava, once lady of the Lady of the Lake, who also wishes you well. With my knight I have fought and defeated the Chimaera and Charybdis of the Sicilian strait, and I will give my life to save you. You have this one chance, and so has your people — choose quickly, while the night protects us, or face Mordred yet this night in the dark, alone. Choose, Queen Guinevere!"

"How? How shall I ..."

"Choose freedom and live! Find your worst-looking cloak — oldest and most tattered works best. Take a rope, or a sheet, or a gown, and tie it to the rail by the parapet, then lower yourself down. From here we must escape as we can. Please hurry!"

Within minutes Guinevere slid down a long gown she had twisted into a rope and tied above, and before she reached the ground, Lilava caught her and helped her gain her footing. "We must find the quickest way out, now," Lilava whispered, "regardless of peril or pleasure."

"Yes," said the queen. "I have an idea. Your face tells me I should trust you, so I ask you now to trust me." Guinevere led Lilava through the garden, across a stony wall that ran close to a window that opened onto a large, lighted hall, and around the keep to a little-known refuse passage. "Hardly queenly," she said, "but I must do something to save myself and you too, since you have placed your life in danger for my sake. This filthy passage runs down beneath the city wall, where it ejects orts and offal — I have seen the exit point outside the city. No one would look for a queen in it. Do you know what to do once we get out? I cannot spend another instant with that horrible Mordred — the very thought is worse than death. I must tolerate what I must to get free of here. Lead now through the passage if you can see better than I, or follow if you can't; now that we have come this far, I will flee with all speed!"

"But if we end up outside the wall, we may have a problem."

"No greater than we'd have inside. Follow me!"

"Wait! My stone will light our way. Hold your nose, and let us find how quickly our feet can carry us."

Lilava held the illuminating stone before her. The passage, slick with refuse but remarkably protected, led them more quickly than they could possibly hope out of the stronghold. At that late hour no would come near it except for a servant emptying pots or a soldier eager to relieve himself. Its trough followed a sinuous path among the buildings and walls, though as it emptied out, they had to crawl under sharp iron bars to exit beneath the city wall. They emerged unseen, but filthy.

"Ick," said Guinevere as she tried to brush the muck from her cloak. "What do we do now?"

"That's what I tried to tell you above. You have got us out, but our horse is still inside the wall, where I stabled her."

"Not good."

"I thought we should need her from within — you have helped us escape almost too easily. But maybe our situation is not impossible, if I have prepared well enough," Lilava said. "Here: take my cloak. It is cleaner and will provide more warmth than yours. No, don't worry. I have learned to increase body heat when I need to, and the stone will help me. When we reach the front gate, we will want the guard to see me, but not you — the cloak will help with that as well. Wrap your old one inside-out. Let us keep close against the wall, and perhaps no other sentries will see us."

They crept around the wall nearly silently, and Nineve's fog had remained to cover them. As they came within sight of the gate amidst a growing, swirling mist, Guinevere, beneath Lilava's protective cloak, clung close against the wall, while Lilava still at a distance from the guard began in low tones to hum her "Non Nobis." When she could see the guard, she began to sing the tune just above audibly. She could see the guard straining to hear. Singing the words more clearly, she stepped into his view.

"Who goes there?"

"Sir, can you help me? For I'm in trouble."

"Who are you, young woman? What are you doing outside the gate after dark? Persons are normally arrested for being where they shouldn't be at this hour!"

"Pardon me, sir, but I was out walking and got lost."

"You have ignored the curfew, and the gates are closed for the night. Do you know what danger lies outside the walls?"

"I do, sir, so I sing my "Non Nobis" to protect me. Can you help me?" Lilava began whistling the song.

"I may not open the gate this late. You must fend for yourself until morning. And you should not be whistling a holy song. That must be blasphemy."

"Pardon again, sir. I am untutored in religious refinements, but my father will beat me if I don't get home, and being alone here frightens me. May you not open the gate just a sliver so I can get in?"

"No, I may not. You must find shelter somewhere else."

"I know of none, and the fog frightens me. Please, can I not persuade you to help me?"

"Persuade? By no means."

"Then I must whistle to keep fear from me." Lilava began to whistle the tune again, more loudly than before.

"Stop that, young woman, or you will have the soldiers after you and the priests after me. Come closer, and let me see your face."

Her words having disarmed the guard's concerns, Lilava approached the base of the gate, and the guard raised a torch to get a better look. Lilava shaded her eyes with her hands, trying to keep her face shadowed and her vision clear.

"Now, you must — oh," the guard stuttered. "Perhaps we can do something for you. Just let me have a better look." When he spoke, Lilava was not listening, but attempting a spell beneath her breath, just enough, she hoped to get him to open the door.

"Yes, come down from your watch and open the gate. You are a good man, and surely you will help me." Lilava began whistling much louder, and she noticed along the wall at short distances on either side other heads peering out into the fog. She thought she heard the sound of hooves approaching from inside the wall.

"What's that?" she heard a male voice, not that of the guard, croaking a short distance away. Lilava motioned back to Guinevere to hurry and hoped she saw the gesture.

Then with a bang of the bolt and a creak of the door, the gate opened a sliver, and the guard's head poked out.

"Maybe we can come to some sort of agreement."

"I believe we should agree on little. Dancer, come!" As Lilava called, from inside the gate the mare rose on her hind legs and kicked the door wide open. The guard sprawled forward, then scrambled to get out of the way of the rearing horse.

Lilava deftly leapt onto Dancer's back, found Guinevere in the fog, and pulled the queen up behind her. Before the guards could do anything to stop them or even get off a bowshot, they rode into the mist, out of sight. "Run, Dancer, with

all the speed you can safely manage, run north, for we must save the queen!" Lilava whispered in her ear, and run Dancer did.

* * *

Guinevere clung tightly to Lilava. "Where will you take me? I cannot go to him — you know who. Will you take me to Arthur?"

"Not prudent now, I think. I know of a haven, not all you'd wish, but safe, even from Mordred, unless he would call the army of the Church as well as the army of the king down upon his head, assuming he can even find you there. North and east of here lies an abbey... ."

Once they had cleared the danger of Carlisle, the fog lifted, and even carrying the weight of the two women on her back, Dancer ran for all she was worth. In the dead of night they rode past the fort at Stanwix, and in a spot where the Roman Wall had fallen into disrepair, clear of the sight of a milecastle and its guard, Dancer jumped it and ran on.

At first light Lilava roused the gatekeeper at the abbey at Netherby. Reasoning that Guinevere was safer north of the Wall, Lilava left her there in the care of the sisters. Soldiers along the Wall, Nineve had told her, had not yet declared themselves for Mordred and so were less likely to allow him free reign there, even if he could guess the queen's whereabouts.

Guinevere, caught between the mixed relief and trauma of her escape and her desire to return to both Arthur and Lancelot, allowed herself to be taken in by the nuns. By afternoon, with clean clothes and a fresh horse, leaving the faithful Dancer there for a well-earned rest, Lilava, with the protection of the magic cloak recovered from the queen, borrowed a work horse from the abbey and road back toward Carlisle to confront Mordred. With her she carried only a tiny pouch of gold, all that she had of it in the world.

Carlisle was madly astir with the search for Guinevere. Dozens of soldiers patrolled the city wall, and sentries questioned everyone who entered, though of course they didn't reveal their mission — Mordred would not want the people to know that the queen had escaped, either under her own power or by kidnapping. When the sentry, a younger man than had held the post the night before, stopped Lilava, she merely asked that she be permitted to see a smith to have her horse re-shod, and he admitted her with no quarrel.

"What cheer?" she asked, having received his clearance.

"Can't say," he grunted. "Prince orders that we question everyone and limit traffic." He waved her on with glance over her face and figure and began questioning the next traveler.

Lilava passed the stable where she had left Dancer the night before and rode farther into the city. She left the abbey horse to have the shoes checked at a stable and walked to the castle stronghold, gathering her energies, since she would have to talk her way in to see Mordred, then talk her way back out again. Amidst the hubbub she reached the main door by weaving in among groups of townsfolk hurrying along on their business. Beneath Nineve's cloak she passed unnoticed, practically unseen, with a group of foodservers right through the door. She got all the way to the main hall before a tall, grim knight stopped her.

"What business, woman?"

"I must see the prince."

"Get out. He's seeing no one, not even — ladies. You must be stupid to ask." He snorted dismissively.

"On a matter of safety."

"Whose, yours? I said get out."

"His."

"Arrogant witch. The prince can take care of himself."

The word witch took Lilava aback, since she was hurriedly whispering a spell under her breath, trying to get him to let her pass. "His safety and the queen's."

"What do you know about the queen?" The knight gripped her arm, squeezing painfully. Lilava, by then experienced in various arts of battle, thought to knock him down, but wished to call no more attention to herself than the knight's loud voice already had.

"I know enough to help the prince, and if you hinder me, I will suggest he remove your head from your shoulders and place it somewhere where it may do more good, say, on a pike on the city wall."

"Little bag of a beast, it'll be your head on the city wall, and worse yet if he allows me my way with you. All right, you'll have your audience, but I'll stand right at your side, waiting his order to throw you out into the refuse hole you deserve." He relaxed his grip only slightly and pulled Lilava beside him down a short hallway and through a door into a room lit only by high windows.

Sunlight round as Roman columns poured down through them onto the floor. The prince sat sprawled in a chair, his legs stretched out, a foot wiggling nervously, and his hand playing with the small, sharp beard on his chin.

"What do you want" — not a question, but a command.

"This baggage insists on seeing you. Says she knows something about — you know — the queen." The knight whispered the last two words.

"Leave us." Mordred betrayed no semblance of interest. "Speak," he said tonelessly.

Lilava remained silent.

"I have no time to waste with you. If you think you know something, tell it, or I will have you whipped and thrown to the soldiers." Only Mordred's twice regripping his hand in a fist exhibited his agitation not with Lilava, but with the problem he hoped to solve. Otherwise, he acted his usual surly self. Finally he turned his face halfway toward her.

Lilava, standing tall, walked straight toward him, staring directly into Mordred's eyes. His nostrils flared, and iron-gray eyes burned in his stony face. His lips made a move to call halt, but her step and steady gaze mesmerized rather than frightened him. Lilava stopped ten paces from him, too distant to cause or receive harm, close enough for her eyes to bore into his. She gathered her power for the speech that must buy time for Arthur, Lancelot, and Severus.

"Listen, prince of Britain." She allowed the exotic rhythm of her southern tongue to inflect her British words, and the pitch and tone carried them to his ears with the hypnotic, enervating urge to listen and then sleep. "Time beckons you to hear the voices of the ancients, whose spirits walk these halls. Join the powers of the ages, whose shades walk in your midst, who accompany you to your destiny. Like rivers the days flow into endless waters, waters that engulf enemies, wash clean the pathway to your dreams. Carefully you must swim within them, lest you to fail, as shall many. The queen has fled, and you must forget her, forget her, for those same powers that will you on your way to destiny protect her now, and her fate carries her clear of your realm and your rule. Accept the place, secure now, that the ancients have prepared for you, where the truth of your blood leads you. Take power, build strength, rule what befalls you by the will of fate and your right of birth. Hear the council of men warily, and let these your own thoughts guide you. Trust in your reason to build your forces, avoid the haste that dissolves your enemies, and you rise like the tide, inevitable, inexorable, as from the beginning of the world, from the act of Creation. Prepare, make each measured detail pure, and each of many days yours alone, as enemies spend their vitality far away clearing your course. As they are spent, so I am sent to you, truth spoken through me, that you may find your destiny."

Lilava drew deeply on her reserves to keep from passing out, so much had she expended on the speech, but she could see her words were already having their effect. The dreadful gleam in Mordred's eyes had given way to dull, unfocused oscillation, as though he were trying to see a gnat that zigzagged restlessly before his face. When he spoke, his words lacked conviction.

"Yes," he said dully, "I can see, hear the wisdom of your words. They come not from you, but from, can God wish my victory, or the old gods? So it would seem; so it would seem. You must go now and leave me to think, to think." He waved a hand as if brushing her aside. "Just call my aide, the knight who brought you in, Sir Vortigern, and tell him I want him, yes need him. What was it I wanted to do today? Find — yes, that's it, but she's gone beyond my grasp now. Forget her. I shall find a hundred like her. I must prepare for battle, prepare to march, prepare. Go away, you, go."

Lilava nearly stumbled, gathered herself to go, took a deep breath, bowed, and retreated through the door. She spoke the knight's name with all the commitment she could summon.

"Sir Vortigern: I have delivered my message, and the prince summons you. He will need your strength and will repay your service: heed his summons."

"You baggage, you had better not have done any harm, or I'll have you yet, whole or in pieces."

"Vortigern." Mordred's voice came weakly but audibly through the door, and the knight answered.

"Coming, my prince! I have not done with you, woman. You had best be here when I return. You shall be paid for good or ill, by the old gods!" He passed through the door, and Lilava closed it behind him.

With all the haste she could muster without calling attention to herself, Lilava fled the hall into the street, reclaimed her horse, and through the bustling crowd mounted and rode. The sentries at the gate shouted for her to stop. She paused, took from her pocket the small pouch of gold, and tossed it to the lead sentry. "A gift from the prince to you — use it well. I must speed on my way in his service!"

The guard opened the pouch, and his eyes grew wide. He waved her on with no further delay, and she rode out the gate, the old horse gamely gaining speed with each stride. The gold, like her spell, had done its work.

Lilava, willing to spare no more time, rode the poor horse nearly to death. She knew that Severus' life might depend on her speed — when she told the guard that she must hurry in his service, she had not in her own mind meant Mordred.

Luck remained with her when the passed the great wall, but she had nearly to drag the poor horse the last quarter mile through bleak darkness to the abbey. The watch there responded reluctantly to her call and admitted her only on the word of the abbess herself, whom he had had roused with the message that their peace had been disturbed again. Lilava found Guinevere well and sleeping and explained to the abbess what she had done and what they at the abbey must do: hide and protect their queen, the fallen, imperfect, but still dignified and imperial symbol of their people.

"You, young lady, must get some rest yourself," said the abbess. "I insist on it. Then you must eat and pray with us. You look not far from death yourself, wasted with toil and trouble."

"Yes," Lilava said, "I must rest and eat, for I am deep-down tired, and pray, too, yes, but I must also get on my way as soon as possible. A life I value more than my own waits in the balance."

"You will not get there, wherever you intend to go, without taking care of yourself first. Heed my advice: rest, repast, prayer. Then you may do your saving, once we have saved you. I will have a place prepared for you to sleep. You will enjoy the quiet here."

* * *

When Lilava woke, she could hear the sound of rain, and dim light insufficient for clear sight filtered into her room. She hardly remembered having got into bed. She rose, washed her face from a basin of clean water, dressed, and walked into the hall. She saw several nuns returning from prayer service. They nodded as they passed, and she walked on toward the main hall of the abbey with her stomach, regardless of the actual time, growling tierce. She passed the chapel and spotted the refectory, where she found an old nun cleaning.

"You, finally," the woman said. "I suppose you must eat now, after I've got everything clean and sparkling. Well, here, I'll get you something, and I'll tell the abbess you're back among the living. The food won't be much for fancy tastes, but it's healthful enough."

Lilava ate the bread and butter, milk, cheese, and gritty, rooty vegetables with gusto, wondering vaguely what the old nun meant, since from the quality of the light, she guessed she must have slept only a very few hours. She rose and bowed when the abbess entered some quarter hour later.

"Welcome back from the darkness, daughter," she said with a sly grin.

"The sister said something like that, too. As late as I got here, should I have got up at first light for prayers?"

"Which first light? You have slept through a night and a day, another night and nearly another day. It is evening again now, and I hope you feel rested. I hope also that you have not made yourself sick with eating too quickly."

"Has it been so long? Och, I must hurry. Have you my horse, Dancer? I may waste no more time, or all will have gone for nothing!"

"Calm now, dear. You might as well sleep another night. When did you last eat? And you must take time for prayers."

"Pray for me, Mother, and for Severus my husband, and for Arthur and his people, and Guinevere the Queen, and pray that, if my Severus needs me, I come not too late."

Brooking only so much delay as she needed to beg what healing herbs the abbess had at hand, Lilava found the stable, where a well-rested Dancer whinnied her eagerness to go, even in the dark, since she had been as long away from her beloved Courage as had Lilava from Severus. The rain fell steadily, and against the remonstrance of the nuns, Lilava began her ride east, warm and dry under Nineve's cloak, following their directions as best she could, not knowing how soon she could reach Joyous Guard, but intending, despite bad weather that looked to get worse, to get there and find Severus before she allowed herself another moment's rest.

* * *

Severus had with the greatest reluctance parted from Lilava, yet he knew that the course they had agreed upon offered the best, perhaps the only hope of success. As he rode to the northeast, sturdy aboard his long-time companion, he watched from the corner of his eye as Lilava, riding Dancer, disappeared to the west.

He determined to ride as far and as quickly as Courage was willing to carry him — quickest to Arthur gave him the greatest time to find a way to persuade him to make peace with Lancelot. And the resolute Courage carried him quickly indeed. After a long rest, the horse felt almost glad to have his knight in saddle again as they hurried to a new adventure. Courage had the sense of Severus' urgency, and while not the fastest of horses, he was far from slow and had as firm and sturdy a step and as much heart as any horse of his time. And he ran as he had never run before.

Like Lilava and Dancer, they kept as well as they could to rural ways to maintain their pace and avoid stoppage. Along the east coast many folk in the small towns and settlements knew little of Arthur. They greeted the few knights they met warily, but assisted them readily enough and sped them through. Their greatest worries came from marauders from the sea, whom even Arthur's far-reaching power couldn't stop, and they needed no additional troubles from passing knights.

Still, from the second day on rain slowed their progress. Courage drove on patiently for a horse who had so long been free of his rider. Near Tees-Mouth a local official, spotting an unknown boat coming toward shore and needing a knight to help him, stopped Severus and asked him, as an agent of the king, to defend his town if the boat should prove to carry pirates. Eager to press on, yet fully conscious of the man's problem and his right to ask for help, Severus dismounted, prepared his weapons, and waited with the local men who clearly felt wary of a battle — they had seen such hit-and-run bands and what they could do, even in small numbers. The official hailed the sailors with no success. As they got near enough to disembark, about fifteen of them, Severus hailed them in the name of King Arthur, asked that they identify themselves. They answered in a language Severus didn't know, but in a tone he did: they had responded, he understood, with nothing but curses. The local men arranged themselves behind Severus, hoping he could do something if not everything, ready to flee if he couldn't.

Severus, after all his adventures and battles, had never yet developed a taste for fighting against other men. Even in such an instance, saving a town from men who appeared more brutal ruffians than organized soldiers, he fought reluctantly. But he had learned long before that once he had engaged battle, he must win, and time allowed him no negotiating. He saw the marauders draw weapons — mostly short swords or axes, but two with bows.

He took his own bow from his back and felled the enemy bowmen with his first two shots. The others kept coming. He withdrew the dirks he had recovered from the battle with Scylla and with four quick tosses dropped three more of the pirates. Several began to run through the waves towards him, their axes in front of them, but he had firm ground beneath and they did not. Wielding his staff, he disarmed the first of them nearly to reach shore and struck him on the forehead beneath his iron helm, plunging him into the surf. With that man's axe he cut a knee from the next, then chucked the axe into the throat of the third. Finally the others stopped to reassess their position. Another still in the boat had collected the bow of a fallen comrade — Severus armed his bow, and shook his head, appealing to the man to restrain himself. One man yet among the breakers approached Severus with his hands empty and his arms above his head.

"Ve stop, ya? Ant you stop, too. Ve come for supplies, no trouble, but now ve go on. You too much for us. But ve see you again sometime, ya? Ya, no more. Tell you Artur King ve no stop here no more, ya? Maybe not."

Severus pointed his drawn bow at the speaker, then with the tip of the arrow motioned him back to his ship. Those pirates still alive reboarded and departed, leaving their dead bobbing in the wash.

"Ya, ve go, no serve King Abra no more, right," the leader called as the remaining men rowed back to sea.

"Abra again," Severus sighed. "How could he have stretched his influence so far?"

Severus didn't stay for whatever lukewarm thanks he supposed the locals would offer. He spoke tersely.

"Remember that your king does his best to watch over you, but you must communicate to him your needs, make an effort to defend yourself, and remain loyal to him always. Thank him for what I have done for you today, for I have fought in his name only. Remember it, and support him when he asks you. And God save you from such pirates."

Severus remounted, and with no further ado or any reward he and Courage ran on north. They needed another day and a half of steady riding before on a

178

cool, crisp morning Severus could see in the distance Lancelot's tall castle, Joyous Guard, once the gift of a loving king, looming against the slate-gray clouds.

Severus recalled what he had seen in Ambrose's magic mirror. He and Lilava had already made choices, probably eliminating some possibilities, or at least suspending them. Mordred had assembled his power in Carlisle rather than London, so the scenarios he had witnessed would change, had already changed, by the choices of another. Yet nothing had changed, as far as he knew, with respect to Arthur and Lancelot: they would receive him the same way. Severus had to find a way to win the confidence of Arthur or Lancelot or both, and he little knew how.

He climbed a small promontory and watched as, in the field before the castle, two horsed knights rushed together in joust. At the first pass they struck each other so powerfully that, though it took a full three seconds after impact for the echo to reach Severus' ears, it reverberated like thunder. Each was flattened backward on his horse, but neither fell, so they prepared for another pass, but by then Severus had recognized the knight closer to the castle as clearly Lancelot — no one else looked so tall in the saddle or rode with such presence and conviction. On the second go neither struck firmly, but on the third the knight farther from the castle — Arthur's representative, whoever he was — was thrown backward so forcefully that he flipped in the air. The successful knight, Lancelot, pranced over to his adversary, who struggled admirably to recover himself — Lancelot sat still on his horse and let him rise. When the fallen man staggered to his feet, he pulled his sword. Severus, closing, could hear him shouting, but couldn't yet identify him.

Nobly, calmly, Lancelot dismounted and drew his sword, as the other man waited just long enough to regain what composure he could muster before rushing to attack. Lancelot parried blows for some time without striking, but gradually his attacker began not only to recover, but actually to appear to gain strength, until he had forced Lancelot to defend himself with vigor and return the attack as well. They continued for some time with Arthur's knight gaining in speed and brilliance, having backed Lancelot nearly to his castle gate. Severus noticed that the sun, now streaming through the clouds, had risen to its zenith, and he realized that the attacker could be none other than Gawain, whose strength always waxed at midday, and who in the wild spin and swing of his strokes looked almost demonic.

Some hour later the fight continued, but the balance had changed. Gawain, who had nearly driven Lancelot to his knees, was now in gradual but forced retreat. As Gawain's strength appeared to wane, so Lancelot's had risen, and he drove his opponent backward with every stroke, until one finally broke through defenses and struck Gawain smack on the helmet with a ringing ping, an expert stroke delivered in workmanlike battle without the disrupting intervention of thought, like that of a skilled smith's hammer striking an anvil. Gawain's knees buckled, and Lancelot stepped back as though astonished at the stroke, having had so many blows parried and dodged, watching his opponent fall face downward into the turf.

Lancelot threw down his sword and raised his visor, dropping to his knees to find if any lifesbreath flitted across the lips of the man who had once been his greatest friend. Other knights from Arthur's side charged, perhaps hoping more to catch Lancelot at a disadvantage than to save Gawain, but as many poured out the gate of Joyous Guard, drawing in a stunned and unwilling Lancelot even as Arthur's men collected on a litter the limp body of their champion.

Severus urged Courage on and rode for Arthur's camp.

IV Reckonings

[A long-dreaded battle tests the knight's skills and powers of healing.]

Severus had never considered himself much of a public speaker, but he did his best to talk his way into the tent where Arthur himself along with his physicians attended the doomed Gawain.

Gawain was speaking painfully and intently to Arthur, who bent over him, listening for the last, faint words, his face red and strained and his eyes wet.

"What does he want here?" snarled Aggravayne, who, unknown to Arthur, was Mordred's spy in the king's camp, when he saw Severus waiting patiently.

Severus wasn't sure whether Aggravayne remembered him and dismissed him because of his lack of court standing or whether he didn't recognize him and wondered why someone with the dirt and sweat of a long ride still on him dared enter the king's tent. But one doesn't survive such battles as Severus had fought without acquiring some commanding confidence. He was concerned about Gawain, and he was angry at having killed the men at Tees-Mouth. Since they were pirates they had probably killed often enough themselves, no one could say they hadn't deserved what they got, but Severus had never felt justified in doling out what we in the world often call justice. His spirit guided him to save people and free them from their fears, not to avenge them for ill deeds done by bad men — though of course one may argue the public good of such actions. He brushed Aggravayne aside and strode to Gawain's bedside, addressing Arthur.

"My king, you may not remember me. I am Sir Severus le Brewse. I have achieved the quest of the Chimaera, freed the Italian Strait of the monster Scylla, and saved your town of Tees-Mouth from attacking pirates, for which they thank you. In a distant land I have seen into the future of these battles that you now fight, and in the name of Britain and chivalry I have come to urge you to reconcile with Sir Lancelot, that you may defend your people from a growing host that will, without you to lead them, drive your land into centuries of darkness. You have little time. Will you let me help you?"

Having said it, Severus could still hardly believe himself capable of such a long speech.

"Sir Severus, you have returned at an evil time, and you do ill to interrupt the last converse of a king and his dying nephew. I remember you as a rustic knight, so I suppose I must forgive you for lacking courtly behavior, but if you believe in God and goodness, unless you have some means beyond our ken to heal Sir Gawain, I ask you to depart whence you came before I set these knights upon you."

"Wait," Gawain whispered from the field-cot where he lay. "I would speak to this man."

Severus knelt down, bent his ear to Gawain, and grasped his hand. Gawain coughed up blood, but made great effort to speak.

"As my king knows, I have little life left and few words, but the strength of your hand gives me sufficient vigor to speak. Odd that I never thought much of you before, Sir Severus, as I know my dear brother Gareth did. Perhaps by some means you could heal me if you had time, but as responsible men we must do what we can, not what we would. I must tell you: you appeared in my dream last night, where I spoke to you as I do now. I hope that dream, now unfolding, came from God and not from the devil. I have erred, Severus, and someone must put things right. Forgive me if I speak slowly: I find the movement difficult.

"The guilt for insisting on this war belongs to me and my family. We were wrong. Despite my love for my brothers, I should not have urged the king against Sir Lancelot, the greatest living knight and his champion. Had I given good counsel, we should have peace, and not the growing storm that in my last minutes I can feel rising in the west. Severus, do what I should have done: make peace between King Arthur and Lancelot. I don't know what makes me believe you can. I don't know that I do believe it. But in my desire to do one final good act, I beg you to try. Now I must have last words with my king, for my breath grows short."

Severus gently squeezed Gawain's hand and nodded assent, then he stepped back, and Arthur knelt beside his nephew. Gawain whispered in the king's ear, and the king shook his head. Gawain whispered again, and Arthur answered, "If you wish it, I will try." Paroxysms gripped Gawain's body, which heaved like a wave. The body shook, then heaved again, and after two hisses of breath, the body bent once more, then stilled. Arthur knelt stroking the head of his nephew, but the great knight's spirit had flown.

"Get out, you, and let a family grieve," Aggravayne hissed from behind a large knight who stood armed, attending Arthur. Severus glared at him and turned to leave, but Arthur grasped his wrist and held him.

"May I speak with you, sir?" the king said. "You must allow me a minute here with my nephew, but then I would have parley with you outside." Severus bowed and stepped through the tentflap. Outside the wind blew steadily, and the late-afternoon sun had dispersed the clouds to shine gaily as if it were to be a very fine day.

Several minutes later, followed by two sergeants-at-arms, Arthur emerged, distracted by grief, and he looked almost surprised to see Severus waiting for him. "You? Oh, yes. For reasons I can attribute only to blood loss and a result-ing unsound judgment, my nephew tried to convince me that I must trust the next move in this siege to you. I have no idea if you can accomplish anything or how, but if you think you can serve me, then I enlist that service."

"Of course, my king."

"Then you must do this task for me. Avenge my nephew in battle against Sir Lancelot."

"Sire, I would undertake any honorable task to bring about peace, but I must counsel against combat — we must cease hostilities, not renew them."

"Any sensible man would counsel me against sending him into combat against Lancelot. No one can defeat him. But he has killed my sister's-son, and I too must defend the honor of my family, even as Gawain did. Without honor, I can-not be king: the people will not follow me. If you call me king and would serve me, do as I ask. If not, leave here, and knowing Lancelot's prowess, I will try not to think of you as a coward, if I should ever think of you again at all."

Arthur stalked off, and Severus could see that the king had reached his break-ing point. He wondered how Lilava had done with Guinevere, but knew he couldn't wait to find out. He had to choose and act, and no scenario that he could think of could work, unless he could somehow fight Lancelot to a draw and while doing so persuade him to beg Arthur's pardon, so that, honor sat-isfied, they might be reconciled. So Severus prepared for individual combat, choosing the weapons he must for the formal exchange, praying as he checked his gear that God would grant him to see Lilava once more. Without her, he thought, he should quickly tire of life anyway.

As he rode through the camp toward Joyous Guard, an old woman covered in a cloak called up to him. "Sir, would you allow a word with an old woman before you go?"

"Certainly, ma'am." He dismounted beside her, and she pulled aside her hood enough that he could see her face. At first his heart thrilled, thinking she was Lilava, but then he noticed that that thought came more from his heart than his eyes. She wasn't an old woman, as she'd said, and she looked familiar, though not like Lilava, except for a certain glow in the eyes. She pulled him aside and spoke quietly.

"I am Nineve, Lady of the Lake, friend to Lilava. I have come to serve the king. I'd hoped to keep you from battle with Lancelot, but now I see that I can't do that. Rumor says that Lilava has got Guinevere into safe keeping, but I haven't seen her myself since she stopped at my lake on her way to Carlisle. She is, I believe, riding here as quickly as she can, but bad weather and rough terrain will slow her — I came soon after she departed from me.

"Here's the worst news: Mordred comes with his army. Lilava's spell slowed him a little, but Morgan le Fey intervened. I thought I had seen the last of that old witch, but she has never given up her ambition to unseat Guinevere and diminish Arthur, though her powers have waned with the years. Maybe we will find ourselves better off in the long run: the conflicting sorcery has confused Mordred enough that he comes at less than full strength, which leaves Arthur with a chance, even if he must fight without Lancelot. The loss of Gawain has hurt us; not only does he fight well, but he inspires other men to fight well. Lancelot could secure us victory, particularly with you fighting beside him, but you will find winning him over more difficult than any monster fight. I don't believe he will parley, and in the heat of battle how can you reason with him, since you must try to save your own life? We have spoken too long and call attention to ourselves. Ride on, sir, and go with God. You have friends here of whom you know little. Trust us to do our part."

Severus thanked her, remounted, and rode through the last of the milling troops, turning over too many thoughts, trying to remain aware of what he must do, to make sense of Nineve's words, but at the same time to clear his mind for combat. As he passed the front line of troops, he noticed the last man wore a long, brown cloak clasped at the shoulder with a green pin. The man's dark eyes shone beneath black hair, and as Severus passed him, he nodded encouragement. As a courtesy Severus bowed his head briefly in answer, not recognizing the man, but feeling heartened by the goodwill of at least one of the king's men who wished him well. Severus wondered if the man had something elven about him.

As he rode onto the field before the castle, Severus could feel Courage's nervousness, such as he had never before detected from his horse as they approached battle. He tried to whisper in his ear, but the horse just shook him off, the head moving back and forth as if to say, why are we doing this stupid thing? Severus patted him on the neck and stroked his head, so Courage did his best to prance forward confidently, though knowing better in his equine heart.

As he neared the castle wall, Severus could see archers perched atop it. He stopped before the main gate, sitting straight in the saddle.

"I have come for parley. Would Sir Lancelot speak with me, please?"

"You look, sir knight, as though you have come to fight, not to speak," a voice called back to him. It sounded like Sir Bors.

"To speak, certainly, to fight only if necessary."

"Lancelot has fought all he wishes to fight today. He grieves at the injury to Sir Gawain. He will speak to no one but the king."

"I come at the king's order, but I bring bad news for the cause of Britain. Sir Gawain has gone to God."

"Then Sir Lancelot shall grieve the more, for he never wished that knight's death nor even harm to come to him. Sir Gawain himself insisted on pursuing war, day after day, and not even such a great knight as he can stand up to Sir Lancelot indefinitely."

"With whom am I speaking, please?"

"You have come here, not we to you. You should announce yourself first. Your failing to do so suggests you are a man of little quality and hardly worth our trouble."

"You instruct me rightly, and I ask you pardon. I am Sir Severus le Brewse. I have never willingly sought harm to any man, but I do come on King Arthur's business, so I hope you will treat me accordingly, for his sake."

"He should have come himself instead of sending a no-name knight. Well then, I am Sir Bors, cousin to Sir Lancelot, and I suggest you return whence you came before Arthur must grieve for a lackey as well as a nephew."

"Can I not persuade Sir Lancelot to parley?"

"No, but if you persist, we may reward you with some lesser knight to kill you. Now go away, and don't return."

"Then I must give you the rest of my message. The king, by right of honor, seeks return combat through me as ritual for the death of his nephew. Will you send forth someone to have a do with me?"

"Your delicacy in delivering your message betrays your cowardice. If you come here for battle, you should have said so. I will consult my lord and have him send someone worthy of your quality." Severus noted the bite in Sir Bors' words and recalled once again why he so detested court life. He waited in silence, wondering at such a reception from a Grail knight.

Some minutes later a fully armed knight emerged from the castle gate. Severus could see he was a young man, aiming to impress his fellows with a victory between the two armies.

"Prepare, recreant knight, for you will have the do you seek! I am Sir Hector, vassal to the world's greatest knight." The voice sounded young, and Severus considered how best to handle the young man. He sat his horse well and had probably practiced considerably for such a joust, though Severus doubted he had ever greeted the fact of his own mortality. Not the world's best jouster, Severus nevertheless eased Courage into a charge and with a quick movement at impact unhorsed the young knight at the first pass. He realized he was sufficiently out of practice that he should have trouble against a better knight. He gently dismounted before the young man, who lay flat on the ground, breathing with difficulty. Voices from the wall of the castle rained insults down upon him and called for him to let the young man live. Severus unlaced the youth's helmet.

"You have killed me, sir," he said, breathing rapidly and unevenly. "I only regret that in serving my lord Lancelot I have failed to destroy his enemy. Please dispatch me quickly."

"Young man, I don't think you'll die today. You ride well, and you will fight again. I think you've just had the wind knocked out of you. No, I'm not going to pull my sword and behead you, so don't worry. Just try to breathe steadily and slowly. In a minute here we'll get you up and have you on your way back to the castle. No dishonor when you give your best, courageously. Yes, you may just have had a bit of bad luck. Yes, I'll joust with you again sometime, if any of us lives beyond these awful days. Here now, up you go."

When he had got young Sir Hector safely up, and several squires had returned him inside the castle, a second knight emerged.

"You have had an easy time against a boy, sir. Let us see what you can do against a true knight. Now you must fight Sir Bors. Prepare yourself."

Severus had in fact recognized the voice of Sir Bors, then found he must face one of the most famous of the Round Table knights. Remembering the magic mirror, he knew he must win, but not too obviously. He hoped he was enough in training to take a lance without falling. He knew at least that Sir Bors would not kill his horse, as an evil knight might have done. He got the sense that Courage wasn't so sure. He remounted and rode back to begin the next run.

They jousted three passes. On the first both blocked the lance with shields. On the second pass both struck, but neither man fell from his horse. On the third Severus allowed himself to fall, taking care to avoid wrenching Courage as he did so. Preferring lighter armor even in joust, he managed to regain his feet briskly, ran behind Bors, and jerked him from the saddle.

"I should have suspected treacherous tactics of such a fellow," Bors complained, as he pushed himself to his feet. "Draw your sword then. Where were you when good Christian knights quested for the Holy Grail? Have you no faith as well as no honor?"

"Not all knights may follow even the best of quests. I had my own tasks, such as God saw fit for me."

"Likely excuse," Bors grunted as he renewed his attack.

Severus did his best, using up valuable energy, to make the fight look competitive without taking any damaging blows. After about ten minutes he managed to duck beneath a swordstroke, throw Bors from his feet, unlace the helmet, and immobilize him in a chokehold.

"Evil tactics" Bors spat, trying not to pass out, "but you have got me, and I must yield and trust myself to a traitor's mercy."

"What makes you think I'm a traitor? I would see the King and Lancelot at peace. I tell you this man to man: for whatever reason King Arthur sent me, I have come only to see them reunited."

"Then you will have to convince Lancelot, since before I left he joked that if neither a youth nor a Grail knight could not beat you, he would have to do so himself."

"I would say to him what I have said to you."

"You will have no chance to talk once he has begun to fight, and you can feel sure that you won't have the chance to wrestle him down as you have done with me, since he is watching from the wall and now knows your methods."

Severus looked up toward the wall, which actually stood overhead and backwards from his perspective, so he couldn't make out any faces. "Then I may safely accept that you yield, on your word as a Christian?"

Bors struggled for a bit longer, until Severus tightened the grip at his throat just enough to make clear that Bors had nowhere to go. "Yes," croaked Bors, "I yield," and Severus immediately loosened the hold.

"You could have killed me, sir," Bors said, dejected. "I believe now that you could have done so earlier if you had wished."

"Please don't tell anyone. I spoke to you truly, I don't wish to harm, but to bring peace."

"If so, then God will speed you in your task."

Severus rolled free of his opponent, then offered a hand to help him up. "Please try to get Lancelot to talk."

"Not possible. Look yourself to the gate."

Lancelot had emerged, horsed, fully accoutred, and ready for battle.

"I can tell by the way he sits his horse when he is serious," Bors said, "and I believe now that your best chance is simply to pray, for no matter what you speak, he will not hear you."

"Then I ask, Sir Bors, that you will pray for us both."

"I pray you, horse yourself, sir knight, for you will find in this encounter all the fight you need to satisfy you," Lancelot called from the end of the field.

"Here goes," Severus said, partly to Bors, but mostly to himself.

Severus walked slowly back to Courage, stroked the horse's face, and mounted. "Poor fellow," he said, "you've had a tough few days, and it won't get any easier now. Maybe his battle is your Chimaera. You have proven your name a hundred times over. Please do so once more, and what extra heart you can find, share with me."

Lancelot raised his lance, and when Severus nodded, with no more words he charged. Severus intended to take any chance he could find to parley. Since Lancelot had seen his battle with Bors, Severus suspected he would have no chance to grasp him, even if he could get hold of the larger man. So as they passed, Severus ducked and swerved to miss the blow.

"Cowardly knight!" Lancelot remonstrated.

"I came to speak with you rather than to fight."

"Too late for speech. You have come for the king's vengeance, so show some heart, and fight or die. Either way I shall probably kill you."

"Will you not hear what I have to say?"

"No."

As Lancelot prepared for another pass, Severus surveyed Arthur's ranks, which he could see once they had changed positions on the field. Hundreds of soldiers watched, but he had hoped to see a certain woman there.

Lancelot attacked at full speed. Severus defended as well as he could, turning aside from the brunt of the blow, but he received enough nearly to propel him from horseback. He dug his knees in to hold, and Courage neighed loudly at the shock of the blow and Severus' grip. His shield had held.

On the third pass, knowing he had to do something to shake Lancelot's deadly aim, he angled dangerously inward toward his horse, so that the two animals brushed as they went by, barely averting injury. Severus avoided the point of Lancelot's lance and with his lance nearly punched Lancelot's shield from his arm, though the edge of his own shield was splintered. He knew that from the force of his blow Lancelot must be feeling intense pain in the shield arm.

"Would you pause to speak, Sir Lancelot?"

But Lancelot simply rode to the other end of the field, then charged again, his whole figure and force bent on felling his opponent.

At the fourth meeting Lancelot struck a clean blow, reducing Severus' shield to fragments, while Severus' own lance broke on Lancelot's shield. He eased his grip so that Courage would avoid injury in a fall. Worse for the monster-slayer: the blow struck so powerfully that it threw him backward from his horse, and when he landed for an instant he lost consciousness.

Few men had done better than four passes in joust against Lancelot, but the battle had not ended, nor would it likely end before death had taken its due, one knight of the other.

By force of instinct, or practice, or will, or luck or despair Severus swirled back into consciousness and rose to his feet. Lancelot spoke, but Severus' head was spinning, and he could make no sense of the words. Lancelot chivalrously dismounted, and Severus attacked with his sword, his body taking over before his mind could clear to make a reasonable decision. Lancelot was no ordinary man, tainted as he was with the blood of the monstrous, and since he was therefore Severus' natural enemy, Severus attacked powerfully and without thinking.

While Lancelot had fought men better trained in weaponry, he had never fought anyone with such natural quickness and feel for combat or such acquired endurance and persistence. When Severus returned fully to his senses, he was driving Lancelot back toward the gate under a rain of blows so fast and heavy that any but the world's finest swordsman would already have fallen. Lancelot had become accustomed to letting other men spend their strength, then returning the attack as they ebbed, but Severus had shown no sign of ebbing, and only when he penetrated Lancelot's defense and struck a clean blow against the left shoulder did he pause. The thought struck Severus that he had got the advantage and could use it, but his clearing mind told him he must not kill his opponent or even disable him: Arthur would soon enough need him.

Lancelot, however, took Severus' quarter as a waning of strength, and then he began his counterattack. Fighting less well when he directed his strategy by thought rather than by instinct, Severus found himself twice driven to the ground, but he managed each time to regain his feet without injury.

The old stories tell of day-long battles, of the ebb and flood of individual combat — who can prove the truth of such stories? But Severus and Lancelot fought with swords without pause for more than an hour, and during all that time soldiers on either side of the field could not have told who would conclude the battle victorious and who dead. Severus did his best to avoid attacking the injured left arm — he could not tell if that tactic angered or inspired his opponent.

188

As darkness inked the field and neither man could gain full advantage, Lancelot finally paused and spoke.

"We must decide this battle, you and I."

Allowing Severus no words, and seemingly beyond the limits of human capacity, Lancelot rushed with every fiber of his being committed to the attack and redoubled his strokes. With a powerful blow he drove Severus nearly into the ground, so that his knees buckled, shattering the sword-blade with which Severus had parried the stroke. Lancelot staggered forward, unbalanced by the power of his own blow and surprised by the failure of Severus' inferior blade, but he found his breast plunging toward the still-sharp, broken edge above the reinforced hilt. Uncertain whether the stroke bore his enemy's death or his own, and with an instant's doubt about the justice of his own victory, Lancelot somehow halted the descent of his own sword toward Severus' neck, though he opened a gash between the shoulder and the center of the breast. What had looked to bring Severus' certain end became in that instant, as all time seemed for the two soldiers to condense into that action, Lancelot's imminent death, as the upturned, broken blade grazed the great knight's throat.

But Severus' body reacted where the brain could not. He dodged to Lancelot's left, the side he had been avoiding, turning the sharp edge aside, grasped the dull bottom of the blade in his left hand, and as he had squatted against his heels, repelled against the ground so that his shoulder, rising, rammed Lancelot in the chest, stopping the descent of his weight even as Lancelot tried to pull away. With the hilt of his sword Severus caught Lancelot behind the knee, and with the force caused by his rising and his opponent's attempt to retreat, in one fluid move he threw him onto his back. When Lancelot hit the ground, Severus tossed his broken sword-end away and thrust his short sword into the ground beside right the other man's head.

More surprised than injured, Lancelot rolled and jumped to his feet, relieved that he had not suffered injury, expecting to see his enemy right above him, pursuing his advantage.

Instead, he looked around, saw no one, and then turned to see Severus, unarmed, kneeling behind him. Severus had used what could have been his advantage to yield to his enemy. Lancelot grasped his sword in both hands, felt the pain shoot through his shoulder, and readied a death blow.

Severus spoke calmly and clearly, bleeding badly from the wound in his chest.

"Before you kill me, my lord Lancelot, I ask that you observe that I am no longer armed. You will see my short sword buried in the ground beside where you fell. You have spared me once, just now, and you will see by the position of that sword that I spared you as well. If you would hear my words first, I will die at your hands hoping I have done my duty to you, the king, and God. Considering my bleeding, I must speak quickly." Severus could see the fire-red glow in Lancelot's eyes, the same fire that overtakes a monster in the heat of the kill. But he didn't flinch. He stared directly into those eyes, and he watched the flame dim, and he pressed his hand to his wound to try to slow the flow of blood he knew he couldn't stop.

"Speak, then."

"You have throughout your life proven yourself the greatest of martial knights that the world has known. You have served perhaps the greatest of kings. Right now, Prince Mordred is preparing an attack on your king. Unless you make peace with King Arthur, he shall fall, and you shall fall thereafter, and Britain and Gaul will be plunged into an age of horror and blood worse and longer than anything poets dare imagine.

"If you still believe in right and honor and God, find a way to make peace and join your one-time king and friend to defend all those people for whom you have lived. If we are lucky, the queen is safe, but she may not stay safe for long when the world has spun into turmoil and madness. I came here not to fight, though our fight may have been inevitable, but to do what I could to save what I believe is good. If these are my last words, believe I would use them for nothing other than the truth as I know it. Consider well, please. I don't think you shall need a final stroke. My senses fail me."

Lancelot puffed, nervous, uncertain, wanting both to strike and to still his hand, to justify himself and to defend those he loved, for deep in his heart the love of his body and soul, Guinevere, and of his reason, Arthur, would never leave him. "How do I know you speak truth? Do not faint! Tell me how I can trust you!"

"Trust him," said a voice.

Lilava, having arrived in time to see the last strokes of the combat, fell to Severus' side, cradling his head in her lap and applying a poultice to the throbbing river of his wound. She spoke rapidly and quietly, unsure herself if she were peaking magic or prayer.

"Believe him," said another voice, male, gentle and musical. "You do not know my name, Lancelot, but we have met, and you have seen my folk betimes. We, too, have much to lose, should you fail, and peace to gain, should you succeed." He knelt beside Lilava, speaking to her in low tones. His dark eyes pierced into Lancelot's heart, stilling the rest of his anger. He unclasped the green brooch that held his cloak, and threw the cloak over Severus' breast to keep him warm in the chilling air.

"Hear him, and believe me," said another voice, baritone, and there Lancelot saw the face of an old friend. "I have lost my nephew, and if what these people say is true, and I believe them now, without you I will soon lose not only my kingdom and my life, but all that I have loved and striven to create and preserve. Can you forgive and once again support a man who has made bad choices, but who has loved you as his friend and champion, the greatest knight and greatest man a king has ever known?"

Lancelot looked first at his king, then down at Severus, whose eyes were beginning to roll back into his head as his arms and legs shook as though with cold.

"I am sorry for this business," he said. "I did spare him, but I see that he also spared me. I must learn more of what has happened. And, my lord king, I want more than life to make peace with you and return Britain to her days of glory. Let us parley. If you will lead, I will follow."

The great soldier solemnly followed the famous king to his camp. Lancelot's men, who had filtered down from the castle wall, fell in behind, and in moments they had spread amidst the campfires that glowed fleetingly in the growing, swirling darkness, seeking old friends.

Severus lay on the field with Lilava and the dark-eyed man, King Arawn. They did their best to tend him. Nineve, the Lady of the Lake, reappeared as well.

"My only beloved, there must be a God, since I have got what I prayed for," Severus said, fighting the darkness that was shadowing his eyes. "Selfish — I should have spared you this sight of me, but I wished that I might see you once more. Funny, as though I had a bad memory for your face: I see your eyes, but your face fades. But I love that face and the spirit that shines through it. Forgive me that wish, will you?"

"You shall see many more years of me, my love, and then an eternity, if you will have it," Lilava answered, pressing the wound tightly. She looked at the others. "What can we do? He has lost oh so much blood. I don't have the skill. Have you? Have you?"

"Doubtful," said Nineve.

"Perhaps," said Arawn "if we can get him to my carriage. My horses are swift. If we can reach the Shining Lands before he fails, I may save him, but we must hurry, though moving him presents a danger in itself. He has much to offer in the Other Lands, if we can keep him alive until we get there. The evil of Britain spills into my kingdom, and you and Severus can do more for us than you can for Arthur now, since Lancelot has returned to him and his life must take its course."

Nineve nodded.

"He is strong; he has always been strong," Lilava said. "And he is good, good in heart and deed. Lady, can you meanwhile do nothing for him? If only I could have got here sooner! Weather and some force, Morgan perhaps, slowed me."

"The spirits at my call will follow you, for now, to speed your way, but I must stay with Arthur. His soldiers are too few. Mordred marches from the west, and when they will meet in battle, it must take place on better grounds than these, with Arthur on the attack rather than besieged. I must march him north, around them, to better ground from which to attack or defend; Mordred has ever been weak in the flank."

"Courage," Severus muttered.

"Yes, my dear, courage."

"Horse, my horse — his own horse, really. Have I got him killed?"

"I have sent my lieutenant to check on him," Arawn said. "Report, Bran?"

"Injured a bit in the fall, my lord, but he will live, and with luck may fight again."

"Good," Severus said, "best of horses — tell him I said so."

"You will tell him yourself, love" Lilava said.

"Someone must bring Courage," Severus managed.

"We cannot bring him," Arawn answered, "but I will make sure we leave him in trustworthy care."

Lilava looked into Severus' eyes as they beamed at her, and then he fainted. "The pulse is weak. We have no choice but to try to move him. At least the bleeding has stopped," she said.

"Horse spirits of the land, come — your king calls you at great need," Arawn whispered. And the horses came, grand, earth-brown horses full of strength and speed, pulling a green carriage. Arawn's men lifted Severus into it. Lilava sat beside him. Arawn himself leapt into the driver's seat.

"Thanks to you, great king," Nineve said. "Blessings and luck go with you, friend and daughter. You are both young and strong; may your youth, love, and all that you have suffered together serve you well in your time of greatest need. If my next adventure goes well, I will see you both again. If it fails, so will I, and my powers will pass away, for I have placed them all at Arthur's disposal. Should Morgan make her presence known, we shall have one grand battle, she and I. As the land and its king go, I go. Fare you well!"

Arawn nodded and called to his horses to run. Lilava watched as Nineve waved to them — the coach disappeared into the whirl of night and mist, moving beyond the speed of humans toward the Other Lands, and Lilava whispered, half-praying, half beseeching her beloved to live.

* * *

$\mathfrak{M}$any accounts tell of King Arthur's final battle against Mordred at Camlann, how Arthur's inferior forces won the day, and how Arthur sorrowfully killed his son. Mordred, however, left his father with a mortal wound. Some say that there Arthur breathed his last, while others tell that the Lady of the Lake got him to Avalanna, where she healed him to return at the time of Britain's greatest need. The following years brought darkness and trouble to Britain, but not so irrevocably as they would have had Mordred emerged victorious — yet no hint of Arthur's return.

Other stories purport to tell of Severus and Lilava thereafter. One, recorded by a Northumbrian cleric, says that a local chieftain, a man for whom Severus had once done a small service, not the king of the Other Lands, appeared on the field and carried Severus' body to one of the great forts along the Roman Wall, perhaps Wallsend or Halton Chesters. But despite Lilava's care, he died before they reached it and was on the next day buried there, outside holy ground, in land that had once been a Roman cemetery.

That tale gives no additional account of Lilava. If one were to read it alone, one would have to guess whether she joined Guinevere in the convent, returned to her family in the Mediterranean, or if perhaps with the waning of the influence of Nineve following Arthur's death, she took her teacher's place as Lady of the Lake to watch over and protect British waters for future generations.

Another story, better told and which I prefer to believe, tells that Arawn drove faster than an eagle can ride the wind, and Lilava wove about Severus a net of prayers and spells, so that when they passed the barrier into the Other Lands, he still had life's breath. Arawn's physicians had strong medicine, but the elf-king himself had stronger yet: he breathed a part of his own immortal strength into Severus' lungs, calling him back from the Road to the Dead. By those means and through Lilava's love and a long convalescence, Severus not only survived and recovered fully from his wound, but regained the best part of his abilities. He and Lilava for a time joined Arawn's court, since, because of the tragedies of the world, that kingdom, too, had its share of monsters and quests for individuals or teams to pursue. In the Other Lands — as they had in the world of humans — Severus and Lilava preferred their own company to that of a courtly crowd, even one generous and kind to its heroes. They roamed the hills and fields of the Other Lands, says the story, and enjoyed many adventures together, for folk, even humans, live a long span in those regions. That story ends so: they returned to Arawn's court occasionally for news of the lands from which they'd come, though never to Arthur's, for they had done their part in those events, and, desiring no more converse with the people there, they disappeared from the general memory.

But you and I have the story of the Arthur's reign, the many legends that inspire us to believe in heroism and in the value of working for a greater equality for people everywhere. One may say only that events would have gone much worse without the heroism of Severus and Lilava, two people from opposite ends of the world who met, fell in love, and joined together to defend their lands against such monsters as walked the earth in those distant times.

Yet one final story purports to tell the exact events that occurred upon Severus' and Lilava's entering the Other Lands, and the next part of this book recounts them. These parts I hold as truest and most worthy of telling.

V The Paths of the Dead

[Severus finds rescue from the Road of Shadows.]

Nausea struck him, and he retched, trying to fight off the clouds that covered his eyes, trying desperately to train his attention on Lilava's loving words, which gradually faded to a warm but distant purring and then to nothing. Severus felt as though he were falling, falling, falling into a chasm darker than night, darker than dreamless sleep.

He came to his senses, or what passed for them, and found himself seated upon a road. A gray landscape rose around him just visible in dull light of which he could distinguish no source. A gray plain stretched on either side beyond the road on which he sat, rising into slowly sloping hills that disappeared into a misty haze. Along the road, short, dry, gray trees bent over, as though choking on the dust, their limbs hanging like weary arms. Someone passed him, two shadows, in fact, and one spoke.

"No laziness, now, lad. You'll find rest or not at the end. Come along, eh?"

Neither waited; they passed along quickly, their dusty laughter swallowed by the haze. Severus did his best to rise to his feet and follow them.

Yes, they felt like feet, if rather numb and spongy, more like someone else's feet than his own. Several more shadows passed him. He heard them sometimes muttering, sometimes sighing, sometimes crying, sometimes grunting with resolute laughter. Feeling embarrassed at being passed by mere shades, he tried to pick up his pace, and in time he fell in beside what appeared to be two other men, with human shapes and features, though at first they had seemed little more than vague figures emerging out the mist, taking clearer shape as they went. As he walked and grew accustomed to the dull, gray light, they emerged as more fully corporeal, as did his own hand, which he held before his face to assure himself that he was conscious, not dreaming.

Shades, he thought. I must have died on the field.

He felt an intense wave of sadness, not at death, but in the fear that he should never see Lilava again. Longing and loneliness bit into him so keenly that if as a shade he could have passed out, he would have.

One of the other shades spoke to him, the voice distant and dusty but understandable as human.

"You look familiar, what? Ya. Horsa, you know this yarl?"

"Oh ya, ya: ve meet him on da British beach. He get you vit der arrow, me vit der dart. Ha, ha. Not so long till he join us, ya?"

"Ya, ya, pretty funny, dat, ya. So it goes. Who are you, soldier, and vat bad luck got you? You de bad luck vat got us. Ha, ha."

Severus knew them then for two of the pirates he'd fought at Tee's-Mouth, but they appeared to bear him no ill will whatever, so he walked with them and joined in their conversation.

"Yes, I suppose so. I am sorry about that, but then you shouldn't have attacked those poor folk."

"Ya, guess ve shouldn't, ha! But dat's our living, ya. Ve do vat Wodan and Tor say: live by the svord. Ve harry, and ve eat."

"Live by the sword; die by the sword," Severus muttered.

"Ya, dat's a good one: live by da svord, und die by da svord. Vat you tink of dat, Horsa? True enough, for you as vell as us."

"True enough," Severus said. "And what happens now?"

"Who knows?" Horsa answered. "You know, Offa?"

"Don't know notting," Offa answered with a guffaw that would have been loud had not the gray landscape swallowed it like a crust of dried bread. "Never did know noting but how to sving an axe and love a voman."

"Always look to me like you love an axe and sving a woman," Horsa joked, his snort also gobbled up by the gloom.

"Dat's you vat don't know da difference," Offa retorted, "'cause you vere good with neider. Elsa tell me you take your axe to bed and leave her outside to cut vood in der morning, ha."

"Elka say dey call you 'Offa' 'cause your horse trow you offa her."

"And Elsa say dey call you 'Horsa' 'cause sometimes you ride de horse, sometimes she ride you."

Horsa let his head fall back and grasped his belly as his long laugh trailed into the mist, swimming tunelessly from a dull choughing to something akin to the sound of fallen leaves fluttering in a winter wind. Offa slapped his friend on the back with pleasure, but he merely raised a thin cloud of dust that fell like soot upon the gray road.

Severus noticed out of the corner of his eye something oddly green that seemed to slither around one of the flaccid gray trees that stood like etiolated weeds along the road.

"And you, young soldier, son of Tor: vat your people called you?" Horsa asked Severus.

"They call — called — me 'Severus,' Sir Severus. I was a knight."

"A knight, vell! If only ve had known. Vouldn't have fought a real knight. You ever kill a knight, Offa?"

"No, not one, only ten or tventy maybe, odervise no knights at all," and the two guffawed again. "Severus, eh? Roman name. Hey, Horsa, he sure 'sever us,' don't he, ha? Sever us right from life. But somebody sever him, too, poor fellow. Just like us poor fellows, ha?"

"Ya, poor fellows, not much good to Elsa and Elke now. Hey, you, Roman boy, you have voman to mourn you?"

"Yes," Severus said slowly, "a woman lives who I believe will mourn my absence, but no more than I shall mourn hers." The thought of Lilava would have sent a shiver through him and caused his stomach to free fall, if his body had felt more substantial. He tried amidst circling thoughts to shape a prayer for Lilava, but wondered if in that place even God could hear him.

"Ya, Offa, our soldier's a lover, too. Von't do him no good now, but at least she vill mourn him — some last pleasure in dat. Hey, you not going to stop by the road and cry, eh? Ve saw dat, some vay back: two or tree folk, not going at all, just lying by da road, crying. You tink ve should stop and cry some, Offa?"

"Ya, let's stop and cry like girls who lose deir dollies, ha? Ha, ha."

"Can we stop?" Severus asked. "Now that I am walking, I hardly feel that I can. The road seems to pull me along. What does it mean?"

"Maybe good for you, maybe bad. For dem, dat you see sitting, dey can stop for now, but not forever."

"Do you feel as though you can stop if you want, Horsa?" Severus asked.

"Vant? Who vant to stop? I alvays vant to see vat Hel look like, and soon enough I know, eh, Offa?"

"Ya, Horsa, soon enough. Ve meet her vit our head up, eh, ya? Her and all her frost giants, ha!"

"Vit head up. And ve give her such a battle shout so all de dead vill hear us coming."

The two pirates shouted for all they were worth, but their voices, which would have rung over land or sea, faded like shadows into midnight.

"Der ve find her, lads, vatever she is," Offa said.

For what seemed to Severus like a long while, the three men, shades or men, walked together. They talked as though they had known one another for years. Offa and Horsa joked, and Severus tried to clear his thoughts, which drifted ever back to Lilava.

Finally, ahead Severus observed what appeared as a black cloud, a null darkness that emerged from the gray landscape into more gray shadows. Again Severus noted something along the side of the road, something making sinuous curves between a pair of brackish trees that had somehow leaned together and intertwined. He caught but a glimpse, but he sensed the thing: beast. Beast of some sort, but not malicious, like something he had sensed before in life — life! — but not exactly like: cool, ophidian, aware, intelligent. Two red, glowing eyes just caught his.

"Vat's der?" Offa hissed to Horsa, drawing Severus' attention back to his walking companions.

Either Severus' eyes had adjusted to the dull light, or they were closing more quickly than he'd expected toward some force or boundary. The road ahead seemed to funnel into a slowly moiling black chasm.

Severus heard from ahead of them, seemingly from amidst the chasm, a sound like a wailing cry. "What's that, I wonder?" he said, barely audibly even to himself. He heard something like singing, in the distance, soft to his ear as lambswool. He realized that he had begun to feel his feet again, and a breeze, which he had not felt since he had regained his senses in the gray landscape, blew warm and rejuvenating over his face.

"I don't hear noting," Horsa said, "dough I listen. But I see: deep and dark — deep and dark and cold. Hey, you, ya, Sev'rus: your face look funny. Brighter dan before. You sure you supposed to valk dis road now? I tink not, maybe, eh, Offa?"

Again Severus felt a breath of breeze, and notes of a song, soft and longing, distant but trenchant, played in his ears. Warmth scattered through his limbs, touching here and there the gray cold of his shade, until he felt himself breathe with a jerk of air into his lungs.

"Come back, Severus, come back to me! Don't desert me, my love! We have come too far, tried too hard. Severus, oh!"

Light seemed to draw itself around him like water, and he bobbed upward, the sound of real human voices, warm and alive, rinsing his ears of the dust of the gray road.

"Farewell, Severus, Tor's son soldier! Vish us vell on the black road!"

Without time to reply, but wishing well, Severus heard no more of Offa and Horsa as he felt himself yanked back into the silvery light of day, the hint of two red, phosphorescent eyes lingering in his thoughts.

"I do. I do, and forgive me," he said as his eyes opened to see the face of Arawn bent toward his, the brow wet and gleaming, the eyes focused, intent. He felt hands wrapped around his head, and knew the smell of the skin: Lilava cradled his head in her lap.

"Forgive you for what?" Arawn asked.

"Thank God and elven medicine!" Lilava said, and the sigh that escaped her lips fell over Severus face like warm water.

"My one dear, Lilava: that's you?" Severus tried to turn his eyes up to see her face.

"Of course. I thought we'd lost you. Your face had turned gray with — with blood loss and pain."

"What did you see?" Arawn asked, coolly seeking information once he had brought his patient back to the living world.

"Maybe we should let him rest?" Lilava asked. "Though of course I thank you with all my heart for what you've done, great king, he deserves a rest before questions."

"My folk know little of the fate of humans beyond this life. For knowledge's sake I would have him speak what he has seen before the images pass from his memory. What do you do, and who must forgive you?"

Lilava tried to hold Severus still, but the knight waved his hand to suggest that he felt all right. He raised himself to his elbows and paused to look into her eyes: they were grim and tired and still wet with tears. He saw that for his sake she forced a smile to her lips, but in those tired, dark eyes he saw more than a smile: he saw love and impossible, unexpected relief and exhausted joy. He tried to return her smile, then turned back to Arawn.

"I do wish them well, and I asked them to forgive me."

"Asked whom?"

"The pirates. Two of those I killed on the way to Joyous Guard."

Lilava gave him a long draft of fresh spring water, such water as flows on in the streams of the Other Lands, and then Severus told them the whole story, from his journey after he and Lilava had parted until his waking. Arawn spared him rehearsing the battle, which he had seen and already related to Lilava.

"Interesting." Arawn said. Lilava merely nodded.

"You have seen it before, haven't you?" Severus asked her. The recognition in her eyes was undeniable.

"Please, love, try to sleep now. We will have much time for talk after we have drawn you fully back among the living."

"You have seen the Gray Road. How? Why? But tell me first, please, how you brought me back."

"Lilava has many abilities, in this case aided by the power of love," Arawn interrupted. "I have some abilities that come from my office, granted me by the Eternals who watch over this place. I breathed the air of life back into you. You were strong enough to respond, and your love for Lilava was great enough that your spirit, once we reached it, flew back to her of its own accord. I have heard of the Road of Shadows, the Road of the Dead, before, but have known few to return from it. Are you sure of what you saw?"

"I'm not convinced that it was more than a dream. It felt real at the time — as dreams sometimes can."

"Yet dreams may mirror truth. Regardless: now that you have wakened, I welcome you to my lands."

Severus clasped Arawn's hand in thanks, and he kissed Lilava gently on the lips, and then he dropped into a profound and healing sleep.

"I, too, must rest now," Arawn sighed.

"And I," Lilava responded. "Here next to him."

* * *

"The elf king gave a good deal of his strength to bring you back," Lilava said. Both had slept for what seemed to them like days. Food and drink from Arawn's tables was restoring them both as Spring does the green fields. Lilava and Severus walked arm in arm under a copse of brilliant linden trees, and Lilava pulled him closer to feel the slowly returning warmth of his body.

"So did you," Severus said.

"But that was mine to give and yours to take. Arawn made a sacrifice for you: his strength comes from his tie to this land, and the place itself breathes power — you wouldn't have recovered so quickly in Britain, if at all. He borrowed energy from the place, mediated it through himself into you. In the future he will lack something of what he had."

"I'm sorry he did so," Severus said. "I wouldn't wish to inconvenience him, especially since he has brought you to safety. I owe him my life. Him and you."

"You gave my people a new life, free of fear of the Chimaera, and you have given me love: you owe me nothing, and I would do the same for you a thousand times over and more. But you may owe Arawn recompense for his gift — though I would warn you of the need for prudence: beware of giving up too much in return. Others give of their own accord; if the time comes when you must give, give as he did: because you wish, not because you believe you must."

"Do you speak as a counselor or as a wife?"

"Hmm. Let's keep walking. We can talk about it, and the exercise will help us regain our energies."

"I have been thinking of the Chimaera," Severus said some time later, a vague notion of red eyes hovering at the edge of his memory. "It haunts my dreams more than does the Road of the Dead — of that journey I can remember more of what you told me I said than of what I saw myself. But the Chimaera: where has it gone? Whom does it haunt now? And your people: is there a chance they were better off with the Chimaera than without it? Lacking the fear inspired by the monster, will more populous, better armed neighbors besiege them, hoping now to have the chance to subjugate them?"

"We can't think that way," Lilava sighed. "We must remove the immediate dangers, then deal with others as they arise. The world has never treated anyone with kindness for long. New — I almost said 'tasks' — challenges arise, and we must do our best to meet them, enjoying the time we have. Haven't we had this conversation before, on the beaches of Valencia?"

"Yes, but they have returned to my thoughts again. Notice: you have made me a thinker. Once only a soldier blundering along from monster to monster, trying not to hurt anyone who got in the way, I have become a philosopher. You're right to laugh. That exaggerates my efforts a bit. I must make sure that action doesn't inhibit my ability to think, and that thought doesn't restrict my ability to act quickly and precisely. Perhaps that's why few thinkers make good soldiers. Sad to think of it: violence without thought brings horror, but thought without action brings malaise — yet each hinders the other. Such thoughts keep returning to me: how to balance the changing aspects of myself and yet remain myself. That's funny: until Valencia I'd never even thought that I have a 'self.' We must talk with Arawn regarding these problems."

"And others. I get the feeling that something else is agitating you."

"You have often shown me a talent for empathy."

"You often glance aside as though something else has entered your field of vision, and yet I can see nothing there."

"A memory, vague, from the Road of Shadows: a creature, I think, serpentine, with glowing red eyes. Don't know if it was real or dream. Still don't know if the whole thing was a dream. That's hard, when you can't tell if the image that haunts you comes from waking or sleeping. And I sense something out of balance here, but I don't know what, whether the problem lies in me or in this place. I find myself often saying 'I don't know,' probably because when I try to understand what I'm sensing, I don't understand it."

"One thing you know." Lilava smiled at Severus.

"Yes, love, one thing I know."

As they strolled into an apple grove showered in the peculiar silvery-gold light of the Other Lands, they found Arawn leaning against a tree and munching on a bright red fruit from one of the trees. They bowed, and he nodded in return.

"After all the ages I have lived here, I still love these things," he said, smiling as he swallowed a bite of apple. "Yes," said the king, "now that you are recovering, we have much to discuss. We must not hurry action, but we must take counsel. Even here, in these beautiful lands, my beloved country far from the crowding desires of people, a new trouble rises, though yet far to the east. Here, have some fruit — I think you will like this one — and we will walk and talk together."

* * *

"Tell me what troubles you," Severus said, looking into the king's large, dark eyes as the three of them strolled under the trees. "Lilava hinted at what you lost in saving my life. For your sacrifice I'm grateful, but I fear that for your own sake you have given up too much."

"Not so much for my sake as for that of my folk, who depend on me. Royals here in what your people call the Other Lands have rather different responsibilities than do your kings. In one sense we are the land: with the acceptance of kingship comes the ritual of Tir-banna, what you would call an 'earth-bond,' a deeper link to the landscape, to the place, than have any other of elvenkind. The bond gives us the ability to borrow energy from the land, to draw power from it into ourselves for defense against the elements, against outsiders, against chaotic forces. You have already noticed I'm sure that bad weather seldom troubles us here: with the earth-bond we can limit it.

"But occasionally some difficulty arises that taxes the king's abilities, and on rare occasions such a problem may exceed his strength, particularly if some recent event or service to another has drained it. I sense that you perceive the truth of what I speak, if so far but dimly. I am weaker than when we met after your battle with Lancelot. And you have sensed something out of balance here, in my lands, something distant but disturbing."

"He has," Lilava spoke for Severus. "But he has a long way to go to regain his own strength yet."

"I know," replied Arawn, "and I would loathe to shift any of my own responsibilities to another, particularly a human, if I had any hope of fulfilling them. Like you, I need to recover, even as another necessity calls me elsewhere in my kingdom."

"What may I do to help you?" Severus asked.

"Love, right now you're ready for nothing but rest and recovery," Lilava interrupted.

"Yes, I know," Severus answered, taking a deep breath. "Yet when I can, because I owe this king a debt, I will readily repay it. He has brought me back to you from the shadows. He did, in that sense, answer my prayer, the only one I made on the Gray Road."

"I did not answer your prayer, Severus. That power lies beyond me. But I did what I could for you, and I hope that, in return, once you have recovered, you will assist me where your powers exceed mine."

"I will," Severus responded, shivering slightly with a sudden chill.

"He will, and so will I," Lilava added, shaking her head sadly but resignedly.

And Arawn told them of growing Troubles, of strange energies and whisperings, of threats and thievery and sudden attacks in the Northern Forest, of strange creatures and portents along the coast to the west, and of strangers and spies in the east.

VI Body Temperature

[Severus convalesces and undertakes a new adventure to repay his hosts.]

"Cold," Severus mumbled. "Probably the worst of it is that I always feel cold. I didn't so much notice the feeling there, while I was walking on the Gray Road, but now I can never quite shake it, though the chest wound feels as though it has healed completely." He exaggerated that point to ease Lilava's concern.

"Time will help, time and, I hope, my presence, and this soup" Lilava said, smiling. They sat together over steaming bowls of vegetable soup.

"Secret family recipe?" Severus asked.

"It will be."

"The smell alone is heavenly. No, that's not it: homey, that's the word for it, homey."

"Pretty simple stuff, really."

"That suits me. Homey: funny word, that, especially for someone like me. I'm not sure I've even known what home means, except that it must be wherever you are."

Lilava leaned over and kissed him.

They sat together over their light but satisfying supper in a comfortable room with a tall window that allowed them to relax and gaze at the emerging stars. The last purple of sunset lingered in the sky to their left. The room abutted the large, pleasant apartment that Arawn had allotted them off the northwest end of his great hall — Severus had always particularly loved the northern sky, where on occasion in his journeys he had watched great waves of light that people called aurora-nacht dance and shimmer. Trees stood to the east of their sightline, but directly north the hills rolled gently upward as though creating a pathway into the sky, as if some magic mariner could use them to sail off to the stars. Beyond where they could see, Arawn had told them the Great Northern Forest stretched vast and dark.

Severus wore a cloak over his shoulders, though the gentle breeze that eased through the window bore warmth rather than cold. Occasionally he would shiver, then he would dip his spoon again into the soup, which swathed the edges but not the depths of the death-chill that Lilava tried to cleanse from him.

As he glanced to the northeast, into the trees, Severus thought he saw a wisp of sinuous green glow.

"I wonder what that is," he mumbled.

"What do you see?" Lilava asked, following his sightline with her eyes and rubbing his forehead with her warm fingers.

"Not sure. It reminds me of something I think I saw along the Gray Road."

"A creature, green and glowing?"

"You've seen it?"

"No, but you've mumbled about it. It seems seldom to leave your thoughts."

"Do you think it's real?"

"I don't know, but I can see that to you it has substance and meaning. What do you think it is?"

"Can it be a spirit that has followed me back from the Gray Lands?"

"I wonder. A thought has crossed my mind... ."

"Chimaera."

When he whispered it, Lilava almost leaped from her chair. Her face looked almost white in the growing moonlight. "It can't be that — can it?"

"No," Severus said, drawing out the syllable and slowly shaking his head. "Doesn't feel like that. I don't think I could ever mistake that feeling. The Chimaera has a deep resonance of absence more than presence, of chasm, abyss, as if one were standing at the edge and the ground beneath one's feet were giving away. Fighting it, I felt as though I were tumbling into a hot, fetid mouth, and the teeth were closing tightly. It feels like the weight of fear and confusion and disgust all at once, with one's legs rooted to the spot, shaking and unable to move."

"You certainly moved in its presence," Lilava said, moving toward the window and peering out. "I have never seen anyone move so quickly — almost super-naturally. Much faster than you moved against Lancelot, though there I saw you only from a distance as I hurried to reach you in time."

"I felt odd, as though I were fighting myself. The — beast — its malice, willed me to melt into my own tracks, but instead of stilling me, its malice pulled me taut, as though I were a stone in a child's slingshot, and the monster's own desire to harm shot me toward it like a lightning bolt, more than could my will alone — that, of course, and the power I drew from your presence: whilst I had a drop of blood in my veins, I wouldn't have let it nearer you than I could possibly prevent."

"My dear one. But you don't feel that presence — or that absence — now?"

"I don't. But I feel a force that I don't know, an odd thing: spiralling, will-of-the-wisp, frivolous, but not foolish, the way you feel after someone has just played a joke on you and everyone laughs, but you're not quite sure why."

"I've never had that happen to me."

"Forgive me. I feel so close to you that I forget that others find you dangerous and frightening. Even king Arthur's knights wouldn't play a joke on you."

"The ladies would, but then they would regret it."

"What would you do to them?"

"Oh, nothing — just make my eyes go round like pinwheels or make my hair stand up on end and float about in wavy black flames. I wouldn't turn them into salamanders or anything really awful."

"You can't."

"You sure?"

"Of course. You've taught me enough about magic to know better than that."

"I shouldn't give away so many professional secrets. Keeping up a reputation is almost as important as actually having the ability to use the spells. Fear can have as great effect as any magic or manual skill. Hey: I think I did see something out there, among the trees: chartreuse, with two tiny glowing red coals like eyes. Sevy, come look... ."

A gentle knock at the door interrupted them. The door opened slowly, and Arawn stuck in his head. "May we come in?"

"Of course," Lilava answered.

Arawn, dressed in a stately, purple evening robe that fell all the way to the floor, covering all but the ends of his toes, entered, and behind him fol-lowed Prosperpina, his queen. They had so rarely seen the queen that Severus jumped to his feet, and both he and Lilava bowed deeply and formally to their hosts. Severus forgot to offer the formal greeting, but Lilava as always came through for him. Elven queens, you see, are even more retiring than elven kings. By choice they seldom leave their intimate circles, even to greet the most important of guests. They have a grander presence than their kings: in their company one feels profoundly connected to the world and its history. Senses heighten, breathing deepens, the heart beats slowly and powerfully, the limbs feel light and supple, and the mind feels calm and attentive. So we can forgive poor Severus, both inexperienced and weary, for merely standing there gaping at his hosts.

"Miralla lanna, Lei maradal la plenu-ere zhamas." Lilava not only knew exactly the right thing to say, but also spoke it fluently in Old Elvish. From the bit of Elvish Severus had heard, he thought he recognized a version of the ritual greeting of respect; he guessed the words meant something like, "Great Lady, your presence here graces us forever," but he could do no more than nod his assent. He felt his face shape itself into a smile with no conscious effort on his part.

The lady's laughter fell smoothly as water from a bubbling fountain. "Dear guests," she said in Severus' Cymric language, "how kind of you to greet me in my own tongue. Few folks but the elves learn it these days, and fewer still remember it. I should so enjoy sitting with you for a bit, if I may."

Severus' voice cracked as he tried to regain his manners, but he pressed on as best he could. His first impulse was to try the Elvish, but he quickly realized the futility of such an effort and fell into the Cymric he knew they all could understand and in which he would be less likely to fumble. "May the sun light your path and the moon soothe your dreams," he said, hoping he had got the phrase right. "Please accept my chair, Great Lady, while I find another for your lord. May friendship fill our days."

"Elvish tongue or no, gallant knight, you have captured our spirit, and I thank you for those kind words."

Lilava beamed at her knight, proud that whatever words he lacked, he showed no shortage of grace. Severus saw in her eyes the emotion she seldom spoke, and its power over him made the monster fighter's knees grow weak. The gentle, silvery plash of the queen's laughter echoed in his ears, as he drew his eyes from Lilava's loving face and stumbled after a chair for Arawn. Lilava poured the king a drink from their table, and she and Severus waited politely for their hosts to speak.

"I'm sorry to disturb you so late, my dear friends," Arawn said softly. "But trouble has not only crossed our borders, but spread, and I fear it will not pause for our deliberations."

"It comes, you see, not from our lands, but from yours," Prosperpina said. "The signs tell us that we can slow it, but not still it. We do not yet know what it is, but we know that it purposes harm and will fall only before something — how can I say this — something closer to its own nature."

Lilava leaned back against the window sill. Something in the look in Prosperpina's eyes caused her to tremble, and she had to exert her will to stop shaking. Something about those eyes, brown, but with a green, mossy glow, Lilava thought: why do they look familiar?

"Tell me more, please," said Severus.

* * *

With the aid of a palliative sleeping draft that Arawn had prepared for him, Severus had got such a rest as he hadn't known in months, and he slept past lunch the next day. When he rose, Lilava had gone, and so he washed, then went immediately to the stables to collect the arms he and Arawn had discussed the night before. Outside the stables by the armory he found Lilava debating with a smith about the virtues of a shield she was none too happily examining.

"Too small," she said, "and hardly likely to repel flame."

"Light and strong," the smith countered, "and not designed for flame — the shell and armor must do that. Feel the slick surface."

"Hardly impervious to steel, sir, nor particularly warm against cold nights," Lilava said, shaking her head and squeezing between her fingers s thin, black, skin-like cloth that Severus guessed must either cushion or replace body armor.

"That's why we have the shield," the smith explained in a tone that suggested he had obviously made that point before. Tall as a tree, he towered over her, bending down so that they stood almost face to face. Lilava stood with one hand on her hip, peering up at him, a look on her face like that of a child who intends to scale a tree and leap down into the garden beyond. "Each accoutrement serves its own purpose, and the skillful knight must know the virtue and limitations of each."

"We don't seem quite to understand each other here," Lilava continued, but Severus interrupted.

"Lovely lady, you fear that the king's smith won't take adequate care of me?"

"Well, Mr. Sleeping Beauty, good thing for you that someone's watching out for you. I may yet save you a good toasting."

"You have before, and no doubt you will again." Severus felt the grain of the thin leather armor that the smith had prepared for him as the elf gazed down into his face, expecting more trouble such as he had got from Lilava. "Fine work — it must fit nearly skin-tight: thank you, sir." The smith nodded crisply but said nothing, apparently wondering if complaints would follow. Lilava frowned.

"May I try the shield?" Severus spun it several times, thrust it forward, upward, downward, struck it in several spots with the side of his fist. "Light and firm, but a bit smallish perhaps." Lilava nodded, and the smith frowned darkly. "May I see what else you have?" Severus quite liked the shield, but knew he must placate Lilava as well as the smith, so he sought a compromise with both. He could see that the smith had labored over the exact size of the finely wrought leather suit, so he could hardly turn it down; he could, though, humph and hoom and nod sagely over the collection of shields that the smith showed him hanging on walls of his workshop. Severus tried three or four, then finally selected one a bit larger than the one the smith had proposed. Large enough to cover head and torso, it had a fine coating of unpolished metal, thin enough that the shield remained maneuverable, but sufficient to keep the linden substrate from burning on the outside. Lilava looked at him, apparently feeling somewhat better about that choice, though short of certain. "Don't worry about me, dear Lila: that sleep has made a new man of me, and this fine gear shall keep the new man alive."

"I'd feel better if you had a few more days to rest and exercise," she said hesitatingly.

"So would I. But I appreciate Arawn's anxiety, and I have enough of my own that I want to get busy and find what we have out there. Sir," he said to the smith, "has the king a horse that will suit me?"

"I doubt it," said the smith dourly, "but I will certainly try. Perhaps the lady knows horses as well as she knows armor," he mumbled petulantly. Lilava humphed, and they entered the stables.

An hour later Severus stood at the gate with Arawn and a small retinue, and with his arm around Lilava's waist. "I'll return as soon as I can, lord, at least with news if nothing else. Whether the sorties your guardians report come from elves or men or monsters, I should be able to tell as soon as I encounter them. What strength they have I must test by arms."

"We seldom encounter men here — they know not how to find us. And elves do not cause such restlessness among ourselves. You can determine better than we what sort of difficulties monsters may present, for I feel sure that we face an extraordinary enemy. While you try the shores to the west, my soldiers and I shall search the forests to the east. Our bravest scouts patrol the Great Forest to the north. Lilava shall accompany Prosperpina south: there our wisest folk gather from all over the kingdom to share the bits of knowledge they have acquired. We may hope to know from them if the Troubles represent some kind of unified threat or mere random acts that by chance have converged on us — common attacks we may disburse by conventional means.

207

"Truly, my heart bodes ill, or I should not have hurried you in your recovery. These lands have held secure for many centuries, and they have provided safe haven not only for us, but for the various peoples of the world in their time of greatest need, as you have found yourself. We must remain, if not impregnable, at least stern in our resistance. We cannot allow the chaos without to infiltrate this bastion of calm resiliency. Not only our lives, but the shape of the world depends on our ability to stand firm. Ride safely, friends, and may the sun light your path."

"And the moon soothe your dreams," the others answered in chorus.

Arawn called his horsemen to him, and with a wave to Severus and Lilava, he led their swift, light-footed mounts north around the walls and toward the east.

Severus and Lilava allowed themselves a long, passionate kiss.

"Don't worry," he said. "I'm fine. The tiredness will fade as I ride and rebuild my muscles."

"I wish you had Courage with you. I have always particularly trusted that horse," Lilava said.

"Ah, poor Courage. Arawn told me that his squire placed the dear fellow with Sir Lancelot before he left him, after our battle. I hope Lancelot sees the horse's worth and treats him accordingly."

"If not, Dancer shall rescue him," Lilava smiled.

"In that case, I hope she already has. Meanwhile, Starlight here is a fine horse, too, eh?" The elf-trained horse whinnied, shook her head and stamped her foot. Shall we run then, you and I?" Severus leaped into the saddle, reached down to touch Lilava's hand, then turned and rode west, urging Starlight on to test her speed, and he wasn't disappointed. Lilava watched after them until they disappeared beyond the range even of her excellent sight. Interesting, she thought, that the elves should call their uncertainties "The Troubles," as if such upsets to their lives occurred seldom — for her and Severus trouble had long seemed a way of life. When she could see Severus no longer, a tear dropped to the grass at her feet.

* * *

For some time Starlight ran without tiring. When some hours later they reached a dale and a copse of trees, Severus dismounted and uncorked a water-skin for each of them. The knight allowed the horse to move about untethered, while he sat down and leaned against a tree to enjoy the pleasant warmth of the late afternoon sun. In those lands, Severus thought, the sun shone a gentle milky gold, the perfect sunlight to lull a man weary with endless travel and fighting into a nap. Echoes and images darted, warped, and melded as he fell into swirling dreams.

208

The Gray Road and endless shadows, walking, walking, dust clouds at his feet; ya, ya, he sever us, don't he, dat Roman? blasted trees, gray, slouching, too dry and crumbled to weep; dragon, teeth and fire; I am a vampire — ha! poor old blighter with his satchel, sitting at the roadside; wolves, many wolves, salivating; rain, rain, go away, come again some other day; deep brown eyes — Lilava, the soft skin of her cheek, the rich smell of her hair, the warmth of her embrace; cold, the dead swirling, cold, and giants hiding among the snowbanks; snowbanks turning gray, growing into hills, hills that grow into mountains, down from the mountain the enormous shape, lion, troll, Chimaera! neighing, someone, something neighing nearby — something wrong? sweat on the brow and into the eyes, wet eyes, twitch, clear the vision, twitch! what's there?

Before his mind fully woke, Severus' arm shot forward, and he grasped his fingers tightly around the neck of something that had lowered itself down before his face.

He fought the dull gray of sleep, willed his eyes open.

A long, green, glowing head, upside down. Small, round red eyes. A tongue shot out and licked his face.

"Leggo my t'roat, you brute!"

"Who?"

"Too soon for da' — leggo you me! ffffft." The tongue shot out and licked his face again.

"Stop that — ugh."

"Den leggo, leggo: I don' hurt you!"

Awake now, Severus saw that he held some sort of creature by the throat as it hung upside down, clinging by a long, prehensile foot. It glowed green, with the exceptions of a long, pink belly and small, round, red eyes — yes, red eyes — that fixed themselves on Severus' face. He yanked the creature down, so that it lost its foothold on the limb above, but feeling himself oddly in no danger, he twisted his fist around and set the creature down on its feet in front of him.

He had seen it before: on the Gray Road and among the trees. It stretched out wide, gray-green wings as if to uncramp them, shook itself, sneezed twice, and spoke.

"No need to grip so tight, silly silly fellow. You in no dangeah from me, mahn."

"You licked my face."

"Could have bitten off youah nose nose nose, bitten it right off if I want to, mahn." The beast made slithering motions up and down its body, so that it seemed to vibrate in waves. "Ha, ha: you sleep in the middle of the day, like a baby, but I don' blame you, baby — you come back from the Path of the Dead.

Not mucha anybody come back from deah, no' but me. I come and go as I please. Hey: guess what I am. Guess guess."

"Hmm: dragon of some sort, I should say by the look, smallish. At least now I know you're not just some phantom of my imagination. I saw you on the road, and I've seen you since then, lurking."

"Lurking? Not a nice word. Le's say watching, waiting. Le's say protecting."

"You, protecting me? From what? There's no one else here."

"Yah, man, nobody — but deah might have been, might have been been been, might have been ... Ooo." The odd creature repeated itself, singing, shuffled its feet in quick little dance steps, spun round twice on one foot, knelt on one knee and threw its wings wide, as though waiting for Severus' applause.

Severus, confused, tried at least to be polite. The beast — no, not really a beast — apparently intended no harm, and Severus sensed none. "You're a fine dancer, my good — ah.... ." Severus didn't know what to call the creature, nor did he know whether to think of it as friend, assailant, or passing curiosity.

"Guess again, guess what I am. 'Dragon' he says, funny funny. Yah, guess, guess! Yah, mahn, you nevah seen the likes of me befoah, huh? Guess guess guess."

"I don't know. Can you tell me?"

"Guess guess guess."

"Well, at first I thought you were a Chimaera, but ..."

"Ah, mahn, shhh!" The creature placed its wing tip to its mouth. "Don' even say dat name, bad fellow! Be sensible, mista monstah specialis' who don' even know me when he see me."

"I should know you?"

"You should, you should know, you should know me, yah yah." The creature sung its lyric, danced a few quick steps, tried a triple spin and tripped itself. "Blas' — still have trouble wid da triple. Ha, da' funny: 'trouble wid da triple.'"

"Do you have a name?"

"Impolite little knight! You don' know me da' well to be askin' my name. But I tell you somethin', yeah I tell you somethin', yeah yeah."

"What will you tell me?"

"Wyvahnn."

"Why what?"

"Wyvahn. You would say: 'wyverrrn.' Oo, das' a hahd sound to make, like a dog growlin'! Das' what I be: wyvern. Da's it, yah, da's me."

"Wyvern," Severus said, searching his memory.

"Yah, smaht guy. Look: see da sleek body? See da wings? See da bee-ay-u-tiful pink belly? See da long, clawed feet? See da bright red eyes and da fetchin' green cullah? Oh ya, wyvern, da's me!"

"Wyvern — yes, wyvern! I remember. I had thought you a myth."

"Myt! No, mahn, no myt. Why, you myt me when I no' show up? Ha, you myt me? Oh, mahn, I crack myself up!" The wyvern fell on its back and held its shaking pink belly as it laughed and laughed. Suddenly it stopped laughing, held up its head, and stared at Severus. "Okay, mahn, you seem okay to me, bu' a little dumb, maybe. Ahsk me my name."

"All right. What's your name?"

"Ah, mahn, you think I gonna tell you my name?"

"You told me to ask. Sorry if I offended."

"Sokay. Ask anyway."

"I am asking, please."

"Why, Vern."

"Your name is Wyvern? You told me you are a wyvern."

"No, silly fellow. My name. Verrrn."

"Your name is Vern? Vern the wyvern. Not very imaginative, that."

"Ask me why," the wyvern said, trying to look inscrutable. "Ask me why dey name me Vern."

"All right. Why Vern?"

"I don' know, mahn, I don' know. Must have been unimaginative parents."

"Did you ever ask them why?"

"Oh, no man: bery bad mannahs to ask a wyvern dat. I have to teach you everyting, mahn?"

"Not everything." Severus tried to think of something he knew unequivocally.

"Whatchew know, mahn?"

"Well, I know someone who loves me."

"Oh, I know, mahn. Da' one sweetiepie wife you got: she full of spit and shimmy. Good ting for you I a wyvern an' no mahn, or I steal her away from you."

"Will you tell me why you're here, and why you were hanging from this tree with your face immediately opposite mine?"

"Oh, you too hasty. Le's dance a bit firs.'" The wyvern hummed a tune, did several more steps, tried the triple spin again and got it without stumbling. "Ah, mahn, you see dat! Parfit triple! Oh, dis fellow can dahnce, mahn, don' you think, don' you think?"

"Yes, quite impressive. Now about my question ..."

"Mahn, I already tol' you: watchin'; protectin'."

"Protecting me from what?"

"Anating."

"Anything?"

"Yah, anathhing. Da's anudda hahd sound in youah language, but I can make it sometime, thhh. You tell me: anathing bothah you while you take youah little nappy?"

"No one but you."

"Tha's right, an' nobody would have, 'cause I heah to stop dem so you get youah rest, get your rest, get your little beauty sleep — mahn, you need da' beauty sleep! ooo — an' den you ready to fight again."

"Fight what?"

The wyvern pulled in its feet, fluttered its wings fast as those of a humming-bird, and hovered before Severus, staring at him.

"Fight what?" Severus repeated. "Can't you tell me, or won't you?"

"Ah, mahn, to tell you true, and I always tell you true, I don' know wha'."

"How can I fight it if I don't know what it is? Do you know if something dangerous has reached the borders of this land, the trouble that so concerns King Arawn? Tell me, please, if you know."

"Embarrassed, mahn. Oh, I don' know I don' know I don' know. I can't tell no more than he can, though I should know bettah. I been all round wit' da livin' and da dead, but I'm no' sure, mahn. It look like a mahn, it smell like a mahn, but it got something else wid it, something much more dangerous. Don' doubt me now, mahn, for I tell you true, tell you, tell you true: something very bad, probably a mahn, dis guy, a sea captain, and something else, too. He come by ship to dee beaches west of heah. He not even supposed to be heah. Human, like you, but he got something wit' him, ya, mahn, something very bahd."

To Severus the wyvern actually looked worried, and his tone echoed absolute sincerity.

"I'll do better if I have a sense of what it is before I fight it. I've seen my share of monsters and bad men, sea captains among them."

"You da monsta' fighta, mahn, and you da mahn, too. You go get him, an' I go wid' you."

"You say he came here by ship, a human, but with something odd about him — or with him?" Severus felt strange about calling a fellow human odd in the presence of a creature so unusual as the wyvern.

"Ya, mahn, da's it, big ship, big sails, no' alone."

"Have you seen him?"

"Oh, ya, of cahse I seen him, from a distance, but dees eyes very good, oui."

"I wonder. A short man, round face, receding hairline, cold brown eyes. Pilots a large ship with golden sails? Don't know if you heard him, but he talks with a hiss."

"Ooo, mahn, you mus' be smahter dan you look: das' da bery mahn, berry-berry mahn, mahn, an' ship wit da golden sails. You know dis guy?"

"I think I do. Calls himself the Witch King. Abra, Abracadabrax: that's his name."

"Oh, you know dis guy's name? Da' will help us."

"A bit. But I wonder what else he has with him. You say he's not alone, and I have had a feeling of something dangerous lurking about. Abra must have more power than I thought for him to have got to these shores at all."

"Yah, mahn, I think he got some sort of powa' moah dan his own. You got to find out."

"We must find out. You know where he is?"

"Yah, mahn, da's what I meant, we. I know wheah he was, and we can staht from deah'."

"Yes," Severus said, "we can start from there. Though first I must find my horse, which you seem to have scared away."

"Sorry, mahn, but I'm no' tha' scary, am I?"

"No, not so very scary."

"No? But a little bit scary, oui, mahn?"

"Yes, a little bit scary. Scary enough. All right, pretty scary, but in a friendly way." He could tell the wyvern didn't believe him. "Well, you're less scary now that I know who you are, and you've trusted me with your name. That helps."

"Well, mahn, you betta' hope I get scary, 'cause we gonna need everythin' we got 'gainst dis dude and whatevah he got wid' him. Hey, mahn, you look warmah than you did: little beauty sleep musta been good for something."

VII Old Friends, Old Fiends

[... wherein Severus rescues Courage, but finds another problem.]

"Hey, mahn, how come you no' tell me your name, now I tol' you mine?" The wyvern asked Severus, after about an hour's unsuccessful hunt for the horse Starlight. The wyvern floated alongside the knight, his wings flapping rapidly but nearly silently.

Dusk was giving way to night, and the only Starlight they found fell from above.

"You already know my name. You've been following me around at least since the Paths of the Dead."

"I tho' you offer to tell anyway, jus' to be polite."

"Sure and I'm wondering what else you know about me of which I'm not aware."

"I know wha' my good eyes an' my good eahs can learn. Da's more dan mos' folk can say."

"What do your eyes and ears tell you about Starlight?"

"Da' stahlight deah for everybody to see, mahn."

"I mean the horse, the one I rode here."

"Oh, dat — I dunno, mahn." Then the wyvern burped loudly.

Severus looked at him, astonished. "Tell me you didn't."

"Didn' what, mahn?"

"I heard you burp."

"Burp? Oh, yeah, I was jus' eatin' a few berries and such while we hunt tru da trees. Why, you — oh, no, mahn, tell me you don' think tha' I ate her, da hoahsey! Ah, come on: you know I don' — how can you say, even think, such a thing! Da' I would eat — oh, you not such a nice fellow afta all, to think tha'. Bahd fellow, bahd!"

"So what happened to her then?"

"I not talkin' to you no more." The red eyes that had watched Severus so carefully turned away from him, and the wyvern alit on his feet, folded his wings across his chest, and stood still.

"Well, forgive me, but what am I supposed to think?"

"You no judge of charactah, mahn."

"It's those red eyes of yours."

"Red eyes? You got a thing about folk wid red eyes? So da's it, eh? You one a' dem. Fellow's got red eyes, you right way think he eat hoahses. Fine thing, afta

215

I protect you while you beauty sleepin'. You don' like red eyes, and you da one need da beauty sleep. Yick! Bery bahd."

"No, no — my goodness, but you jump to conclusions. Look here, now — just look here!"

The wyvern slowly turned its face back toward Severus, but he kept his eyes shut tight.

"Open your eyes, please, and look at me."

After a moment, the eyes sprung open, shining bright red, but to Severus the expression didn't look happy.

"Please listen: I didn't mean to imply anything about the color of your eyes, which in fact I quite admire. I simply don't know how to read the expression. After meeting hundreds of be — ah, creatures of all sorts, I've never encountered eyes so ... distinguished. Yes, that's the word: distinguished. So I just need time to understand their, ah, nuances.

"You really mean dat, mahn, or you jus' playin' wid me?"

"Not at all: with such impressive eyes you must be a prince among your folk. I mean that sincerely." Now some people saying such a thing might have intended merely to placate their companion, but Severus did his best to mean what he said. "Please forgive me if I have insulted you. I've done so twice already, but, believe me, I intended neither instance. I'm a bit overwrought with worry about Starlight, the horse that is. She's a fine creature, and the King was kind enough to allow me her help, and I'd feel terrible if any harm came to her."

"No worries, mahn, ho hahm: she run home houahs ago."

"What: you saw her, and you didn't tell me?"

"I tho' you figure it out eventually, an' I wan' you to feel like you gave a good effaht. Turns out you polite enough, jus' no' so smaht."

"So people have told me."

"It's okay, mahn. You a distinguished looking creachah, too, in youah way. No' that I think so, you unnastan' — I figah you mus' be to have such a hot looking wifey as you got. To me you look kinna bland: no' much cullah."

"Thank you very much."

"Youah welcome."

"Now what am I to do for a horse?"

"Look like you gotta go back, or go on widout one. If you ahsk me, you do bettah wid'out one, anyway. About an houah's flyin' from here we get to da shoah, you know?"

"An hour's flying to the shore. You intend to carry me?"

216

"No way, mahn. Oh, da's right: you canno' fly, ha ha. Well, we find you some food and watah, get you a little moah beauty sleep, and in da morning I take you deah — I fly, you run. Good foah dee muscles, ha?"

* * *

In the morning Severus did run, following Vern the wyvern at as rapid a pace as he could keep.

"You not a bad runnah for a human, you know?"

"Ran pretty well when I was younger — puff — through the old forests of Britain. Didn't even have a horse — puff, puff — so I got on as best I could."

"You do bettah if you can fly like me, mahn."

"I can't fly, but I could do better than this if I were in good shape. At this rate, soon I will be," Severus said, and he increased his pace, faster and faster, until the wyvern began to get winded himself.

"Mahn, you not doin' so bad — puff. What you say we take a break by da woods ahead, find some watah and food. Hey, you tryin' to prove you as fahst as I am?"

"Water, good, too far to go to eat now — puff, puff."

As they reached the edge of the wood, Severus eased to a stop. He bent over, clutching the pain in his side, drawing as much air as he could. Even Vern had little to say as he, too, caught his breath.

"Yah, mahn, you jus' take a little break, tha's a good fellow, and I hunt for a stream or something — ah!"

Vern screamed as someone from inside the wood threw a large sack over him. Severus could hear Vern inside the bag shouting and cursing, but he had his own problems, as several angry looking elves had quickly slipped out of the wood and surrounded him. They were armed with bows and wooden staves.

"We know this fellow in the bag, but who and what are you? You look human," one of them said, speaking Latin. "How did you get here? What are you doing in the company of this creature?"

"Too many questions to answer at once," Severus said, "until we change the odds a bit."

With one foot Severus swept one of the elves off his feet and into the air, so that he landed with a thud. He leaped behind another, grabbed the bow from his back, wrapped it around his body and slung him down. A third came toward him with a swing of his staff, but Severus caught it, felt the reverse tug, and with a twist threw him off his feet as well. Then he scurried behind the fourth so that the remaining three instead of having him surrounded stood in a line before him, having lost their advantage of numbers. He pulled his sword from the scabbard that lay across his back. One of the elves, though, had armed his bow and was prepared to shoot.

"Stop! called the last. "Don't shoot, yet. Sir, you defend yourself well, but our numbers and bows have you at a disadvantage. We had no immediate intention of killing you, or we could have shot from the wood. Perhaps you have nothing to do with this wyvern, in which case we have no quarrel with you."

"I must tell you that despite your advantage, he is my friend, and I will defend him as I will myself."

By then Vern had wrestled his head free of the bag so that it alone stuck out through the opening, though two elves held it tight enough that he couldn't escape. "Mahn, you mean da', you really my friend? Oh, da' be touchin', mahn, if it be true."

"Then you had better guard yourself," said the elf to Severus, "for you have named yourself any enemy to our folk."

"Hardly that — I am serving as vassal to your king, and I happened here on his mission." Hearing that, several of the elves whispered to one another.

"Why should we believe you?"

"Don't you recognize the suit and shield as elvish craft?"

"You could have stolen them."

"Then I volunteer you my name: I am Sir Severus le Brewse, once knight of King Arthur of Britain, now hoping to help you rid your land of the Troubles." Giving one's name readily, especially in the Other World, suggests trust in the listener, and Severus made points with his assailants by doing so.

"And what of your 'friend' here, the wyvern? Will he name himself as well?"

"No' a chance, mahn, and let me outta da sack."

The elf turned to Severus. "Will you give his name? That would go far toward convincing us you mean no harm."

"I will not. And you, sir, should know better than to ask me."

The elf who had been speaking to Severus whispered to his comrades in words Severus couldn't understand. They helped their fallen comrades to their feet and dusted them off. Then he spoke again to the knight. "Then I offer you two choices. You may give up your weapons and come with us peacefully, or you may defend yourself and die here."

"I will go with you if you free my friend."

"You will go with us regardless, alive or dead."

"What grudge have you against him?"

"He falls upon our village at night. He has stolen our food, and worse, a child is now missing."

Severus cast a quick glance at Vern, whose red eyes burned brighter. His mouth fell open, and he shook his head vigorously.

"No, no: no' me, mahn, I nevah take no children! Da food I take, but I alway leave something foah it. If I can no' bahtah witchew, I still trade."

"He left us stones where we had placed food. Stones have no value here."

"Ah, mahn, dey was emeralds and a ruby. Men kill one anothah foah dem."

"Perhaps you have killed for them," the elf said, "but we are not men, and we do not value the trinkets that men and wyverns do."

"Den you give dem bahk to me, and I trade you something else. We bahtah, see? It's easy. Hey, how about I help you fin' dee little one?"

"How about if I look inside your belly for him."

"No, mahn, you don' touch my nice pink belly! If da little fella missin', I sniff him out fo' you."

"How did you know it is a male child?"

"I didn' know, mahn, it jus' an expression, fella, you know? Ayii! dees people so lit'ral!"

"May I suggest a compromise?" Severus offered. "I will give you my weapons and go with you, but you release the wyvern. I know creatures as well as does any man, and perhaps as well as most elves, and I believe he has not intended you any harm. He was hungry, so he ate — I suspect you can spare a little food. If you didn't like his pay, we will find something you value. My friend and I will help you find the lost child, and you will let me continue my task. What say you?"

The elf thought for a minute. "The wyvern goes before us, where we can see him, and on a leash."

"No leash, mahn, no, no!" Vern protested.

"You can hardly blame him, especially if he has done no harm," Severus said. Hear, then: he goes beside me, free of restraint, and you may hold this sword point at my back." Severus reversed his sword, offered it handle first to the elf. "If you find any harm in him, you may dispatch me for misjudging him."

The elf again whispered to his comrades, then nodded to Severus. "I accept your terms, and to show you I wish you no ill, I am called Vostrandard."

Another of the elves spoke quietly to him.

"Your comrade says you should not give your name," Severus said.

"I am old and experienced enough to know you have not learned our language, Sir Severus, but you have shown me that you have wisdom enough to guess his meaning. I choose these two items in recompense for what the wyvern has taken: that leather suit you wear and an account of your mission."

"Done," Severus answered.

* * *

"**Y**ou a true frien'," Vern said to Severus as they hurried toward the elves' village. The wyvern hovered easily alongside as the man and the elves kept a good pace. "Like, you really touch me back theah — touch me to the heaht. No' many mahn-types would do da' for anything else no'a mahn. We definitely even now."

"Even?"

"Yah, you owe' me foah protectin' you while you sleep."

They had been traveling for some time, and the evening had swept in and was rapidly swallowing the amber light of dusk. They had passed several hillocks and copses and forded a stream, but the land ahead lay flat before them, and Severus caught a hint of salt in the air. A substantial wood, nearly of forest size, stood straight ahead. Severus thought he could hear the sound of the sea coming from beyond the wood. He noticed that Vern was sniffing rapidly.

"You never told me how you found me on the Gray Road?"

"Da Gray Road?"

"In the Land of Shadows. That was where I first saw you. I had begun to believe that was a dream."

"Yah, mahn, mus' have been a dream."

"I don't think so now. Why were you there, and how did you get there?"

"Slow now," the elf-leader interrupted. You are near the entrance to our village. I would normally blindfold guests — do not worry, wyvern. Since our hungry friend has got in before, that would merely waste our time. Vostrandard led Severus and the others into a field of tall, fingery grass to a spot where a pool bubbled at their feet, while Vern continued sniffing. "Here is the entrance," he said. Let us hurry, please since we must rejoin the search as soon as possible."

"If you want to fin' de child, no help to look in deah," Vern said resolutely.

"How do you know?" the elf-leader asked.

"He in de wood yondah: I can smell him. He alive, but scahed."

The elf looked at Severus, who just shrugged, then spoke again to Vern. "Why should I believe you?"

"You want dee chil', no? So you follow me, an' I fin' him foah you."

"I believe him," Severus said, "and I will help. But we should hurry if we wish to beat the failing light."

The elf nodded. He directed two others into an opening in the ground beside the bubbling spring. As they reached it, it opened wider to allow them entry. They emerged seconds later with torches. He posted the two elves at the pool

220

as guards and handed one of the torches to Severus, who looked at Vern for directions.

"You boys folla me," Vern said. I have dees eyes, so I don' need no torch. We fin' da little one, no worries.""

With Vern leading, Severus and the elf-leader right behind, and the remaining elves following, the hunters moved almost silently into the woods. They hardly needed their torches: Vern's coat of green, glowing scales produced a cool, eerie glow. Vern darted one way, then another among the trees, sniffing. Suddenly he stopped and turned to Severus, his eyes shining bright red. "Something wrong heah, my friend. Someting bahd — I can smell it."

"Yes, and I can feel it," Severus whispered, "and hear it." Something familiar, something I have met before, but not exactly the same, Severus mused to himself. He thought he heard a voice, quiet as the sigh of a breeze, up among the treetops, but he could see no source for it.

"If harm has come to the child, I will have difficulty not finding you responsible," the elf whispered to Vern.

"Shh — follow, follow."

Severus listened intently: yes, a voice, but too low for him to make it out — something in it, a malevolence, quiet, lurking.

They came to a small clearing, but Vern hurried through it, then disappeared among some thick trees opposite. For a moment Severus and the elves stood still, waiting, just long enough for Severus to worry that Vern had abandoned them and fled. Then he heard a rustling of leaves, and a small child, with the look of a boy about four years old, edged his way into the clearing, rubbing his eyes. Vern hovered behind him, pushing him along gently with one wing.

"Dis da crittah you lookin' foah, elf-mahn?"

Severus heard in the distance, among the trees, the soft tread of large feet moving slowly and carefully.

The elf-leader knelt down and whispered to the boy, who answered sleepily. The leader lifted him, hugged him tight, and spoke to Vern. "I thank you, wyvern, and I offer apology if, as it appears, you had nothing to do his getting lost here."

"Of coahse I don', but you welcome anyway."

"I suggest that we move along now," Severus whispered. "Something in the wood is trying to lull us to sleep. I don't believe it has good intentions toward us."

"Yes, the wood has been troubled lately, though we don't know why or with what — or whom. Come quickly," said the elf, and Vern hurried to lead them by the shortest if not the clearest path out of the wood and back into the field. The troop conversed no more until they had found the guards at the spring, entering the earthen doorway that enlarged into a tunnel as they walked down into it. The doorway appeared to close behind them, and Severus and Vern found themselves in a cool stone hallway that wove among multiple paths slowly underground. The boy had fallen asleep in the leader's arms, and almost as one they all let out a sigh of relief as they emerged from the passageway into a large, open cavern.

"No' to be too much trouble, chief, but I bery, bery hungry, and I bet my frien' be, too." The wyvern placed a protective wing around Severus' shoulder.

"You'll be well fed, but I suggest that you follow us rather than proceed us: don't want a stray arrow reaching you before we can explain your presence here. Thieves and worse have been circling our borders lately — that's why you met our patrol."

* * *

Severus had the good fortune to spend a comfortable and uneventful night at the thriving if not overlarge village that had once been a mere outpost, but that the elves had recently begun to garrison for what even distant settlements had come to call "the Troubles." No one there seemed to have any better sense of the cause than had Arawn, and they spoke of it uneasily. The folk there spoke a language different than Arawn's, but most also had fluency in Latin — they studied the recorded learning of humans — so Severus could communicate with nearly anyone he pleased; no one, though, could give him much useful advice.

Before sleep Severus and Vern had eaten heartily of the elves' vegetarian fare. Elves, you see, don't eat meat, but if you like their sort of food, you'd have found it a feast indeed. They had eaten warm herbed breads and salads with sharp cheese and elvish beer, which calms, but doesn't inebriate. They had fried eggplant and spinach pie and squash soufflé. They had soups and curries and roasted potatoes and bowls full of berries with cream and even hot sweet rolls with fruit icings, and cold, clean spring water: elves enjoy a good meal even far from their great halls. Severus hadn't had such food since he and Lilava had eaten with her family in their city in the south where the sun shines bright and breezes blow warm. He tried not to think too much about Lilava — they had shared so little time together, and yet her absence hurt worse than a wound. He tried, but mostly he failed.

As Severus watched Vern eat, he realized that the wyvern would no more eat a child than would he: the wyvern consumed more vegetables with more pleasure than Severus would have thought possible. The child, waking once he was returned to the loving if scolding embrace of his mother, said that he had sneaked out to go to the beach and upon returning had heard voices and got lost in the wood. He had found water and berries and had slept under piles of moss and leaves to hide and keep out the chill. Even young elves know how to survive.

While they ate, Severus had recounted several of his adventures, sticking mostly to the minor ones to establish believability and avoid overstating his own accomplishments. In fact, he relied mostly on descriptions of terrain, weather, food and drink, and means of travel: always safe as well as informative topics for elves as well as people. He realized, too, that he missed not only Lilava, but also Courage; once again he hoped the horse was, if not free to roam as he wished, then at least healthy and well cared for.

When he woke in the morning, Severus washed, as was the custom among the elves, and drank a warm, slightly sweet, rooty drink with his host, to whom he outlined the mission Arawn had given him: to search the western shore for hint of the nature of whatever invader he could find. He mentioned the gold-sailed ship and asked if the elves had seen it.

"Yes, we have, and I myself have spoken to its captain and pilot. He is, like you, a human. Two of my scouts and I found him coming ashore in a rowboat. He had several of his sailors with him, stout, silent fellows, and he tried to entice me to 'trade' — despite what he said, I could hear that by that word he meant to steal from us."

"You seem to have a good deal of difficulty with thieves here."

"We had not until this equinox past. Since then, we have had humans on our shores — unheard of! — whisperings in our woods, evil creatures swimming far up our rivers — even the birds seem to have come from elsewhere, and if we set our gear down for lunch and a moment's rest, they poke around in our packs and fly off with what scraps or crumbs they can disentangle."

Later, after the exchange of much information to their mutual benefit, Severus prepared to leave, and he offered the elf his leather suit, as he had promised.

"Sir, you remain true to your word, but I have no intention of accepting it. I asked to test your mettle as a negotiator and to try your generosity: one does well to learn the quality of either opponent or friend, to determine which he may ultimately become. On your mission you will need the suit more than I. It will not protect you from all attacks, but it will repel water and resist heat or cold — I don't believe you could have found better anywhere in our lands or in your own. You appear to have good fortune as well as good manners: I noted you did not name our king, either. I suspect you were yet unsure of our allegiance here. And if your demonstration with my hunters yesterday mirrors your true skills, you may have success in your task, however difficult, and I heartily wish you good luck."

"You'll note, too, that neither did I ask your name," Severus said.

"I gave you my ..."

"Title. You gave me your title, not your name: 'Guardian of the West Shore.' Some of your words have parallels among languages I have heard elsewhere, though your Elvish differs from the little I have been able to learn from the king's folk."

"You are a linguist as well as a soldier."

"Kind of you to say so, but no — indeed, I wish I had such abilities. I learn what I can by paying attention, without special ability to retain all or to guess the rest."

"Are you then asking my name now?"

"No, but thank you. Rather, because I trust you, I'm going to give you the name of one dear to me, so that if she happens in her own venture to find you, you will treat her well and tell her that you saw me and sent me on my way hale and strong. Her name is Lilava. She is fully able to take care of herself, and when she can, she also does her best to see that I avoid harm. I love her more than life, and for her honor I perform what deeds I can and help other folk whose needs bring them in my way."

"Then I call you thrice-blessed, in our language trech-bennatha, for you have skill, the greatest of elven patrons in our king, and the love of a worthy woman. I have known few men, but I can hardly guess that one could ask for more than that. Trech Bennatha shall be your name among my folk, and when you speak it to them, they will help you — we shall spread the word."

"Perhaps you should have named me 'Four-times Blessed': you have forgotten my friend."

"The wyvern? I am not so sure he is a blessing."

"A friend is a great gift, even one who stumbles occasionally, and I believe him trustworthy. I have a sense for such things."

"I hope your sense will prove correct," sighed the elf.

* * *

By mid-day Severus and Vern had already searched the wood they had entered the night before. They found it free of encroachment — whatever they had heard and smelled there either had gone or came only at night. Through afternoon they combed the beach many miles to the south, finally giving up that way and returning north.

"Notting dis way, mahn. I say we have some lunch, den turn back nor'." The elves had provided them with packs of food and drink, as light as possible without skimping.

"Didn't I see you eating an enormous breakfast, and after that meal we had last night?"

Vern turned beady red eyes on Severus. "Wyvern need plenty of food: we store it, then can go days widout if we need to — but don' you tell nobody da'. I eat when I can, because you can no' count on people when you in need: dos' elves say I steal from dem! Steal! Me! As if."

"Can you eat as we go?"

"Oh, bahd hahbit, mahn. Good ting you got me to civilize you. Jus' sit heah and we have a little bite of — hey! what's dat? Deah, on dee horizon, you see?"

Severus' eyes were good, but not as good as Vern's. He peered where the wing pointed, and in a moment he spotted a speck in the vast, blue distance. In another moment the speck resolved itself into a ship.

"Bery bad, mahn: gold sails."

Into the early evening they ran north along the coast, following the direction of the ship, assuming that the pilot intended to make land somewhere along Arawn's coast.

By dusk they saw ahead a forest that extended north along the shore, beyond shallow bay. The ship had set anchor two stones' throw off the beachhead, and two rowboats, empty, were run aground. Severus and Vern hid behind a dune and considered a plan.

"I know the ship. It belongs to King Abra, Abracadabrax — calls himself the Witch King."

"Wid all dos names you know, must be some magic you can use on him."

"I don't have any magic. Lilava could use it, if she were here, but I have no doubt she has problems of her own."

"Didn' she teach you notting, mahn?"

"Magic isn't my way. Not everyone has talent for it."

"You musta had a little magic to win such a babe."

"Babe?"

"Yeah, you know: dolly, peach, hot tomahto, hoochy-coochy — come on, mahn, you know: cutiepie, female!"

"Well, actually, at first I think she just needed a monster fighter. I can do that, and she can do magic, and we ended up making a pretty good team."

"If you were a team now, rathah than by yoahself, we'd be bettah off."

"I know, but we must make do. So first question: shall we wait for Abra and his ship to return, or shall we plan an attack?"

"We should plan for you to attack. Me, mahn, I a lovah, not a fightah."

"You're not allowed to fight?"

"Canno' do it, mahn, no' in the wyvern code. We can protec', but we canno' attack."

"If you don't get caught in a sack."

"Ah, das' no' the kinda thhing one friend say to anothah. You jus' lucky dey got me an' no' you."

"I know. You're right. Sorry."

"I accep' your apology, 'cause you be my frien', but' don' you be makin' it a habit. Learn to be nice."

"You're right, but I've had to scrap all my life. I'm a fighter, and not a lover."

"Das' almos' funny, mahn, bu' don' try too hahd and hurt yoahself. Too bad, too, for tha' female of yoahs. If you no' a lovah, maybe she like me bettah."

"Don't bet on it. But if you can't fight, you may help me plot a strategy."

"Now da' I cahn do, buddy-o."

After some discussion Severus and Vern decided they could reasonably make no attack until they knew how Abra had got to those shores and what he was doing there: they had no right to initiate violence. He was almost certainly the source of at least part of the trouble to Arawn's kingdom, but they needed evidence, and they needed information. They chose to move back inland, out of sight of the ship's crew, then enter the forest from farther north. There they would wait, catch Abra's returning men unaware, and incapacitate them sufficiently to learn what they were doing.

The first part of the plan they carried out with fair dispatch, and little more than an hour later they found themselves safely perched on a small platform created by some thick branches of a sturdy old oak tree, far enough above ground to avoid detection but not so high as to induce serious injury by a fall alone. The elves had given Vern a dark cloak to throw over himself to cover his green glow, so the two friends sat together with little likelihood of being detected. They ate a snack of fresh fruit, sweet dark bread, and goat's milk from their elven provisions, and they settled in to watch. They could just see the first evening stars through the tall limbs above. To pass the time they conversed, though so quietly that you and I could hardly have heard them if we had passed directly underneath.

"I assumed that they would return directly. It hadn't struck me until right now that they could actually be gone for some time."

"You already gettin' tiahed of my company?"

"Perhaps we should have tried to reach the boat, board her, and surprise them. Maybe Abra is there, waiting unguarded, thinking himself safe. We could learn what we need and return to the king with a report. I have a bad feeling for Li-lava, as if something's about to go wrong."

"No, mahn, no' to the boat. I canno' swim, an' if I fly, maybe they see me comin'."

"I don't swim so well myself. We could build a raft."

They'd gone over those options before, but people ready for action seldom wait patiently.

"I cahn fly pretty fahst — maybe I could surprise them. But dis plan bettah. I think Abra go wid his peepo somewheah to do mishchief. I see him inland before. I think he go to make allies himself, to take dem weapons."

"What kind of allies could he make here, among the elves?"

"No' elves, but othahs, othahs you don' see yet. Dey live heah among da many trees, and in da cold nor'. Dey some bery bahd things deah, who don' like elves and dey won' like you. Sea captain bring dem what dey like, make friends of dem."

"What does he bring, besides weapons?"

"Dey like gold — I dunno why, mahn — an' dey like cullahful stones an' animal pelts an' some kinna drink he bring, an' dey like fresh meat."

"Abra brings them meat?"

"No, mahn, but das' what dey do wit you if dey catch you."

"I see."

"You bettah hope you see dem befoah dey see you."

"That's why I have you with me, right, my friend?"

"Ah, right, my frien', das' why you have me! You know, I been gettin' to like you, mahn. If you were no' married and were better lookin' — sorry, mahn, but is' true — I would introduce you to a nice wyvern female."

Severus tried not to wince. "That's very kind of you, but I'm quite happy with the wife I have. I just wish she and I didn't end up apart so often."

"She a sweetie, all right, yah. 'Sokay: female wyverns would no' take der eyes off me, anyway, so you no' have a chahnce."

"I take it that you also find human females — attractive. That strikes me as rather odd."

"Oh, mahn, I like all females, an' dey like me, too. Well, almost all females: deah was dis one look kinda like a big possum, you know, way in da wes', back by my home. She had a bahd eye, so she woah dis magnifyin' glass crunched ovah her eyeball — mahn, she like me, but she no' so be-ay-yu-ti-ful, so I keep to a safe distance, you know?"

"What I really want to know is how you found me on the Gray Road?"

"Oh, da' again?"

"You never have answered me."

"We keep gettin' interrupted. Well, okay den, it was dis. I was chattin' up dis really cute dolphin — beach vacation, you know — and I heah dis ..."

"Shh."

"Yah, mahn, I hear it, too. Dey comin' back."

"Yes. Ready?"

"Always ready, mahn."

Severus listened intently. He could make out seven or eight sets of footfalls, but could see no lights: they hadn't yet lit torches. "I was just thinking," he whispered, "that I should have put holes in the bottom of their rowboats."

"Too late now, mahn."

"But I will make good use of this fishing net that Vostrandard gave me."

"Thas' no' his real name, mahn."

Severus smiled. "I know."

"I keep sayin' you no' as dumb as you look."

"Well, do keep saying it, and perhaps I'll come to believe it, too."

"You know, I notice you say 'pe'haps' a lot."

"Shh."

"Right-y."

The tree in which they perched stood just over a slightly worn path through the woods. Severus had scouted the path before they climbed the tree, and he had guessed correctly that Abra's sailors would take it. He lowered the fishing net, almost invisible in the growing gloom, so that it would catch the first men who walked into it just like a spider's web. He heard them talking and laughing, crunching their feet along the forest floor, apparently assured that no one haunted their way.

"Light a torch, someone," a voice said.

"Not now. We're almosst back to the boatss, and I don't want to wasste what's left of thesse torchesss. We will need all we have tomorrow, and you know thiss path well enough."

Severus recognized the voice, with its odd sibilants: King Abra.

"It'ss getting dark, and we're beginning to sstumble, and I don't want to lose the cargo."

"She's tied tight," said another voice. "Nothing to worry about. Just step carefully and don't injure her any more. She's exactly what we need for tomorrow's trade, so we want her alive and her injuries healable."

"Hey! What's this!" a voice screeched, as the first two of Abra's men caught themselves in Severus' net. He dropped the rest of the net overtop of them, and they struggled and tripped and fell to the ground. A third, who hadn't seen them fall, fell overtop of them.

"Look out!" called a fourth. Severus leaped down from the tree upon two more shadowy forms. The force of his fall knocked them cold. He rolled free of them, regained his feet, and kicked another man to the ground.

The small, roundish shape before him, the last one standing, lit a torch. Severus shielded his eyes from the sudden light, but immediately recognized the face.

"You!" Abra spat.

"Yes." Severus took a step forward. Abra stood his ground and aimed a kick directly into Severus' crotch.

Severus raised a foot and blocked the kick, catching Abra directly on the shin.

The little man screeched a howl of pain, dropped his torch, and began hopping about on one foot. Severus felt a body directly behind his, drew his sword, and turned in a flash.

There was Vern's green body, glowing, free of the elven cloak. The man who had stumbled over the two characters caught in the net had risen, drawn a long, nasty knife, and prepared to attack Severus from behind, but Vern had interposed his body between them.

"No so fahst, bahd mistah sailah."

The man swiped his knife at the wyvern, but Vern just floated overtop of the blow. He swiped again, higher, and Vern ducked beneath it. Then he growled. "What kind of a devilish thing are you?"

"I youah wuhst nightma-ah, mahn," Vern said, and as the man drew back to thrust his knife again, Vern raised a foot and kicked him in the solar plexus, dropping him, heaving for breath, to the ground.

"I thought you said you don't fight," Severus observed calmly.

"I don' attack, mahn, but I do protec', eidah you oah myself. Hey, wheah did de little faht mahn go?"

Night had fallen, and the only remaining light was the wyvern's green glow.

"We hahd bettah fin' him, or dis little dance wid dees men all foah notting."

"Listen."

Severus heard whistling, then he noticed the sound of footfalls running — toward the forest's edge and the boats.

"Foah a faht little mahn, he run pretty good."

"Let's catch him."

They made sure the first two men hadn't yet disentangled themselves from the net and then began to follow, but they immediately met an impediment. Before them lay a large bundle carefully bound to a pole, that Abra's men had left behind. Beast! Severus thought, sniffing, and an injured one at that. He could smell the blood. The beast hissed at him as he passed.

By the time they reached the forest's edge, Abra had entered the water and was swimming toward a boat that was rowing rapidly toward him. He hadn't even bothered to try one of the rowboats on shore.

"We must stop him before he gets in range of the ship. He has archers there," Severus said. They reached the edge of the surf, Vern hovering beside Severus. He could see three men in the rowboat, two rowing powerfully and a third poised with his bow ready to shoot. Abra must have warned them to be ready for his return, in case he ran into trouble. One had to admire the fellow for his ability to plan for contingencies.

"I canno' believe I sayin' dis, mahn, but grab my feet."

"Why? Really? You intend to carry me?"

"Oh, dey such pretty feet, so sensitive. If you evah tell anothah wyvern I done dis, I have to call you a liah. No time to waste: hold on tight." Vern hovered above him, and Severus grasped his feet and was immediately pulled from the ground.

Vern faltered for a moment with the extra weight, and Severus heard an arrow whiz past his head.

"Careful!"

"Sorry, but you heaviah than you look, wid all that soldiah geah!" Vern flew a serpentine pattern, right, up, left, down, up, right, and Severus watched the archer trying to get a fix on them. "Leggo now!" Vern called, and Severus dropped into the surf directly atop the swimming Abra. Vern shot upward and off at an angle as quickly as he could fly.

When he struck Abra, Severus knocked him under the water, and in the swirling surf Severus flailed until he grasped the wriggling man tightly and began to pull him toward the shore. Abra hadn't got far into the surf, so Severus soon got a foothold and began to pull back forcefully. Only one more arrow passed Severus, narrowly missing, then he and Abra were too nearly tangled for the king's man to risk another shot. Vern swooped down on the archer from behind and kicked him headlong into the waves. Grasping both of Abra's arms, Severus held the pirate like an enormous sack of potatoes, hauled him up on shore, and disgustedly threw him onto the sand. The two remaining sailors in the rowboat cowered low to avoid the flying enemy who by then must have had them thoroughly terrified.

"I believe you tried to bite me, you wretch," Severus said.

"I'd do whatever I had to do to get away from you, you corpsse, and don't call me 'wretch.' I am a king, ssir."

"Right. Now let's make this quick and simple, your majesty, and if you're lucky, I'll either turn you in to the authorities here or let you go your way. If you're unlucky I'll kill you where you sit."

"We've been through thiss before, Ssir Sseverus le Brewsse, and you will not kill me, even if you can, which I doubt. You forget who I am and what powerss I control. As for you, some necromancer must have raissed you, and I can as eassily ssend you back. Aaeeii!" he screamed as Vern flew within a few inches of his head and then settled down beside him.

"You jus' listen to my sidekick heah, you Abracadabrax, phoney witch king. Yah, I know youah silly name. If you do what he tell you, maybe I no' scratch you to death with these bee-ay-yu-ti-ful feet of mine!"

"Yuck, wyvern — never thought to ssee such a thing as you, ugly beasst. You can't kill me, either. You have no power to attack. I know all about you."

"Ugly! Ugly? You in foah it now, for suah. My whole family kick youah tail for da' one. Ugly! Imagine da', with such a bee-yu-tiful creachah as me! An' you wi' dat funny accents, too, da' sss-stuff! Les' jus' kill him now, mahn; whatchew say?"

"I'll give you one good reasson not to kill me, Sseveruss and if you're a man, and not a zombie, that'ss all you'll need."

"Speak quickly and exactly."

Abra put two fingers in his mouth and emitted a whistle so loud and harsh that it exceeded the pounding of the surf. The pitch rose and fell twice, then held for two seconds and fell again. "Look on the deck of my sship."

Severus looked and saw nothing, then turned again to Abra.

"It will take a minute, dummy. Even the Witch King can't move men instantaneoussly."

"You which king? I think you no king, notin' but a thief and swindlah — no, no, don' you try to move! Jus' sit an' be nice, if thas' possible foah you," Vern said.

"Look now, ssoldier. And tell your puny dragon to get his claws off me."

On the deck of the ship several men came forward with torches, then two more came to the gunnel pulling an unwilling horse.

"How good are your eyes, ssoldier? Do you know who that horsse iss?"

"No. It can't be."

"It iss."

"He looks so thin and drawn."

"Shouldn't have left him with Lancelot, you idiot."

"Courage!"

"Yess, Courage."

"If you have harmed him, I will kill you."

"If you let me go, my men will not kill him."

"Ungentlemanly, this hostage habit of yours."

"Fine comment from you: hardly a gentleman yoursself, lowborn sscum."

"I accept your offer. If Courage is unharmed — no, too late for that — if Courage is in such a condition that care will allow him to recover, I will exchange you for him. He deserves better ransom, but I will pay what I have to save what I may."

"At lasst I have made a businessman of you. Now you will just let my ssoldiers claim me and we shall arrange to have your horsse put ashore at a convenient sspot... ."

"No, I will hold you here with my sword at your throat until your crew have found a way to bring the horse to us without doing him any further harm."

"That will be very difficult. I highly advise you to ..."

Severus interrupted Abra to swipe his sword just below the man's chin, cutting off the tip of his beard.

"Ha, we have reached thiss impasse again, for I don't believe you will kill me."

With two steps Severus stood behind Abra, grasped both of the man's wrists in one hand, and pressed the sword edge to his throat.

"I say we jus' kill him anyway, den go save da hoahsey," Vern suggested. "You canno' trust dis guy."

"My ssoldiers will kill your horsse long before you can reach him, and you shall have both the blood of a man begging for mercy and of your own sstallion on your hands." Abra wrestled himself down to his knees. "I beg for my life. If you are a true knight, a religiousss man, or a persson of any ssort of decency, you must sspare me."

"Call to your ship, and tell them by however difficult means, they must free Courage to me immediately." Severus eased the blade into Abra's skin until it drew blood.

"Wait!" he shrieked. "Let me talk to them. I will do as you assk." Abra called to his men in a language Severus didn't understand.

"Speak to them in Latin," he said. "They'll understand, and so will I. Tell them to bring the horse to land, but to bring no archers. They will have you only when I have the horse. Any further attempt at parley, and they will leave here without you. I shall have to learn to live with my guilt."

After shouting to his sailors several times across the crashing surf, Abra got them to understand what he wanted done. The remaining sailors rowed the boat back to the ship, and after a short time Abra's men had set together some broad planks to make a ramp. With great difficulty three of them got a thin, angry, beleaguered Courage into the wash, where with great flailing and a brave bit of swimming they finally managed a foothold. If the men had left their ship with weapons, by the time they neared shore, after considerable struggles, they no longer had them — Severus anyway couldn't see them. A rowboat followed them at bowshot distance from the shore.

But Courage wouldn't come ashore.

Thin and boney, cold and afraid, he looked at Severus, shook his head back and forth, tossing his bedraggled mane, and neighed with dismay.

"Come on, my good fellow," Severus encouraged. "You can do it. You're free of them now. I am alive, and I will care for you myself. Trust, Courage: no more harm shall come to you. Don't you wish to come ashore?"

Abra would have spoken, but Severus held his blade tight to the man's throat. The darkness had grown thick, and only torches from the ship and Vern's chartreuse glow lit the night.

"Oh, mahn, I think I know dee problem. Le' me talk to him." And Vern approached the horse, then whistled and hooted, neighed and bleated, beeped and whirred. In reply Courage whinnied and whined, then concluded with a long huffing sound. "I see it," Vern said to the horse. "Bery bahd, bery bahd, but you got to come, you know. Come on now, hoahsey: my friend an' me take good care of you, oh yah." Still Courage wouldn't come.

Abra's men were standing on the edge of the sand waiting to receive him. Once they had got out of the water, Severus could see daggers at their sides, but they little worried him. With a push he thrust Abra down at their feet. As they scurried to pick him up, Severus grasped the shield from his back, held it before him, and dashed into the wash to place himself between Courage and the men in the rowboat, in case they were armed with bows. He called to Vern: "Come behind the shield: they may be armed!" Just then an arrow whistled by, nicked Severus' shield, and flew just past Courage.

"I right behind you, mahn, don' worry. We got to get outta heah." Another arrow whistled by — though Severus was defending in the dark, the archer in the boat was also shooting in the dark. The boat drew closer. Vern ducked as an arrow flew over Severus' head. Severus backed up until he could feel Courage's boney ribs right behind him. Vern had slipped back behind the horse and was whistling and cooing in his ear.

"Why won't he move?"

"Heah's da problem, old mahn: if he come ashoah, he can nevah return to youah land again. Dat is sometime dee way wid elven magic."

The rowboat came closer, and Abra's sailors helped him into the surf and towards it.

"Never return?"

"Das' da fac', Mac: da magic heah too strong. He afraid he die if he cross da boundary, or he nevah see his beloved lady hoahsey bahk home." An arrow struck the center of Severus' shield and fell into the wash.

With his free hand Severus stroked Courage's neck and whispered into his ear. "Look, my old friend. I stand here, alive. If you don't come, you or the three of us may die. Trust, and hurry now: come!" With his back Severus pushed the horse toward the shore, and finally with a kick and reluctant resolution Courage dug in as well as his weak legs allowed and bucked onto shore. He neighed loudly as he passed clear of water onto the sand, a sound filled with sorrow and worry.

The sailors had helped Abra into the rowboat, which began to move quickly toward the ship. Archers on deck began to fire toward the shore, but Vern and Courage, with Severus holding his shield before them, had already moved out of range of the longest bow.

From the rowboat Abra called to them. "I doubt you shall ssee me again, Sseverus the ssentimental. I left something in the foresst for you — an old friend of yourss, I think, that you will feel glad to meet again, or at any rate one who will gladly meet you. It was ssmall when I brought it here, but it iss growing, quickly. If you have no chance to kiss your lovely bride good-bye, maybe she will sseek me out, or I her, when you're gone. You should have tried to kill me while you had the chance. I sstill have my foothold here, and Arawn shall learn the wrath you've raissed in me. Ah!"

Abra screamed as a dart that Severus had drawn and thrown brushed his shoulder and struck the man rowing behind him. "You will regret that casst, too, if you live long enough. You will need every weapon you have. Die soon, Sseverus, you and your ssick horse and your ugly, infernal friend." A second dart grazed his forehead, knocking him over and almost upsetting the boat.

"Le' me have a go a' him, Sev," Vern whispered. "I will knock him in da watah and let him drown."

"Don't try, my friend. See the archers? No need to take a chance on their hitting a wild, lucky shot, and you have done wonders already. You have helped save this poor fellow, my oldest friend and comrade in battle."

"Pthsst!" Vern spat in Abra's direction. "Nasty fellow," he said, disgustedly. "Les' take ca-ah of da hoahsey."

Severus led Courage, weak and weary, back toward the forest, and there he shared with the horse provisions from his pack. They were both soaked — Vern, of course, was waterproof — so Severus toweled down Courage as well as he could and patted his head warmly. A cool breeze had blown in, and he began a shiver. Only at the edge of the forest, they decided to dare a small fire for warmth. In the distance, they could see a dark shadow — Abra's ship — merging into the purple horizon.

When they had eaten a bit, Severus rose to examine Courage more carefully by torchlight. The skin looked blotchy, the coat uneven, the nose and mouth dry and dull, and the eyes shone with sorrow and suffering. "What has gone wrong? Before I ... left, I requested that Lancelot take care of you — did he fail in my request?"

Courage took his right front hoof, touched it to his forehead, and shook his head.

"Le' me try to talk to him," Vern said, and he proceeded to emit another series of whistles, whirs, and whinnies. Courage responded with a long series of disgruntled nickerings, whines, and fricatives.

"What did he say?" Severus asked, knowing it wasn't anything good.

"Sorry, mahn, I no' so good at hoahse language, bu' to me it sound like dis. You leave him wid a knight, bu' tha' knight give him to anothah knight who not value him so much oah treat him so well. Tha' knight sell him to Abra foah a few pennies, as much to get rid of him as foh da little money. Bery sahd story, mahn. He upset dat you give him up, and he moah upset ye' da' he canno' get back — he have a beloved back deah, you know, a bee-yu-ti-ful creachah, he say."

"Pretty fair interpretation for someone who doesn't speak horse. But thank you. I didn't give him up, you know. I died. If it weren't for some kind folk and perhaps for you, prince among wyverns, I wouldn't have been here to find him now."

Courage nodded, made some conciliatory sounds, and hung his head and nodded his acceptance. Severus almost cried to see the poor state his old fellow was in and then again when he realized how glad he felt to have his horse return to him. But whether Courage would share any more adventures was another matter, and, remembering how he had felt when he thought he might never hold Lilava again, his heart sank that the horse should never again see his mare.

"I wonder," Severus said to Vern, "if like Courage I too am stuck here, if I may never return to human lands."

"No' so bahd a fate, if you ahsk me," Vern said. "Who want to be among such people as dis Abra fellow anyway? You have yoah female, you have yoah hoahse, you have yoah life: be happy and don' worry."

"Yes, you're right. Now we should find a place to sleep. Let's try the woods, not where we sat before, but near there, just in case Abra decides to make another sortie upon us."

"I don' think he be bahk, mahn. He gonna lose some blood from dat daht you trew, and his men don' come widout him. Les' get some sleep — even I tiahed now."

"But first, we've forgotten something." Severus took a fresh brand from the fire, and they returned to the spot of their battle in the forest. The men had all fled, but they left behind their prey: a long, sleek mountain cat, injured, bloody, but alive, bound to a pole by which the men had carried her. Severus tried to feed her, but she would take nothing, and when he released her, she eyed the three of them menacingly, then hunched and crept off into the dark forest. She made one low growl, then disappeared in silence.

"You should no' have le' her go — she be back, even if Abra's men don' come."

Courage clearly felt the same. He shook his head as if to say that he couldn't believe it, either. "We had no right to harm or hold her," Severus said. We must return in the morning to the elves to warn them of her presence. She may seek food nearby and try to heal herself, or she may head for the fastness of the forest — not up to us. Anyway, we must get Courage medicine as well — but first a place to rest for the night. Here now: what's this?"

Severus found, near where the cat had lain, a long sword with a light but strong blade, with thin serpentine figures incised in the metal and a lion's head carved in the base of the hilt.

"Fine weapon, mahn. You should take it — much bettah dan what you have."

"What I have is fine elven craft, but you're right about this creature — funny I would call it that: the word just came to me. It almost feels alive, this sword, it swings so easily. One of Abra's soldiers must have left it."

"Don' swing it too close to me. It make a nahsty sound, and look how it glow! Put it away, Sev. If I don' feel you find it foah some puhpose, I tell you to bury it heah and fohget about it."

"I think I understand. It does seem an odd thing to find, odd for someone just to drop it. He must have failed to notice — all the more reason they may return: such a weapon is worth the risk. Right: we should get some sleep."

"We mus' take turn watchin' for da' caht," Vern added.

"Yes," Severus said. "Can you take the first shift?"

"Yah, mahn, you can count on dee wyvern."

"Thank you. I feel so tired."

"You still not recovahd. Sleep, an' when you ready, you take second shift."

"Thank you." The knight yawned profoundly.

"Eh, Sev?"

"Yeah?"

"Ambrose."

"Sorry?"

"Ambrose, da magus. You kep' askin' why I follow you on da Gray Road. Ambrose an ol' friend of dee wyvern. He call me foraha favah, send me down an old cavahn in Italia. He ask me to fin' you if I could, an' of coahse I could. He tell me to try to help you out."

"Ambrose, right, thank you. Talk about in the morning. Thank you. *Zzzz.*"

"I hope he don' decide to snore too loud," Vern said to Courage.

Courage whinnied and shook his head.

"Sev, mahn?" Vern whispered.

"Ah?"

"Ambrose tell me to tell you dis, an' I jus' remembah: some people don' have a special quest, he say. Dey jus' have work to do. 'Tasks,' he say 'tasks,' yah. I don' know why he say da', but he say it. You okay wi' da', mahn?"

"*Zzzz.*"

Part 3

Lilava in Search of Severus

1 Lilava Among the Shamans

[While Severus seeks the west coast, Lilava meets with the elven prophets to determine the source of the Troubles.]

Lilava spent a warm and pleasant day in Arawn's library, though her thoughts often drifted to Severus, wondering how he was getting along. She stayed into the evening over a manuscript of formulas for herbal medicines, spells for the safe extraction of honey, and treatments to keep armor from rusting, and she actually fell asleep right in her chair, with her cheek nestled comfortably on a leaf of papyrus.

Early in the morning a librarian roused her, and she returned to her apartment to wash and have breakfast. She walked in the sunshine toward the stables, where to her surprise she saw a group of ostlers trying to calm Starlight. A shiver ran up her spine.

"How has she come back so soon?" Lilava asked them. "And where is Severus?"

"I'm afraid, milady," one answered, "that we know the answer to neither question. But we shall inform the queen about the horse, and I suspect she will send a party of our best trackers after your knight."

"I will go myself. Please find me a horse if Starlight isn't ready to travel."

Lilava dashed to her rooms to collect her gear, and as she emerged Proserpina stood at her door.

"I know what you are feeling, my dear, but you must not go until we get some word of what has happened."

"I can't just wait here. Maybe I can help him."

"And maybe nothing at all has gone wrong, and he needs no help."

"Why would Starlight return without him?"

"We will soon know. Though few elves live in that region, many hunt, track, and patrol the land between here and the sea. Be patient. We will know more soon. Besides, you must come with me to the council, which should begin in the next day or two, as soon as we can get to the sanctuary. Severus has his duties, and we have ours."

"My first duty now is to him."

"You may serve him best by joining me at the council. We do little good, and perhaps much harm, by rash action. Good or ill may find anyone at any time. We choose best when we follow our talents to their best use. Come: I have some texts to show you."

"But I ..."

"... love him, yes, and you want to do something, and you will do something: we two together will spend this day in study for the council, and we will wait for news, you of Severus, I from Arawn. In the morning, whatever we have heard, we will ride for the council. Now please come with me to the library: I must tell you all of what we know, and we must study the signs. When word comes, the messenger will know where to find us. Please come — some mint and chamomile tea will calm us. I will show you some manuscripts that even the librarians do not know, and we can talk privately."

"Surely you have no worries of spies here."

"None. I wish to go where we can worry no one, for the concerns of which we must speak imply the greatest dangers, the only real dangers my folk have faced in more than a thousand years."

* * *

When they were comfortably ensconced in the observatory above the library, sipping mint tea and carefully unrolling some very old scrolls, the queen told Lilava all she knew of the Troubles. That was hardly enough to satisfy an inquisitive enchantress with a personal stake in their nature, but it helped fill the time as they waited. Prosperpina also explained to her more than she had heard before of the history of the elves and of their prophets.

"Men, you see," the queen said, allowing her eye to scan the garden far below them beneath the observatory window, "reach us only by invitation or accident. They may stumble in when the moon is right or when the earth's energies have gone awry and disaster has followed: earthquake, volcano, the strike of a meteor. The fact that they come now not merely openly, but repeatedly, is for us unprecedented. They never trust us, and we hardly have reason to trust them: with them come theft, violence, further disruption beyond what the earth herself causes. And men seldom have moral conscience. Yes, dear, I know they talk of it, preach it, and the most thoughtful among them even write of it, but they seldom if ever practice it. Those who come here do no better than the rest."

Lilava sighed, knowing the truth of the words.

"They come out of desire for gain, not desire for peace. Typically they take, do what harm they can, and then depart, hardly able to find us again. Now, they come, do their harm, and return. They have some new power or someone — or some thing — helping them to do what never before they could. We, the prophets among us, must determine what has changed and how to set it right. There, we believe, you can help us."

"Prophets? I didn't know that you need prophets. You have a greater awareness of and connection to the earth than we do, you see more of the past and present than we do, and you can guess the unfolding of the future in a way far

242

beyond our abilities, even those of the most studious and attentive of humans. When all among you can do so, how wise your prophets must be!"

"Prophet is perhaps the wrong word. I have never spoken to one among humans who tries to understand us as you do, so you must forgive me if I have difficulty finding apt expressions for our experience. The word councilor may better serve, or counselor, or perhaps shaman: we who participate in the council and who spend our lives pursuing the most arcane subjects may with diligence gain what is for us special awareness of how to perceive and use ... dimensions. Here: let us look at some manuscripts that will help me explain. More tea, dear?"

"Please." Lilava dropped into a comfortable chair near the window. She felt a touch of dizziness and disorientation.

Lilava did her best to concentrate as they pored over Classical texts on geometry, astronomy, and magic. Finally, several hours later, they turned to the Great Elvish Encyclopedia. While Lilava could speak a little of the language, she couldn't read it — she had in fact seen only short inscriptions, because the elves prefer to keep both the spoken and particularly the written word secret — so Prosperpina guided her through the sections on what we call the Other World and its relation to our own.

"Even we have less than full understanding of the nature of the world, Lilava," Prosperpina explained. "As we determine it, our lands exist side-by-side with yours, but with only occasional conjunctions. We know how to find them, but most humans do not — and we prefer to keep that advantage. We seldom take interest in human affairs: we believe we have no right to interfere except in such cases as when they endanger us or our friends or allies. We have in fact learned and chosen to eliminate some of those conjunctions, because too often someone who should not have done so has stumbled through them, either to his injury or our own. Usually it has been a man blindly chasing an elven woman he has seen while she was unwisely searching for mushrooms or herbs or medicinal crystals in your lands. Most of our women are like you, what humans call sorceresses or enchantresses — or, among the less wise, witches — in that our preferred studies lead us to medicine and natural philosophy. For that reason we occasionally befriend humans like you, the Lady of the Lake, and others of your order, so that we may share some of our learning to our mutual benefit.

"We seek serenity and peace above all else, for our greatest joy comes in communing with the earth we love. Our lives exist, if you remember from the Greek geometry text, in what we envision as a parallel to yours. You will recall that by definition parallels do not meet, but where physical accidents of some magnitude have occurred, or occasionally where time has worn barriers thin, the conjunctions arise. We have probably used them more often than we should: we too, like you, may fail to resist our curiosity, though need or, as in the case of Severus, compassion may as well move us to cross over."

"Never love?"

Prosperpina looked for a long time into Lilava's eyes, until Lilava began to grow uncomfortable.

"Has love for humans never moved your folk to seek us out?" Lilava elaborated. "We have stories... ."

Prosperpina lowered her chin to her breast, then nodded ever so slightly. "Yes," she said quietly, "in a very few instances elves have crossed over for the same reason as humans, for love — though I should call it infatuation, since it occurs before opportunity has permitted the continuing, deep, meaningful exchange that we value as the true pathway to individual love."

"In childhood I heard stories," Lilava said, "and the Britons tell many of them. Forgive me, but I'm weary with study." Feeling exhausted and less attentive than usual, Lilava failed to notice the hint of discomfort in Prosperpina's eyes. "Will you tell me a love story, one from the elves' point of view? Consider it cultural exchange."

Prosperpina paused, her eyes fixed on the floor. She shook her head and sighed sadly, then looked out the window at the moon that was just rising, large, somewhat flattened, above the horizon. "I am not sure I can," she said.

"You know no such stories?"

"I know them, one quite well. But I am not sure I can get myself to tell it. And you may regret having heard it."

"Forgive me, then, for asking."

"No need for forgiveness, dear. One can study only so long without a break. Perhaps we should take a turn in the garden. I believe you will love it as I do, but I warn you, its restfulness often so relaxes the mind that the mouth speaks before thought intervenes to stop it. The garden has a tendency to bring unspoken concerns to the surface. And I perceive that you have buried worries deep within you that you have yet to release."

"I have?"

"You have."

Lilava felt emotion beginning to stir from deep within her — yes, Prosperpina was right: she could feel something, something that she had hidden, driven deep into her heart by necessity. Her thoughts were interrupted by the sound of footfalls in the corridor. Both women remained seated, but looked toward the door, where in a moment they heard a soft knocking. Lilava thrilled, thinking it might be news, but her knees felt too weak for her to rise from her chair.

"Yes," the queen said softly. The door opened slowly, and a messenger put just his head through the opening. His eyes looked calm and kind.

"News from the northeast, Great Lady: the king has found little difficulty, but intends to ride on toward the eastern shore. He sends you and the human lady his greetings, and he hopes to return himself within three days, if the patrol remains unmolested. And the human knight: the Guardian of the West sends word that he has seen the man..."

Lilava couldn't stifle an exclamation.

"He has found him in the company of a — I believe he called it a wyvern. The knight is unharmed. He helped them find a lost child and is by now continuing along the coast, on foot, with his odd companion."

"Thank you for your welcome message," said the queen.

"My pleasure, great ladies." He bowed his head toward them and then shut the door behind him.

Lilava felt her head spinning and her stomach churning, the unfortunate but powerful effects of relief and weariness, but she controlled herself to say, "Wyverns: are they then real? I've heard of them as legends or symbols, but have never seen one."

"Yes, and there we find another odd sign, since we should not see them here: they come from your lands, not ours, though I believe far from the part of the world you know," the queen answered. "Let's look them up in the Encyclopedia; then we shall take a walk in the garden. May I help you up?"

"No, thank you, lady — I shall be fine, with just a moment here to steady myself."

"Quite so. Ah: here is the entry. A shortish description and also a diagram: look. They are unpredictable creatures, as I understand, but loyal enough to their friends. Come now to the garden, and we will enjoy its peace. The trees have the power to heal, you know, though one may have to cleanse her thoughts first to experience their virtue, since it comes largely from their capability to encourage restfulness. And there I will tell you a story."

* * *

"You seem a bit shaky, dear — worn out, no doubt. Over here by the apple trees we will find a bench. There is a font, and I will get you some water."

Lilava thought she had stilled the spinning in her head before they had descended the stairs from the library, but it had returned as soon as they had entered beneath the light canopy of trees in the garden. Dusk was spreading, and the moon was rising. She eased onto the bench and gladly accepted a drink from Prosperpina. She felt unexpected and unwonted words welling up from deep inside her — the garden, as Prosperpina had said, seemed to want to draw to the surface all the pain and worries she had long buried. She took a small sip of the cool water; it tasted clean, light, only slightly metallic.

"Give me your hand, Lilava."

Oblivious, Lilava placed her hand in both of Prosperpina's.

"Do not worry. You need to speak. Let the words come. Speaking will ease your suffering."

"Oh, I don't feel much like talking," Lilava said, feeling suddenly as though she were back home with her own mother. "I'm thirsty, though, and terribly tired." She sipped again, then took a long, deep drink, draining the water from the cup.

"But if I did feel like talking, there's so much I could tell you, though I shouldn't trouble you with it all. I haven't slept well in I can't remember how long, since long before Sevy — Sir Severus, my husband — and I left Britain. First, in the early days of my search, it was for worry, worry whether I could find someone to accompany me back home, then knowing Sevy was the one, probably the only man who could ever have fought the beast, then fearing lest he wouldn't come with me or that Lancelot would kill him or he Lancelot, and then his actually getting there — he has trouble crossing water, you know, though he's getting better and can actually swim a bit now — and then the battle came so soon, before I could fully prepare him, and I truly thought, feared, he must die, and Liletta, too, and yes I feared for myself as well, and we nearly did, you know, more than once, die that is — odd thing to say, that, 'die more than once,' as if one could, but then poor Sevy shall, since he has died once already, and thank God for your husband and his powers, and I've been forgetting to ask you if we can ever leave these shores again, not that I feel so eager to do so, since it's so peaceful here, and I need peace for a time, oh how I need it, and you should have seen Sevy after the battle: for some time I felt as though, even though he survived it, I had lost him anyway, he simply couldn't recover from it, as though my adventure, with the monster, had drained from him all the will to live and act and do anything, but I loved him so dearly, yet I dared not tell him so, and to tell the truth — another silly saying, that, 'to tell the truth,' as if I should ever tell you other than truth — I wasn't sure for a time that I should marry him, you know: would that have done him or me any good then? but of course I did, we did, and I felt so good that he accompanied me not just to fight the monster but for me, and he didn't even give a thought to risking his life, never even mentioned it, now how can we, I, ever repay him for that? and how could I ever have expected anyone, especially him, to risk his life for me? but all the time I was holding back from him how tired I felt — you know how you can force yourself to go on just a bit more, to get through things, and then all the world falls down around you for your weariness, but I never got to rest, to sleep, though love gives you more energy than you ever thought possible, and then that beast of a fellow Abra — have you ever heard of him? well, I hope you don't — it must have been he who lead Sevy so far out in his swimming, which as I said he doesn't do so very well, though that doesn't stop him from trying — so it must have been he, Abra, who set us on our way back to Britain, where I suppose it was fortunate we arrived just in time, I to save Guinevere from that toad Mordred — wonder what has happened to him by now? — and Sevy to try to reason with Arthur and Lancelot and make peace, which he did, though I think not for long, and you probably know the rest of that story from your husband, for he brought us here, and I do thank you so much for that, but even with the restful rooms and gardens I still haven't slept fully, deeply, and I do so need it: I feel like a towel that someone has wrung dry, a tea kettle that has been boiled and boiled and drained and drained for so long that it sits lower than empty, corroded inside, and seeing death so close so many times has made me feel old, old — funny, when we went home, and I looked at my parents, they looked younger to me than I felt; isn't that funny? — and I'm not old, you know, but young, at least as enchanters go: that's what I need, what I want, to feel young again, to walk and talk for years with Sevy under these beautiful trees and the clear skies and away from monsters and British weather and tasks, stupid, stupid tasks — have you noticed how he always talks about tasks! does your husband do that? all husbands must do that ... and I don't want to hear about them, tasks that is, any more and I certainly don't want to send anyone on any more of them, particularly Sevy — I have not got over his death, you know, even though we have got him back: you know, don't you, that I too have seen that road, the Gray Road? he asked me about it, saw it I think in my eyes, and I haven't told him, but then we've had so little time to tell each other things, though he told me some stories on our way across the sea to my home — when I think of home I can't help but feel a need for my sister, for she's so dear to me, and our closeness has nearly got her killed, too, twice, same as Sevy, oh dear mother I'm scared, you know, but I can't be, for everyone depends on me, and I on them, but then I think of that funny look that Sevy gets on his face when he's about to fight, it's so precious, the funny fellow: you wouldn't think that he were about to fight, but the look on his face says, as though he were speaking it right out, "Now look here, you monster, you — that's just the sort of tone he'd use, that serious, deadpan, scolding tone — now look here, you monster, just be off and let's not have a fight, because you must know if we do, I'll just womp the stuffing out of you, and that's no good for either of us, is it? he's just the funniest thing because he doesn't want to hurt a fly yet look how he makes a living and I love him so much but I'm so tired and I need so badly to sleep sorry to keep going on like this why am I telling you this anyway? oh, must be the trees, as you said, the garden is making me speak, oh, if they could only make me sleep, too, but I seldom even hope for that anymore, who can sleep, can you? I know I never really can, even when ... zzz."

Lilava had curled up into a ball on the end of the garden bench with her head resting on Prosperpina's knee. With her last words her chest heaved, she sobbed, and several drops of the tears, tears of emotion and suffering and love that she had long held back, fell like raindrops to the ground at her feet. Before she could clear her spirit of all the tears that had stored up inside her, sleep overcame her. Prosperpina's presence and the healing power of the garden had drawn the poison of enduring suffering to the surface of Lilava's consciousness, and because she had held it in so long, its release so emptied her of strength that at that moment a score of brass bands strutting by playing marches at full volume couldn't have waked her from that dear, deep rest.

"Your elven love story, will have to wait," whispered Prosperpina, brushing some stray hairs from Lilava's forehead. "But you have told me a human one, and if I had a daughter of my own, I wouldn't wish from her more loyalty, more courage, or a better story than yours. Sleep well, sleep well. You have a long road ahead of you."

* * *

In the early afternoon of the next day, Lilava woke in her bed in her apartment. At first she felt woozy and only half-conscious. When she found a mirror to brush her hair, she thought that all the flips and tangles looked much like a poor nest built by disreputable birds. When she had washed and had a cup of tea, memories of talking to Prosperpina began to return, and the burn of embarrassment rose from her belly to her shoulders, across her face and all the way to the top of her scalp: had she indeed said all those things to the queen of the elves? How could she have been so rude, so indiscreet, so childish?

Then she heard a knock at the door. She feared that in a state of utter mortification she must face the queen again. Rather than calling out, she opened the door tentatively, uncertain of whether she could speak at all.

In the hallway outside stood a young elven maiden carrying cloth towels and a healthy-sized basket. She smiled gently, her cheeks the color of roses, her teeth whiter than the full moon and her hair dark as the night sky. Her face shone with the open friendliness and desire to please that one sees in a loving little sister.

"Good morning, ma'am," said the girl in a voice gentle as milk, speaking halting Latin. "I have brought you breakfast and fresh towels. I hope you have slept well. May I do anything for you?"

"Thank you, miss, no. Oh: may the sun brighten your path. Oh: do you know how I got here? I don't quite remember anything last night after the library and garden."

"Yes, poor lady: you had studied so late that you fell asleep from pure weariness right on a bench in the garden, so one of the librarians called two of my sisters to bring you back here — my sisters tucked you in. They said you were as light to carry as a puff pastry, so please do not worry about having caused them any trouble. We so seldom have guests of any sort, especially human ones, that we feel happy to serve you. They said you are beautiful for a human — I should have said you are beautiful even for an elf, begging your pardon if that sounds too familiar for someone who has just met you."

"Thank you — everyone here is so kind. And your lady queen: do you know if I am still to see her today?" Lilava hoped that by oversleeping she hadn't delayed the queen's plans.

"Yes indeed: she has written this message for you." The elf maiden handed Lilava the basket, towels, and note, bowed, smiled brightly as sunshine, and left.

Lilava expected to have a headache, but to her surprise, once she had eaten — a marvelous breakfast of warm bread with cream and honey, freshly cut apples sprinkled with cinnamon (which Lilava had tasted only once before), a small cake of bean-curd sprinkled with savory herbs and olive oil, and juices made from pressed cherries and blackberries — she felt enormously better. Even her sense of regret at having said so much, which she became more and more certain she had actually done, began to ease, if not entirely disappear. In fact, her heart felt lighter than it had in years, despite the ache of missing Severus, who was, to her delight, once again still alive and adventuring.

She read Prosperpina's note, composed in a patois of Severus' Cymric language and Lilava's variety of Latin: "I hope you have slept well. Please do not hurry. Breakfast, rest, and when you feel ready, come to see me in my hall. Today we will travel together to the council — I believe you will enjoy the ride, through some of our loveliest lands. Please don't feel a wren's breath of concern about our conversation. As I warned you, the garden encourages one to cleanse the spirit, and I took you there so you might, if you wished or needed to, speak. From you I have learned to love humans better. Thank you." She had signed the note with a single elaborate P followed by a dot.

Lilava placed the note carefully among her few belongings, scrubbed her face for fully five minutes, finished dressing, and left for the Great Hall, an enormous building of many floors and angles built of bright white stone.

She found Prosperpina talking with a number of elves, some with sunny faces, some looking serious, if not grave, in the foyer of the Great Hall. Together their voices made a soft, deep music, like flowing water. She noticed that no matter how many elves one had about, one never felt crowded among them. They seemed not to impose on space as humans do, but to glide smoothly through it. They seemed seldom to touch each other or anyone or anything else, and they moved more gracefully than a light summer breeze through a wind-harp.

249

"Dear Lilava," whispered the queen with her gentle smile, drawing herself away from two tall, absorbed looking elves dressed in floor-length robes. "Welcome to the Great Hall — it is grand, is it not? You must meet some of the councilors who have come here to join us for the ride, and then we shall be on our way."

The two tall elves, thin and grave of face with blond hair hanging to their shoulders, Prosperpina called Vainen and Jouka. Another, broad across the chest but with short, stout legs, thick black hair, and enormous brown eyes she called Manawa. Several steps away two elven women whispered mouth-to-ear in a ray of sun that poured down through a skylight: Prosperpina introduced them as Rhia and Brianna.

"Miralli giundi, mai verna Le tennele zhamas beandi zu stolli," Lilava said as confidently as she could.

Hearing her Elvish, they all smiled appreciatively.

"May the sun light your path," Vainen said in good Latin.

"And the moon soothe your dreams," Brianna added.

"You got even the inflections right: well done!" Manawa added. "We must share carefully, for this human has no fear of learning."

"We have all gathered now, I think" Prosperpina said. "I have arranged for Starlight to bear you, Lilava. I hope that pleases you. We have a day and a half's ride south to the council grounds and its sanctuary. The sooner we begin, the better rest we shall get tonight, and the sooner we may continue tomorrow."

"You have forgotten me again!" said a voice from below, and Lilava looked down to see a small but ancient looking figure tugging at Prosperpina's robe.

"I beg your pardon, my good Hod, but you will find we have not forgotten you: we have a beautiful cart with two ponies to pull it, and it rides soft as a pillow."

"Thank you. That's better," replied Hod. He tipped his tall toboggan hat to Prosperpina and winked at Lilava, then stalked toward the door in strides that looked far too long for his short legs. A tiny crystalline trail of ice remained in the footprints of his thick boots.

"Snow gnome," Prosperpina said. "Odd creatures, but highly aware of the earth and its power, learned in spells, dangerous as enemies — despite their stature — and nearly as dangerous as friends. Look that you do not step in his tracks, unless you do not object to falling: he leaves ice in his wake. We draw councilors from far and wide when we need them."

"I had thought you'd all be elves."

"The more varied our friends, the wider our knowledge. That is one of the reasons we are so pleased to have you with us."

"Thank you!"

Prosperpina linked her arm through Lilava's, and they strolled toward the door. "Dear Elf Mother, I hope you'll forgive me if I babbled on and on to you last night. I have only a vague memory of it, but as it comes back little by little, I feel appalled at what I think I must have said."

"Give it not one moment of worry. I took you to the garden for that very purpose. No concern: I had no curiosity about what you would say, only hope that you would say it and so cleanse yourself of it. Most visitors go on far longer and more revealingly than you did, and they have seldom had nearly so great a need to speak. You have great weariness. You have noticed that elves are not loquacious, but even we can manage no better restraint than did you." Prosperpina's laughter fell like snowflakes, and Lilava felt her embarrassment melt away.

* * *

The ride began easily, through orchards of cherry and apple and pear trees, and then it opened out over many miles of rolling hills and stream-fed valleys. The party talked little and quietly. Any but the most attentive person would hardly have noticed their passing, even with the steady click-clack of Hod's cart. At last they reached an abrupt crest, beyond which descended a sharp gorge to a rushing river below. The elven tracker who rode in front of the party guided them down a delicately twisting pathway. Hod drove his rig down the path with far greater skill than Lilava would have thought possible. Several soldiers followed in the rear of their party — Lilava wondered at the need for them so deep in elven lands. Beneath her Starlight felt light and sure-footed, and Lilava thought something must have frightened her badly for her to flee Severus. She wondered about the wyvern and what sort of companion he might be.

When they reached the bottom, the tracker took some time finding the best available ford, so that when they crossed, dusk was already fading into night. They paused briefly to drink and fill water bottles, then pursued a steady pace up the gentler hill on the other side of the river. At its crest they found a small campground, surrounded by sturdy oaks and sporting several small, wooden shelters, on the edge of a forest that stretched as far as the eye could see into the slowly sloping valley. There they made small fires and set up for the night. The stars spread above them bright and varied as clouds of fireflies.

As they toasted long rows of succulent vegetables skewered on sticks over the campfires, Lilava sat next to Prosperpina and Manawa and practiced her elvish. Manawa's large, round, brown eyes repeatedly grew even larger and rounder as Lilava quickly gained phrase after phrase and nuance after nuance. Later, after much mutual pleasure from the language lesson, he asked her a question.

"I have heard that your husband walked the Gray Road into the Land of Shadows. Is that true? We elves have little knowledge of it and much curiosity about it, since our paths — in life or death — do not take us there."

Lilava sat wrapped in a warm blanket and found her eyes growing heavy: all day she hadn't entirely shaken off the fuzziness of sleep from the night before. While she wished not to be rude, and so to answer the question, even amidst the pull of sleep, the images she recalled — of Severus' journey and her own — caused her to shiver.

"Forgive me for asking you at so late an hour. You will tell me another time. For now, may your thoughts rest and your dreams be free of trouble." Lilava wasn't sure, but she thought she noticed the elf waving a hand gently before her eyes. She fell asleep on the spot and remembered no more of that evening.

Early in the morning Lilava awoke on the very spot where she had fallen asleep the night before. She felt a pillow beneath her head and an extra blanket around her shoulders. She took a drink from her water bottle, which rested just arms-length away. She rose to waking with surprising energy — her legs felt light, springy, younger than they had for some months, despite the previous day's long ride. She felt the pleasurable desire in her legs to break into a run, such a desire as a child feels on the first day of spring after spending winter pent inside, at the time of life long before cares and years have the power to weigh down the body. Her own lightness delighted her, and though it made her feel undignified, she couldn't help but leap to see if she could touch a branch that stretched well above her head. She laughed, leaped, and astonished herself that she could actually reach it. Then she lay down, rolled on her back, kicked her feet up and laughed.

"The water from that river often has that effect on someone who tastes it for the first time," said the dignified Vainen as he passed by on his way toward the woods. He frowned, picked out a branch higher than the one Lilava had reached, giggled, and leaped and touched it. Then he laughed gleefully, danced a little two-step, and disappeared among the trees.

"Not just first-timers," said Manawa, who had begun to clean up the campfires from the night before. "Something about its clean tang and the way it gobbles up air as it whisks over the rocks makes one feel giddy. He-he," he said, spinning his body in circle after circle as he headed to pack his horse.

After a simple breakfast of water with dissolved berry-powder and grainy brown bread with butter, everyone mounted, and together they rode into the forest. They moved steadily but slowly, picking through the slender, many-forked pathway with care. Only the beauty and quiet of the trees kept the way from being too tedious, and though by early evening they hadn't traveled a great number of miles, they had reached a small clearing with two large, limestone boulders in its center. There all the riders stopped and dismounted.

"Here is the entryway to the council chamber," Prosperpina said to Lilava, drawing alongside her. "Forgive me, but I must ask you to cover your eyes for a moment."

Lilava did. She heard several voices chanting in harmony, followed by a low rumble. When she opened her eyes, the two stones had separated, and a pathway opened before them down into the earth. "To the council," Prosperpina said. Several of the elves lit torches, and the group who were members of the council descended, while the guards spread themselves outside, about the clearing.

The ceiling of the passage stood two armslengths above Lilava's head, and the passage itself wove serpentine and gently downward. It had many branches, each branch often with multiple doors, each pair of doors labelled unobtrusively with "la" or "ta," carved in runes, Old Elvish for "here" or "there": "here" invariably meant the nearest door, while "there" meant the farthest from the point of the label, until they reached a final fork in the path with two round openings leading into what appeared to be total darkness.

"I observe you have understood the directions," Prosperpina said to Lilava. "But here they reverse, and one dare not take the wrong way. Here we choose the left doorway. But before we do, go just to the righthand opening and no farther, and listen."

Lilava did so, pausing. She heard a low swirling deep below and tested the pathway with her toe. The path appeared firm, but a mere foot ahead it tumbled into an enormous chasm. The stone in the arch absorbed light, making the chasm difficult to discern even by torchlight. Deep down she thought she heard water bubbling and roiling. "Follow me along the lefthand path," Prosperpina said, "but watch closely. You will notice that we elves do not have the human prejudice against the lefthand path." As the elves crossed into the opening, they jumped. Though the pathway looked firm, when Lilava followed, she too jumped. "Now test again behind you with your foot, keeping the other firmly planted," Prosperpina said, after they had all entered the new hallway. Lilava touched her foot tentatively into the spot over which they had jumped: there, too, a chasm opened into the deep. "Elves are careful folk," Prosperpina said. "Not paranoid, but careful."

Maybe paranoid, Lilava thought. Her people had lived for years beneath the Chimaera's mountain without conceiving any such device as these elaborate tunnels. She wondered where all the other doorways had led, if into mazes, other steep drops, or just back where they had begun, and from whom they protected the elves who used them.

The councilors followed the new path straight forward for several minutes until it emptied into a large, well-lit chamber that smelled of fresh air — Lilava wasn't sure how, since she concluded they must have gone well beneath the earth's surface. Several figures stood about a central creche full of logs that looked as though it were set for a fire. They carefully descended a steep, slick staircase, then Lilava found herself on a soft, sandy floor. She preferred the feeling of earth rather than stone beneath her feet. Those of the party already there called what sounded like greetings in Old Elvish to the newcomers, and someone lit the fire in the creche, which caught immediately and spread both light and shadows across the floor. Manawa stepped alongside Lilava and took her elbow.

"Now you will have a fuller test of your language skills," he said, "but do not worry if you fail to keep up. We will make sure everything is clear to you before we conclude, and you can feel confident you shall have your say." He winked at her then hurried ahead, hugging an elf of about his height but with very dark skin and greeting him warmly. They moved on arm-in-arm to several others and, with their arms around one another's shoulders, began an intense conversation, smiling, but bent attentively to one another's words.

Vainen and Jouka loped in their long-legged, dignified strides with Hod tramping rapidly behind them toward three other figures, one tall and blond like them, but with a round face and toothy grin and wearing a tall cloth hat. The second looked more like an enormous shrub than an elf or human, lithe, dark-skinned, covered with vines, leaves, and sprays — Lilava couldn't tell immediately if they were natural or decorative. The third was short, hardly bigger than Hod, with dark but graying hair and a large, round belly, clothed in a floor-length robe with a rope tied round the ample waste. As they neared, they began a chant that rose in volume and pitch until it concluded in a shout, followed by various hand-graspings and back-pattings. Rhia and Brianna moved quickly toward the central creche to help with the elves who waited by the fire.

Lilava cast her eyes over what appeared a large, round chamber, large enough that only with difficulty could she perceive the far side of it. As she walked forward she felt drafts from many different directions — they had come from the north, but the chamber must have openings from other directions as well, she thought. She followed Prosperpina toward two other elves of shorter stature. In the rising firelight she noticed they had reddish faces, and their skin looked wrinkled as with considerable age. With only a hint of a smile, both bowed deeply to Prosperpina, who embraced them and spoke in what to Lilava sounded like an entirely different language than she had heard before. Lilava was struck by how, like humans, the elves are not one homogeneous people, but a diverse group who must inhabit many and varied regions of their own world. They also got along with gnomes better than people did. Once the thought crossed her mind, it seemed obvious, and she wondered why she had not thought of it before.

Prosperpina turned, raised her hands, and called in Latin in a voice louder than it sounded, "Come elves, gnomes, sylphs, naiads, and human to the Council of Shamans. While I greet you always with the greatest pleasure, you know we have convened over matters of the utmost gravity."

She spoke then several sentences in Old Elvish, which Lilava could barely follow, then continued again in Latin. "I suggest we take our places around the fire and begin the Ritual of Convergence. We must determine what force, which we all have called the Troubles, has invaded our marches. It encroaches daily further into our lands, and while our losses have yet been few, the rising plague of anxiety — of harried visions, of chilling whisperings, of the shadow of malevolent creatures — has seen no precedent since our departure from the lands of the humans a millennium ago. We must combine our powers of foresight, discernment, and earth-bond to identify the intruder and excise it. We must not allow these vexations to end our long age of peace and tranquility, those virtues upon which our spirits feed and by which our bodies endure." Prosperpina again spoke briefly in Elvish, then let her hands fall to her sides.

All the others bowed deeply to her and began moving to positions in a circle around the central fire. Prosperpina nodded to Lilava to follow, and she directed the enchantress to sit next to her — Hod sat just to her left, wiggling his eyebrows at her before he closed his eyes. Clearly the queen felt as though they had no time for a full round of introductions. Lilava wished she could have had time to meet and talk with all the councilors, to learn about them, their ways and their wisdom. But she saw that any hope of exchange would have to wait — the council had assembled on business, and they intended to engage it as directly as they could. Lilava wondered at peoples who could collect themselves and cooperate at the hint of danger, when humans often ignored wars fought not far from their homes, as long as they didn't interrupt local commerce.

All the councilors sat, crossed their legs, let their hands fall open, palm up, over their knees, and closed their eyes. The fire had risen to burn warmly, and they sat not close enough to be burned, but close enough to feel its heat. The elves began a slow, steady chant, which Lilava heard taken up harmoniously by other voices in higher or lower registers. She couldn't discern words, but felt herself drawn into the harmony and soon began humming along. Gradually Elvish words and hints of phrases began to take shape in her mind, and she wove them amidst her humming. Then words began to rise and fall, swirl and pass before her eyes as though they were banners, whole sentences as if she heard them in her native dialect of Latin.

"What troubles the land?"

"A foreign enemy, long asleep."

"What woke the enemy?"

"The arrival of its demise."

"What did it do?"

"Fought for its life."

"Did it die?"

"It survived."

"Where did it go?"

"It came here."

"What does it seek?"

"A new home — and flesh to consume."

Lilava, absorbed in the chanting, barely noticed that the Latin words in her mind and the Elvish words of the chant, though of vastly different languages, had fallen together into perfect rhythm. She felt her heartbeat quicken, and her forehead and palms began to sweat.

"Who brought it?"

"A traitor and fraud."

"Whence did he bring it?"

"The land of the humans."

"What does he seek?"

"His own power when it sleeps."

"How long will it reign?"

"Centuries untold."

"How can we stop it?"

"We cannot."

"Who then can?"

"Two together, if not one."

Lilava suddenly felt cold, despite the heat of the fire. Sweat covered her entire body, and her head began to swirl until she thought she must faint. She began to perceive not just words, but an image rising from unconscious thoughts, an image she had tried to bury, but that would not yield to her powers.

"Where can we find them?"

"They have come."

"Will they help us?"

"One is trying."

"Where is the other?"

"Here in our midst."

"What must she do?"

"Help stop the horror."

"Name the horror."

Lilava staggered to her feet and shouted. "Draagakkileo! Draagakkileo!"

Prosperpina and Hod leaped to their feet to catch Lilava before she fell. She could just see their pale, horrified faces as though through a thick mist. She fought to remain conscious.

"What did you see?" Lilava didn't hear the words, but perceived them as though Prosperpina spoke them directly into her mind, without need of sound.

Lilava spoke but one word.

"Chimaera!"

And then she lost consciousness.

* * *

When she returned to herself, Lilava had a vague sense of folk scurrying about her. She sat, propped against a stone. Before she was even aware again of who and where she was, Hod placed a bowl of thin, hot soup in her hands and motioned for her to drink.

"I've got to stop this fainting thing," she said. "I've never had this sort of weakness before."

"Under such pressure even I would faint," Manawa said, emerging into vision from beside her. He was checking her pulse, and he placed the back of his hand against her forehead to test for fever. "I have lived a very long time and have seen horrors outside of even your experience, but the vision you saw suggests perils far beyond the powers of mortals or elves."

"I have faced it before."

"Sadly, you may have to face it again," Manawa said.

"Have to?"

"You may make your own choice, of course," Hod responded. "But likely this monster will not elude, but rather seek you out. Where we would not usurp your choice, it may give you none."

After several sips of the soup, warm, salty, and herby, comforting and restorative, Lilava was beginning to collect her thoughts, and the full import of the situation, beyond its immediate horror, began to dawn on her.

"Severus! We must go immediately. He may already ..."

"He may," said Prosperpina, who reached her hands down toward Lilava to help her up. "How much did you see in your vision?"

"I didn't actually see much of anything. The chanting cast me into some sort of trance — it felt like twirling in a mist or in falling snow, as though my spirit had risen from my body — and I felt the presence rather than saw it."

"Near or far?"

"Farther than nearer, to the north, I think, and then perhaps east — oh, forgive me, queen, but I should have thought also of your lord. He too may face the danger."

"By now he has reached our eastern coast, unless an understanding of the danger has called him back — I must hope rather to our home than to the Northern Forest, where I suspect the beast should first gather and test its strength, since there most often come stray humans."

"Severus had a sense of its presence, I think, soon after he returned from the Gray Road. He hinted at it rather than affirmed it, but some credible feeling must have moved him to think of it. We believed after our battle that we had rid the world of the Chimaera for many long years."

"Rid your world of it and brought it to this one," Hod said, increasingly uneasy with what he was hearing.

"Rather sent it than brought it," Prosperpina said. "You sent it fleeing, and someone or something with malevolent intent found a way to bring it here. It will feed on the energy of the land: I understand now why Arawn has remained so wearied, more so than he should have been merely by bringing Severus back from the Shadows. Arawn draws strength from his bond to the land. I am surprised, though, that I have not more strongly felt the beast's presence, for the land is near and dear to me as well. The Chimaera is something foreign to the nature of our lands: that may make it less dangerous to us — or infinitely more so."

"You think it to be the source of the Troubles?" Manawa asked.

"I feel it to be the means," Lilava replied. "But it has not got here under its own power. I sense that as yet it feels — out of place, disoriented, but it is gaining strength. The power of its presence is growing."

"We must learn more of it so that we may derive a proper defense."

"We must not waste another minute," Lilava said, staggering as she tried to free herself from Prosperpina's helping hands. "We have endangered not only your husband, but all your folk and all your lands. No one knows better than Severus and I what sort of monster we face — and I mean we, he and I. Whether we brought or sent it here or not, we must take responsibility to fight it: no other living person has had such experience. Of all the monsters in all the lands in all the world, this one had to find ours," she said, lamenting.

"We seldom get to choose what evil we face," Prosperpina said ruefully, "only how we face it. Come: the guards will be waiting with the horses. As you said, we must ride. We can inform the others as we go. Perhaps Arawn has reached home with news, and if Severus has indeed learned of the beast and prepares to confront it, we may, with all our diligence, reach him in time to help. The Northern Forest is vast, full of tricks and turns. Unless the Chimaera seeks him, he may need days or weeks to find it."

"If it is strong enough, it will seek him," Lilava said.

As soon as they had departed the caversn, they rode through the remainder of the night and into the next morning. When they reached the Elvenhome, no one had yet heard news of Arawn. The councilors met briefly in the Great Hall.

"You must sleep," Prosperpina told Lilava.

"I can't. I must seek my love. We have lived too much of our lives apart, and I would not have him alone at his time of greatest need."

"He may have acquired allies of whom we have no idea. My folk do not lack due diligence, and the world is a strange place, full of unexpected good and ill. He may still have the wyvern or some other creatures to help him as well."

"Or he may be entirely alone. I must not let that happen."

"Milady Queen!" called a messenger, entering the hall, "news of the king: he rides toward Elvenhome and should arrive within the hour!"

"Thank Mother Earth," said the queen.

"And may he have Severus with him," Lilava whispered, knowing she was hoping without hope.

II A Battle Rebattled

[... wherein Severus must once more face an unbeatable enemy.]

Severus, Vern, and Courage struggled along through the increasingly dense forest as best they could. In its darkness Severus had lost track of time since their encounter with Abra: two days, or maybe three? Courage, following, occasionally whinnied his disapproval of their direction — deeper into the forest — since he would be unlikely to find any decent grazing pastures there, and they would all more likely encounter enemies than friends. Though Severus and Vern shared their failing food supplies liberally, Courage had to make up for long weeks of meager fare, and as he would grow stronger, he would grow also hungrier.

"Mahn, dis fores' really someting," Vern said, whistling. I nevah see anyplace wid so many twist and turn, so many tree. Don' we evah get outta dis place? Wheah I come from, we get dee great heat, bu' at least we get dee cool breeze. Dis place feel like a house made of all closets, wid no rooms!"

"Yes, hoomph, I know, humph," said Severus, equally irritated, pushing his way through incredibly dense growth. "Forest shouldn't be this dense." Many hours before they had found open forest floor beneath a tall canopy of trees, but now trees and shrubs seemed to grow more closely about them even as they moved. "Could be worse, though."

"How could i' be worse, mahn?"

"We could run into a rain gnome or some such thing."

"Hee, hee, hee."

They heard tinkling laughter from above.

"Oh, no," Severus lamented, expecting buckets of rain to drown them at any moment. At least, he thought, it will wash the sweat of all this closeness from me, though briefly.

"Hee, hee, hee."

"Ah, mahn, i' jus' got worse."

But Severus didn't feel any rain. So he looked up. Peeking down through parted branches just beyond jumping distance sat a dark-green face topped by a tall brown hat. A wide moustache and gray-green whiskers parted to show firm, straight yellow teeth with a toothpick hanging out over the lower lip.

"Wood gnome," Vern uttered in utter disgust.

"Blast," said Severus.

"Hee, hee, hee!" repeated the gnome, his beady eyes aglow with happiness at having the chance to torment unwanted guests. A tendril worked its way into Severus right ear, tickling the sensitive skin.

"Please stop that, my good fellow. Now: what do you want?"

The gnome climbed higher, trying to be sure he was out of their reach. He wanted to look assured, but Severus saw he wasn't entirely worry free: he must have sensed Severus' strength, and he certainly had seen that Vern could fly. Beneath him several sprouts grew out almost instantly to make him harder to reach by sudden attack.

"Too late," the gnome hissed. "What I want is for you not to be here. Since you are here, just tree to get out. Hee, hee: just tree, just tree, hee hee!"

"Not only a irr-ee-tating little fellow, but also a bery bahd punsteh," Vern said.

"Bad pun?" hissed the gnome. "Good pun!" and he spat at Vern, who, surrounded by groping limbs, had just enough room to dodge. Severus couldn't even see Courage behind them anymore: he had got bogged down in the growing filigree of tendrils.

"You may think this is funny," Severus said to the gnome, "but you shouldn't stay here now. I tell you for your own sake that you are in danger."

"Not from you, nasty little man," the gnome said, "or from your ugly green friend."

"What is dis wid dee 'ugly'?" Vern asked. "Don' folk heah know bee-yuty when dey see it?"

"Phaw!" hissed the gnome.

"I'm not saying you face danger from me, you little ... my good ... master gnome. From something far worse than I am. Something wicked this way comes, and you know, despite whatever you may say, that I am not wicked. Something lurks that will take your forest from you and eat you whole without even bothering to notice you're gone."

"Phaw! Liar!"

"Attend for yourself. Feel. Listen. Smell."

"I can smell. Smells bad: it's you!"

"What's to be done with such fellows?" Severus whispered to Vern. He felt a tendril wrap itself around his other ear.

"Forget about me, master gnome. You have me safely trapped. Test the wind above for yourself. Climb and sniff."

"Liar."

"Test!"

Severus heard the gnome climb higher, then heard him sniffing; he must have reached the top of his tree. Then Severus heard a distinct whimper.

"I told you," he called up, yanking his hand free from another tendril.

"Bad man — you brought it here!"

"No, you foo ... master gnome. I came here to rid the forest of it, if I can."

"You can't."

"If you let me go, I will try."

"No use. You can't." The gnome whimpered again.

"Mahn, you shown youahself a friend to me, and now I gonna be a good friend to you. I gonna get us outta heah."

"Can you do it?" Severus asked.

"I cahn. But dee bahd paht is, I got to leave you alone an' get dis guy outta heah wheah he canno' be trouble to us."

"I would be in your debt."

"We would be even," Vern said. "Now if you cahn twis' aroun', watch closely." Vern was able to shake open his wings just enough turn in a circle. He began to spin, more and more rapidly, like a top, and, as he spun, he began to hover, and the sharp edges of his wings cut through the tendrils, freeing him from their grip. The rapidity of his spin and the open space he had created for his wings allowed him to rise quickly, and like a green ember up the flue, he sailed up into the tree tops.

Severus heard a scream and then a long stream of curses.

"Got him, mahn." Vern's voice echoed down to Severus from the treetops. "I got me dee ugly little fellow, and I gonna take him above the trees away to somewheah safe — oah maybe I jus' drop him out to sea, eh?"

At that the gnome emitted another high-pitched scream.

"Mahn, you cahn get yoahself an' dee hoahsey outta heah?"

"Yes, I can cut through the brush now that nothing more is growing, I think. Just a minute. Yes, got my sword — I tell you, this new sword is amazing: never felt anything quite like it. Not of European make — Abra must have got it from some land far away with more advanced smithing, and the grip: so tacky, and the curve of it just fits in the palm, but light enough that the fingers can move it with a touch ..."

"Okay, okay: I got dee idea. I'm not so big on swoahds, if you know what I mean, mahn. Now while I gone, you take good ca'ah of yoahself: don' go fighting notting nahsty da' you canno' handle widout me. Be a good boy, an' I be bahk soon to help you. An' you, my ugly wood-guy, gnome oah whatevah — das right, you da ugly one! — jus' keep still, oah I drop you on someting shahp. I wish you could see dis, mahn," Vern called down to Severus. "Dee feet not jus' foah bee-yuty — dey also fully functional! I got him locked tight!"

"Fly safely, my friend! I will head north and east once I'm free."

"An' you stay outta trouble, mon ami."

"Oh, fuss and bludgeon," harrumphed the gnome. Though gnomes' words don't always make sense, one knows what they mean.

Severus could just hear Vern take off over the last leaves atop the trees and the gnome calling something that sounded like yeeee! and he set about the tedious task of cutting himself free.

* * *

262

Some hour or so later Severus had not only freed himself and Courage, but had also begun to make considerable progress through the Great Northern Forest — apparently the wood gnome had been slowing them down for some time by causing trees, shrubs, and vines to rise in their path. Without the gnome to raise its tendrils, the Forest raised no unusual hindrance in the knight's path.

Severus had of course since his youth shown great facility at speeding along through difficult terrain, particularly woods, which he had often scoured for his lord, keeping them safe from trouble. He didn't even think of riding the poor, skinny Courage, who followed along behind as gamely as he could.

Shortly he heard the sound of bubbling water, and with little difficulty he found its source: a cool, clear, spring with a makeshift stone font built around it, just the sort as would make a delightful stop for elf or human, in a green clearing that would have given the impression — had it not sat deep within an enormous forest — of a pleasant arbor gracing one's back lawn. Severus sat on the stones, cupped his hands and dipped them in the water, treating himself to several draughts of cold, sweet refreshment. Courage, happy for the rest, also came over and dipped a grateful snout into the water. The growing gloom of dusk had begun to fall around them, but a gentle ray of light poured down from an opening in the canopy directly above the spring. Exotic flowers of the colors of daffodils and azaleas, seeming to rise up to lick the light, occasionally punctuated the greenery.

Severus noticed on the other side of the spring a well-worn pathway opening out beyond the arbor. It ran north-south, with a gentle curve toward the spring — this font must be a regular stop for elven trackers and rangers, he thought. He leaped easily over the spring and let his eyes follow the path north. Ahead he saw the path broadening, and from what he could discern it twisted and turned before appearing to lead to a grander clearing. Some pasturing there, perhaps, he thought, glancing over at poor Courage's prominent ribs.

"Come, my friend," he said to the horse. "If you can manage just a bit more, we'll find a clearing and some decent grass for you — and for me, I hope" — there he drew his new sword and flashed it about — "a place to practice a bit with this sword and then to sleep." Courage bowed his head and whinnied, Severus wasn't sure whether at the thought of decent food or in mutual appreciation of the weapon or desire for sleep. "But first I can use a good wash," Severus added.

He sheathed his sword and bent over the spring. Eager at the thought of a clean face and ears, but cringing at the imminent sharp tingling of a cold plunge, he paused, then thrust his head into the spring. The crystalline cold sent a shiver all the way from his scalp to his heels, at once chilling him and charging his muscles with life. Like a cold slap, the water jerked him into full waking —

he realized how sleepy he had felt for days on end. Despite the chill, he held his head beneath the surface, flicking water down his neck with both hands.

Cold washed the dusty weariness of labor from his face, then continued down his back and all the way to his feet. It recalled to his mind the icy stillness that plagued his body after he had walked the Gray Road, but this feeling brought life rather than death. He clenched his hands into fists, fighting off a stiffness that began to spread through his fingers.

Suddenly he heard a deep, distant, growing rumbling. He yanked his head free of the water. Beneath his feet, the ground began to ripple. Courage, startled, neighed and reared up with fright. Severus could see the horse's eyes round and glowing — they looked like mirrors reflecting the starlight that was beginning to rain down from the white-dotted cobalt of the sky above.

Severus sniffed the air. He listened: a low, angry, ancient, malicious, familiar growl, still distant, but approaching. A feeling in the air: yes, Severus knew the feeling, the sound, the source.

If he could have spoken, and he nearly could, Courage would have shouted to his knight, "Run!"

"Take cover," Severus almost whispered in the deep tones intended to comfort when one knows nothing can, "back into the forest, the way we came. Try to find Vern. Keep you both safely away."

"No!" Courage would have insisted. "Run, but not that way! This way!"

Severus was already running, not away, but ahead, toward the clearing, the very spot toward which Trouble and that deep sinister growling were converging. The heat of battle rose in him, fighting the icy stillness of the cold water that penetrated his fingers and the gray memory of death that hovered at the edge of conscious thought.

As he ran along the elven path, the hairs on his neck stood straight up, his heart rolled like a drum, and the water dripped down his torso. Severus quickly felt for and took inventory of his weapons: a decent but unremarkable bow and a very few arrows; some dirks and darts; a long, dependable knife sheathed at his side; the amazing, exotic sword that some distant smith must have forged for exactly such a purpose as the one at hand. He glanced along the path, wishing he also had a stout staff, but he could spot nothing useful: the newly falling night was bringing with it a mist that rose from the ground and filtered out onto the path from among the trees. He rounded a curve in the path.

Before him stood a figure outlined in golden light. It looked like a Christian monk, youthful though not young, dressed in a long, greenish-white robe with a simple rope tied around the waist. Severus stopped before the figure and inclined his head in a brief but respectful bow.

"Severus" — the voice sounded deep and kind, but grave — "if you continue on this path, you will almost certainly die. You will fight alone. No help will reach you in time."

"Yes, I know."

"If you turn back, you may survive for a time, but great harm will come to many others."

"I suspected so. I will not flee."

"By coming here your enemy has lost some powers, but has gained others."

"Who are you, sir, and why do you stop me?"

"You ask as if you believe me a ghost."

"I ask so that I may know if you intend to bar my way."

"What will you do if I say 'yes'?"

"Request that you allow me to pass."

"Polite even at the brink of battle. You are a good man. No, I will not stop you. Should you prevail, you will help me, for I am the spirit of this wood. To guard it now, against such an adversary as you will find ahead, lies beyond my knowledge. I stop you only to tell you this — remember it well. Strike for the heart, the exact center of the breast, with that sword you carry. Luck, and not ill luck, has brought the weapon to you. With an apt thrust, and by no other means, you can end this woe. The one who brought the sword knew that, hoping to protect himself if he needed to, but I arranged that he forget it so that you might find it."

"Would that I could stop this creature for good and all."

"You can, if any luck remains with you. But as for escape ..."

Severus again heard growling in the distance.

"Our knowledge holds that the creature will only change its shape and flee, to return again in time," Severus said.

"It has lost the ability to change shape: our land differs from yours, and different powers hold sway here. When it arrived here, it was no bigger than a small bird. Through the nature of this land, the strength that it could draw from the earth here, it has resumed its original shape. If you kill it in this shape, its power and evil will pass away from this earth forever. Its strength has doubled since you last met it: it continues to draw energy from this land, from my forest. You have met it. You know it. The longer it dwells here, the stronger it will become. But remember this: though its strength has increased, as has its hatred of you, its speed has not. Regardless of what it says, it will try to crush you as soon as it can. Your speed is yet in your favor."

"I thank you, but I believe I must wait no longer."

"You are ready for what you face?"

"Yes, I believe so."

"May Mother Earth and all the divine spirits protect you."

"Thank you." Severus bowed deeply before the figure, and when he raised his head again, it was gone, leaving no sign that it had ever been there at all. Severus uttered a prayer and took off like an arrow shot toward the source of the growls that grew and rumbled ahead.

By the time he reached the clearing, the low, rumbling growl had risen to a high pitched scream that careened into him from the far end, where the trees rose again. There, at about the distance the fastest of runners can cover in a minute, aspens bowed and rocked, and the wood creaked, and something with incredible power tore trees up from their roots and tossed them aside like toothpicks.

Severus drew the sword. It seemed to vibrate in his hand, as he wrapped his fist around the hilt, and it adhered to his palm, drawing the skin and muscle to itself, making itself part of him. A series of runic letters, glowing in the darkness, resolved themselves along the length of the silver-blue blade. But the words were in Latin, so Severus could read them: "Weland-smith made me for this purpose, that I might slay what no one else can." He couldn't have released the sword from his hand even had he wanted to. It would practically have fought without him.

The clearing was still bare. Long — what seems to us a long time, as we wait for incontrovertible disaster — before Severus could see his adversary, he knew it was near. He felt it in the air, the earth, in the prickling of his skin: the abysmal malice, like nothing else he had ever encountered. And with a sudden rush it emerged from the wood. No doubt then.

Chimaera.

It extracted itself from the trees, raised its voice to the sky, and howled with the rage of a thousand banshees.

The head and mane of an enormous lion, the talons of an eagle, the long, snaky body of a winged dragon with a sinuous, barbed tail: it didn't change shape, either because as the forest spirit had said it no longer could or because it didn't want to. It sniffed, saw Severus standing opposite, tiny in comparison, and glared at him through two bulbous, golden eyes. And it laughed: a low, rolling, vicious, vengeful laugh.

In a voice as deep as the caverns of the Gray Road, it spoke in a malicious growl.

"You again. I have wanted to find you. Puny mortal, I thought you should have died first. You should have. Now I will avenge myself as I choose. I will rip you and slake my thirst on your blood. Then I will find the female. She is not so very far away. Her friends will feed me for millennia, and your frozen

spirit shall hear my laughter from the pits prepared for you in the depths of time." The enormous lion-head began creeping toward Severus.

"You should not be here in these lands."

"Nor should you. But you are already dead — I smell death on you."

"I have friends with greater power than mine."

"They have brought you back. And now I have friends, too. We have a mutual friend who has brought me here. Now I belong here much as you do, and I stake my claim to this place and to you."

"You're right: we neither belong here. Let us return to our own place and settle our battle there."

"I like it here. This place gives new strength to me. I have more power than I had. I will toy with you like a cat with a mouse. Then I will kill you in what manner most pleases me. You will lie here alone. I will find each of you alone."

The voice vibrated in Severus' heart and raced icily through his bloodstream. He knew he must give the beast no quarter, and he knew it was gaining confidence even as they spoke. He knew he must attack. The sword in his hand felt ready to strike with or without him.

But before he could spring, he felt a rush pass alongside him: Courage was dashing with all the speed he could muster straight toward the Chimaera.

The Chimaera, taken aback only for an instant, uttered a hollow laugh and raised a huge claw to swipe the horse from its path. To his surprise the sword allowed Severus to sheathe it. Less than confident with his bow, he nonetheless armed it and fired straight for the monster's open mouth.

The arrow missed its mark, but struck close enough that when the great claw swung down, it too missed its target. The force of the blow upon the air was enough to throw Courage from his feet, and the brave horse slid into the trees at the edge of the clearing. The monster roared thunderously.

Severus was already running at full speed toward his adversary. He fixed his mind that, whilst he lived, the beast should wreak no harm upon any other creature but him alone, and he must summon every fiber of his being to destroy it utterly.

"You cannot defeat me," Severus called out, leaping forward. The magic sword practically leapt back into his hand, and he struck at the great claw that, having missed its first mark, was preparing for a return blow upon its second.

The sword struck the Chimaera with a sound like a steel hammer on a steel anvil, and the beast shrieked in a howl that shook the woods about them. It drew up on its hind claws, glowered down at Severus, and pounced.

* * *

"**M**y heart tells me that we must hurry," Lilava said.

"As does mine," Prosperpina answered.

They rode in the cart with Hod, as deft a driver over hill and through forest as he was on the open road, along with Rhia who, Lilava had learned, was among the best of the elven physicians. Arawn and two of his best trackers led them, and behind followed Manawa, Vainen and Jouka, all expert riders and tireless as the elven-bred horses that carried them. Dozens of soldiers fanned out to the sides and behind.

The forest, Lilava noted even in the failing light, looked blasted, scrapped, as though a fire or whirlwind had passed through.

A deep growling sound filtered through the woods to where they rode, echoing menacingly among the trees.

"Haw!" yelled Hod to his horses, and the whole company accelerated its pace until Lilava thought they all should smash to death against the great oaks and beeches.

"The battle is about to commence," Prosperpina said. "I can feel it, hear them. We shall not arrive in time."

"We must try," Lilava said, wringing her hands as though she held her heart between them. "I wish he had his full strength. The battles have so weakened him."

"He has his love for you and his zest for life," Prosperpina answered, "and the uncountable wealth of experience. Even weakened, he has abilities bred for this work. Where strength may dwindle, resolve and heart may prevail."

* * *

Once Arawn had reached Elvenhome, he explained that before he had got so far as the east coast, word had found him of the extent of the horror that had infiltrated the Northern Forest. He and his band had immediately returned, dispatching what soldiers they could to the north, urging others to warn the settlements nearest the forest to find what protection they could. No sooner had he seen Prosperpina's eyes than he had given orders for fresh horses, soldiers, and gear, and within minutes the troop had begun the difficult ride north. While the land was beautiful, it was sculpted with woods and fells, rivers and chasms, making the ride tortuous and slow for all but the best riders, those with beyond-human skill.

In the face of disaster Lilava felt glad for such friends. Yet they had ridden with her not only for her own need, but for theirs as well: they knew that with the Chimaera loose in their lands and gaining strength, they should have no peace, and they believed that Severus, if not Severus and Lilava together, offered them the best chance of subduing an enemy foreign to their land and to their skills. As they rode, Lilava had shared with them all she knew of the beast, but Prosperpina guessed that in elven lands one would need different skills than Severus and Lilava had employed before to defeat it. Together Lilava, the gnome, and the elves had traveled straight north from Elvenhome, following first their best guess and later Prosperpina's keen senses to try to find Severus and join him in the battle they knew he couldn't avoid and probably couldn't win.

* * *

Severus ducked the beast's leap, rolled and swung the sword in a rapid arc, slitting the skin of its belly and barely avoiding the monstrous talons that crashed to earth beside him. The earth shook with the Chimaera's weight. The knight stumbled to his feet in time to parry the barbed tail that swung whiplike toward his head. The sword, miraculous in defense as it was in attack, repelled such a blow as Severus thought must yank his arm from the shoulder. The tail recoiled from the parry, then flared back toward him again, but he had already darted closer to its slower base, and as the barb swung broadly and missed him, Severus leaped upon the base and ran straight up it onto the monster's back. He tried to thrust the sword into the body, but even the magic blade could not pierce the thick dorsal skin. The Chimaera trembled like a dog shaking off water, and Severus lost his footing and felt himself airborne, thrown toward the trees. Confused, the Chimaera roared its anger, and the rumble thundered off the roof of the sky and through the forest with the force of a hurricane.

* * *

"Just ahead lies a wide artery," Arawn called, "one of the main forest roads. When you find it, turn to the west and ride at full speed!"

"Not far from there," Prosperpina uttered hurriedly. "We may reach in time after all, if the horses survive the ride."

Lilava saw the queen waver, growing faint, and she caught her in her arms. Opening her eyes, Prosperpina spoke weekly. "Close — its nearness weakens me. It draws great power from the earth and so from me. How can something have such strength and malice? Who could dare face it? Oh, my dear, sorry — I know — we must ..."

"Lady, sing with me if you can. I will teach you the words. It is a great spell, and it worked once. It may have no power here, but I must do something. Please sing with me!"

And Lilava began a low, alto chant, the spell she had once used in her own land against the monster, but in a different register. If the effort for the spell had not risen from her heart, one overhearing it would have believed it had come from despair.

Then she heard the roaring tempest of the Chimaera's rage echoing through the forest. Amidst the darkness they came suddenly upon the open road and swung wildly to the west, careening onto the Forrest Road nearing the clearing where two adversaries battled to the death.

* * *

Severus, regaining consciousness, found himself lying amidst the trees with a substantial lump taking shape on the side of his head. Shaken off the Chimaera, he had been thrown all the way through the clearing. Slowly and unsteadily rising to his feet, he heard the beast stomping and fuming not far away. The sword clung to his hand: its gentle glow of the runes on the swordblade gave him just enough light to make his way through the trees. Through gaps among the trunks, he caught glimpses of the beast, aided by the starlight that fell like a shower upon the clearing. The Chimaera snuffled, trying to find him by scent, and Severus, not one normally to seek other than plain frontal assault, looked for an angle by which, in the limited light, he might find a way to surprise the adversary to whom he felt he must otherwise certainly lose his life.

Having run a quarter turn around the opening, he shook his hand free of the sword, sheathed it, shinning up a tall tree, crouched upon a high but stout limb, redrew his sword, which clung to him anew, and he waited.

The snuffling neared, the hot, fetid breath almost searing bark from the trees. Talons poked along the ground, ripping at roots and low lying branches. Cold sweat dripped from Severus' forehead, burning his eyes. A lionish snout poked itself into the brush beneath him. Severus leaped down upon it, swinging his sword toward a gleaming, burning, golden eye.

When the sword edge struck that gleaming orb, flame shot from it, and in a billow of smoke it went dark.

The howl of the Chimaera's pain shook the earth, and Severus fell to the ground directly before the monster whose only thought concentrated on devouring the man who had brought it so much pain.

The talons rose as the monstrous body of the beast surrounded Severus and prepared to pounce upon him. A great drop of saliva splashed on Severus' breast as the Chimaera drew up to its full height, preparing the final blow for its fallen victim. And then in mid-descent, crouched for the blow, it stopped.

* * *

$f$rom the eastern edge of the clearing road a band of warrior-elves led by King Arawn. Lilava and Prosperpina sung their spell, ineffectual as a spell, but in its varied pitches and odd harmonics it was enough to distract the beast in its last-ditch fury.

* * *

$f$rom the western edge of the clearing bolted a shot of brilliant green, flying toward the Chimaera with all its speed.

The Chimaera looked left, hearing the noise of horses and carriage and voices, then right, seeing a pale green, glowing dart that bore directly toward it.

* * *

With the last of his strength Severus raised himself upon aching legs, fought the sharp pain that ran up his spine, found the center of the creature's breast, and pointed the magic sword: the runes glowed brilliant blue. Just as the remaining fiery golden eye returned to him from distractions on either side, Severus had taken three steps and leapt straight up.

The sword point found soft tissue and penetrated deep into the cavern of the body, piercing the heart. Severus heard what sounded to him like a wind whipping off the sea, and bilious scarlet-yellow blood poured down overtop him, and he fell back. In the jerk of the body's death throes, a razor claw swung down, ripping clothes, skin, and muscle from Severus' belly.

The Chimaera lurched forward as though it would fall and crush the knight, but it recoiled and stood straight up, then began to teeter.

Vern the wyvern, having found his friend Severus at his greatest need, paused in flight before the Chimaera's forehead, waited until the Chimaera tilted away from Severus, and then gave the already dead body a gentle push backward. Slowly, slowly, it fell to the ground, clear of Severus, landing on its back with an enormous thud, the spiked tail rising like a whip, then striking its barbed point deep into the ground.

A foul mist rose around the body, and in moments muscles, sinews, and nerves dissolved into the air. Teeth and talons fell to the ground like coconuts. The thick blood spouted and spread into a fetid pool, then boiled away in a ghastly, ghostly cloud. The bones stood like the ruins of an ancient shrine.

For once and all, beyond all hope in the human world, the Chimaera was dead.

As Severus struggled to prop himself on an elbow, a familiar green flash of light appeared at his side. His head felt as though it were spinning like a carousel. His sword's blade had dissolved away from the creature's bilious blood, and the hilt fell heavily from his hand. Vern's feet tugged Severus away from the growing pool of the Chimaera's blood.

"Vern?"

"Oui, mon ami, and a lotta uthahs, too, but I think we got heah too late. You don' look so good, mahn. Breathe, mahn, breathe!"

"You! Back away or die!" Arawn shouted to the wyvern as the elf band and Lilava closed. Lilava's feet had already reached the ground: she had jumped from the cart and run toward her love. Her feet flashed, though her heart felt frozen with fear.

"Don' mess, mahn: I his friend! Anybody a doctah? Hurry, hurry!"

Severus had fallen back. His body felt crumpled, and the stars swirled above him. Drops of the beast's blood clung to him like glue. Only then did he realize he too was bleeding profusely, and he placed his hands over the wound, which was beginning to burn, to try to stanch the bleeding belly. The one face he most dearly wanted to see swirled into sight.

"Hang on, Sevy, hang on!" Lilava propped up his head.

"Dear one. I think we really got it this time."

Lilava wasn't sure whether he meant that he had killed the Chimaera or received his death wound.

Despite the stench of the beast's foul blood, which oozed about them, Rhia plopped down beside Severus and began searching his wounds. Arawn and Prosperpina swung into Severus' view: he recognized the king's brown cloak with the bright green pin. Even poor, skinny, battered Courage had emerged from the wood to attend his friend at last. Severus looked around as best he could, trying to burn the faces into his thoughts so that he might carry them wherever he had to go.

"My friends are with me. Dearest Lilava, one and only. Vern: forgive me for saying your name, but you're with friends here, too. King and queen, thank you for coming. We've done our task. We've won. Your land is free and safe again, at least of this awful curse. Abra and his men may return. Please see, King, if you can, that my friends reach home safely."

"Shh, dear. Save your strength," Lilava whispered. Her tears felt warm on Severus' face as a chill sifted through his limbs like fog through the forest.

"Breathe deep, mahn; just breathe."

Rhia was cleansing, testing, wrapping Severus' wounds, praying as quickly as she could. "Someone: hold the compress tight on that wound!" she called.

Hod dropped down beside Severus and held Rhia's white cloth to Severus' bleeding belly.

"We hadn't enough time," Severus said, looking into Lilava's deep, brown, frightened, loving eyes. "I would have liked a little more time, just for us, without tasks. I know the world gives us what it shall, not what we wish. But I did so wish for that."

"We will have it yet! Hang on! Rhia, can you do nothing? King, we saved him once, you and I."

Arawn too knelt beside Severus, touched his head, felt the cold, widening lump there. He turned to Prosperpina. "The wisdom says that no one returns twice from the Gray Road. I have no power to help him. Can you do anything?"

Elves don't cry — it isn't in their nature. Prosperpina, fervently chanting a soft prayer, shook her head, and her chin fell to her breast.

"Live well, Lila, my love, and remember me. Friends all, may the sun light your path, and the moon soothe your dreams."

"Sa-esse," Arawn answered.

"Sa-esse," chanted the other elves in chorus. Lilava toweled her husband's forehead with the hem of her cloak.

"Breathe, mahn, relax an' breathe!" Vern urged.

"I love you," Lilava whispered.

"And I you. Now and always." Severus' heart stopped, and his body lay still, not far away from the ruined beast whose end was that excellent knight's final task in this world.

"Do something," Lilava said. "We must do something. I, someone: do something!"

"The spirit has flown," Arawn said.

"Then it must have flown somewhere," Hod said. He looked around at Lilava, Vern, Arawn, Prosperpina. "Do you know where?"

"We brought him back before from the Gray Road," Arawn said.

"Where does it lead?" Hod asked.

"We do not know."

"Has any one of you been there?"

"I have been there," Lilava answered.

"Yah, man, I too," Vern added.

"But I can't go again by the same road," Lilava said. "I was warned the last time."

"Do you know of another road?" Prosperpina asked.

"No," Lilava said.

They all stood or knelt there, silent, grieving.

"Ahem: I believe I know another road," Hod said. "In my land, in the North. It is far, it is cold, and it is dangerous. But if I understand what you seek, I think it is at least possible to find. If you wish to try it, I can show you, though I advise against it."

"Will you take me?" Lilava asked.

"If you wish. I should rather you had an army to go with you."

"I go wid you," Vern said, "and dat almos' as good as an ahmy. He da bes' side-kick I evah hahd, an' I want to help you. I go as fah wid you until we reach da snow — dee wyvern canno' go pahst da'."

"I will go," Lilava said.

"Daughter," said Prosperpina, "I know the road of which Hod speaks. Humans do not take it, nor do elves, nor do gnomes. You must rest, recover. Severus would not want you to waste your life or your death."

"Thank you, but I will go. And I will find him. I promise," said Lilava, looking up at the stars and stroking Severus' dead hand, "that I will find him."

III A Turn

[The body must go, but the spirit may stay. Lilava bears her burdens.]

"The monster has passed from this world, both the land of elves and that of humans. I feel it," Arawn said.

"As do I," said Prosperpina, "and thanks to Earth Mother and to Severus for that. We must look to the good that has come of this sorrow. Only so can we move on from it, and that we must do as long as we live, never forgetting those who have sacrificed for us."

The last embers among the fire had died down. All remant of Severus' body upon the funeral pyre had turned to ash. In the land of the elves songs of honor and appreciation normally accompany death rites. Those rituals come more seldom there, and they often bring as much joy as sorrow: the elves believe that their folk who die bravely, in good spirits, or in sacrifice for the general good pass into the Light of the Immortals. But the funeral of Sir Severus le Brewse, greatest of monster fighters, brought no joy. Lilava mourned as she would have for no other creature; she could find no joy in the honor and glory her husband had won, but only pain and longing, wretchedness and woe. And the elves had no certain sense of the ends of humans beyond this world other than what they knew of the Gray Road, though for Lilvava's sake they recalled and articulated better than they ever had the stories of heroes past, weaving them into recent events, bringing the hope of legend into the sorrow of experience. Truthfully, they feared for the man who had once already walked that Road. Their legend said that, with luck, one may walk that Road once and return, but no one escaped it twice. Such words, though, they did not speak. Their songs, too, laments as well as praise, remained quiet and subdued.

Tired elves took light food and drink. Lilava could but sip cool water.

"I must find the way to the Gray Road," Lilava said, finally.

"Lilava, have you not received warning against taking that road?" Prosperpina asked.

"Against that, but maybe one may take another path. Regardless, I must try that road if I can't find another."

"I can find it, as the snows grow thin," Hod said. As I said, I know any pathway within my own lands, though my folk would think one foolish to take some of them."

"It must get treacherous with ice, so far north," Rhia said. She had stayed with Lilava since they had returned to Elvenhome, tending her for shock and sorrow as only elven physicians can.

"The entry itself, yes," Hod answered, "but the path warms quickly enough. I have told no one else, but once I ventured down it only a few hundred els — I had no reason to go farther — and found it more than toasty, even 'so far north,' as the lady says. Hod sniffed. He didn't like what he heard, a hint of disdain in the way the elf pronounced north. To him it meant home, not discomfort and dismay. All but the unluckiest of us will defend home in a pinch.

"You will take me there?" Lilava asked.

"What feels like home to me may feel quite unpleasant to others," Hod said, sniffing, directing his eyes at Rhia. "Yet one may do a lot to make the journey more comfortable, and you must try what you think best. Of course I will help you if you wish it."

"I'm not thinking of comfort. I'm thinking of speed. I wouldn't wish anyone to hurry from Elvenhome, my good Hod, but I would ride as soon as I may and as soon as you will. May I borrow Starlight for yet a while, Queen Prosperpina?"

"You may take her until snow covers the ground. She was not bred to go beyond that, and I don't wish it for her, though I have no doubt she's game enough and cares enough for you to try."

"I understand," Lilava replied, "and I have no intention of abusing your kindness or hers. Thank you, my queen."

"You may find another horse insisting on accompanying you," Arawn interjected. "Courage."

Rhia, a physician of special skills even among folk noted for healing, coughed gently. "I must remind you, Lady Lilava, that even with the best of horses, you need think of no journey for at least the next seven to eight months. Beyond that you must let your conscience dictate."

"I would begin tomorrow as early as you're willing."

"I shouldn't advise it in your condition," Rhia whispered.

"I shall regain strength soon enough. Waiting hurts more than traveling, and with the perfect guide, traveling will feel easy."

"Forgive me, then, if I speak more clearly about such things than your folk prefer to do," said Rhia. "Your choices now involve another besides yourself."

"Of course they do," Lilava said. "I know my Severus. He will wait for me, or if that land where he has gone permits it, he will seek me himself. If not, I will follow wherever he has gone."

"He is not the other of whom I spoke."

The weight of the recognition, the truth she had tried so hard to keep from herself, fell so heavily upon her that Lilava nearly passed out.

"A baby," she said. "God save us."

"We must take care to foster what's left of Severus in this world and what shall remain of you, too, after you have gone from it," Rhia added.

"Good to know," Hod humphed. "You must not enter the Lower World in that condition. Neither of you would survive it. I know only my bit of magic, which little concerns humans. But I know that much of medicine: such a journey strains the body to its limits. I may not wait these long months to return home. When you are ready, if you wish it, I will send a guide for you, to bring you to my lands, where I can show you the entry. But perhaps now you have other concerns that will keep you from your quest."

"Nothing will keep me from it, at least not indefinitely."

"We will go with you, if you still choose to go," Vainen said, Jouka nodding. "The North presents no difficulties for us, and we have visited Hod's lands, so that he need send no guide. We will only too gladly remain here at Elvenhome until you feel ready to travel. We have much to study, and we get less time than we would like among the councilors."

"How soon can we begin?" Lilava asked.

Rhia frowned, sniffed. "I would not encourage her. But you, Lady Lilava, must first learn to eat again, if not for yourself, for the little one."

* * *

277

One evening, two months later, Lilava, Prosperpina, and Rhia strolled together in the library gardens. Lilava had had spent nearly every day in the library, but that day she lagged not only with heart-sickness, but with morning sickness also. Her elf-physician picked medicinal plants: chamomile, peppermint, licorice, lavender, motherwort, and white peony root to ease her discomfort.

"Once I promised to tell you an elvin love story," the queen said.

"Anything that will take my thoughts from their usual haunts I will value greatly."

Rhia cast a questioning glance at the queen, but said nothing.

"More than ten years ago," the queen began, "a young elf, having seen the span of our lands, decided to cross over into the realm of humans. As he had the wandering spirit and a touch of the melancholy, he seldom stayed anywhere for long, but always sought new sites, constructions of beauty that he could study. The art of building, as practiced by elves, humans, or any other creature, had always fascinated him. Tall and slim, with fine cheekbones and deep brown eyes with an emerald glow, he turned the hearts of elven and human maids alike wherever he traveled, so he took to wearing cloak and hood to cause less of an intrusion and allow himself greater anonymity to pursue his studies. He carried with him only scant supplies and a small book in which he drew or described, in a fine, easy hand, what he saw and felt in his travels. He also recorded human myths and legends about love, life, and death: he had always wondered why human and elven beliefs about the continuation of the spirit differ.

"He crossed a boundary, sojourned in Egypt, asking questions no one could answer about the Great Pyramid, sailed to Greece for the Parthenon, to Rome for the Colosseum and the Caracalla Baths, to Jerusalem, that troubled and holy city; he traveled with a caravan to China to see the Great Wall of the Emperor Qin, by ship to Alexandria to discover the wonders of the great Lighthouse; he sought out the Mausoleum at Halicarnassus and Stonehenge, the Roman Wall, and the New Grange passage tomb in the western isles. Impressed with what humans had accomplished despite limited tools, he learned what he could of each architectural marvel, but found nothing that could grasp and hold his imagination for long — until one cool, fateful day in southern Europa, near an inn where he had paused to rest and reflect, in a town where elves stop occasionally, because it lies near an intersection where the two worlds meet.

"There, he wrote, for all his searching he had never seen anything more beautiful than a young human woman, little more than a girl, he saw in a market town in Italia. She had raven hair, dark, flashing eyes, and a look at once kind and strong-willed, and she moved with elven litheness, without the heavy clumsiness that sometimes burdens humans.

"The girl sat in a piazza, waited patiently until an older woman came for her. That woman led her to a small shop not far away. The elf followed them.

"The shop was filled with curiosities: antiques, dried herbs, amulets, simple weapons, and many primitive devices for healing. But the elf took interest in nothing there but the young woman. To arouse no suspicion, he purchased a fine but simple dagger and a sheath — all he could afford. When she left the shop, he continued to follow her. Cloaked and quiet of foot, he had little worry that she would hear him or notice him in any way. He found he couldn't take his eyes from her without feeling a sadness as profound as anything he had experienced in his life.

"The young woman walked to the river bank, where a man greeted her, one who had apparently been waiting for her there. He quickly untied the line that held a flatboat to the dock and boarded; the young woman leaped lightly onto its deck after him. As the boat embarked, she turned, looked directly at the elf, and spoke. 'Young man, are you following me?'

"Her voice rang clear, but not stern. The elf, surprised to have been noticed at all, nearly could not reply. As the boat drifted off, he called, 'Apologies, young woman: I intended no harm. I thought you might be someone I know, you look so familiar.'"

"'I have never seen you before, young man, but as you intend no harm, I wish you well,' she replied, and she turned away, helping the boatman turn their little craft into the current. More than disappointed, the elf knew not what to do, other than that he must find a way to pursue. In an instant he had lost his heart to her — a romantic tale indeed, but something that occasionally happens to humans and even, though less frequently, to elves, who do not give away their hearts easily.

"By boat, by horse, but foot, at a distance, hoping to arouse no alarm, uncertain of what to do, the elf followed the human girl, as quietly as a shadow. Soon he assured himself that she was indeed human and no elf, and with that certain knowledge his heart sank: humans and elves have bonded in marriage but three times in our remembered history, and while the couples loved well, their necessarily different ends bound them also to sadness. When the spirits depart their bodies, as far as we know, they fly to the fate to which their birth-world has bound them. So the elf, a creature of conscience and kindness, had no intention of intruding on her; he simply could not free himself of thoughts of her, and the mearest glimpse of her face fed his desire never to stray from her in her world or ours, for as long as life might permit him to share her vicinity.

After a journey over sea and land, she reached her homeland, he not far behind. For two years he lingered on the edge of her world, unwilling to hazard his affections, knowing he could not fathom the distance between them, but unwilling to approach any nearer. He had great skill with his hands and could easily acquire human crafts sufficient to earn a meager subsistence while never taking his thoughts too far from the unknowing beloved. Despite his sadness and loneliness, and that fact that she did nothing to encourage him — we believe that she knew nothing of his continuing presence — he felt his spirit draw closer to her. Though, unlike many other girls, she cared nothing for looks and ornaments and clothes, she grew only more beautiful to him.

"One day the young woman departed her home, journeying alone, by horse, east toward the shore. Easily gathering his few belongings, he followed her on foot. Lest he lose her, at a farm he bought a horse, using nearly all that he earned through the practice of his crafts — had he not done so, he would have lost much more, for she rode well, and swiftly as elves can travel, he could not have kept up with her otherwise.

"He caught up with her at the edge of a valley. She had reached the bottom of the dale as he crested the top on the road by which she'd entered. Ahead, from his vantage point, he could see what she could not: a group of thieves hiding, waiting on the hill beyond, at the head of her path.

"He rode at full speed after her; when she heard the sound of horse's hooves in pursuit, she glanced behind, then hurried her horse up the slope ahead, fearing danger from him, not ahead, where it truly lurked. As she neared the top, she looked ahead to find the bandits, five in all, barring the path before her, in addition to what she believed was an assailant following. She turned her horse abruptly off the path, and using such magic as she had — she was a sorceress, you know — she cast an explosive powder at the feet of the horse of the first bandit. The horse reared, tossing its rider. When she turned to face the figure approaching from behind, she was surprised that he rode right by her and attacked head-on the assailants who awaited her.

"The elf had about him only the dagger he had bought at the curiosity shop. With elven speed and agility, but unaccustomed to fighting, he felled two of the bandits, before a third struck him down with a sword. Fallen from his horse, the elf was yet able to bring down the fourth man before his strength left him. The young woman must face the swordsman alone.

"She had, though, other resources of her own, and the elf's attack had given her time to prepare them. She drew from her traveling pouch a strong sleeping powder, and when the swordsman approached her, she blew it into his face. He staggered a few steps, and he too fell, lost in a deep sleep.

"She went directly to the figure who had helped save her life and found him, so she believed, a tall, thin, handsome young man. His brown eyes shone with an emerald glow that faded even as she watched. She could do little for him: he had received a deep wound just beneath the heart. He spoke to her in hesitant but understandable Latin. 'I have but a few minutes before my spirit must flee this body and this world. Please, draw from my pocket a small book and the quill and ink you will find there. I am already losing my strength. Thank you. I must record in it one more note. Unless you are even more learned than I know, you will not be able to read it, but I would ask you to take it to the curiosity shop in the village where we met. You will remember that I followed you to the dock, and you spoke to me. I know that too great a request: I am sorry to ask. Leave it there with the proprietor along with instructions that a man dressed in brown and green will come to claim it, not in days, but surely in less than weeks. As for the other meager belongings, please dispense them as you will, except for the small hand-harp you will find also in my pouch: please leave that with my person. Forgive me, I grow faint. I understand if you cannot fulfill my request — you brought nothing of this misfortune upon yourself — but if you can, you will do a great service to me and my family. In recompense I can say only that they will one day return that favor, if you have luck, when you most need their aid. I can give you only this reason, dubious as it seems, to believe me: that if I had lived, I would have loved you all the remaining days of your life and for all the days time would have given me. Where I go from here, I will try to wait for you. If I cannot, may love and goodness attend you always.'

"He scribbled a few faint lines in the book, handed it to the girl, smiled and thanked her, and he died to this earth and yours."

Lilava shook her head and sighed. "I can tell you the rest of the story, dear queen," she said. "The girl took fishing line from her pouch and with it tied the sleeping bandit securely so he could not move, but must trust his own fate to passersby. She placed the book, a small volume, bound in leather, full of drawings and of a written language she did not know, in her travel pouch. With great effort, she managed finally to lift the body of the young man — the elf, rather — onto his horse, for the loyal beast had hardly moved a step from them. She mounted and rode ahead toward the sea, keeping more watchful than she had against attacks, drawing the second horse behind her.

"A mile along the road, she looked back to check that the body was secure. It seemed to her as though a mist had gathered around it, that it had become insubstantial, and though she did her best to keep her eyes fixed on it, it disappeared entirely from her view. She dismounted and checked the horse, but no remnant of either body or clothing remained. The horse carried no physical burden beyond the youth's pouch. With that horse she paid for her journey abroad.

"So she returned to that little shop far away, left there not only the book, but all the elf's remaining belongings, with a brief note in Latin describing her sorrow and gratitude for his help and what had happened to the body, however unbelievable her account might seem. She tied the note around a green stone that she had carried for many years as a keepsake — it reminded her of the fading color of his dying eyes — placed the note and stone in the middle of the book, and tied the book closed with fishing line. She had no knowledge of her benefactor's name or heritage nor of his quality, beyond what he had done in her defense. She mourned him as best she could, then stayed that night at the inn.

"She dreamed. A figure appeared to her, kingly, dressed in brown and green and wearing a long, gray cloak. He had kind eyes and a gentle but commanding voice. 'One who meant much to his folk has spent himself to aid you. Fear not: I am honored for him. But he has made an error, for your sake, that he may choose not to amend. He has gone to a place he should not, believing he should wait for you there. Please, for his sake, go to him, convince him that he must take his own path, not yours. You will find him on the long road that proceeds from the passages below Cumae.' The dream faded from her sight, but not from her memory.

"In the morning she pondered her course, but soon decided what she must do. But two days ride from Cumae, she went there and found the sybil and with her aid sought the deep caverns beneath her lair, leaving her horse above. She had no idea how long she spent there searching, but she found a gray road, a path of shadows. About her she sensed rather than saw the shades of others who took that road because they must, not because they would. She pressed on, feeling that she must. She felt as though not only shadows, but also benevolent spirits accompanied her every step, or she couldn't have continued, for she was young, and the place filled her with terror.

"She walked on until there arose in the distance a growing cloud of smoke so dense that she believed nothing that passed into it could pass back through it again. She stood still and trembled.

"Then, just ahead, beside the road, she spotted a figure, reclining. She heard coming from it the faint, tinkling sounds of a hand-harp. She moved closer, and though the figure seemed cloaked in mist, she recognized it as the youth who had come to her aid. The pale skin emitted a greenish glow, and the drawn body showed little sign of strength, but the fingers strummed gently on the ghostly harp. As she approached, the eyes turned toward her, and the thin voice spoke.

"'So soon! Some ill has befallen you! Or has time passed so quickly? I have no idea, but I have waited, and I would have waited as long as necessary.' The poor spirit flickered, even as the speech drained it of nearly all the energy that seemed left to it.

"'Sweet youth,' the girl said, 'I have not died, but have come with a message from one close to you. He asked me to find you to tell you this: that you have taken a path not your own, and for your sake and your family's you must not wait here, but find your own way. I will not make light of what you have suffered for me: I know and value your sacrifice. But I beg you not to wait for me, who must walk a path different from yours. I free you from your earthly love, that you may seek the realm of the spirit that awaits you beyond. Take it happily, for there you will find love untainted by such earthly failings as mine must show. Find your way, youth, for I must follow a course of my own, one for which my own people need me, a long way that you may not travel. Your own eternity awaits: go bravely! go happily!'

"The face seemed at first forlorn, and then a smile crossed the pale lips. 'Yes, you are right,' said the thinning voice, barely audible. "I have long forgotten myself. I must go now." The limp body rose slowly, and with silent footfalls the ghost stepped, almost floating, away from the rising black cloud in the distance. He passed by the girl, and as he did, his body flickered, and in a wave of light, brighter and faster than the mist that had drawn it from earth, what was left of it disappeared. She waited for a moment, but she saw no more of him.

"Then she heard a voice call to her. A tall figure emerged out of the darkness far down the road. Though at first far away and seeming to move but slowly, in a few strides it came upon her, spectral, dark of hue, and robed in gray, with a long beard that fell to where it should have had feet, eyes that, from rims darker than night, yet burned in their pupils as though with noon sunlight.

"'You,' it said, in a voice as deep as the caverns themselves, 'you should not have come here. You don't belong here now. I know why you have come, at the bidding of another, but you have not reached your time to walk this road. Return to your own world, and do not take these paths again. You shall not escape a second time. Go quickly. Heed my warning: come not this way again for any reason other than that Death has called you. Go!'

"At that she lost sense of her whereabouts. Some time passed, and she found herself stumbling through the mouth of the cavern, the sybil helping her to sit upon a rock bench so that she wouldn't fall. When she had recovered, she began the long journey home, uncertain of what had happened and what had not, but certain that she must never dare that path again by any choice of her own."

"The young woman is you," the queen said. "The young elf was my son."

"I don't think I even heard him say his name."

"Orfey. We called him also Poinamen, which in your language means "maker." As a boy he designed the quarters where you lodge now. The smiths built it not because we ordered, but because, seeing his plans, they wished it. He composed poetry and music as well. Being long-lived, we elves have few children. May the stars guide his path to peace."

"Sa-esse," said Rhia.

"Sa-esse," echoed Lilava. "I should have seen him in your eyes: the same eyes.

"I have something to show you," Prosperpina said. She drew from beneath her cloak a pendant, a gold chain that held a green stone mounted in amethyst and yellow gold. "Do you recognize the stone?"

"I don't think — yes, maybe, can it be? The stone that I placed in his book?"

"Yes, Arawn claimed it and made from it this pendant for me. Elves wear little if any jewelry, as you've probably noticed. This piece I wear for my son and for the young woman he loved, if briefly."

"I don't know what to say. I am so sorry. If only I could have known what to do."

"Please don't feel sorry, dear Lilava. Rhia will chastise me later for telling her patient this story, but I wanted you to know the whole of it. We love you not only for yourself, but because Orfey loved you. Elves don't love blithely, but they love fully, and with good reasons. Please know that we hold you not less, but more dear for what has passed between our families. Arawn has ever been your friend since with no thought of risk to yourself you carried out our son's request.

"Now you know an elven love story, and you know that they can turn unhappily as any human love story. But they do not end — one would make a terrible mistake to say that a true love story ever ends. It continues forever — love has that power, you know. Your love story has not ended, nor has it paused: you simply add to it as you go. You will soon have another to add to it, regardless of the course you choose afterwards. You will love her, and we will love her, too. Where I have temporarily lost a blood-son, I have gained forever a spirit-daughter, and from her a granddaughter."

"She:

you know it will be so?"

"I know."

"I'd hoped to have a son, someone to carry on his legacy."

"She will do so, not as a beast-slayer, but as a paragon of learning and good will. She will build such a bond between elves and humans as the world has never seen. She will look so like you that by image alone one could not tell you apart."

The two elves and the human lady emerged from the garden back into the library. Lilava's eyes welled with tears; the queen felt as though a burden had lifted from her heart. Rhia worried that an additional shock would do her patient's health no good. A voice from outside the window interrupted their thoughts. A green body with a pink belly hovered outside and thrust its nose through the window.

"I tho' you ladies nevah goin' to come back. Anybody foah lunch? I been jus' about starvin'. I make you somethin' nice an spicy but foah the pretty lady carryin' da child. Anybody foah a nice veggie bahbacue?"

* * *

$\mathfrak{S}$ix months later, with Rhia tending her every minute, Lilava gave birth to a beautiful, healthy daughter. In honor of her hosts, she named the wee girl Orfila.

Three months after the birth of her daughter, who was growing quickly in the healthy atmosphere of Elvenhome, Lilava began to make plans for a journey. Daily she would exercise Courage, who had regained his strength and confidence, but who had not forgotten the knight with whom he had had so many adventures. He nonetheless approved of his new human companion, who carried much less weight, rode with nearly equal facility, and appeared to possess the good sense not to go chasing about alone after monsters. While Starlight would have made the journey that Lilava intended, she knew that Courage would not allow himself to get left behind.

When another month had passed, Lilava paid an official visit to Prosperpina and Arawn in their Counseling Chamber. Rhia attended, and Vainen and Jouka as well.

"She must not even think of it," Rhia insisted, "not only for her own health, but for that of the child."

Lilava addressed the queen. "You once told me, elf mother, that my daughter would be to you as a granddaughter. I now ask that I may leave her in the care of your folk while I make the journey I must and will."

"She needs her mother," Rhia protested, "and someone of her own kind. The mother has a duty to the child that outweighs that to the husband — and I hope you'll forgive me for saying it, lady, but I must speak bluntly — particularly to a dead husband. His spirit has long since passed to wherever it must go. Let it rest peacefully. Such a journey bespeaks folly at best, mere madness now. The lady herself knows the journey forbidden to her. I speak, my queen, only out of concern for those involved."

"I know you do, Rhia, and so does Lilava. I must say, Lila, that I agree with Rhia. I honor the strength of the love that moves you, but to me your duty looks clear."

"I have the duty, great lady, of a promise. All of you here heard me speak it. And who among us knows with certainty where Severus' spirit has gone? He saved my people, and he did much for yours as well in ending the Chimaera for good and all. I fear, I feel, I know that somewhere he waits for me. I owe him this much: to return to him if I can, with him if I may, or to show my living love this one last time. Not easily have I resolved. I love Orfila, but she can find no better foster-parents, temporary or otherwise, in all the world. In this gift I return to you as best I can a life that means as much to me as your son did to you. I am no monster. But I have vowed to seek my love, and seek him I will."

"Mad, she's gone mad with birth-trauma," Rhia said. "I have read of that in humans, foreign to us. We must recognize a medical condition for what it is."

Arawn stood, breathed deeply, and spoke. "I doubt the wisdom of this choice, but I have no doubt of the right to choose. We have never denied it before, and I have no wish to do so now. I, too, believe, Lilava, that you should not go. But I know in your place I would go: I would seek Prosperpina to my last breath. Will we deny you, then, because you are a woman rather than a man, a human rather than an elf? What seems wisdom to us may seem punishment and imprisonment to you, and we would willingly do that to no creature. Even the horses that serve us stay of their own accord, not because we chain them. I fear that, if you go, we will see you no more. Yet I value the fulfilling of a vow as I do the moral choices of fair kingship. Who can see into the depths of another's heart and know the right or wrong of it? We can only hope that decisions come out of love. Lady Lilava: do as you will. Wherever you fare, you will remain, as will your child to us, heart-daughter, spirit-daughter. I wish only that I had a better hope for the success of your journey."

"We will see her safely to the pathway," Jouka said. "Beyond that, she must go without us, for that realm offers no welcome to our folk. I suggest we wait one more month. By then we will have missed the worst of the snow."

Vern waited impatiently outside the hall.

"You talk her outta it, right? Oh, mahn, tell me you no' gonna let her go! Wha's wrong wi' you peopo! Come on! I see da' look in youah eye, pretty lady, and I see you no' gonna listen to dee wyvern. But I tell you wha': I no' gonna desert you. I go wid you. If ol' Sevy still deah, he maybe need me, too, and you, to help him escape, even if it mean bravin' da snow. All right! We get goin', but dees feet o' mine no' gonna like all da' snow, no way. I hope dey at leas' got you to wait a month or so. I need to eat a lot to get ready foah dis. Somebody bettah feed da hoahsey well, too."

* * *

"Don't worry, my love. I'll wait for you," said the voice, distant, weak.

"How long, my love: how long can you wait?"

"As long as you need. Don't worry. Don't hurry. All in good time."

"What should I do?"

"Take care of those who need you."

"Are you in pain? Where are you? Can I find you?"

"Take care."

"Where are you? It's dark here. Don't leave me! Sevy!"

Lilava woke in a sweat, vague images fading, a voice lingering.

* * *

286

$\mathcal{T}$hree weeks later Lilava had packed supplies, and Vainen and Jouka had mounted their horses. Vern was humming and twirling absent-mindedly, hovering a foot off the ground, waiting for his companions to begin.

"Everybody should prahctice rotation," he said. "Good foah da concentration."

Lilava said good-bye to tiny Orfila, kissed her forehead, and placed her in Rhia's arms. Rhia shook her head and would not meet Lilava's eyes. Lilava bowed to Arawn and Prosperpina.

"What little girl could ask for more than to grow up in the home of the queen and king of Faeryland?" Lilava asked.

"She could ask for her mother," Arawn answered.

"And her father," Lilava replied. "She may yet get both. I must try. I have spent these weeks studying in your library. I know more of the world and its magic than I have ever known. I have enough strength for the journey now. I can allow myself to wait no longer. Happiness to you all, and thank you for all you have done and all you will do."

"May the sun shine on your path," Arawn said, "though the paths you seek admit no light."

"Mai ioia besta tui solve lei. May joy greet all your days."

"Please, if you must go, take with you this small gift." Prosperpina handed Lilava a pouch made of blue cloth and gray leather. Inside it Lilava found a beautiful hand-held harp, carved from deep-reddish mahogany. "Orfey made it when he was a boy. It makes a gentle but lovely sound. It may comfort you on your journey."

Lilava bowed deeply to her hosts.

"Come on, Lila. Youah elf friends ah right, too, but if we gonna find Sevy, we bes' get goin'. I have a feeleen' about him, you know. He gonna find a way to wait for you you you. You one hot lady, and he no' gonna give you up so easy, if I know dee mahn atoll. Les' go, les' go: soonah stahted, soonah home, say dee wyvahn. Ciao, elf king, an' grazi, elf queen, au revoir, physician — you da bes', you know. Vern floated after Vainen and Jouka, who had already begun riding north. A long journey lay ahead for all of them.

[Where Lilava makes contact, and the world changes ...]

"We will have some days before we reach the melting snows of the North," Vainen said that afternoon. We should tell stories to pass the time."

"We should sing songs," Jouka said. "The harp that the lady carries should make nice music not so different from that of a kantalette — our version of the instrument, if you've not heard of it. May I try to play it? In our home, as far to the north and east as one can go and still find land, all the children learn to play on it and sing, even if they play and sing badly. He nodded toward Vainen, then winked at Lilava.

"Know you any songs, Lady Lilava?" Vainen asked.

"I hope you will forgive me, but I have no heart to sing. I would gladly listen, though."

"Our friend Jouka tells truly: I sing badly. But he does not. I would not call him the best of our singers, but he remembers as many songs as any elf I know."

Lilava noticed an accent in the speech of the northern elves different from that of her hosts. It carried over to their Latin — a musicality of speech, with evenly periodic accents not of Latin, but of their own, a softening of consonants, and a tendency to prefer very long vowels — she heard those sound in their Elvish as well, despite her limited experience with its dialects. She used their own polite form of address when she spoke, as she handed the elf her harp.

"Please do sing for us, Jouka-tolo. I have no facility, but I would see so fine a gift well used."

Jouka accepted the harp from Lilava. "Lovely instrument indeed. If we have enough time I shall teach you how to play it, at least a simple melody or two. The world looks better through the mist of a song, we say. What shall I sing, Vainen?"

"How about 'The Song of the Finicky Dragon'?

"Yes, a good one to begin, a human song, which we learned long ago from them — maybe it will appeal to our young friend, as more familiar than those of our tradition." Jouka tuned the harp as he rode, strummed thoughtfully for a time, and gradually began to hum along with the sound of the strings. As Lilava began to drift away on wafts of music, she noticed that the elf had started to chant along with the music.

288

"Bring the rope to hang the man,
The young fellow, the mother's son,
The rope will rid us of these troubles,
The one who brings the bane upon us."
Then they called the Elder-woman,
Village Counsel, old and wise.
"What has he done, what offense,
The frightened youth, the mother's son?"
So they told her how the dragon,
Come to feed, to still its rumblings,
Came to find the proffered maid
That they had left him, as was custom.
But something stopped him, something wrong,
Something caused the dragon pause.
Around the maid the dragon sniffed,
Sniffed and sniffed, quite unhappy,
Flicked its tongue to taste the air,
Examined closely, gave a snort.
"Not a maid!" the dragon shouted,
With wrinkled brow turned up its nose.
"You've chosen wrong," the worm complained.
"She's a woman, known to man.
This is no maid. How could you?"
So up he flew and circled round,
Hungry and offended, too,
Spewing flames that scorched the clouds,
Circled thrice and flew straight off,
Angry with such sacrifice.
So the men released the girl,
Rebuked her sternly, blamed her folly,
Called the mob to join their anger,
Combed the town for the intended,
Sought the youth who loved the maid,
The one who wanted her in marriage,
Made the girl a maid no more.
"So we'll hang the lusty traitor,
He who raised the dragon's wrath.
Think what evil he has caused us
When the dragon comes to burn."
"Wait a bit," the old one counseled.
"Once you've hanged you can't undo.
Release the maid and hold the youth,

Hold him if your vengeance hungers,
Until the dragon's rage is done."
So they waited, fearful, hiding,
Filled the water barrels high,
Waiting for the dragon's fire,
Expectant of the sound of wings.
So they waited and they waited,
But the dragon never came,
He suffered so from poor digestion,
Could stomach only maids, you know.
Off he went to other towns,
Seeking willing sacrifice,
Those conforming to his palate,
Frightened to obedience.
"I thought as much," the Counselor said,
Thoughtful woman, old and wise.
"They married ere the dragon came,
Wed, you know, as I advised them,
Lusty youth, beloved maid.
A chance to take, oh yes, perhaps,
But none had tried it, I thought it wise:
Find out if we had to do it,
Test the dragon's appetite."
So the townsmen took the rope,
The one they'd got to hang the youth,
Returned it to the water well,
Where it drew the oaken bucket,
Drawing water for the town.
Water they still had a-plenty.
Of dragons, though, they had no more... .

Lilava and Vainen applauded Jouka's song.

"How's that?" Jouka asked? "A human song with a good moral, a good song for traveling. But now I'm hungry. Are we not due to stop for supper? Do I mistake, or can I already feel a fine chill in the air? These are good horses: they do not hurry, but they carry us quickly. Songs help a trip pass pleasantly."

They had a simple dinner of brown bread cooked with nuts and seeds and spread with butter, also a compote of raspberries, blackberries, and blueberries, some cheese with savory herbs, tea made with chicory and sugar, and some light honey brandy.

"We can ride yet before dark and maybe a bit longer before we camp," Jouka suggested. "Another song now. What next, Vainen?"

"Why not sing the tale of the magic kantalette that Kulevo used to charm the bear."

"A naughty tale, my friend Vainen."

"Just good fun, Jouka. The lady is worldly, not a child, and a laugh is the second best medicine; only a song works better, as the saying goes. This tale, too, comes from the humans, in this case those who live in the far north and east." Jouka began again with his hum that turned to a chant, pausing only to say:

"Right, then, and good: if she doesn't like my song, I shall blame you, and so she will still let me teach her some music. Who knows that it may not come to her aid on some occasion when other magic fails." And here is the tale that Jouka sang (translated from the Old East-Sea Elvish into prose, since poetry in that language presents particular difficulties).

* * *

£ong ago, in the old times, before the One hung the sun in the sky, when the sky was lit by candles alone, a man named Kulevo lived in the north with his mother and father. That family were not beautiful people; in fact, Kulevo himself may have been the ugliest man of his time, and his parents lived on the edge of their village, near where the forest began. Kulevo so lacked physical refinement that no girl would have him, so he could not marry, but stayed home with his mother and father. He had large, heavy features and had grown a full beard by the age of five. That problem did not bother him too much: he loved better than anything else to hunt and fish, and so spent nearly all his time in the pursuits he loved, whenever his parents could spare him from chores at home. They did not work him very hard, feeling bad already that they had produced such an ugly child with so few prospects to improve their social status.

Once when Kulevo was away fishing on the eastern shore, a bear came out of the forest and began to terrorize the villagers, stealing food, rooting through compost, scrapping fishing sheds, and leaving everyone more than usually afraid to go out at night.

Townsmen sent out hunting parties during the day, but by then the bear had returned to the cover of the forest, and they couldn't find it. By night they remained too fearful to look very far, but maintained the safety of their homes, while the bear continued its depradations. Folk could sometimes hear the bear's call very early in the morning, before the sun rose, and some claimed to have heard its claws scraping and its breath snorting right at their doorsteps. But no one had the means or the courage to meet the bear at night on its own terms, at least not until Kulevo returned.

He brought back a fine big basket of ocean fish packed in ice, but he had in his absence become a celebrity, since, beginning with his mother and followed by nearly all the townsfolk, people had been saying, "Just wait until Kulevo returns. He will know how to deal with that bear." Now Kulevo, though a fine woodsman, had no experience at all with bears, and no one felt quite sure why everyone had come to believe that he could deal with one then. But once his mother had said it, everyone else grasped at any hope offered them, however irrational, and they repeated it until they nearly believed it.

After they had taken care of the fish, Kulevo's father told him about the bear, and his mother mentioned that the town council would like to talk with him about it, believing that he would know what to do. So Kulevo ate a big meal, then walked into the town center, where he was greeted with cheering, music, and other such fanfare. The council members all came out to meet him, and they draped a banner that said, "Welcome home, Kulabo" across his shoulders — folk did not spell so well in those days, and that shows you about how much they really thought of the youth.

The chief of the council told Kulevo the whole story of the bear and asked him if he had any ideas about what to do about it. He then cast his arms in a broad gesture, as if to suggest that all the townsfolk joined him in this sentiment: that should Kulevo succeed in ridding them of the bear, he should have his choice of the eligible young ladies of the town for his wife. A screech rose from the midst of the crowd. The young ladies, hearing that proclamation, had stopped cheering and quickly gathered together at the edge of the crowd to determine their response to such a revelation. In complete agreement they snuck off to various hiding places, and no one else in town could find one of them for the next few days, so well did they hide.

Kulevo, guessing how all that would fall out, shrugged his shoulders and agreed to face the bear anyway, asking in return only that his mother receive admission as a full member of the Council, something she had always said she wanted while knowing it an essential impossibility. At that idea a lower-pitched murmur arose among the councilors, who gathered together for a quick confabulation; after a few minutes of spirited discussion, the chief of the Council emerged to say that, yes, sure, she could become an associate member, a member-in-training, on probation, as was the custom. They of course had no such custom, and everyone including Kulevo knew that, but he shrugged his shoulders and agreed: from his point of view, he had done his duty by asking.

"I will take care of this bear for you," Kulevo said, and he turned and left them.

Everyone cheered him as he departed, though as soon as he had disappeared from view, the cheering petered out, replaced by doutful hemming and hawing.

"That boy just doesn't seem right in the head to me," said one old woman. "But then again, maybe that's the sort you want to send against a bear."

Kulevo told his mother that she was to receive appointment as an associate council member — not exactly what she wanted, but a step that had once seemed beyond her wildest hopes — and he filled his pack, took a shovel and some other tools, and headed off toward the forest. Night fell shortly afterward. In those days if you wanted to find a bear, your best chance lay in poking around in the woods at night, so that's exactly what Kulevo did, leaving the shovel at the entrance to the forest path. He lit a torch and made his way along the path carefully but with no attempt to keep silent.

At first he met little more than a few owls and beavers, but then he found exactly what he sought: a recent footprint, obviously that of a bear. One couldn't be sure that the right bear had left it, but Kulevo had to do the best he could. Taking a mix of mud, grass, and a binder his father used to make mortar for livestock walls, he made a cast of the footprint. When the cast hardened, he took from his pack an old tortoise shell, and using an awl and a wooden hammer, he reshaped the shell as nearly as he could to fit the footprint cast. He then carved the edges of a small piece of bear-colored mahogany so that it fit neatly into the hollow of the shell, and carefully inserted wooden frets in holes that he had prefricated in the wood.

Next, he found a tall oak tree, and beneath it placed a large bowl that he filled with milk and honey spiced with sweetened sassafras and laced with a strong sleeping powder that his mother had prepared — she had used it on his father when he got too rambunctious. Kulevo snuffed his torch, climbed as high in the tree as he could, sat perfectly still, and waited.

Before midnight he heard the sounds of snuffling and heavy feet not far away. In minutes the bear emerged from among the trees, the smell of the milk and honey drawing it irresistably.

The bear, enchanted with the smell of a drink that seemed a gift from the forest gods, did not bother to look up into the tree, but simply consumed the drink more quickly than you or I would tell a joke. Between the effects of the sweetness of the drink and the powerful sleeping powder, the bear dropped off to deep slumber in a matter of minutes.

Kulevo shimmied quietly down the tree, but found the bear sprawled, belly up, in utterly unwakeable sleep. In those days bears had whiskers longer than a cat's, and from that bear Kulevo plucked them all. He placed them carefully in his pack and returned by the path he had come back to the edge of the forest, making certain to leave both tracks and his scent in his wake. There he found the shovel and dug a pit at the end of the path. Then he took out the tortoise shell with the mahogany face and strung it with the bear's whiskers, making a kantelette. He tuned it carefully, and again he waited.

In the morning he could hear the sounds of a very unhappy bear rumbling directly along the path toward where he sat. As the bear got closer, he began to play on his new kantelette and to sing his deep, throaty, soulful voice a tune that even a bear would love.

As the sound of footfalls got nearer, they began to slow noticeably, and even the snuffling sound faded, replaced by deep breathing with just the tiniest whine.

When the bear turned the last corner and got a good look at Kulevo, he saw not vengeance, but love its eyes. It was in fact a she-bear, and the sound of the kantelette, filled with the natural music of flowing water and of the bear's own decent nature, had turned the animal's heart to rapture. Whatever the girls of the village thought, to the bear Kulevo looked beautiful, and his music sounded heavenly. He sang songs of the beauty of the forest and its creatures and of the loneliness and sorrows of life, and the bear appreciated all those things.

She batted her eyes and swished toward him. Her thoughts elsewhere than on the path before her, she slid right into the pit Kulevo had dug.

When Kulevo looked over the edge of the pit to decide what he should do with the bear, she had such a look of profound disappointment in her eyes that his heart turned in her favor. He found himself rapidly developing admiration for her many fine ursine qualities. He immediately slid a stout branch down into the pit on which she could climb out, and when he could he grasped her paws and helped drag her up. Kulevo and the bear both experienced a moment of joy and wonder when, for the first time up close, they looked deep into each other's eyes.

Not long after candles lit the sky with morning, as people began to stir about their business in the village, they found coming up the main street Kulevo with the bear strolling happily at his side. They fled to the surrounding buildings, looking out of second-storey windows, if they had any, to learn what miracle would happen. When he reached the town square with his companion, Kulevo addressed the absentees.

"None of you young ladies would have me, but I have found a truer mate than any of you would have been or than any of you will find. She came here not to trouble any of you, but simply to search for food and because she was lonely — she could find no one to call her own in the vastness of the forest. We intend to go to north into the forest to live, so you will hear from neither of us again while you live, as long as you agree to appoint my mother as a full, not associate, member of the Council. We ask only that in exchange for your peace of mind. Good-bye, and good wishes to you all."

Kulevo and the bear appeared to smile at each other, and side by side they ambled back the way they had come, disappearing into the forest.

The Council reluctantly appointed Kulevo's mother a full member with all the rights and privileges thereto accruing, and no one there ever heard from the happy couple again, other than gifts of certain hard-to-find but useful forest products that mysteriously appeard on the doorstep of Kulevo's parents' house at Yule-Time, for which they justly gave credit, though they never had the opportunity to offer personal thanks, for which blessing they actually felt relief.

Legends tell that Kulevo and his mate, who turned out to have the name Ursula, lived happily together deep in the forest, and that together they had a son, who entered into many myths and fairy tales, the famous "Bear's Son" stories of a shape shifter with strength, courage, and woodsy skills well beyond those of mortal men.

In later generations the stars of the North shaped themselves in memory of Kulevo and Ursula, he offering her a drink with his ladle, she happily accepting. The stars teach us that with persistence, luck, and a willingness to love, we will all find our mates, and though we may not keep them forever, the world will find a way to remember those that prove most faithful and therefore memorable.

* * *

"𝕱ahscinating da' dee human and dee elf like story about drahgons and beahs. Dee wyvern have many stories about creachahs of all soahts, but especially about dee fishes. No' too many folk know it, but a wyvern actually invented dee sushi bah.'

"Will you tell us a fish story, please, Vern?" Lilava asked, not knowing, of course, anything about sushi bars.

"Of coahse I do, pretty lady, ya ya. Bu' dee wyvern no' equipped to play da kantelette, so I jus' tell you a bery good story, an' it go like dis. One time Wyllium — he a Wise One among dee wyvern many century ago — he out on dee lahge lake fishin', not like dee man wid dee pole, but wid only his famous and bee-yu-ti-ful feet ahnd his brilliant wits. He one of dee best fishahs of all time, and he cahtch pretty much whatevah he want foah him and his family. Dat day he wan' to cahtch a really big fish to make his supah-cute wifey happy.

"Well he floating ovah dee watah and spot undah da wave a nice salmon, jus' a good size foah dinnah. So he wait to jus' dee right time and drop down, cathin' dee salmon up as neat as you please, and he begin to fly home.

"Well da salmon begin to talk to him. He say, 'I heard of you, Wyllium Wyvern, what a good fishah you ah, but you catch me, you catch moah fish dan you can handle.'

"'If da' true,' Wyllium say, 'how I catch you at all? You ah not so big an' strong anyway, but enough to make a good dinnah.'

295

"'You be suhprised a' what I am,' said da salmon. By da' time Wyllium have him almost to da shoah, so he no' worried too much. Bu' dee salmon began to grow lahge, biggah an' biggah, until Wyllium's toes get stretched as fah as dey can go. Den all of a sudden da fish get smallah, so small he slip right tru Wyllium's toes and splash into da watah, and he swim off as fahst as he can go. Wyllium fly all ovah lookin' foah da fish, but he canno' find him, so he fly home dejected and empty-footed.

"When he get deah, his cutiepie say, 'Wyllium wyvern, why you not bring home something foah dinnah?'

"Wyllium say, 'I caught you a nice nice fish, a salmon, bu' he got away.'

"'How he get away?' dee wife ahsk, disbelieving. 'How big was he?"

"Well Wyllium hold his wings apaht about dis far, da size of dee fish when he fihst cahtch it. Den he move dee wings out a bit, den a bit moah, den about moah, till he have dem spread wide as he cahn.

"Wyllium Wyvern!' says dee wife, all mahd, 'why you make up dis big-fish-da'-got-away story! I bet you not fishin' at all, but out chasin' ahftah da cute females!'

"Well da' makes Wyllium bery unhappy, so go out to dee lake and look all ovah foah dee fish, but he no' find him. He bring home some clams foah dinnah, but da' no' da same as a bery big salmon, an' he have an unhappy wifey twice ovah.

"So next day he go fishin' again, an' his wife tell him he bettah no' chase dee females, if he know wha's good foah him, but he mad now an' bery much want to cahtch again da salmon, so he fly fahst as he cahn all round dee lake, and finally he fin' him again, da' salmon.

"Well he cahtch him, but dis time dee salmon get big really fahst, and Wyllium struggle to pull him out, and dee salmon struggle to stay in. Finally dee salmon say, 'Wyllium, now wait a moment, an' let us tête-à-tête, you an' I. I don' want you to take me home so you an' youah wifey cahn eat me, but I don' want you to stahve, eidah. So how about if you let me go, I tell you wheah to find some really nice eels: dey fry up and make nice dinnah.'

"'Oh no, smahty salmon,' Wyllium ansah, 'you no' going to get me to put my bee-ay-u-tiful feet on no electric eel an' buhn my toes up!'

"No, no, Wyllium, I no' do da' to you if you treat me nice. Dees ah good eels, safe to touch, good to eat. Youah wife say you bring home dee bes' meal evah!'

"So Wyllium do as dee salmon tell him, an' he fin' dee eels. He touch one wid jus' one toe at a time, an' when he no' get buhned, he catch a bunch of dem an' take dem home. Well his cutie wife give him a funny look, but she introduce dee eel into wyvern cuisine. She no' specially like dem hehself, but she give some to dee neighbahs, and dey go crazy foah dem, so she get a reputation as a great innovatah in wyvern cooking, and she happy wid Wyllium again. So every now and again Wyllium go to see dee salmon an' ahsk foah moah fishin' tips. From dee fish he find how to cahtch dee uhchin, dee floundah, dee puffah, an' dee calamari. Ahftah da' dee salmon get in all soahts of trouble wid dee uddah fishes foah finkin' on his watah buddies, but Wyllium's wife get bery famous foah exotic cookin', and a' least Wyllium get to turn a big fish story into a whole bunch of little fish stories. An' da's how dis story end."

* * *

With that story and others the small party of searchers made their way north through hills and woods until they reached remnant patches of snow on a stretch of high, crusty, rolling ground. Some while ahead they found a wide lake, still partly frozen, and across the lake they spotted unexpectedly pleasant hills green with pine and fir.

"Do you recall the place, Vainen?"

"I do, Jouka: I believe Hod lives in those very hills. Do you not see smoke, as from a chimney, rising just there? But if I make no mistake, those are storm clouds approaching over the hills, though it's late in the season for them. If we can cross the lake swiftly enough, we may find a warm fire before the snow they carry engulfs us. Look: you can see a few flakes falling already."

The lake had too much ice for them to boat across, even if they could have found a boat, but the ice looked too thin for walking, leaving them no choice but to ride around the lake. They turned east, but soon the ground became too treacherous for riding, as the snow began to fall more heavily and the wind to circle in squalls. Vern felt too heavy and cold to fly, so the elves and Lilava all gave him their spare cloaks, but by then all together were reduced to plodding in slow, slippery steps through the quickly accumulating drifts. Vainen and Jouka distributed snowshoes from their packs, but the horses were having troubles of their own. Lilava clung close to Courage both for his assurance and for her own.

Before long the snow was blowing so hard that they could barely see. Vainen and Jouka led the party, their only guide the lake's edge, which they kept just to their right. Vern had used the extra cloaks to wrap his feet, which had gone from tender to numb. In the strong gusts the group could barely keep a torch lit, and soon even the elves, who had lived nearly all of their lives in the cold north, were reduced to proceeding by feel.

When dark had covered them even more thoroughly than had the snow, and they had decided to try their best to set up a camp, Vainen pointed ahead to where a small but steady light looked to be approaching them at a height of a little more than a foot above the ground. They huddled together and waited.

A short, stocky figure in a tall toboggan hat appeared before them, holding the light higher now so that it could see them and they could see it. It handed Vainen a bottle, made with its free hand a drinking motion. The party of travelers each took a long pull from the bottle: the rich, lightly sweet liquid traced a pattern of warmth down their throats, into their bellies, and out to their extremities. The figure then motioned them to follow and turned back the way it had come. They did their best to oblige.

The figure led them briefly yet along the edge of the lake, then turned abruptly left and up a hill through a tunnel of pines. Lilava wondered how they could manage to climb in the slick snow, but the snowshoes did their job, and someone had treated the path with something that looked like soot and wood shavings and that made it less slippery. They climbed together for what seemed to Lilava like an hour, but must have been less, until they made a turn into a woodland maze: right, left, right, left, left, right, right, left, left, right — Lilava lost track, until finally a bright light shone before them, looking as inviting as the morning sun. A wooden house hid itself among tree boughs and snow drifts, and the welcoming light poured from its windows. A tall, thick door swung open, and the party followed one after another into a Great Room with a rousing fire and the wonderful smell of vegetable soup cooking on the hearth.

* * *

"God!" said Lilava. "You have saved us." The snow gnome had thrown off his coat and shaken off his boots and put them by the hearth, but the knit hat still sat high atop his head. Words tumbled out of him as though he hadn't spoken to anyone in months.

"Not your lives, I think — these elves wouldn't do so poorly as to get you killed, I think — but I have saved you a deal of trouble, I know. The wolves and such cause no real problem here, in fact they're friendly enough for the most part, though I keep away from the bears, but a fine storm has blown up to greet you, and you may well have got lost. An owl spotted you across the lake and alerted me. You certainly wouldn't have found my house in all this blizzard. Unseasonable, you know, as if to keep you away, though I don't believe in such things: the world does what it does, and we must deal with it. But tell me your story now: I was expecting you last year. Talk all you want; my hearing's good. I'll just get you some hot food while you do. Too late at night for proper digestion, but you'll need something to warm you, I dare say, and the soup in the hearth-crock works as well as anything I know, especially together with nut-coffee, a special family recipe, you know. We'll eat with you: bad to expect others to eat what you won't yourself. Go ahead, talk away — don't let me stop you, and I'll be needing to know your plans. You, wyvern: don't fly in here — too easy to hit one of the shelves and break something."

The Great Room was lined with shelves upon shelves, full of knick-knacks of all kinds from books to stones to boxes to musical instruments to figurines. Vern exhaustedly plopped himself by the fire to warm his feet.

As he spoke, Hod darted about the room and into the neighboring kitchen and pantry, faster than Lilava would have guessed he could move. He climbed up counters, desks, and shelves nimbly as could be, and his arms seemed to stretch as far as he needed them to, then he'd drop down softly on the floor to set the Great Room table with plates, utensils, cups, and odds and ends of bread, dried fruits, nuts, root-hash, milk, and biscuits. As Lilava told the story of her last year, Hod finished setting the table and poured everyone bowls of soup from the hearth-crock. When she told about leaving Orfila at Elvenhome, a small face appeared around the corner of the kitchen doorway. It looked much like Hod's, but more feminine, with no beard but large, blue-white eyes, and also a tall woolen cap perched atop the head. The skin around the eyes and mouth wrinkled into a smile, and the gnome nodded kindly at Lilava and handed a pitcher full of steaming liquid to Hod, who lifted it onto the table.

"Here's the nut-coffee — if you don't like it, I'll be very disappointed — and that's my mate, Laud, at the kitchen door. We snow gnomes, though we live everywhere the snow falls, have relatively small numbers and few young. We value them, but we don't pine for them: our son left us years and years ago to work and find a mate, just as we left our elders and found each other. Daughters will sometimes stay with their parents and entertain visiting suitors, if they are very beautiful, but they too may choose to go out on their own, too, to see new snows in new places. I don't know how you humans feel about such things. Our lad visited about ten years ago, and now and then we get news of him from passing crows, if you can trust their sort. As for us, Laud tends the mountain-magic and the high snows, and I tend the lake magic and the low-snows, and we both tend the nut-coffee. If you drink much, it becomes a habit, you know, so start slowly and savor, and stop before you think you should."

"The lad will visit with a mate of his own soon, I dare say," said Laud in a smooth, carefully enunciated alto. "About time for that, old Hod." She smiled and winked at Lilava. Lilava wondered whether the wink implied welcome, understanding, or that, in Laud's opinion, Lilava would make an acceptable mate for their son.

Hod climbed on one of the benches at the table and poured two cups of the steaming beverage. Laud nimbly slid in beside him, and Hod handed her one of the cups. Together they both took a long, slurpy sip. "Aaaah," they sighed together. "Good batch, love," Laud complimented.

A fascinating aroma drifted up from Lilava's cup, an earthy blend of sassafras, pine nuts, berries, hickory root, and walnut — she pieced together the olfactory impressions one by one, but some ingredient eluded identification. While her heart felt frozen, her limbs began to return to life as she sipped coffee and rich soup and milk, nibbled on biscuits and root-hash.

Everyone else ate heartily, and hardly anyone spoke until all had filled their bellies; even Vern said not a word, but ate his fill, occasionally checking his toes for signs of life.

Finally they all pushed back from the table and gathered around the fire to sip elderberry brandy.

"Two days, at least, I think," Hod said. The travelers looked at him, waiting for him to say more, but he took a sip of brandy and stared at the fire. Some minutes later he added, "Unless you're very lucky. This snow, you know, it will have covered the entrance. We'll need two full days for it to blow through, two more for us to find it and clear it. You're still set on trying the passage?"

"Dead set," Lilava answered.

"No' a good choice of words, no' atoll," Vern said. "But I agree wid dee gnome-mahn dat you should wait anyway, get back youah streng'. Dees pahts no' so easy, even foah dee skillful trahvelah."

"The road can be hard, yes," said Lilava.

"You may not get in at all," added Vainen, "and if you do, you may well not get out again, and that's even assuming this path can take you where you want to go."

"Yes, yes, I know," said Lilava softly. "But I will go. I will go." She fell asleep in the chair where she sat.

* * *

Lilava awoke in a soft bed with a down comforter pulled up over her. When she poked her head out of bed to look around, the room felt warmer than she would have believed possible so far north — Hod and Laud's house had a re-markable ability to retain heat, and they were probably doing their best to keep it so for her sake: snow gnomes wouldn't need their rooms as warm as that.

The world has in it much evil, Lilava knew from experience, but it also has much good, many folk both kind and generous, if one has enough luck to find them, and in this case Lilava had found them.

She looked out a window down onto a woodland landscape still covered with snow.

She found a basin of water and a towel in her room, so she washed, then made her way out of her room, down a short hallway, and down a spiral staircase into the rear of the Great Room where she and her companions had dined. A fire still roared in the hearth, and in front of it Vern revolved slowly, hovering about a foot in the air, humming a tune Lilava couldn't follow. "Good morning," she said.

"Good ahftanoon, sleepy head," Vern said. "How you feelin' now?"

"Afternoon? I feel like I had a few good hours' dreamless sleep, and I'm ready to go."

"A few houahs? You slep' a whole day and a few houahs, thhen a couple extra houahs foah good mezhah. Hod say the snow too deep to go yet, howevah. He ahnd dee elves been out clearin' a pathh — I getting' bettah a' dos thhh sounds you make."

"Have you had breakfast — lunch?"

"Oh, yah, bee-u-tiful lady, dey — thhey — been feedin' me bery well, bery well. I jus' about ready to take on da snow."

"I thought I heard voices. Bring you something to eat, human lady?" Laud's blue-white eyes shone as she spoke from the kitchen doorway, and her smile showed just a hint of exactly even, bright white teeth.

"Yes, please, whatever you have that's easy. Have you seen Hod this morn — this afternoon?"

"Just then the front door burst open and amidst a flurry of snowflakes in came Hod, Vainen, and Jouka.

"The sleeper wakes. Welcome back," Hod said. The two elves, having clearly undergone considerable labor, went directly to the pitcher warming by the hearth and poured themselves large cups of nut-coffee.

"Luckily the snow has stopped," Hod continued, "except for a few light flurries. These sturdy elves and I have cleared a path along the near side of the mountain. After that, if you can sled and snowshoe, we should be able to begin the trip north tomorrow just after sunrise."

"I only hope that after all we have done, it proves the right path once you find it, Lady Lilava," Vainen said.

"Will you take care of Courage for me, dear Laud? No journey for horses ahead."

"Of course, dearie. When the snow's really done, we'll take him back to Elvenhome."

"Can we not start north today, after you have had lunch and rest, of course?" Lilava asked.

"Tomorrow morning. If we get lucky, we will then make the entrance around noon of the second day, assuming we can cut a path directly in this snow. More yet may have fallen north of here." Hod was adamant, so Lilava reluctantly waited another day. She was dressed and waiting outside Hod's front door at next sunup.

* * *

301

While the uphills, even in good snowshoes, proved slow and difficult, the sledding felt to Lilava, even in her sorrowful state of mind, positively exhilarating. The cold bit into any exposed skin, but the blood leaped as she turned corners and whisked down hill as smoothly atop the snow as a bird would soar to earth on a current of air. The sleds, made of light linden wood with a surface of thin, highly polished metal, seemed to float over the snow. They carried the shield-shaped sleds on their backs as they walked, then used them as floors for their tightly woven woolen tents at night. Having a short journey — so they hoped—they carried small rations, melting snow for drink. Even Vern, who floated up the hills, fanning his wings rapidly to try to keep them warm, used a sled for the downhills, just for the fun of it.

Down hills, through dales, over crests and frozen tarns, past scraggly copses, and then finally to a barren, icy plain they moved steadily and surely following Hod's lead, and even with his short legs, in his own element he led them faithfully and truly, never sinking beneath the surface of the snow, to a remote entrance to a cavern, which they reached just before noon on the second day. "That's it," he said, the Northwest Passage. "Easy trip. Now the hard part begins."

They had found the entrance to the Underworld, but it was covered with thick sheet of ice.

* * *

Jouka hacked at it with a double-headed axe, the only weapon he had brought, and Hod tried his spells on it, but they could not penetrate the icy cover that shut the cavern from the upper world. Lilava, knowing no spells for ice, felt lost, ready to beat on it with her bare fists.

"I b'lieve I can do dis job," Vern said. "You all look like you tryin' so hahd I hate to stop you, but let dee wyern have a try."

Vern floated over to the frozen portal and began slowly to spin, to revolve in place. Then he held out his wings so that just the tip grazed the surface of the ice. He spun faster, and faster, and faster, and the sharp edge of his wings cut a growing groove in the wall before them, making a sound louder and higher pitched than that of a lathe sharpening an axe blade. Finally he slowed, then stopped, looking tired and dizzy, but leaving a deep gash in the ice.

"Yow, da' sting! Always good to prahctice spinnin'. Good ting dee wyvern have da bery shahp wing tip — I nevah hahd to test it like da' befoah. Legend say da' Wyllium Wyvern once make shoes wi' clippins of dee wing tips, in case his bee-u-ti-ful feet get soah, but I dunno if da' true or no'. Wing-tip shoes, he call dem. Give it a swipe oah two wi' youah axe blade now, elf mahn."

Jouka did just that, and in three swings he had burst through — Vern had cut through far enough to weaken the ice wall for Jouka's blows to finish the job easily. With the first blow to clear the wall, a cold wind rushed out, followed by a warm blast that smelled of ash and sulfur. No one in the party looked anyone else in the eye: they knew that the warm air meant that they had found the right entrance, but also that they would not be able to convince Lilava to return with them.

In a few minutes they had cleared the opening to the cavern, the elves having brushed the ice-chips away. Lilava peered into the passage, saw nothing but darkness, smelled only dust and desert dryness and sulfur. She turned back to face her companions.

"Thank you all. No one has truer friends in this life than have I. But you must not come with me. Here I must go alone."

"We may not go there," Jouka said. "The Creator did not make this path for elves, nor for living humans, I think. But we have got you safely here. We will gladly take you safely back as far south as the ground still bears snow. But otherwise we must return home. We have been gone long, and though we are far from the most important of our folk, families, friends, and community need us, and we miss them. Will you not relent at last, Lady Lilava?"

"Come home with me, Lady," Hod said. "Laud and I will treat you as we would our own daughter or, better yet, an esteemed guest, and we will accompany you to Elvenhome when you're ready to go."

"I cannot, may not, will not, but thank you, thank you for all you have done." She hugged the elves and the gnome, then turned to Vern. "You too should make your way home. Vern the wyvern, you have been the greatest of friends to Severus and to me, but I can hardly ask you to go any farther. Only the dead walk these paths."

"You no' ge' rid of youah buddy so easy, Lady-o. I gonna help you find Sevy. We rescue do Monstah Specialis' from dee greates' monstah. Vern Wyvern goin' to have annuda great story to tell when he get home. I be jus' as famous as Wyllium. Dee wyvern has seen almos' everting dey is to see in dis world, but no wyvern has gone to the Human Dead Land twice. I be a hero all ovah, an' all dee wyvern females come from fah an' wee to see handsome an' famous me, jus' beggin' to get a kiss. Le's go. No time to waste. Sevy waiting foah us. Maybe if we no' find him, you come home wid me instead! Bye-bye elvies an' gnome-mahn: you have good trips home, an' remembah youah wyvern friend."

They drew out their good-byes, as friends will do, but as soon as she could free herself, Lilava dropped all her gear but a back-pouch inside the entrance and threw herself into the cavern at a trot.

* * *

Vern came floating up behind Lilava. "Slow down! I know you ah eagah, but you got to go safely, too, and quiet quiet quiet!" he whispered. "Livin' folk don' go dis way."

Together they worked their way down a treacherous path, a kind of rough stairwell, for what might have been hours — to Lilava it seemed like days — until finally they reached an open cavern broader than they could fathom. Lilava's hurry turned to steady plodding as the air grew thinner.

"Vern!" Lilava whispered, "do you hear voices?"

"I been hearin' da voices for some time now. Same as las' time: dee dead ones walking, all aroun' us. Can you no' see dem?" When Lilava looked at him, Vern's eyes glowed bright red.

Then Lilava saw the road, the Gray Road, on which they were walking, lit only by strange, dull blue lights off the path. She heard the dull echo of tinny voices, odd bits of grotesque songs, wails of lament, meaningless phrases unconnected to life or logic. And amidst the growing darkness she saw shadows of outlines, some hurrying by, some plodding soundlessly, no more quickly than herself, some lying faint along the barely distinguishable path, clinging to the bent, gnarled gray trees that jutted like scars from the blasted landscape.

"Come on, Lila, we got to keep goin'. I know it hahd. Try jus' to keep da feet movin'."

Lilava hadn't realized that she had stopped right in her own tracks. She coughed up dry air, took from the slim pack she'd kept with her a leather water pouch, and offered Vern a drink.

"No no, Lady, we canno' do da' heah, no watah!" Vern hissed. But Lilava was already absent-mindedly taking a drink, and a drop fell from her chin to the dust below.

Suddenly shadow after shadow flung itself upon them, thin and clinging as cobwebs, biting like dust mites. The echo of dusty voices grew to a din: "Water, water, water!" they howled, digging desperately with ghostly fingers for a drop of comfort they could not touch.

Vern covered Lilava with his wings and hurried her along until the heat and rising dust nearly made her faint. When he freed her, she stumbled forward and nearly fell, voices faint but fewer dogging her steps. "No moah wa — no moah, Lady, we cause big trouble!" Vern hissed. The two travelers drove themselves forward until the voices all but faded, and nearly all sense but the dull plod of foot on dust passed to oblivion.

* * *

"**W**ha's that?" Lilava asked dully, her lips parched and her eyes burning. She felt as though her whole life had been consumed with walking, walking in endless gray dust.

"Dahk," Vern answered finally. "Dahk da' is dahker dan dahk."

"The abyss," Lilava thought. The growing black that consumed the spirit, that plummeted it — where? Severus had spoken of it. "We must reach it. Maybe he will be there."

"We canno' go deah — nobody go deah and come bahck. No no, bahd bahd, we mus' no' go."

"Sevy, Sevy will be there. He must be there." Lilava plunged ahead with more will than strength, feeling as though she was running, but barely stumbling forward. The growing cloud of unrelenting darkness grew, extending its fingers toward them. Lilava could feel its grip about her ankles, its eagerness to draw her in, to suck her body and soul into the hole that was opening at her feet.

A sound. A call? From the left, a voice: yes!

"Lila!"

A faint light, swirling, light only by contrast to the infinite black raising its grip about her knees.

"Lila! Go no farther! Lila! Vern! Come, come toward the light!"

Lila felt something try to pull her toward the swirling mist of light taking shape at the side of the path.

"Resist the darkness! Come, come to the light!"

Lilava wrenched herself from the abysmal fingers and, grasping at what tried to hold her up, thrust herself toward the light. She felt Vern close to her, then dropped in a confusion of limb and wing, and she fainted.

Hands. White hands. Misty hands, cupped, cupping her face. Eyes, dull white eyes, but familiar, loving. A face. A familiar face, the most-loved face, right before hers.

Sevy, Sevy my love, my darling!

She had the will, but not the strength to speak it.

"I have waited, and my foolish love and my foolish friend have come for me. How I love you both. But what shall we do?" Beyond doubt the figure of Sir Severus le Brewse had taken shape, misty and insubstantial, but clearly identifiable, before Lilava, a long swirl of light trailing behind him. Vern perched there beside them, his worried eyes glowing red.

"We mus' do sometin', silly lovahs, to get outta heah! Dee dead-abyss comin' foah us again!"

"Come with me!" spoke the voice of Severus. "Come, toward the light! The light flows behind and above me. I have resisted it, waiting. It will take me now, and you will come with me. Peace and safety dwell there, love, too! Come, follow!"

"No!" called a deep, resounding voice. "You, living ones, may not go!"

Out of the dark abyss emerged a tall figure, stretched, robed in gray, dark, bearded, with black eyes, from the center of which grew burning suns.

"You three again. One has come through my portal for the second time. Two have come as fugitives, living. One has been warned never to come here alive again. One was not made for human paths. What must I do with you now?" The figure stared down at them, his glaring eyes grim and unyielding.

Lilava licked a dry tongue over her dry lips and tried to speak, coughed up dust. "You said — you said not to come by that road. I have come by another. Nothing could keep me from my Severus."

"I can, if I wished to do so. I can cast you in — see just there? — if I wish."

"You will send us into Hell?"

"Hell? Certainly not. Send true lovers into some imagined torture for loving too well? Balderdash. Where do they get these ideas? No, no 'Hell' for you, but something fitting, certainly, for all the trouble you have caused me. You, missy, thought to get off on a technicality. Not going to happen. You wyvern, think you can bop your "bee-ay-u-ti-ful" feet along any path you choose, just because you want to or somebody asks you. No good sense! None among the three of you. You know what that means, hmm? You, silly man, keeping the Living Light waiting, as if you had any right just because of some transient human love. You died, man! Twice! Let it go, already! You think the Spirit of Love will deprive you of your love forever? Grrr! Folk had patience in the old days.

"So now, first: mini-dragon, say good-bye. You're going home. You won't like the journey, but you'll get there fast and safe. Fortunate for you there's a portal right over there. Didn't even see it, did you, for all your great eyesight. Hurry up: say your good-bye. So sentimental, the living, and some of the dead, too!"

"Sevy, Lila, whachew gonna do widout me?"

"Vern, best of wyverns, best of friends."

"We'll never forget you!"

"Bye-bye, lovahs! Maybe we meet again some day! Remembah me, an' someday I name a little wyvern ahftah each of you, an' — hey! Hey!"

The gray figure had raised his hand, and in a flash of gyroscopic light, Vern flew backward and out of sight.

"Don't worry about him," the specter said. "He'll be home in about five top-side minutes, dizzy and disoriented, but safe and sound. Now, what about you two."

306

Lilava did her best to cling to Severus, who felt in her arms like no more than a mist.

"Nobody dies twice and goes back. Nobody visits twice and goes back. You don't want to go to the light: you're both still body-mad — hug hug, kiss kiss, human foolishness, blech! So I will send you through another portal to a different place or time. Alive you'll be, but with nothing familiar but yourselves, nothing and no one else upon whom you may rely. No wyverns, no Ladies of the Lake, some place and time where nobody believes in real magic, and silly sleight-of-hand tricks fool almost everybody. That will test you! Yes, I know just when. Now: no arguing. Do as I tell you, and you, dead man, when you die the next time, just go to the light. Understand me? Say it with me now: go to the bloody light! Now look what you've done: you've made me swear, which I haven't done in several top-side centuries! You, live woman, go away, and don't come back for any reason. Go live out your lives, and then go to the light! Off with you both! Go!"

The specter raised a hand and gave a little push, and Lilava felt herself flung backward at a pace that she thought must kill her. She tried desperately to cling to the mist that was all she had left of Severus: she felt nothing, but saw a spiralling glow beside her. She tried to call out, but the wind caught her breath. She felt a scream rising from her lungs, but before it could escape, her body struck what felt like an enormous cushion, and all the wind was knocked from her lungs.

* * *

Eyes open? Check. Limbs all connected? Check. Breath in the lungs? No! Breathe, breathe, try to breathe — oh, that's painful! Breathe, breathe. Lilava! Severus looked beside him, drawing painful breaths. Lilava was half sitting up, holding her ribs, gasping for air. He put his hand out to touch her: nothing. No, he had just missed. He tried again: solid! She turned her face toward him, the eyes wide with wonder and disbelief, but with life, life! Then for a moment he passed out again.

When Severus awoke, he was lying in a field beside a haystack, the cushion onto which he and Lilava had fallen. Lilava, his beloved Lilava, held a wet cloth, torn from the hem of her tunic, with which she dabbed his forehead.

"Sevy?"

"Lila!"

They fell together in a kiss so complete, so perfect, that they both passed out again.

Lilava awoke to find Severus dabbing her forehead with the wet cloth. "You're alive!"

"We're alive."

"What happened to Vern?"

"The spirit sent him home."

"Oh, yes, that's right. Where are we?"

"I have no idea."

"Should we look around?"

"First, kiss me again. I can't believe it. You found me!"

"The only man to escape the Gray Road twice."

"Your love did it, both times. We destroyed the Chimaera, for good and all."

"We did. But what do we do now?"

"Live. Love. The rest doesn't matter so much. Must be some sort of monsters, or something."

"Let's look around."

"Let's."

They found themselves in the middle of green fields woven together with stone walls. They heard sheep bleating. Sun poked uncertainly through blue-gray clouds, a gentle breeze was blowing, and a light rain began to fall.

"Looks like Britain. Feels like Britain. Smells like Britain, sort of" Severus said. "Can that be?"

"Who knows. The spirit might have sent us back to my home, so I could explain to my parents and my sister, tell them how much I love them. But home doesn't look like this."

"I just thought of something: didn't the spirit say "place or time"? Maybe it sent us to a place we know, but a time we don't.

"That could create significant problems."

"What if they don't have monsters and magic? What will we do?"

"As you said, Sevy my love: live, love — we'll start with that, and go on from there."

"What on earth is that sound?"

"I hear it, too. Maybe they do have monsters here."

"Let's go see!"

Severus' fully corporeal hand took Lilava's hand, and they got up and ran. Stumbling at first, but stronger than they expected to feel, they ran toward the crest of a hill to find the sound they heard.

In the distance beyond a small lake they say a thin, gray strip twisting serpentine through the countryside. They saw several small, wooden structures, oddly shaped.

Something strange, something they had never seen, dashed at a mad pace along the gray strip, screamed as it rounded a corner, continued on at such speed as only an eagle or a soaring dragon could reach, and disappeared into the distance.

Another dashed back from the other way, paused, turned, and stopped by one of the wooden structures, which looked like a stable. What looked like a man squeezed out of it and entered the stable.

"It's gray. The Gray Road," Severus muttered.

"A gray road," Lilava responded. "The creatures look alive, not dead, at least the ones that get out of those awful running things. What do you suppose they are?"

Severus sniffed. "Not monsters, at least not of the classical sort. They smell bad, though — phew! Like burning peat, but worse, harsher. Metal and something else, something not natural. No sword with me — not sure what to do about them. The spirit said "no magic" here, either. Look: there's something by that gray road, just there. Let's have a look."

They walked together, hand in hand, down the hill, and looked at it: a green rectangle held up with metal posts. On the rectangle, three words with numbers and arrows:

Carlisle 15 ↑
Keswick 17 ←
Penrith 3 ↓

"Do you know what they mean?" Lilava asked.

"No, though the third, you know, looks familiar ..."

"Carlisle! though the letters look different ... Do you suppose it refers to Arthur's court and other places in the kingdom? But that can't be, not with those running beasts that look like enormous beetles. Can't have come all this way just to find beetles. That did look like a man we saw from back there. We can stop and ask directions."

"We should try to work it out ourselves," Severus suggested.

"Wouldn't hurt to ask. I feel so disoriented."

"I think we should go toward the one called 'Penrith.' See the little arrow? And the three after it? That may mean it lies closer than the others. Didn't Arthur have a getaway in a place called Penrith? We may find knights and ladies there."

"Then let's not go there," Lilava said.

"Right. Feeling any better yet?"

"Still strange, weak — as I said, disoriented. But not all that bad. How about you?"

"Not all that bad."

"We have a daughter."

"A daughter!"

"Or had one. If we're now in a different time, she may not yet be or have gone long ago, but I'm sure the elves have taken good care of her."

"Oh!"

"I'll tell you all about her. Look, in the field there, horses! At least we've found something familiar."

"Should we speak with them first, before we try the people?"

"The people may not like it if we speak with the horses first."

"You're right. I'll miss old Courage, you know."

"We must find New Courage. Shall we go on?" Lilava asked.

"Let's do. We'll just walk together over there and see what happens."

End

Walking Tree Publishers
Zurich and Jena

Walking Tree Publishers was founded in 1997 as a forum for publication of material related to Tolkien and Middle-earth studies.

Please also visit our web pages:
http://www.walking-tree.org

Tales of Yore Series

The *Tales of Yore Series* s provides a platform for qualitatively superior fiction that will appeal to readers familiar with Tolkien's world.

Kay Woollard, *The Terror of Tatty Walk. A Frightener*
CD and Booklet, Zurich and Berne 2000, ISBN 978-3-9521424-2-4

Kay Woollard, *Wilmot's Very Strange Stone or What came of building "snobbits"*
CD and booklet, Zurich and Berne 2001, ISBN 978-3-9521424-4-8

Edward S. Louis, *The Monster Specialist*
Zurich and Jena 2014, ISBN 978-3-905703-23-8

Beowulf and the Dragon

The original Old English text of the 'Dragon Episode' of *Beowulf* is set in an authentic font and printed and bound in hardback. Illustrated by Anke Eissmann and accompanied by John Porter's translation. Introduction by Tom Shippey. Limited first edition of 500 copies. 84 pages.

This high-quality art book will please both Tolkien fans and those interested in mythology and Old English.

Selected pages can be previewed on:
www.walking-tree.org/beowulf

Beowulf and the Dragon
Zurich and Jena 2009,
ISBN 978-3-905703-17-7

Cormarë Series

The *Cormarë Series* collects papers and studies dedicated to the exploration of Tolkien's work. It comprises monographs, thematic collections of essays, conference volumes, and reprints of important yet no longer (easily) accessible papers by leading scholars in the field. Manuscripts and project proposals are evaluated by members of an independent board of advisors who support the series editors in their endeavour to provide the readers with qualitatively superior yet accessible studies on Tolkien and his work.

News from the Shire and Beyond. Studies on Tolkien
Peter Buchs and Thomas Honegger (eds.), Zurich and Berne 2004, Reprint, First edition 1997 (Cormarë Series 1), ISBN 978-3-9521424-5-5

Root and Branch. Approaches Towards Understanding Tolkien
Thomas Honegger (ed.), Zurich and Berne 2005, Reprint, First edition 1999 (Cormarë Series 2), ISBN 978-3-905703-01-6

Richard Sturch, *Four Christian Fantasists. A Study of the Fantastic Writings of George MacDonald, Charles Williams, C.S. Lewis and J.R.R. Tolkien*
Zurich and Berne 2007, Reprint, First edition 2001 (Cormarë Series 3), ISBN 978-3-905703-04-7

Tolkien in Translation
Thomas Honegger (ed.), Zurich and Jena 2011, Reprint, First edition 2003 (Cormarë Series 4), ISBN 978-3-905703-15-3

Mark T. Hooker, *Tolkien Through Russian Eyes*
Zurich and Berne 2003 (Cormarë Series 5), ISBN 978-3-9521424-7-9

Translating Tolkien: Text and Film
Thomas Honegger (ed.), Zurich and Jena 2011, Reprint, First edition 2004 (Cormarë Series 6), ISBN 978-3-905703-16-0

Christopher Garbowski, *Recovery and Transcendence for the Contemporary Mythmaker. The Spiritual Dimension in the Works of J.R.R. Tolkien*
Zurich and Berne 2004, Reprint, First Edition by Marie Curie Sklodowska, University Press, Lublin 2000, (Cormarë Series 7), ISBN 978-3-9521424-8-6

Reconsidering Tolkien
Thomas Honegger (ed.), Zurich and Berne 2005 (Cormarë Series 8), ISBN 978-3-905703-00-9

Tolkien and Modernity 1
Frank Weinreich and Thomas Honegger (eds.), Zurich and Berne 2006 (Cormarë Series 9), ISBN 978-3-905703-02-3

Tolkien and Modernity 2
Thomas Honegger and Frank Weinreich (eds.), Zurich and Berne 2006 (Cormarë Series 10), ISBN 978-3-905703-03-0

Tom Shippey, *Roots and Branches. Selected Papers on Tolkien by Tom Shippey*
Zurich and Berne 2007 (Cormarë Series 11), ISBN 978-3-905703-05-4

Ross Smith, *Inside Language. Linguistic and Aesthetic Theory in Tolkien*
Zurich and Jena 2011, Reprint, First edition 2007 (Cormarë Series 12),
ISBN 978-3-905703-20-7

How We Became Middle-earth. A Collection of Essays on The Lord of the Rings
Adam Lam and Nataliya Oryshchuk (eds.), Zurich and Berne 2007 (Cormarë Series 13), ISBN 978-3-905703-07-8

Myth and Magic. Art According to the Inklings
Eduardo Segura and Thomas Honegger (eds.), Zurich and Berne 2007 (Cormarë Series 14), ISBN 978-3-905703-08-5

The Silmarillion - Thirty Years On
Allan Turner (ed.), Zurich and Berne 2007 (Cormarë Series 15),
ISBN 978-3-905703-10-8

Martin Simonson, *The Lord of the Rings and the Western Narrative Tradition*
Zurich and Jena 2008 (Cormarë Series 16), ISBN 978-3-905703-09-2

Tolkien's Shorter Works. Proceedings of the 4th Seminar of the Deutsche Tolkien Gesellschaft & Walking Tree Publishers Decennial Conference
Margaret Hiley and Frank Weinreich (eds.), Zurich and Jena 2008 (Cormarë Series 17), ISBN 978-3-905703-11-5

Tolkien's The Lord of the Rings: Sources of Inspiration
Stratford Caldecott and Thomas Honegger (eds.), Zurich and Jena 2008 (Cormarë Series 18), ISBN 978-3-905703-12-2

J.S. Ryan, *Tolkien's View: Windows into his World*
Zurich and Jena 2009 (Cormarë Series 19), ISBN 978-3-905703-13-9

Music in Middle-earth
Heidi Steimel and Friedhelm Schneidewind (eds.), Zurich and Jena 2010 (Cormarë Series 20), ISBN 978-3-905703-14-6

Liam Campbell, *The Ecological Augury in the Works of JRR Tolkien*
Zurich and Jena 2011 (Cormarë Series 21), ISBN 978-3-905703-18-4

Margaret Hiley, *The Loss and the Silence. Aspects of Modernism in the Works of C.S. Lewis, J.R.R. Tolkien and Charles Williams*
Zurich and Jena 2011 (Cormarë Series 22), ISBN 978-3-905703-19-1

Rainer Nagel, *Hobbit Place-names. A Linguistic Excursion through the Shire*
Zurich and Jena 2012 (Cormarë Series 23), ISBN 978-3-905703-22-1

Christopher MacLachlan, *Tolkien and Wagner: The Ring and Der Ring*
Zurich and Jena 2012 (Cormarë Series 24), ISBN 978-3-905703-21-4

Renée Vink, *Wagner and Tolkien: Mythmakers*
Zurich and Jena 2012 (Cormarë Series 25), ISBN 978-3-905703-25-2

The Broken Scythe. Death and Immortality in the Works of J.R.R. Tolkien
Roberto Arduini and Claudio Antonio Testi (eds.), Zurich and Jena 2012
(Cormarë Series 26), ISBN 978-3-905703-26-9

Sub-creating Middle-earth: Constructions of Authorship and the Works of J.R.R. Tolkien
Judith Klinger (ed.), Zurich and Jena 2012 (Cormarë Series 27),
ISBN 978-3-905703-27-6

Tolkien's Poetry
Julian Eilmann and Allan Turner (eds.), Zurich and Jena 2013
(Cormarë Series 28), ISBN 978-3-905703-28-3

O, What a Tangled Web. Tolkien and Medieval Literature. A View from Poland
Barbara Kowalik (ed.), Zurich and Jena 2013 (Cormarë Series 29),
ISBN 978-3-905703-29-0

J.S. Ryan, *In the Nameless Wood*
Zurich and Jena 2013 (Cormarë Series 30), ISBN 978-3-905703-30-6

From Peterborough to Faëry; The Poetics and Mechanics of Secondary Worlds
Thomas Honegger & Dirk Vanderbeke (eds.), Zurich and Jena 2014
(Cormarë Series 31), ISBN 978-3-905703-31-3

Tolkien and Philosophy
Roberto Arduini and Claudio R. Testi (eds.), Zurich and Jena 2014
(Cormarë Series 32), ISBN 978-3-905703-32-0

Patrick Curry, *Deep Roots: Essays on Tolkien*
Zurich and Jena 2014 (Cormarë Series 33), ISBN 978-3-905703-33-7

Paul H. Kocher, *The Three Ages of Middle-earth*
Zurich and Jena, forthcoming

Information for authors

Authors intersted in contributing can learn more about the services we offer by reading
the "services for authors" section of our web pages.

http://www.walking-tree.org/authors

Walking Tree Publishers
CH-3052 Zollikofen
Switzerland
e-mail: info@walking-tree.org

Walking Tree Publishers, Zurich and Jena, 2014